The Pretender
(Book One in the Liar's Club)

Celeste Bradley

St. Martin's Paperbacks

THE PRETENDER

Copyright © 2003 by Celeste Bradley.
Excerpt from *The Impostor* copyright © 2003 by Celeste Bradley.

ISBN: 0-312-98485-5

Printed in the United States of America

St. Martin's Paperbacks edition / June 2003

St. Martin's Paperbacks are published by St. Martin's Press, 175 Fifth Avenue, New York, NY 10010.

10 9 8 7 6 5 4 3 2 1

To my sister Cindy, who is always there.

I must thank my husband, for being my best friend and foremost cheerleader and for putting up with being called "Fabio" at work.

I'd like to thank my daughters, for loving me even though I never remember to thaw out the good stuff for dinner.

Many wonderful women helped me with this book. Some writers, some patient readers. Darbi Gill, Robyn Holiday, Sherrilyn Kenyon, Cheryl Lewallen, Joanne Markis, Jennifer Smith, Alexis Tharp.

Everyone should have such friends.

The Liar's Creed

In the guise of knaves we operate on the fringes of the night, forsaking home, hearth, and love for the protection of all.

We are the invisible ones.

Chapter One

She had married Mortimer Applequist on April 7, 1813, in a moment of mingled exasperation and imagination. He wasn't much of a husband, being merely a name to offer up when people dived too deeply into her affairs. Still, in that he had suited Miss Agatha Cunnington very well indeed.

Until now.

On the outset of her journey, Agatha had been stalled and stymied more times than she could count. Every time it had been by some well-meaning soul trying to save her from herself.

As if a woman were incapable of purchasing a ticket and traveling from Lancashire to London without the supervision of a husband!

Upon announcing her "married" state, however, Agatha met with nothing but assistance and polite respect.

Truly, she should have made up a husband years ago.

Because she disliked leaving poor Mortimer as merely a name to spout when necessary, Agatha had spent many a pleasant moment on the journey visualizing him in precise detail. After all, he was her creation, was he not?

He would be tall but not bulky. Elegant but not foppish. Dark but not swarthy. If only she had been able to make his face come into focus in her imagination, she would have been entirely satisfied with her invented spouse.

Mortimer had become increasingly handy when she had arrived in town, allowing her to rent her little house—her very own!—on respectable Carriage Square and hire a few servants.

Most important, Mortimer had allowed her to fully pursue all venues in her search for her missing brother, James.

But all of that would end today if she could not come up with some sort of plan.

The hall clock chimed the hour, and desperation began rising within Agatha. She turned to pace back up the front hall of her lovely new house, ignoring the rose-covered wallpaper and gleaming dark woods that had lured her to select it. With her arms folded tight and head down, she was lost in her scurrying thoughts.

Why was it the men in Agatha Cunnington's life were never about when she needed them?

She could dress up Pearson—no, too old and too stout. She could pass Harry—no, too young, just a boy, really. She'd given Harry the footman position as a favor to Pearson, but the butler's nephew could scarcely see over his two enormous left feet.

She needed a man, and she needed him immediately!

Simon Montague Raines, aka Simon Rain, paused outside the servants' entrance of the house on Carriage Square to check his disguise. His face and hands were blacked with soot, and the long brushes slung across one shoulder were believably well used. As well they should be, having been his bread and butter once upon a time.

His target's house seemed ordinary enough from the outside, with its tidy entry and scrubbed steps. It was amazing the corruption that could hide behind such a harmless facade. Vice, lies, even treason.

"Mrs. Mortimer Applequist," said the lease. Yet the rent was paid from a certain account that Simon had been watching for weeks. The account of a man who well knew the definition of treachery.

Simon should have sent one of his operatives in on this one and remained aloof and objective, as any good spymaster should.

But Simon had to admit to himself that this case had become personal. Someone was killing off his men. Men with identities so secret that they scarcely knew of one another's existence.

Only two men within the Liar's Club had the information necessarily to bring down its members one by one. Simon and one other. A man who hadn't reported in for several weeks. A man with a sudden increase in his account at the London Bank. A man who had, according to Simon's sources at the bank, paid well to rent and furnish the tidy little house before Simon.

With a grim smile, Simon hefted his brooms and prepared to play the hated role of chimneysweep one last time. All in defense of the Crown, of course.

The situation was becoming most desperate. Agatha had been combing her fertile mind for a solution all morning and still nothing had occurred to her. The rug in the front hall might never recover from her frenzied pacing.

Agatha turned to pace again—and ran full force into an obstacle that had not been there a moment before. Stunned, she staggered but didn't fall.

" 'Ere now, missus! You all right? Didn't see you coming."

Agatha blinked and focused her vision on the black expanse before her. Black coat, black vest, black hands on the sleeves of her dimity morning gown—

"My dress!"

She was set swiftly back on her feet.

"Oh, well, it were a close one. Had to decide if you'd rather dirty your sleeves or your bum when you hit the floor. Guess I called it wrong."

Agatha was being teased and rather freshly, too. Ready to let the fellow have it, she looked up—

Into the bluest eyes she had ever seen, in a face as black as midnight. Or soot.

Soot! All over her dress, right when she was expecting Lady Winchell—

Soot.

Chimneysweep.

Man.

She looked up again. Tall, but as lean as a greyhound. Just like Mortimer. Even the soot couldn't disguise his even features.

"Sorry I am, missus. It's a pretty dress, or it were. I don't suppose the soot'll come out—"

He was perfect.

"Never mind the soot," she interrupted. "Come with me."

He only blinked at her, and she couldn't help her sudden fascination with the sapphire brilliance of his eyes. Then she noticed he hadn't moved yet.

"Well, come along then."

With another blink, the chimneysweep shrugged and fell into step behind her. She led him up the curved stairs and down a short hall.

Before a paneled door, she turned and held up a hand. "Wait. Did anyone see you come in?"

A knowing gleam entered those lovely eyes.

"I come in through the kitchen, mum. Blokes like me knows better than to use the front door."

Agatha shook her head. "No, I care nothing for the people on the street. Did any of the servants see you come in?"

"Well, Cook let me in, but she 'ardly looked at me. Up to her elbows in flour, she was." He grinned at her. "If you're after a bit o' fun, Simon Rain's your man. After a wash, o' course."

Agatha was barely listening. Was there enough time? "Yes, yes, I'll get a bath for you."

Agatha opened the door to the bedchamber she'd lovingly prepared for Jamie. She ignored the few of his possessions she had brought with her from home. There was no point in mooning over his books and his personal items. Sentiment would have to wait.

In an hour, three of the most influential women on the Chelsea Hospital Board of Volunteers would be calling upon Agatha and her husband, Mortimer, of whom they had heard so much.

Oh, why hadn't she kept her mouth shut? She could have simply listened when the other women talked about their husbands. She could have answered vaguely when they had asked about hers.

Instead, she had carried on about "dear Mortie," enumerating all his attributes and virtues. He was a scholar, a musician, a man of enormous charm and appeal—

And he was at home.

Well, she'd had to say that.

Lady Winchell, with her smarmy smile and her gimlet eyes, had wondered if it was quite proper for such a young bride to be working amongst the men at the hospital all day while her husband traveled abroad.

Now, Lady Winchell and two other highly placed ladies were coming to meet Mortimer.

Agatha remembered Lady Winchell's suspicious manner and couldn't help a shiver. If she were found out, she would never be allowed to stay here in town alone. Her self-proclaimed guardian would fetch her home within days and she would never accomplish her mission.

Her choice seemed clear. She could admit to her situation and return to Appleby, and all that awaited her there.

Or she could lie. Again.

Well, in for a penny, in for a great many pounds. Putting one hand on the chimneysweep's back, she gave him a little push into the spacious bedchamber.

"Get undressed behind that screen. I'll have your bath brought up immediately." She had best not let the servants in on this little bit of playacting. Newly hired, they had certainly never seen Mortimer. She could always say that he'd been "called away" on another adventure by supper, and then things would go back to normal again.

After shutting the door on the bemused chimneysweep, Agatha pasted a happy smile on her face and hurried back down the stairs.

"Pearson," she called to her butler, "I've just had the most delightful surprise. Mr. Applequist has come home! He is terribly weary and wants his bath straightaway."

Coming from the parlor, where he'd been overseeing the preparations for her guests, Pearson raised a silvered brow and looked askance at the front door, which of course hadn't admitted a soul all morning.

"Yes, madam, happy news indeed. Shall I attend Mr. Applequist until a manservant can be engaged?"

Agatha folded her arms to disguise the black hand prints on her sleeves. "No, Pearson, that won't be necessary. I'll tend my husband myself. After all, we have so much to . . . talk about."

Now why was he looking at her that way, with both eyebrows nearly to his hairline? Couldn't a woman talk to her own husband?

"As you wish, madam. Nellie will bring the water directly."

"Thank you, Pearson. I shall be down in just a moment to greet the ladies."

By the time Nellie went back downstairs with the last of the hot water pails, Agatha was freshly changed and her hair repaired. Quickly she slipped into the other bedchamber.

The room was the finest in the house, much better than her own. Green velvet draperies framed the bed, and the hearth was nearly the size of a kitchen fire. There was no one in sight and only the large steaming tub in evidence. Had he left?

"Hello? Mr. Chimneysweep? Are you here?"

"That you, missus? Crikey, a bloke's like to freeze his you-know-what off by the time he gets his bath round here."

From behind the painted Oriental screen that stood in a corner of the room, she heard a rustle.

"Oh, no! *No,* don't come"—it was too late—"out." From behind the screen had stepped a man who was quite very nearly naked.

She should turn away. Yes, definitely.

She couldn't turn away. She could only stand and stare, without blinking or even breathing.

With the majority of soot wiped from his hands and face, the man before her was as beautiful as a Greek statue. Lapis blue eyes shone in a poetically boned face, with a mussed shock of black hair and the body from her dreams, dreams she hadn't even known she'd had.

Whipcord muscle wrapped around his lean frame. Even his stomach rippled in a most diverting way. His shoulders weren't enormously broad, but they were square with strength, the muscle twining down his arms to wide hands that grasped the toweling at his narrow waist.

Agatha blinked at the size of those hands. Heavens. Were his feet as large? She let her gaze travel down. Oh my.

Jamie's boots would never fit him. "Blast!"

The fellow's grin disappeared and he looked down. "What's wrong w' me feet?"

"Let me see your boots."

"Whafore?" His voice rose in indignation. "They're mine. I ain't stole nothing!"

"I need to examine your boots to see if they'll do."

Still scowling suspiciously at her, he bent to retrieve his boots from behind the screen.

Agatha almost swallowed her tongue at the view.

"Let me see." She held out a hand and he gave her the boots. She examined them closely, her eyebrows raised in surprise.

"These are rather fine. Yes, I think they'll do well enough. Let me have Pearson give them a cleaning while you are in your bath."

She turned to go. "We'll be expecting you downstairs in a quarter of an hour. Do be sure not to say a word, not to anyone."

"But, missus, wha' about"—the fellow gestured to the bed—"you know?"

Agatha looked at the bed, and then back at him.

"You may have a nap later if you like, although I shouldn't think you'll find any of this terribly exhausting."

She smiled brightly at him.

"Yes, you'll do nicely. Your new things are on the chair. Hurry now. And remember, *not one word*."

Agatha shut the door on her beautiful chimneysweep and drew in a long breath. My, oh my. Did all men look like that underneath? Somehow she doubted it.

Then she shook off the spell of his masculine charms. She must focus on the problem at hand. Trotting downstairs to see to refreshments, she firmly denied herself the imagining of that perfect body in the bath.

Wet.

Covered in soap.

Oh my.

Simon twisted his lips cynically as he squeezed the sponge over his already perfectly clean torso. Here he was, in Mr. Applequist's house, in Mr. Applequist's tub, with Mr. Applequist's lady awaiting him downstairs.

If she was indeed Mrs. Applequist, for that was not the name on the account that had rented this house and hired these servants. That account belonged to none other than James Cunnington, Simon's fellow spy, former best friend, and probable traitor.

At the thought of James, Simon's fingers tightened on the sponge until it was wrung dry. Years of friendship and trust, sold out for a bag of gold or possibly no more than a woman's favors.

For James was a man in love, or at least in lust. Simon had heard it from his protégé himself, when last he'd seen him. James had sat across from him in Simon's private office, preoccupied with his latest mistress.

"She's incredible, Simon. As limber as a snake, and as

lusty as a mink. Like no woman I've ever known. The things she does! So much energy . . ." James had thrown his head back on his chair and given a great sigh of weary satisfaction. "I'm exhausted, but I'm sure I'll recover before tonight. You should find yourself such a woman, old man."

Simon had only grunted, too engrossed in the recent reports from the front to take up the challenge.

"You don't have to marry a woman, Simon. You don't even have to love one. But you need a little fun, Simon. A bit of muslin to take your mind off work. Just the thing for you, to get you out of this dusty office. Get your juices flowing before you become as rigid as our dear founder, cold in his grave."

James had eyed the portrait of Daniel Defoe that hung behind Simon's head, squinting as if to make out something not usually seen. "Although I'll wager he was a juicy fellow in his day. A man of adventure. You'd never catch him moldering behind a mountain of paperwork."

Simon had finally looked up at that. "What do you call penning hundreds of novels and works of political satire, if not paperwork?"

James had only grinned affably, happy to have gotten a rise from his mentor and superior, even if it meant losing the point.

"I could find out if she has a sister. Or a friend."

"No thank you. James, I've been where you are, and I decided it was seldom worth it. It makes one too vulnerable. So I'll leave the womanizing to you."

James had dropped his clowning and leaned forward, his elbows dislodging a week's worth of counterintelligence reports.

"Seriously, Simon, you need to get about more. Get a bit of perspective. There is more to life than the Liar's Club. Hell, there's a whole world outside of Europe that doesn't give a damn about Napoleon, nor how many horse soldiers he has, nor how many spies in London!"

Simon had gazed at his young friend. There was so much that James didn't understand. He was a good operative, quick-witted and dedicated, but the only one James put at risk was himself. If he was caught, the only neck in Napoleon's noose would be his own. At least until he took over Simon's position as spymaster of the Liar's Club.

Simon couldn't afford mistakes. He held in his hands the lives of every one of his men and, in a grander scope, perhaps even the lives of everyone in England.

There was no time for play, with a burden such as that. Not a moment to lose, nor a fact to disregard.

He had to remain on top of the mounting pile of clues, in order that the next time he sent out one of his Liars, perhaps even James himself, the man would go with the best and newest information that Simon could give him.

So that when one of them died in the service of his country, Simon could try to ease his own pain with the knowledge that he had done his best. Perhaps someday it would work.

James apparently had no such concerns. Taking his new assignment in hand, James had given Simon a half-salute and a grin. He'd left, whistling, to cadge a last drink from Jackham behind the bar.

Simon had never heard from him again.

That alone would have only given rise to worry, not accusation. But it then became obvious that someone was supplying descriptions and identities of Simon's men to the opposition. One man after another turned up dead or injured.

Simon had entertained the possibility that the leak was someone higher in the chain of command than himself, so sure had he been of James's loyalty.

Then a large amount of money was suddenly deposited in James's account, so large that Simon had been forced to suspect that worst of all conclusions.

His spy was spying for the enemy. There was no way to know precisely how it had happened. So many things could turn a spy, from sedition to seduction.

He hadn't discovered the name of James's mistress, more's the pity, but he'd kept a watch on his protégé's bank account. Finally, a certain little Mrs. Applequist had made her appearance, freely using James's money to set herself up in style.

That's when Simon had made his move.

And only this morning he'd wondered how he could gain entry into the house in Carriage Square. The chimneysweep guise had worked well for him in his youth, but that had been before he'd reached his full height.

He'd planned everything carefully and had deliberately picked a moment when the cook was likely to be busy in which to knock on the back door. A quickly muttered, "Chimbley cleanin' for Missus Applequist," and he'd been inside.

Once he'd been admitted, he'd slipped through the house with an eye out for the butler. Fellows like the fine silver-haired houseman downstairs would look suspiciously indeed on the arrival of a chimneysweep when none such had been ordered.

He'd been hoping to make his later job easier with a quick casing of the layout and possibly the unlatching of a likely upper-story window. And to be honest, he'd been very curious about the lady of the house.

Then Simon had run smack into the comely Mrs. Applequist herself. Her curvaceous form had packed quite a wallop, and it had taken him a moment to get his breath back.

Luckily for him, the lady didn't seem too interested in his purpose. Nor did she seem to realize that most chimneysweeps were either boys or poorly grown men the size of children. She obviously had something else on her mind.

What was her game?

Deciding that lingering in the bath wouldn't help him learn much, Simon stood and let the water stream from his body.

As he rubbed the toweling over his chest, his eyes narrowed at the memory of Mrs. Applequist's face when he had stepped out from behind the screen.

She hadn't missed a beat, but her eyes had gone wide with what Simon wasn't too modest to call appreciation. Well, it was mutual. She was a ripe little morsel herself.

Oh, her dress was perfectly demure and her house perfectly respectable. Nevertheless, a woman built on those generous terms was more likely to be at home in the bedroom than the ballroom. A lady of healthy appetite, she was.

And now it appeared she had an appetite for Simon. Not that he minded so much. He liked an armful as much as a handful, but he knew better than to get involved with the subject under investigation.

Unless it became absolutely necessary.

Agatha's panic simmered as she waited impatiently in the parlor. Who could have known being married would be so complicated?

She tidied the tea tray for the fifth time and eyed the clock on the front parlor mantel. The ladies would be calling within half an hour and her chimneysweep had yet to come downstairs to hear his part in the charade.

Biting her lip, Agatha reminded herself that all this would surely be worth it if it meant finding Jamie.

James Cunnington was a soldier, away fighting Napoleon the last Agatha had heard from him. He had written her every week, and had for four years, until two months past.

Then there had been no word from him in any way. Despite all her inquiries to the army, she had received no answers, even after all this time.

Spurred by her need to find Jamie, a need that became more desperate by the hour, Agatha had packed a trunk and bought a ticket on the next coach, leaving her estate of Appleby for London. Her servants had aided her escape, and she knew they would keep her whereabouts hidden for as long as possible.

It wouldn't do for Repulsive Reggie to find her before she found her brother. She'd be forced back to Appleby and to the altar with all the speed of Reggie's thwarted ambitions.

"Marrying" Mortimer had simply made the journey easier. No one questioned a married woman's morality in traveling alone, not in wartime with so many husbands gone.

When she had been inspired to investigate the Chelsea Hospital in London for news of dear Jamie, it had been her married status that had allowed her in and enabled her to volunteer to care for the wounded.

Still, creating an alias to travel under and presenting the world with an actual false husband were two entirely different kettles of flounder.

"Hello, love. Here I am."

Pulled back to the present, Agatha looked up . . . and up . . . to see one of the handsomest men she had ever laid eyes on.

Jamie's trousers fit the fellow a bit closely about the hips, although not excessively so for the current fashion. Rather too much for Agatha's peace of mind, however.

She yanked her gaze from dangerous ground and followed the rest of the transformation upward.

Jamie's snowy shirt and dark green waistcoat gave no reason for dismay, but the morning coat, oh my. While the cut across the shoulders was quite fine and the nipped waist fit perfectly, the cobalt color gave far too much emphasis to those twinkling blue eyes.

His cravat was only loosely tied round his collar, in a way rather more suited to a pirate than a gentleman, showing a bit too much of strong brown throat.

A lethal combination indeed. It was very odd how her imagination proceeded to remove every one of those articles of Jamie's clothing from his frame, until in her mind's eye he stood as nearly naked as before.

"What? Don't it fit?" The chimneysweep flexed both shoulders and twisted at the waist to see behind him. "I thought it looked right nice, I did."

"Oh, no, you look wond—adequate, perfectly adequate." Agatha forced her wicked imagination to re-dress him. "Please, come in and sit. I have a boon to ask of you."

The fellow smiled slightly at her, and Agatha had to fist her hands to keep from tracing the dimples indenting each side of his mouth.

She was attracted to him. How unthinkably inappropriate of her. Not to mention inconvenient. Really, was there no end to the obstacles in her path?

Agatha shot a look full of her irritation at the fellow before her and watched his beautiful smile fade. Good. If she could maintain her vexation for a while, the day would go easier for her. Yes indeed. A brisk, no-nonsense manner was called for.

Agatha indicated the seat opposite her. "Please sit, Mr.—?"

"Rain, Simon Rain." He sat and continued to look at her expectantly.

The clock chimed three-quarters of the hour, and Agatha knew she didn't have much time to explain.

"I have a need for a gentleman to attend me today. You need do nothing, really, merely smile and greet my guests. I will do all the talking." Agatha sat back and smiled. There. Rather succinct, if she did say so herself.

"Whafore?" Mr. Rain frowned. "I mean, I'd like to help you, mum, but I won't do nothing what's wrong. This here don't sound much close to right, not a bit of it."

"Oh, no. There's nothing wrong here at all. I shall simply introduce you as my husband, you shall bow over the ladies' hands, we shall all sit for the standard fifteen minutes and take tea. You shall never have to say a word."

"Your *husband*?" Mr. Rain stood abruptly. "Here now, we ain't married! What if your mister finds out? He'll make a spot of trouble for me, he will. I would, if'n you was mine."

"You would? I mean to say, of course you would. But there is no need to worry about Mr. Applequist. He—"

Sounds of arriving guests came through the closed door to the entrance hall. Agatha panicked. Oh, this was going very badly indeed!

"He doesn't exist at all, Mr. Rain!" she hissed, even as Pearson opened the door to announce her guests. "I'm *not* married, there will be *no* trouble made for you, and you mustn't utter *one single word*!"

Chapter Two

Agatha's chest tightened with anxiety as she smiled fixedly at her guests. Or perhaps her corset was laced too snugly. Surely the cause could not be the strong thigh pressed to her own or the clean scent of freshly bathed male.

Whatever the reason, she felt quite breathless as she sat next to Mr. Rain, across from Lady Winchell and her two companions.

Despite the pains Agatha had taken to fill the parlor with colorful comfort, Lady Winchell remained perched on the edge of her brocade chair as if she feared soiling her dress.

The lady made a slight face at her tea and set the cup and saucer down. The movement only accentuated the elegant curve of her figure, clad in her signature shade of mint green, and made Agatha yearn for a little lithesome grace instead of her own dumpling shape.

"When dear Agatha told us about you, Mr. Applequist, I must confess I thought you too good to be true." She turned her piercing gaze on Agatha, then dropped her eyes to Agatha's gloveless hands. "I've noticed before that you don't wear your wedding ring, my dear. Have you lost it somehow?"

The ring. She'd forgotten the wedding ring entirely. "Ah—no, no indeed. But I've been leaving it off to work at the hospital. I feared to ruin it. It's—it's an Applequist family heirloom." For a moment Agatha could even picture the ring. Sapphire, she decided. Just like Mortimer's eyes—wait, those were Simon's.

Blast. The next thing she knew, she'd be believing her own deception.

"Hmm." The lady did not seem impressed. She turned to Simon. "You know she thinks you single-handedly hung the stars, don't you, sir?"

All eyes turned to "Mortimer" and Agatha began to panic once more.

"My Mortie did hang the stars! At least the ones in my eyes!" Agatha dug her nails into her companion's arm. He turned to her with that smile of his, and two of the three ladies sighed audibly. Lady Winchell only narrowed her eyes.

"Ah, you must tell us all about your travels, Mr. Applequist. Only then will we be able to understand how you could tear yourself away from such an adoring young bride."

Agatha watched in horror as her chimneysweep actually opened his mouth to speak. Grinding her heel into his instep, she rushed to answer for him.

"Oh, well! I cannot be so bold as to think my simple company can compare with the excitement of tiger hunts in India, can I, darling?" The ladies turned their attention back to her. Good. Now she must think quickly!

Papa had always been easily distracted by her Banbury tales. Surely she could deflect a more discriminating audience. Her purpose depended on it. She lowered her voice to add some excitement to her yarn.

"Imagine, swaying atop an elephant as the mighty beast crashes his way through the jungle. Contemplate the tension as the party grows ever closer to their vicious prey. Can you envision the sight he must have made, whilst he raised his rifle to fire upon the tiger?"

Mrs. Trapp and Mrs. Sloane were enraptured. Not so Lady Winchell.

"Tiger hunting in India? Truly? While most of our young men fight the demon Napoleon?"

"But Mortimer was on a mission—for the Prince—carry-

ing a message to the Rajah," blurted Agatha. "The tiger hunt
was necessary when . . . when the beast stole away the Rajah's only son! Mortimer saved him with a single shot!"

"While the tiger held the child in his very jaws, Mr. Applequist?" inquired Lady Winchell in a silky voice. "How . . .
precise."

"How heroic," sighed Mrs. Trapp.

"How divine," breathed Mrs. Sloane.

Agatha's smile grew more artificial by the moment. Had
it not yet been a quarter of an hour? Surely fifteen minutes
had never lasted so long.

"Mrs. Applequist, you must bring your charming husband
to my little soiree tomorrow night," Mrs. Trapp said.

The elder of Lady Winchell's companions grew a bit flustered when Mr. Rain turned that overwhelming smile upon
her invitation. Agatha tensed. No, he mustn't—

He did. With a regal nod, he accepted for the both of them.

Blast! She clenched his arm until all the feeling left her
fingers, but he only smiled serenely at her and patted her
hand.

Agatha turned her own witless smile to her guests. "Oh,
how silly of Mortimer. He has forgotten that we are unable
to make a Tuesday event, as we visit his mother every Tuesday. Mortimer dearly loves his mother. But you are so very
kind to include us, Mrs. Trapp."

Heavens. That had been entirely too close. Agatha turned
relieved eyes to Lady Winchell.

The smile on that lady's face gave Agatha a chill as she
watched those glinting eyes travel over "Mortimer." The
woman looked positively hungry. Oh, dear.

"His lordship and I are hosting a supper dance in one
week, Mr. Applequist. I daresay the gentlemen would relish
the chance to hear of your escapades"—she shot a look at
Agatha—"*first-hand*."

Agatha opened her mouth to protest. Lady Winchell held
up a hand.

"Now, now, no need to thank me. I know how difficult it

is for a young couple like yourselves to make their way into Society."

She stood and gave Agatha a polite smile with a gleam of triumph in it. "I so look forward to getting to know you better, dear Agatha." Her voice dropped to a purr. "And your handsome husband as well."

Mr. Rain gave a creditable bow once Agatha had dragged him off the sofa. Mrs. Sloane and Mrs. Trapp tittered appreciatively.

Agatha refrained from rolling her eyes. Heaven save her from ever being so silly. The ladies turned to go with many a backward glance.

Giving "Mortimer" a shove to indicate that he should stay behind, Agatha followed her guests to the door where Pearson stood ready with bonnets and shawls.

"I do hope we may attend, my lady. One never knows when Mortimer must—"

"Oh, you'll attend, Mrs. Applequist. After all, it is not a *Tuesday.*"

Her smirk told Agatha that the lady hadn't believed a single word. Lady Winchell donned her hat and gave Agatha a glacial smile, her eyes hard.

"You mustn't disappoint us. Remember, one doesn't get many opportunities to put one's best foot forward in this world."

Lady Winchell stroked a strand of pale hair into place and cast a lingering glance back into the parlor. "A man of few words, your husband. I do hope he feels more talkative next time. The gentlemen will be so looking forward to hearing of his adventures."

Agatha shivered at the last icy smirk delivered with these words. When the ladies were gone, she wrapped both arms around her against the chill and returned to the parlor. What was she to do now?

"I thought that went right well, I did. It weren't so 'ard at all. Them's real nice ladies, for toffs." Mr. Rain looked very pleased with himself. "And I never said not one word, just like you wanted."

Agatha's jaw dropped. He had no idea what he had done to her, with his irresistible smile and his fabulous anatomy.

Simon had done a terrible thing, he knew, but the lady deserved it for telling such staggering whoppers. Tiger hunting in India? Rescuing the Rajah's son with a single shot? How poisonous. Even *he* hated Mortimer Applequist.

Ah, but there was no Mortimer Applequist, was there? There was only pretty *Mrs.* Applequist and her penchant for fibbing. She was no more married than a Drury Lane actress would be. Although he'd wager she was just as good in bed.

Yet she was no ordinary ladybird. She lied beautifully, if a bit outrageously. She went to great lengths to support the tiniest details of her story. And even more surprising, she comported herself among real ladies without hesitation.

Simon knew from experience how hard it was to overcome a lifetime of class-conscious diffidence to pose as one of the gentry.

All of the above smacked of a great deal of training. Training that quite possibly came from the French. He'd not received any mention of women in their intelligence network, but that didn't mean they weren't there. Napoleon was nothing if not creative.

It made little difference to Simon either way. Whether she was here as James Cunnington's paramour or co-conspirator, he was willing to bet that she could lead him to James himself.

At any rate, he'd accomplished his task and was now well versed in the layout of the house. He'd even left a likely window unlatched upstairs. Tonight would do for a more thorough search. He would have to take care. If he left any sign of entry tonight, he'd be the first one suspected.

Not that she'd ever be able to find him. But he'd be watching her. Indeed he would.

He nodded politely as he passed her. "Nice to be of service to you, mum. I thanks you for the bath. I'll be collectin' me rig and be on me way."

The parlor door slammed shut inches in front of his face.

Simon looked down to see a plump palm pressing the door closed.

" 'Ere now. I thought we was done."

"Done? *Done?* After the mess you've gotten me into? Did you have to be so charming? Did you have to smile so . . . so . . . ?"

Blast. He was doing it again.

Agatha got shivers in her stomach as Mr. Rain smiled down at her.

"Charmin', was I? And me not sayin' a word? Now, how could that be?"

His voice was low and flirtatious and his eyes gleamed as if they held a secret. Only one corner of his mouth actually curled upward, and it gave her hot chills simply to look at it.

But those shivers no longer lived just in her stomach. A great deal more of her person seemed to be involved.

She licked her lips.

He chuckled and his breath was warm on her face. He smelled of cinnamon. What would he taste like?

Good lord, what was she doing?

Quickly Agatha ducked under his arm and scuttled across the room. Yes, distance was good. Enough distance that she couldn't feel the heat of him on her skin.

Smoothing damp palms down her skirt, Agatha resumed her artificial smile and turned back to Mr. Rain. Indicating that he return to his seat on the blue velvet sofa, she herself perched where Lady Winchell had sat.

Distance.

Mr. Rain moved to the sofa but did not sit. Instead, he stood behind it and planted his elbows on the back. He said nothing, only studied her closely, that off-center smile still lingering on his lips.

"You may sit, Mr. Rain," Agatha said with another regal motion to the sofa.

"Oh, I knows it. I'm just keepin' the way clear to the door, in case you're wantin' to snare me again."

"I assure you, Mr. Rain, I have no intention of 'snaring' anyone." The gall!

Well, except she had rather snared him, hadn't she? Oh, heavens, what was she doing? Abruptly the starch and indignation left her spine and Agatha wilted.

Putting her face in her hands, she blocked out the room and the man and her hopelessly tangled situation.

Think. No, not about the fit of Mr. Rain's trousers. Think about how to mend the damage.

She must be allowed to continue at the hospital. It was the best link between London and the soldiers still at war. She was able to ask about Jamie at every opportunity and peruse first-hand the lists of men lost and men found.

"You looks a bit mopped, mum. Don't know why. Them ladies think you're right married now."

"Yes. Married to you," Agatha muttered from between her palms. "What will they think if I do not go to Lady Winchell's supper dance? I cannot very well go without an escort, especially now that they have met Mortimer."

And Lady Winchell had known that no one could easily turn aside such a highly sought after invitation without inviting gossip. Gossip meant curiosity into her affairs, curiosity she could ill afford.

What a blasted muck-up she'd made of things. Blast, blast, blast!

Vulgarity helped, but when Agatha raised her eyes, the central player in the muck-up still leaned insouciantly against her sofa back.

"Well, that's a right shame for the lady, but it ain't got nothin' to do with me then, do it?" He turned to go.

"Wait!" Perhaps this wasn't a mess. Perhaps it was a miracle.

The only other clue Agatha had to Jamie's disappearance was a name. Not even really a name, more of an epithet. On Jamie's last visit home, she had chanced upon a letter in his room, a message clearly in code, signed by "the Griffin."

What did a common soldier have to do with the most famous gentleman spy in Britain? Agatha had no idea, but there was no doubt that Jamie and the Griffin had some connection.

Finding the Griffin might just mean finding Jamie. And

finding the Griffin would be much easier if Agatha could enter Society.

And for that, Agatha needed Mortimer.

Mr. Rain turned halfway back to her, clearly not intending to be swayed from his departure. How could she make him stay?

"It seems I still require a husband. You were interested in making use of a bed. That can be arranged, if you agree to help me." He could nap in Jamie's bed for the rest of his life, if he would help her find her brother.

Simon was startled by her bold invitation. What was the alleged Mrs. Applequist after, really?

He let his eyes travel over her with the intensity he reserved for business, seeking out clues that would tell him who this woman was.

There was little to discover on the surface. Her wardrobe was of good quality, if a bit short on style. Her features were regular and appealing in an apple-cheeked country fashion. Nothing to hint that she was anything out of the very ordinary.

Until he looked at her body.

It was difficult to do so with detachment. Her full, sweet curves made his blood heat. He couldn't examine her without wanting to get a much closer look. Would the reality prove as promising as his imagination?

Would her breasts overflow his hands the way they overflowed her corset? Would her bottom prove as luscious as the swelling of her hips promised him? She was full-bodied and ripe, like the fruit of temptation hanging just out of reach.

His mouth watered.

"I should think you'd jump at the chance to earn a decent wage, Mr. Rain. After all, you're getting a bit large to sweep chimneys, aren't you?"

So lush . . .

"Mr. Rain?"

With difficulty Simon bridled his hunger and wondered if perhaps he should check his chin for saliva. Quickly he pulled on the impudent facade of Simon the Chimneysweep.

"What all will you be wantin' me to do? I ain't interested in nothing what might get me across the law, and no mistake!"

"Of course not. The very idea. There is no breaking of the law involved. The merest bending, perhaps, but truly nothing serious. And all for the finest of causes, I assure you."

"Well, that's good—"

"Oh, Mr. Rain, I cannot thank you enough! It will only be for a few weeks, perhaps slightly more, but hardly any time at all, really. And I will reward you for your pains, most handsomely."

The lady beamed at him and heaved a great sigh. Simon was forced to rip his gaze from her décolletage. *Pains?* He had agreed to perform as her husband? He'd been so distracted, he hadn't even noticed.

She was clever. Too clever, for a mere mistress. Her ingenuity and persistence were something other than ordinary. Simon was forced to move her from "bystander" to "accomplice."

A party at Lord Winchell's London house would fit into his plans anyway. All the better to keep his eye on this woman. And Winchell was definitely on his list of possibles, for the man lived very well, with high standing in both Society and the War Office. Winchell's position close to the Prime Minister alone made him worth investigating.

With the Liars' current manpower shortage—Simon suppressed the pain and loss—every man had to serve more than one purpose as it was. He could kill his two birds with one stone. . . .

Carefully Simon focused his attention on the problem at hand, squelching his odd distraction. Yes, agreeing to her plan might yield a great deal of information.

But he wondered . . . what *precisely* had he agreed to?

Chapter Three

It was a most agreeable dream.

Warm breath caressed Agatha's neck and she sighed. Turning into the heat, she stretched her body in luxurious delight. Reaching out, she stroked her hand over—

—the chill hard wood of the bedpost.

Snapped from her sensual half-dream, Agatha jerked upright. Her nighttime braid had slipped its knot and her hair spilled in front of her eyes. She pushed it hurriedly aside and sat very still, listening.

The chamber was the same unimpressive room as always, its squat furnishings not improved by the shadows. Unlike Jamie's chamber, she had made little effort to improve her own.

Yes, her window was still shut against the last chill of spring and the coals still glowed from her bedtime fire. So why were her nerves trembling? Why was her breath coming short and sharp, and her neck aquiver with sensation?

Why did the room smell ever so very faintly of cinnamon?

Simon.

Mr. Rain to you, my girl, she scolded herself, *and don't you forget it.* Moreover, Mr. Rain was safely all the way down the hall, ensconced in Jamie's big bedchamber for the week.

He hadn't liked the idea of staying in the house, and it had been all that Agatha could do to persuade him that there would be no irate person of the male persuasion coming to defend her honor. Truly, it was the only practical solution.

And it was lovely having a man around the house again. A deep voice, a heavier tread, a solid presence to fill the emptiness. Agatha bit her lip for a moment. She missed Jamie and Papa terribly.

As much as she loved Appleby, the estate had become more lonely burden than loving home in the last few years. Jamie had not been living there for quite some time, even before he went to war.

And poor Papa, gone just two years, had been so devastated by his wife's death fifteen years before that he had retreated into his books and his mathematics. Even when he was with his son and daughter, he was scarcely there at all.

The care of the sheep herds and the orchards had been hers for so long, it felt distinctly odd not to forever be thinking of lambs and apples. Odd, and something of a guilty relief.

But she would gladly tend both for the rest of her life if only she could bring back her family. The way they used to be. Agatha rubbed at her eyes, for they burned just the tiniest bit.

She pulled her determination about her like a shield against the pain. Papa was gone forever, but Jamie was out there, somewhere, and it was left to Agatha to find him.

Mr. Rain was not a replacement but a tool placed in her path to aid her mission.

She was close, she knew it. She could envision the moment when she found her brother, perhaps when the ambulance wagons brought the men into the hospital by the dozens.

She would offer a dipper of water to another wounded man, one who was not too terribly wounded, then raise her eyes to see the gleam of Jamie's wicked grin and hear his teasing voice.

"Got your nose in my business again, don't you, Aggravation? Can't leave you alone for a minute!"

And she would help him from his pallet and he would walk out of the hospital—because he wasn't too terribly wounded—and they would go back to Appleby, where things would be just as they had always been before.

Before Napoleon had struck and Jamie had gone soldiering. Before Papa had died.

Before Lord Fistingham had come to tell her that he was the executor of her inheritance now that her brother was likely dead as well. Hence, she should be honored to join her wealth and her lands to Fistingham by becoming the bride of his son, Reginald.

Before she had been left alone with Repulsive Reggie, with his sweaty hands on her body and his slimy tongue in her mouth.

She had managed to avoid Reggie for most of her life, neighbors though they be. She'd learned very young that he was not to be trusted.

Quickly she shut her mind to that older memory, so swiftly that only a brief vision of Reggie's sweating teenage face appeared, silhouetted against a cloudy summer sky while she fought him off with small childish hands.

He isn't here.

She was safe from him here as she had been for the past several years at Appleby. But that hadn't lasted forever, had it?

It had only been through her reluctance to offend Lord Fistingham that he and his son, Reggie, had managed to be let into Appleby last month.

His lordship had come to pursue an agenda of his own.

"You're an orphan, gel. Not a soul in the world to look after you. It's my duty to see you set."

"Jamie will look out for me, my lord," Agatha had argued. She hadn't thought claiming she could look after herself would have done her any good with an old-fashioned fellow like his lordship.

"Ah, but young James is dead, make no mistake. You must get beyond this foolishness and face the truth. You're all alone in the world, doomed to starve."

"Hardly that," she'd muttered dryly. She was fairly sure that Appleby brought in a larger income than Fistingham, for it was better managed by far. Not to mention that her accounts had not the constant drain of a useless gambling sot of a son.

"Nonsense. No woman can get by without a man. But I've taken care of that. Your father—ah, how I miss dear Jems— would have wanted me to."

Agatha had striven to seem respectful, for Lord Fistingham had been the closest thing her father had ever had to a friend. The unworthy thought crossed her mind that Lord Fistingham had only made the occasional appearance to hit his dear "Jems" up for a loan.

And her father would only blink dimly and write a generous cheque, never questioning the amount and never asking to be repaid. Although knowing Papa's complete disregard for anything but the realm of numbers and formulas, that likely had more to do with a total disinterest in money than actual generosity.

Then his lordship had outlined his plan to bring their great estates together under the name of Fistingham. Agatha had barely listened, mentally tallying her books while she nodded away.

Until she had realized with cold sinking horror that Lord Fistingham's plans included marriage. A proposal that he was not going to let her refuse. At first she'd been afraid he'd wanted to marry her himself.

Then her situation had become even more dangerous.

"You'll marry Reggie straightaway. You've no choice, gel. I've control of everything now, you see. With young Jems gone, your father's will turns it all over to me until you marry, at which time it will go to your husband."

She'd frantically tried to remember the reading of the will, but only the shadow of her grief came to mind. Still, she hadn't doubted for a moment that it was true. How like her father to turn her welfare over to a stranger. And why not? He'd practically been a stranger himself since her mother had died.

"But I've run Appleby for years! I'm perfectly capable of tending my own affairs!"

"Oh, I know young Jems let you play steward now and again, the silly boy. He's fortunate you didn't do much damage." Lord Fistingham had stood then, his formerly mild gaze sharpening suddenly on his son. "Time for you to wed, gel. Reggie, see to convincing your bride."

"Yes, Father." Reginald had smiled winningly at Agatha.

His lordship had left then, removing the key from the lock and closing the door carefully behind him. Agatha could still remember how that click had resonated through her nerves like a screamed warning.

For romantic persuasion had not been part of Repulsive Reggie's plan. As soon as his father had quit the room, he'd been on her. He'd clawed at her bodice and pulled her hair, all the while crudely pushing himself at her like a rutting ram.

Agatha had struggled silently against her own debilitating fear and his superior strength. She'd dared not call out for one of her servants to break down the door to help her, for she'd only condemn her own staff to an appearance before the magistrate if they laid hands on a lord's son. That would not end well, especially when Lord Fistingham *was* the local magistrate.

It hadn't been until Reggie had her down on the sofa, fixed on pinning her whilst he undid his breeches, that a long-ago event had flashed through her mind and she knew what she must do.

When they were young, Jamie had suddenly decided that she needed to learn to protect herself and had demonstrated how to disarm a man completely with one simple action.

With all her might, Agatha kicked out. Her knee had missed, for she was hampered by Reggie's weight on her skirts. But her thigh had made satisfying contact all the same.

Most satisfying indeed. Reggie's face had gone greenish-white and he had rolled off her with a breathless wheeze. She'd clambered out with practiced ease through a large window, leaving her foe writhing on the floor behind her.

When she'd left Appleby early the next morning, her household staff had still been trying to clean the vomit from the carpet.

Remembering that day, Agatha realized that she was rubbing her wrists, although the bruises had been gone for over a week.

She shuddered. Absently rebraiding her hair, she forced herself to focus her mind on the enormous task confronting her.

How to turn a chimneysweep into a gentleman in a single week?

He must be able to converse, to dine, to dance, to walk even, as if he were born to the gentry. It was a daunting task, without the remotest chance of succeeding. Agatha dropped her braid and flopped back onto her pillow.

One thing at a time. She had spent the evening with him, going over a few highly useful phrases that would get him by with the household help for the next few days. He had learned quickly and relieved her mind about his ability to master conversation.

The simplest change would be to transform the outside. Already he had proven to be acceptable-looking, even a bit devastating. With the proper clothes and a modicum of manners, he ought to pass well enough.

After all, it wasn't as though she were trying to find him a wife. She needn't prove anything about him but that he was an ordinary fellow.

If only she hadn't claimed he was a musician . . .

Curling her body around her pillow, Agatha sleepily tried to plot her way out of that one until she drifted off again.

Simon stepped out of the shadows to look down on Agatha. Even in the near darkness, he could see her sleep-flushed cheeks and one round shoulder peeking from the neckline of her gown.

What was her game? She was a consummate actress, with her fresh country ways and her direct sexuality. He had waited for another invitation tonight, half-expecting her to dispense his "reward" for remaining to help her.

Instead, she had brightly wished him a good evening and

instructed a bemused Pearson to have breakfast ready promptly at seven.

Simon didn't know much about the habits of mistresses, but he had always pictured them a lazy bunch, sleeping their days away whilst awaiting their paramours at night.

The house creaked a midnight protest around him. He had searched every inch of it in the last few hours, barring the servants' quarters. But other than some rather incriminating inscriptions in the books lining his own room—"To James, my dear schemer, Love, A"—he had found nothing useful so far.

Agatha shifted restlessly beneath her covers and Simon stepped back into shadow. He was finished here, and he had much to take care of before he could remain in this house for a week. He should go.

This room held nothing more of interest to him. Nothing but the woman in the bed. She was a mystery that he was fast becoming obsessed with.

As he slipped out as silently as he had come, Simon decided that he probably shouldn't have untied her braid to feel the texture of her hair. And he definitely shouldn't have let her scent tempt him into leaning deeply over her as she slept.

The streets of London never truly slept, at least not in Simon's part of town. As he walked swiftly down the cobbles, using the shadows for concealment without skulking, Simon inhaled the damp, sooty smell of the city, overlain with a tinge of dirty Thames.

After the fresh-flower-scented halls of the house on Carriage Square, the city's reek was familiar as his own face in the mirror but not particularly welcoming.

This part of the city was neither the finest nor the worst. A mix of places gone to seed and establishments on their way back up. Londoners of all classes mixed here as they did nowhere else. During the day, gentlemen walked next to beggars and ladies passed unknowingly close to whores.

Neither desperate nor decadent, this area was the perfect

location for the Liar's Club. By day a gentlemen's club of not-too-sterling reputation, by night the lair of England's finest—if somewhat irregular—spy corps.

Simon slowed, his boots clicking on the cobbles faintly. Casually he waited until a cart rattled past, then he ducked swiftly down an alley. Pausing for a moment to listen for any sound of trespassers, Simon let his eyes adjust. The light from the street lamps didn't penetrate into the darkness within, but Simon didn't need a lamp to find his way.

The alley angled sharply and Simon turned with it automatically. Then he stopped to feel in front of him, making a small sound of satisfaction when his hand touched cold iron.

With practiced ease, Simon swiftly climbed the rusted ladder that had been positioned between the two walls of windowless brick.

The ladder led nowhere. The raw iron of the ends was cut, leaving the climber halfway up one wall with nowhere to go but down.

Unless one knew to stand on the topmost rung and jump to the narrow ledge running the length of the opposite wall. There were handholds if one knew where to look.

Simon didn't have to look, having made this journey hundreds of times in the last several years, in wet weather and dry, at the black of midnight and in broad daylight.

Once he was perched on the ledge, clinging to the almost invisible grips chiseled into the brick, it was only a short journey along the ledge to a heavily barred window that rose from his knees to over his head.

The bars were joined with a massive lock and a loop of mighty chain that would have been at home on the docks. Simon ignored these for a small lever hidden in the upper right corner of the window.

With a substantial click and the whisper of well-oiled hinges, Simon was through the window and inside. Once within the storeroom situated above the kitchen, Simon secured the window and dusted his hands together.

Just another ramble to the office.

Chapter Four

Only a few short hours later, Simon yawned as he passed the little maid scuttling down the hall on early-morning maid business. Nellie flashed him a cheery smile and a cheeky giggle.

The sun was not yet up, but Simon was determined not to let Agatha have the complete running of things. If she said seven, he would breakfast at six. He pushed open the door of the breakfast room, fighting another yawn, then stopped short.

"Good morning, Mr. Applequist. Did you rest well?"

Perched, fully dressed, at the table in the yellow-papered breakfast room, Mrs. Applequist cut a triangle of toast and daintily chewed it.

Simon couldn't believe it. She was as chirpy as a bird digging for worms in a pre-dawn garden. Forcing his yawn away with iron will, he nodded briskly.

"And you?" he asked, as she had rehearsed with him the night before.

Her eyes widened appreciatively at his perfectly modulated words. Simon felt a tiny surge of ridiculous pride. Of course he could speak well. He always had. Well, not always, but for years. Why should her approval mean a thing to him?

The gangling footman left the room, and Mrs. Applequist sighed with visible relief.

"You may be at ease now, Mr. Rain."

Simon simply shot her a glare and fixed himself a heaping plate from the sideboard and sat opposite her at the cheerful table with its bright crockery. The lady's cook was better than his own, he decided as he chewed.

He watched her covertly as they ate in silence. The sun had begun to shine into the room, glancing off her hair with reddish shine. Odd. He had thought her hair to be pure black, not a brown so deep 'twas almost sable.

Brown hair, brown eyes. So very ordinary, really.

Except she wasn't ordinary at all, was she? Suspicion sneaked through his thoughts. What more perfect disguise for a woman than to be ordinary? People never noticed the ordinary.

Their eyes would go right over her, to be attracted by the more exotic, the more flamboyant. Like his guise of a chimneysweep, so everyday as to be invisible.

The news-sheet she read crackled under her fingers, and she gave a little gasp of excitement.

"What's afoot?" he asked.

"Read this!" She slid the paper halfway across the mahogany tabletop, then paused. He looked up to see her eyeing him hesitantly.

"What?"

"You . . . you *can* read, can't you?"

Simon almost snatched the paper away with a growl, then decided that his chimneysweep character might well be illiterate. He simply sat back without replying and let her read to him, eyeing the sheet as he listened.

It wasn't a real newspaper but more of a gossip sheet, full of references to "Lady B—" and "Lord F—," nattering on about marital matches and gowns and spies—

Spies. Oh, no. Not again.

" 'Your Voice of Society wonders that England's greatest hero-spy has not been rumored about town recently. Although he is the Crown's closely held secret, your Voice knows that not so long ago he upset an entire attack against the Sons of England with his swift action against the wagons carrying cannon shot and powder.

" 'He crept behind the lines in the dark of the night, risking life and limb in a sure-suicide mission to destroy the very weapons of war that Napoleon wields against our Sons and Brothers.' "

Simon had heard it before, or something very like it. The workings of his secret organization, spread out for public consumption. Facts that only one man besides himself could know. Simon's hands twitched with rage.

Later. Simon quelled his fury, returning his gaze to Agatha. She read on, the praise growing more exorbitant and flowery, until it almost held the flavor of mockery.

Simon had to make it stop. "What's this rot?"

Mrs. Applequist put the paper down with a sniff. "This 'rot' is why I am here. I am looking for someone. He is missing, and I must find him."

"Who is it, then?"

"His name is James Cunnington. He is my—he is very dear to me," she finished.

James. So she gave her lover's name.

"What's it got to do with me?"

"With you by my side, I may move about Society much more easily. I may ask questions, make inquiries. The spy this speaks of is the Griffin. It has as much as said so in previous issues. If I can find the Griffin, then I think I may be able to find James."

"The Griffin, eh?"

"I'm not entirely sure. I have only one clue to follow, so I will begin there. A letter I once saw in James's possession, signed 'The Griffin.' "

"Not much of a clue."

"Oh, I know it is a remote chance. But whatever else, I must find James. He is all I have left."

Her voice was still soft, but Simon could hear the steel determination beneath. This was not good. These were deadly people. Even if she were merely a mistress looking for her lover, she was going to severely shake the tree.

She was not only dangerous, she was in danger herself. She could have no idea what she was dealing with.

· "We've much to do today, Mr. Rain." She smiled and placed her napkin beside her plate. "If you'll join me in the parlor once you've breakfasted?"

Simon nodded as she rose, then was unable to keep himself from watching the way her skirts twitched over her bottom as she walked from the room. He tore his eyes away with difficulty. It was going to be a very long week.

In the meantime, he may as well enjoy the food. Picking up his fork, he attacked his breakfast once again.

A fellow needed to keep his strength up around this one. There was no telling what she expected him to do.

"I ain't doing it! Not now, not never. And if you're thinking of trying to make me, you'll cop a packet!"

The powdered wig hit the bedchamber wall with an explosion of talcum. Mrs. Applequist and Button, the valet she had hired and sworn to secrecy, watched the powder drift to the floor to lightly coat the other items that had suffered from Simon's intransigence that morning.

A horribly wrinkled cravat, collar points, and a monocle lay discarded on the floor, testament to his rejection of dandified fashion.

Mrs. Applequist sighed.

Again.

"Very well, Mr. Rain. Perhaps the wig is a bit much. After all, you'll hardly be making an appearance at Court. If we do without the collar points and the monocle, will you *please* try to accustom yourself to the cravat? No gentleman would appear in Society without his neckcloth intricately tied."

"Oh, *all right*!" Simon muttered crossly, hiding his desire to laugh. He was beginning to enjoy the role of the rascally chimneysweep.

Tilting his chin back, Simon allowed Button to wrap and tie a freshly pressed cravat around his neck. The little valet's hands were shaking, and Simon spared a moment of sympathy for the fellow.

Between Mrs. Applequist's dramatic pleas for secrecy and

Simon's ranting, the man no doubt thought himself in the hire of Bedlamites.

Looking back on the past three days, Simon couldn't help thinking he might well qualify as a madman soon. Every waking moment had been filled with elocution exercises, tableware memorization, and dance lessons.

From dawn 'til night, he was worked as hard as he had ever been worked before. It was nearly as difficult to play a man who had no knowledge of those things as it had been to learn them all the first time.

Mrs. Applequist had been forced to attach a valet for him, but she wasn't taking any more chances on exposure. She prepared his lessons herself, ate with him, and nagged him constantly.

"Remember the *h*, Mr. Rain."

"Kindly recollect the *g*, Mr. Rain."

"That is your *salad* fork, Mr. Rain."

If he had been the poor uneducated man she thought him, he would be a babbling idiot by now. As it was, he was barely able to survive until afternoon tea without strangling the little martinet.

Ah, but following tea, it was time for his dance lesson. That's when his little tyrant would go soft and almost shy.

After sending away the tray and winding a delicate porcelain music box, she would pace slowly to the center of the parlor "schoolroom" and beckon to him silently.

Simon had never danced so well. Previously, there had been no reason to attain any real level of accomplishment, and at first, his clumsiness had not been entirely feigned.

His patchwork education had been centered around stealth and secrecy, not style and Society.

Sadly, until this afternoon he was expected to let her dress him like a mannequin. Button finished his precise tying ritual with a tug and a sniff, and Simon moved to stand before the looking glass.

The man in full evening dress he saw reflected there gave him pause. Button might not be the bravest soul in creation, but he was an absolute genius as a valet. Simon blinked at the picture he made.

Very dapper. He looked an absolute lord. Not his usual style at all. How odd to see himself this way.

"Button, you are a wonder!" Mrs. Applequist clapped her hands in delight. "Oh, Mr. Rain, you look like a gentleman through and through!"

Careful, old man. Mustn't make progress too quickly. He scowled into the mirror. "I looks like a bloody tea leaf, that's what I looks like!"

Roughly he pulled off the cravat and waistcoat. "You can trick me out like this when you must, but I ain't wearin' this rig every day."

She watched with wide eyes as his fingers began undoing the studs of his shirt. Simon was careful to fumble the littlest bit, then he pulled it off over his head impatiently.

She took a tiny step back, but her gaze didn't waver.

"Got your eye full?" Simon snarled.

When her eyes widened and she stopped breathing, Simon finally had to laugh. She flushed at his guffaw and turned away.

"Button, would you be so kind as to prepare Mr. Rain for tea?"

With brisk steps she crossed to the door. When she raised her gaze to Simon's, the delight was gone and her eyes were large and dark with something else entirely.

After beating her strategic retreat, Agatha paused a moment outside Simon's room, leaning on the paneled wood of the hall and breathing deeply.

What sort of weakling was she, to vow one moment to see him as an instrument of subterfuge and the next to be blinded by his masculine appeal?

And he was appealing, wasn't he? It was very disturbing. In—and out of—his new garments, he was any young girl's ideal gentleman. But she wasn't a girl any longer, and he was no gentleman.

"Will you be wanting tea served in the parlor now, madam?"

Agatha opened her eyes to find Pearson gazing at her, apparently unperturbed to find her propped against the wall like a broom.

"Yes, thank you, Pearson." Agatha cleared her throat and smiled brightly at the butler. "That will be lovely."

A bracing cup of tea did sound lovely. Mr. Rain was coming along beautifully with his table manners, although he still had a tendency to eat rather too appreciatively. One really shouldn't make those delighted sounds in one's throat. Terribly distracting.

Tea, and then she would play dancing master. Agatha felt the heat rising within her again. Today she would teach Mr. Rain—no, Mr. *Applequist*—the waltz.

As a married couple, he and his wife were perfectly entitled to perform the somewhat scandalous dance. It was only the maiden woman who was discouraged from pressing herself so closely to her partner, swirling intimately across the floor in his arms.

Heavens. How would she survive it?

Mrs. Applequist looked as though she wanted to kill him. Simon watched as she visibly fought down her growing frustration and began again.

"Place one hand thus, Mr. Applequist. Then lightly—lightly I say, not as though one is handling a coal shovel!—lightly take the lady's hand, here, holding it precisely at shoulder height. . . ."

Simon stopped listening. He was far more interested in watching her mouth move. It was odd how, when you took her features one by one, they did not amount to much in themselves. It was the entire mixture that was so attractive.

She was no classic beauty, but her snapping brown eyes and full lips combined with her fresh rosy complexion, making up a veritable recipe for appeal.

He especially liked her lips. They were highly colored, all

of their own merit, and when she was nervous, such as now, the pretty Mrs. Applequist had a tendency to slide her tongue across them quickly.

There. She did it again. It made him ache a little more whenever she did so.

It occurred to Simon that he had never really seen her smile with those lips. She had made polite faces to her lady guests and been pleasant to her household, but he had yet to see her smile naturally.

He wanted to see that. Very badly. At any rate, he was tired of making himself step on her toes.

"You know, where I come from, dancin' ain't just for those what dressed up for it."

"What do you mean?"

"Me mum used to work in Covent Garden on Market Day. After the whole lot was packed out at the end of the day, the buskers and fiddlers'd sit out in the empty square and play into the night."

"I haven't yet seen the Covent Garden Market. What did your mother sell?"

Herself. But Simon wasn't going to let that tidbit out.

"Oh, this and that."

"What about your father?"

Best not to talk about that. "Are you tellin' this or me?"

"I apologize. Please go on."

He didn't, though, not for a moment. He simply enjoyed the feel of her in his arms as they stepped about the parlor to the sound of the music box chime.

"Mr. Rain? You were telling me about the musicians after Market Day?"

"We'd all gather round, you see, after the regular sorts went home. Them as had coin would buy up the last of the tarts and meat pies for near to nothing, and pass 'em out. Spirits'd be brought out to wet throats dry from hawking wares all day, and things'd get right jolly."

Sometimes they had gotten rather dangerous as well, but she needn't hear about that.

"And then there was the dancing. The baker in his apron

and the seller women in their caps, without a care for their dress, all just dancing for the joy of it, and of a day well ended."

Mrs. Applequist raised a brow. "I've been to country dances all my life, Mr. Rain. Surely it's no more joyous than that."

"I dunno about them country types, but unless they was Gypsy players, I can't see 'em whirling any faster than me mum and the baker."

She looked intrigued. "Whirling? I can't say that I have ever 'whirled,' " she said a bit wistfully.

Simon let her out of his arms and stepped back. Touching a finger to the base of the music box, he ended the sedate chiming.

"But, Mr. Rain, we haven't finished—"

Clapping his hands together sharply, Simon began whistling a sprightly tune. Giving her an encouraging grin, he took her hands and began to clap them within his own until she took up his rhythm.

Then, stepping back, he began a stamping counterpoint to her rhythm, stepping briskly forward to her, then back, then turning in time.

The lady definitely seemed interested, chewing her lip as she followed the pattern of his feet with her eyes and kept his rhythm with her hands. When Simon saw that she had it, he grabbed her hands to send her spinning and began to sing lustily:

> "Go on, fellow, grab your girl.
> Take her hand and let 'er whirl.
> If she comes back, then dance you on.
> If she don't, then hell, she's gone!
> Take the next one, she might do.
> If she won't, then take you two!"

Agatha was whirling. Skipping madly in a circle to Simon's bawdy song, she clapped and whirled until her head spun. Dizzily she reached out, only to collapse against

Simon's sturdy chest. Panting wildly, she grinned up at him.

"You are quite mad, Mr. Rain."

"You honor me, Mrs. Applequist." The formal tone of the phrase she'd drummed into him was at odds with the rakish twist of his lips.

Agatha liked the feel of him beneath her hands. He was solid and truly very tall, when one stood so close. Her breath still came quickly from dancing, and with the air that she drew in, she drew in his scent as well.

Clean and sharp and manly, cinnamon and tobacco.

"Cinnamon."

"What?"

"You . . . smell of cinnamon."

"Aye."

Agatha swallowed. The heat of him was seeping through her clothing, licking like firelight over her bosom and belly. He had grasped her elbows to steady her and her skin tingled where he touched. "Wh . . . Why?"

"Why do I smell of cinnamon?" he asked softly.

Agatha nodded. Odd, how she couldn't seem to catch her breath. Surely she hadn't danced that vigorously.

"Cinnamon drops. The bits of red sugar from the confectionery. I'm rather partial to them."

"Oh. Of course. Drops. Cinnamon." Then she noticed something. "Oh, how marvelous! You are speaking so beautifully."

Simon shook off the spell of her smile and the press of her soft, giving body against his. Damn, he'd slipped. Setting her firmly back on her feet, he moved back.

"Well, I've 'ad me a grand teacher, now 'aven't I?"

"Oh. Well, thank you, Mr. Rain." With a distracted air, Agatha pressed both palms to her face. "What were we doing? Oh, the waltz."

She waved a hand toward the music box. "If you please, Mr. Rain?"

They returned to their formal pattern of steps. Simon moved stiffly, trying very hard not to see the way her eyes had grown dark and the flush of exertion had turned her cheeks a flattering pink.

Her breath still came a touch more heavily than usual, and he could feel it on his neck, warm and moist and fragrant, like her skin.

Unthinking, he pulled her closer, wanting to once more feel her full bosom against his chest.

"Mr. Rain, we must stay a certain space apart! As if another person stood between us."

The phrase hit him with a splash of icy reality. A host of things stood between them. Secrets. Lies. And James. James stood between them as if a mountain had suddenly erupted where they stood together.

What was happening to him? Where was his analytical edge, his cool reason? Was it the disguise? Using the cant of his childhood, taking him back to the man he might have been—a simpler man with no more worries than making a pretty woman smile?

Simon pulled away. "Enough for now."

Agatha's expression softened. "No one expects you to grasp it all immediately," she said. "We have another four days."

"Good. Then I'm goin' out. I need some air." He dodged past her for the door. He had better get to it first. She was fast when she wanted to be.

"Mr. Applequist—"

"Rain," Simon interrupted brusquely. "My name is Rain."

"I know that, Mr.—" Agatha shook her head in irritation. "I cannot become too used to calling you that. I must be able to address you naturally, or this will never work."

"If you're my wife, then call me 'Simon.' Better yet, 'Simon, darling.' " He grinned at her.

"Better yet, 'Mortimer, darling,' you mean to say."

"Bloody hell. Did you have to pick such a name? Mortimer is the lad w' the broken spectacles and the running nose. You should've picked a strong name, like . . . like . . ."

Agatha raised a brow. "Such as 'Simon'?"

"Well, it beats 'Mortimer' any hour."

"I have no difficulty addressing you as Mr. Applequist. Many women address their husbands so."

"Well, how would you know? You ain't never been married, now, 'ave you?"

"Kindly recall the *h*, Mr.—" Agatha bit her lip. "My marital status is not the point. Besides, I could already be married if I wished. I shall call you 'Mortie.' And you shall call me 'Agatha.' Well enough?"

"Well enough," he grumbled. What did she mean, she could be married if she wished? She was a dove, a ladybird, a mistress. No respectable man would take her home and fit her out in an apron.

Then again, he was no respectable bloke, was he?

What was he thinking? She was not only a fallen woman, she was quite possibly involved in something entirely fishy.

He was here to terminate a leak, not to pluck her from her well-feathered nest of sin. No doubt she was perfectly happy where she was.

Air. He needed air. Pausing at the front door, he cursed the necessity of pausing to let Pearson help him into his outerwear. As soon as he had his coat on, he snatched the hat and gloves, then slammed out into the street.

Chapter Five

The long walk through Mayfair and beyond was enough to clear Simon's head, but still his thoughts lingered on his pretty partner in crime. He shook his head, trying to shake her out of his brain. He had work to do.

The club stood directly across the street from where he lingered, but still Simon hesitated. Should he walk in the front door as Mortimer?

Mortimer certainly wouldn't be out of place at a respectable gentlemen's club. Well, somewhat respectable.

The rather Gothic facade before him housed the sort of club that wives and mothers didn't want to know about. A place for the restless set to gather, drink, and game, telling themselves they were experiencing the true streets of London.

Of course, no true Corinthian would waste his time here, for a real whoremongering gaming hell—while certainly full of other amusements—would never serve the sort of cuisine and fine liquor that was found at this establishment. Simon took particular pride in his selection of cigars, although he only occasionally smoked them himself.

No, in reality it was rather tame, at least on the surface. Mortimer was just the sort of poseur to enjoy the blunted badness of the Liar's Club.

His decision made, Simon pulled his top hat low over his eyes and strode across the cobbles, exuding all the snobbery of a gentleman slumming in a moderately shabby area for his own amusement. The doorman gave him a bored glance.

"It's a private club, sir. I can't admit ye without a sponsor."

Simon tipped his hat higher with one finger to show his face. "Open the door, Stubbs, or I'll dock your pay."

The doorman's eyes widened, and he truly looked at Simon for the first time.

"Sir! Yessir, Mr. Rain, sir! I didn't recognize ye all toffed up, sir!"

Simon grinned. "That's all right, Stubbs. I never use the front door anyway."

"Yessir. I mean, nossir!" Stubbs jumped to open the door for Simon.

"Is Jackham about, Stubbs?"

"Yessir. Mr. Jackham's in the office, sir, last I saw 'im, sir."

Simon only nodded, passing into the club. It was a relief to get away from the poor fellow's groveling.

It was even more of a relief to step into the manly, smoky world of his club. Even simply to be in the outer rooms, which were used solely by the young gentlemen and lordlings who frequented the tables and drink provided there. The deep green walls and dark woods were severe and simple. It was a world of men, free of floral scents, tea service, and nagging.

Not to mention free of temptation.

Jackham was grumbling about that very thing when Simon entered the office behind the billiards room. The older man was seated at the giant banker's desk. He had likely been there a while, for his reddish fringe of hair was already mussed from frustrated finger-running.

"We'd be twice the richer if we had some doves in here," Jackham grumbled rudely as he pored over the bookkeeping. "And where the hell have you been?"

Simon only smiled as he lounged on the threadbare sofa that Jackham was too miserly to replace. After days of having the social niceties stuffed down his gullet, Jackham's lack of polish was refreshing.

"You know the rules, Jackham. No opium, no whoring. We stay clean and we stay in business."

"Whores aren't illegal. They're practically subsidized by the ladies of London who want their husbands gone from their beds."

"Jackham, we've had this discussion before. You may bring in the floor shows when the blokes get restless, but *absolutely no whoring*."

Jackham didn't dare do more than mutter when Simon glared him down. There was no possibility that Simon would ever budge on this issue. He had a few sins on his conscience—very well then, more than a few—but he refused to take part in the business of selling souls.

"So why haven't you shown your face around here for days, leaving me to run this place by myself? I don't own it, you know. You do."

"Business."

"Well, I figured that," groused Jackham. "It wouldn't have anything to do with that job got pulled over in Mayfair two nights back, would it?"

Simon grunted noncommittally.

Jackham's black eyes gleamed. "A fine piece of work, that. Worthy of the Magician himself, eh?" He winked at Simon. "Reminds me of my younger days on the rooftops. Hear tell the swag was full of diamonds. You know anything about that job, Mr. Rain?"

"Now, Jackham, you know I never tell tales out of school." Simon decided to throw a few diamonds into Jackham's cut this quarter, just to fiddle with his mind.

"I miss those days, I really do," sighed Jackham.

For a moment, the lines of pain in his face eased and Simon knew he was remembering his own days dancing with the devil on the rooftops of London, a mere shadow man who could lighten the wealth of the most secure establishments.

It was a thrilling life, the career of a master thief. It was also a short life, bound to end badly. For some, it ended in gaol or the gibbet.

For Jackham, one small misstep on a slippery and misted

ledge had landed him on the cobbles from four stories up. He'd become an old man in his thirties, burdened with the never-ending pain from his shattered bones.

It was a lesson that Simon was careful to always keep in the forefront of his mind. He might have gone that route himself, if the Old Man, the old spymaster himself, hadn't plucked him from the streets and dusted the soot off to train him for intelligence work.

Being a sweep was practically sneakwork training after all, with all the climbing and working in the dark. Many a young sweep gave it a try when their bodies grew beyond the diameter of a chimney.

Simon wasn't a thief, although he knew why Jackham thought so. After all, when one masked black-clad man comes across another in the act of opening a wealthy man's safe in the middle of the night, assumptions will be made.

That night, Jackham had generously offered to share the contents with him, confessing that he was strictly a jewel man. Simon had taken the official papers held within but debated taking the money. In the end, he had decided it was necessary to his cover as a thief. Besides, the government-strangled coffers of the Liar's Club could use a bit of padding.

A partnership had arisen that night. Simon would choose the house and obtain the layout through bribery or trickery, and Jackham would apply his genius to the actual act of midnight entry and safe-breaking.

The Liar's Club had prospered, and Jackham had made a quick fortune, which he had just as promptly squandered. When the fall happened, Simon had just taken over from his predecessor, the Old Man. Simon had told Jackham that he was retiring as well, and he needed a manager for the club he was "buying."

It hadn't been easy keeping the real purpose of the Liar's Club secret from Jackham for all these years, but for all the fondness Simon felt for his friend, he had no illusions about Jackham's ultimate inability to refuse money. Not even in the form of a bribe to sell out his dearest friend.

So Jackham believed the boys in the back rooms were part

of Simon's thieves' network and gleefully helped them plan many a break-in while tending the liquor and doing the books.

The club had renewed his interest in life and kept him feeling he was a part of the world he had lost.

Simon could see that the memories were turning Jackham's mood bleak. "You know, Jackham, the woman who danced with the giant snake was a nice bit. Why don't you bring her in for the customers? She can run one show for the marks out front, and then do one for our boys."

Jackham's eyes brightened at the idea of possible profit.

"She did have a right elegant act, didn't she? Brought us in a nice bit of change before. And the marks have seen her once, so they'll want to bring in their mates to prove they wasn't lying." His eyes narrowed. "Now, if even half of them bring a new face in, and even half of those want to join up . . ."

Simon grinned and left Jackham to his calculations, pleased that he had managed to get the man's mind off the past. There was nothing to be gained by looking backward, not when the road still stretched out ahead.

Simon's own road to the future was a straight one. He knew precisely what needed to be done and he knew he was the only man to do it. No matter how tempting the distractions.

Damn, but she was tempting, wasn't she?

The day was nearly gone and Mr. Rain still wasn't back from his outing. Agatha puttered about the house on Carriage Square for as long as she was able, but she wasn't used to idleness. For years she'd been busy with the estate. These past few days, Simon had filled her time and her thoughts.

No. Her *mission* had filled her thoughts.

But who fills your dreams?

Agatha ignored the little voice as she would a nagging fly. One couldn't help one's dreams. And if hers were filled with the noise and clatter of London streets, not to mention a certain pair of blue eyes—heavens, she'd never seen eyes so blue—well, that was a natural result of being unused to city life.

Irritated that she seemed unable to occupy herself without Simon, Agatha ventured into the kitchen. Sarah Cook, queen of her small domain, soon sent Agatha on her way with a sweet bun and a pointed hint. Pearson also had the household well in hand, so Agatha wasn't needed there, either.

She could write to her housekeeper back at Appleby. Surely there were some instructions she'd forgotten to offer Mrs. Bell as to the running of things.

No, to be honest, there was little she could tell her. Late spring was the easiest time of year in Lancashire. The apples were mere green marbles yet, and the sheep had lambed in early spring and had been sheared a month past.

Not that she was eager to return her mind to the tedium that had been hers for years. When the time came to tend Appleby once more, she would. However, the longer she could go without counting lambs or casks of cider, the better.

She'd always been content enough with country life before she'd come to London, although perhaps not entirely happy. She had secretly bemoaned her own restless nature and had done her best to suppress it. Papa had depended on her to see to the day-to-day things—and now Jamie did as well.

Jamie wasn't precisely neglectful of her, but he didn't visit as much as she would have liked. Instead she had to satisfy her need for family contact through his faithful correspondence.

Perhaps she needed children. She liked them very much, and the act of holding a babe had lately brought her near to tears of longing, yet Agatha couldn't think of a single man in Appleby she would want to wed.

Certainly not Repulsive Reggie. Not for his title, not for his lands, not even to stay close to her home. Agatha shuddered even now to think of his groping hands and the way his panting breath had felt on her face.

Forcing her mind back to the present, Agatha shook off the past. She had spent far too much of her life dreading him, certain that he was waiting for another chance to have her in his power. Besides, she had a chimneysweep to train.

And wasn't he coming along splendidly? There was much satisfaction to be found in helping someone achieve his potential. Perhaps she was meant to teach, for she affirmed privately that she had considerable natural skill. Just look what she had done with the man in a few short days!

Of course, she must allow him a certain amount of credit. He certainly was a lovely bundle of raw material. Those eyes . . . and that physique. Such long legs, and the way that the tails of his coat fell just so over his muscular . . .

"Goodness, it's become warm in here," Agatha muttered to herself, fanning her face restlessly.

As she went to confer with Button over the best use of Simon's new wardrobe, Agatha wondered why it should be that feeling Simon's hard body pressed to hers had felt nothing like being pinned by Reggie's vile weight.

Chapter Six

The evening of the supper dance finally came around. Agatha was pacing again. How many miles had she paced since all this had begun? Though the fire burned brightly in the grate, she rubbed her bare arms against a chill.

Her gown lay on the bed, but she didn't really wish to put it on.

If she dressed, then she would have to leave. If she left, she would have to go to Winchell's. And if she went to Winchell's, her lies would ultimately be exposed in a most public and embarrassing way.

Not that her pride mattered precisely, but going home would be bad enough. Going home in shame would only be worse.

Stopping before the gown, Agatha squinted at the rich green satin, picturing it in her mind against Lady Winchell's elegant apparel. Well, it would have to do. Unfortunately, she hadn't thought of needing much fine dress when she'd left Appleby.

The green was really the only thing she had. Not that anything she had left behind would have been any better. Spending all her life in the country hadn't prepared her wardrobe for the elegant competition of London fashion.

Still, the fabric was fine enough, and she had spent the afternoon retrimming it more modishly. Agatha pressed a hand to her middle and attempted to take a deep breath.

She despised lacing up so tightly, but the gown had been made a few years ago, and certain parts of her had grown in the interim.

The little porcelain clock on the mantel chimed. She had best ready herself for the night ahead.

She helped Nellie pull the skirts over her head. It was a pity, really. It would have been nice to face Mr. Rain in something a bit more appealing.

Simon firmly commanded his fists to unclench. Button was only doing his job. The fact that his fluttering and worrying were driving "the master" mad had more to do with Simon's misgivings about tonight's appearance.

He knew he could pull it off, of course. No one would know him for himself. If any did, they would no more claim acquaintance than he would, for their own protection.

And it wasn't that he didn't look fine. He had to admit that while Mortimer might be a nauseating fellow, he was a snappy dresser. Agatha had spared no expense on his wardrobe. He looked quite the first stare of fashion.

It was being the center of attention that worried him, he decided. Now, after all these years of keeping a low profile, it felt distinctly odd to be putting himself forward like this. He might as well dye himself red and flee before the hounds.

He still wasn't truly sure why he was going through with this, and that worried him as well. Oh, an invitation into Winchell's house was handy, but he could easily get in on his own.

As for this place, he was beginning to think there was nothing here. He had searched the house every night for a week and found nothing at all. Not a letter, not a word, not a clue.

By all the signs, the "Applequists" intended no more than the most temporary residence here. There were no hidden safe-boxes, no false-bottom drawers, no mysteriously hollow walls. The house was just as it seemed.

Agatha, however, was not. She was keeping something from him. Her manner was too friendly, too trusting and relaxed. Simon hadn't let his guard slip once since the waltz lesson, no matter how her sweetness had tempted him.

He had to admit, she was a consummate professional. He only wished he could be sure what profession.

Button gave a last aggrieved sigh and reluctant tug on the cravat.

"I suppose that will have to do, sir."

Button looked as though he wanted to cry. Simon examined himself in the mirror but could see nothing awry. Trying not to roll his eyes at the little valet's perfectionism, he clapped the fellow on the shoulder.

"Capital job, Button. Simply capital!" Giving his waistcoat a tug and casting an "I-am-Mortimer-king-of-all-I-survey" look in the glass, Simon sauntered out of the bedchamber in search of Agatha.

If he had to do this, he would just as soon get it over with. He wondered idly what Agatha was wearing.

The blasted gown was too tight. Agatha stretched up on her toes to check her neckline in the gilt mirror hanging over the small table in the front hall. Yes, it was far too tight. Oh, why hadn't she had a new wardrobe made for herself when she had ordered Simon's?

Well, she would, forthwith. But what was she to do tonight?

Agatha blinked at the sheer volume of exposed bosom her reflection presented. There was no getting around it. She would have to fetch some lace to tuck into her décolletage. Dowdy but necessary.

Her appearance was not important, at any rate. She had to remember that she was here to find Jamie, not to parade herself about.

"Are you out of your mind?"

Agatha turned to see Simon scowling at her from the stairs. Well, scowling at part of her, anyway.

"I'm sure I don't know what you mean." Although she thought perhaps she did.

"You are not going anywhere like that!"

Even as Agatha's temper rose at Simon's high-handed tone, she felt pride rise in her at his cultured speech. She had done a marvelous job. No one would ever know him for an uneducated chimneysweep.

Simon hurried down the last few steps to join her in the entrance hall. His scowl darkened as he loomed over her, gazing down at her décolletage.

"You are not decent. Put something else on."

"This gown is the only thing I have that will do." Coolly, Agatha turned back to the mirror. Now that she thought about it, she had seen much lower necklines in the fashion sheets. "Frankly, I do not think it is so very daring. I imagine town ladies wear such things routinely."

Simon had to admit that Agatha was correct in that. Her gown was not so very daring, but her body was.

He couldn't take his eyes off the lush white breasts that threatened to spill from her gown. Well, truly, they weren't so much spilling as they were tempting him to spill them.

Nonetheless, Agatha needn't flaunt her charms to every man in London. It was damned distracting.

That was it. He had important business to conduct this evening and he couldn't afford the distraction of defending her from the lecherous stares she would surely incite.

"Change at once," he commanded.

Agatha ruffled. If Simon thought that would do it, he was sadly mistaken. No one told her how to behave. Not her father, not even Jamie. She narrowed her eyes at him.

"I'm going as I am." She turned to signal Pearson. "Please bring the carriage around."

Pearson stepped forward, bearing her wrap.

"Then you will go without me." Simon smiled a not very nice smile. "I seem to have developed the headache."

Oh, blast. Simon was standing firm. Spare her from men standing firm. Agatha smiled back, a very sweet smile with daggers drawn.

"Pearson, do fetch my husband a powder for his poor aching head." That last was hissed from between teeth still clenched in a smile.

When she turned to the door, Simon put his hand on her arm. "Agatha, in truth, it is not wise to go out like that." His tone was calmer now, less autocratic. "Isn't there any way to cover your . . . to raise the neckline slightly? A bit of lace, perhaps?"

Agatha stopped. Hadn't she been thinking the very thing before Simon had come down? The man had a way of making her forget what she was about.

She ought to keep her wits about her tonight and not let herself be distracted by the way Simon's gaze had trouble staying on her face.

"Perhaps you are right. I shall be back down in a moment," said Agatha grudgingly, and started up the stairs.

It was almost worth conceding the point when she glanced back to see Pearson handing a paper packet of Papa's foul-tasting headache powder to an unenthusiastic Simon.

Chapter Seven

As Simon helped Agatha from their carriage before the elegant Winchell home, she shook out her skirts but never let a single breath interrupt her lecture.

"Now, remember, the precise bowing depth depends on the lady's rank. When introduced to a Mrs., bowing halfway will do. With a Lady, it cannot hurt to dip deeply. Even if you go a bit far, it will only seem flattering, especially if you use one of the phrases I taught you."

Simon gritted his teeth, his patience shredded. It had taken nearly an hour to navigate the crowded London streets, and Agatha had nagged throughout the entire journey.

"*Darling,* a *wife* really shouldn't lecture her dear *husband* in public." He cast a meaningful look at the couples being disgorged from their carriages around them. "One would not want to appear the shrew, would one?"

With a fixed smile, he firmly wrapped her hand around his arm and towed her into the line that was now forming at the door of the luxurious house.

"Oh. I apologize, *darling.* Thank you for reminding me, *darling.* One certainly would not, *darling.*" Agatha glared at him.

Simon only bared his teeth at her. "If you don't let up, I shall strangle you. After two weeks of your correcting my every word, criticizing my every move, and scrutinizing every bloody breath I take—"

"Gentlemen do not say 'bloody' in the company of a lady," Agatha pointed out primly.

"One more word and there will be *no one* in my company except a very pretty little corpse!" hissed Simon.

As she opened her mouth to retort once more, Agatha's mind snagged on one word.

Pretty?

Simon found her pretty? The very thought made Agatha trip on the grand marble stairs leading to the entry of Lord Winchell's even grander house. Simon continued his measured pace, his grip on her hand ensuring that she kept up, like it or not.

Agatha was actually grateful for his domineering attitude at the moment, for it allowed her to pull her thoughts together before being forced to greet the host and hostess.

He wished her to hide her bosom, but he thought her pretty?

A slow smile began as she put the two together. The warm feeling that Agatha had felt during that one afternoon as they had waltzed returned.

She steered Simon to the row of servants who took their outerwear. Then they entered the ostentatious hall and followed the stream of people into a grand ballroom.

While it was not as packed as it likely would be for a true ball, the guests seemed only to enjoy the spacious room the more. Agatha had never seen such expensive elegance. Memories of the assembly rooms that she had experienced in Lancashire faded next to the gleaming gilt-and-rose ballroom.

Her smile now one of excitement and delight, Agatha turned it on Simon.

"Isn't this beautiful?"

He leaned close. "It's a bloody dog 'n' pony show, if'n you ask me," he said, the Cockney thick in his voice.

"Simon! You promised!" Agatha was horrified until she realized from his grin that he was only teasing her. Glad to see his sour mood had dissipated, she smiled fondly at him as they came level with the Winchells.

Still delighted with her surroundings, Agatha found it easy to smile naturally at Lady Winchell as well.

Lavinia raised one perfect brow and twisted her lips in a wintry smile. "Why, Mrs. Applequist! You look quite grand. And I was so worried that you wouldn't find something suitable to wear after your long sojourn in the country."

Well, now the smile wasn't quite so natural, but Agatha refused to let Lady Winchell spoil her good mood.

"Lady Winchell, I pale beside your elegance, I'm sure. Wherever did you find such style? Most of the ladies I know bemoan the loss of French fashion, but you manage to look as if we were never at war at all."

Simon choked. Did Agatha realize that she had practically called a leading member of Society a French collaborator to her face? At the expression on Lady Winchell's face, he knew he wasn't the only one who had read the compliment as a barb.

With eyes narrowed and teeth bared in what hardly passed as a smile, Lady Winchell dropped Agatha's hand as though she held a dead rat and turned to Simon.

Instantly the lady's smile turned from piqued to predatory, and Simon blinked. He took her offered hand and repeated one of Agatha's scripted greetings as he bowed deeply over it. He felt Lady Winchell's middle finger slide up and down over his palm suggestively.

Now wasn't that an interesting development? He glanced up to see Agatha eyeing their clasped hands. She did not look happy.

"We mustn't keep you, my lady," she said sharply as Lady Winchell pulled her hand ever so slowly from Simon's. "I'm sure your other guests grow impatient."

Grabbing Simon's hand and nearly dislocating his shoulder, Agatha pulled him by force away into the circling guests.

"What is your difficulty?" snapped Simon. He wrested his arm from her grip. "I was merely following your instructions."

Agatha stopped her headlong charge and faced him. "You watch out for her, *darling*. She knows something, I can tell. She has always been suspicious of me, I don't know why."

"Could it be because you have been living a lie since you came to London?" Simon straightened his coat and cuffs, not looking up until he noticed her sudden silence.

"How did you know that?" Agatha whispered.

Oh, hellfire. For a moment, Simon couldn't recall what he was supposed to know and not know. "Ah, because you, ah, told everyone that you are married when you aren't and that you, ah, want to keep my real identity a secret. . . ."

Agatha breathed a sigh of relief. "Oh, *that* lie."

Aha. So there was more. As she moved through the crowd before him, Simon wondered how many layers of deception she had woven around him.

The music ended and Simon politely returned Mrs. Trapp to her husband. He dropped a quick bow to the Trapp daughters but avoided their veiled hints that they wished to dance with him again.

Over Mr. Trapp's shoulder he could see Agatha waltzing in the arms of an elderly fellow in uniform. It seemed she had been dancing with one redcoat after another for hours. Gossip had already established Mrs. Applequist's preference for soldiers, he was sure.

Turning aside Mr. Trapp's invitation to a game of cards and sidestepping the elbow in his ribs when the man made a blue joke, Simon laughed, clapped Trapp on the shoulder, and declared his need for refreshment.

Once he was clean away, he hid behind a marble pillar to catch his breath and scout the assembly. The party was getting a bit sloshed by this time, and dinner was still half an hour off. Perfect opportunity for some sneakwork.

"Mr. Applequist! How fortunate I am to catch you alone." The feline purr behind Simon warned him, but he wasn't ready for the elegant hand that cupped his buttock. Damn, but Lady Winchell was brazen!

Turning swiftly, he caught the encroaching hand and brought it to his lips for a formal bow.

"You outshine the stars, my lady. They weep in jealousy of your beauty." He winced as he fell back on the horrendous phrase that Agatha had forced him to learn, but Lady Winchell only looked pleased.

"You may call me Lavinia . . . in private. You speak so well, Mr. Applequist. I must say, I am surprised. You seemed so reticent when first we met."

"A touch of an exotic fever had stolen my voice that day, my lady. I declare, it pained me to be so rude, but my darling wife implored me not to try to speak, so to sooner heal."

"Ah, yes, the little wife. Tell me, Mortimer—may I call you Mortimer?"

"Indeed, my lady, I should be honored." As a mouse is honored by a snake, he'd be honored.

"Tell me, Mortimer, how can a man of your . . . well-traveled nature find fulfillment with such a—you'll pardon me for saying—overblown country milkmaid?"

The lady's lashes fluttered, but Simon didn't miss the hard-eyed stare as she waited for his reaction to her offensive words.

Could it be a test? He tamped down his irritation and kept his smile easy. The lady was going somewhere, and he didn't mind a bit following along until he learned where.

"Oh, Aggie's all right. She's a comfortable sort, easy to please, not a lot upstairs. A man likes to keep his home life uncomplicated, if you take my meaning."

"Leaving you to pursue more discerning company elsewhere, hmm? A masterful plan. I'm sure my husband wishes he had done the same."

"Surely not, my lady. The man who could ignore your charms has yet to draw breath."

She blinked coyly at him, moving closer until her breast brushed his upper arm.

"But I am ignored, you see. All this"—she waved a hand at her luxurious surroundings—"means nothing when a woman cannot feel . . . like a woman." Her pout looked ridiculous on a face meant for feline superiority.

She rocked to and fro minutely, but Simon could feel her nipple hardening against his bicep.

"There could be no one more womanly than you, my lady."

Simon filled time with banal compliments, thinking quickly. If he could get her to lead him to her husband's study, he could save himself considerable time, and time was beginning to be of the essence in this matter.

Agatha was busily combing the crowd for news of the Griffin, and Lord Winchell was occupied with his cohorts in the smoking parlor.

Time to get down to business.

Giving Lady Winchell a heavy-lidded look, he leaned his arm into her breast and slid it slowly back and forth. "Tell me, my lady, have you ever considered taking a bit of revenge on the old chap for ignoring you?"

"Oh, I think it has crossed my mind a time or two," she breathed.

"A man like that, always off playing cards, is he?" Simon knew Winchell was a devoted patron of the arts, but Mortimer wouldn't necessarily know that.

"No, it is his collections. So demeaning, a lady such as I married to a man who would prefer to spend his time with a painting or a statue."

"Now that is a shame."

Simon slid two fingers into her décolletage. He tugged at the fabric teasingly. "Such daring fashion. I wonder how easily I could slip these out and toy with them right in front of his lordship?"

Lavinia shuddered, her eyes closing at his suggestion. "Do it!" she whispered. "Right here, right now. Toy with me!"

"Oh, but that wouldn't be enough for a man like me, would it? Why settle for a simple tease, when I could show you so many interesting pastimes I've learned in my travels?"

That got her attention. Her eyes snapped open, glassy with lust. "Exotic pastimes?"

"My dear Lavinia, I could take you on such a journey you'll never want to come back. In the West Indies, I came upon a technique kept secret by the most decadent of courtesans."

"Show me! Now!" She grabbed his hand. "My bedchamber is—"

Simon repossessed his hand. "Lavinia, I'm surprised. I thought you wanted to explore the exotic. No one of any discernment uses a bed any longer."

"They don't?" She didn't seem terribly disappointed. If anything, her lascivious expression heightened.

"Now, this particular technique I have in mind for you is much heightened by certain . . . accoutrements, if you will. Of course, it requires a table or a desk of some sort . . ."

"The breakfast room. Hurry—"

"And to do it justice, I would really require . . ." How to get her into the study?

"Yes? Anything!"

"Ink."

"Ink?"

"Surely you've heard of the erotic art of tattooing?"

"But doesn't that hurt?" Far from appearing worried by the prospect, her eyes glittered.

"When done permanently, yes, it does. But this method is a sort of short-lived tattoo."

Even through her drink and lust, Lavinia was beginning to look suspicious. Simon pursed his lips and blew a soft trail of air across the exposed tops of her breasts.

"Imagine the sensation of brush and ink as I cover your flesh with mysterious designs. Swirling and wet, the brush is first cold, then, as it warms from contact with your skin, begins to feel like a human fingertip, or perhaps even a tongue."

She was panting now, eyes completely lust-glazed. "My husband's study. A desk. Plenty of ink."

"And imagine the enjoyment you'll feel every time you see him sitting at that desk and you remember your wicked, wicked revenge."

He needn't have embellished. She was completely ame-

nable to the plan now. Grabbing his arm, she almost ran to
the stairs at the back of the hall.

"Here. Down and to the right. Seventh door. I shall meet
you there by another route."

"Godspeed, my pretty." Simon kissed her hand and nonchalantly headed down the stairs. Out of the corner of his eye
he saw her skirts whirl as she took off in the other direction.

As soon as she was out of sight, he flung himself headlong
down the steps.

No one was in sight in the ground-floor hall, which was
lit by an abundance of sconces lining the walls. Simon ran,
counting doorways under his breath.

"Seven!" Quickly he pulled a brimstone match from his
pocket and thrust it beneath the glass shade of the nearest lit
sconce. Once the match flared to life, he ducked into the dark
room with it and shut the door behind him.

A handy arrangement of candlesticks stood on a table near
the door. Simon grabbed the nearest available candle and lit
it, then carefully snuffed the stick of sulfur-dipped juniper in
his hand and returned it to his pocket.

Now, where to start? Moving quickly to the desk, he
swiftly but silently pulled each drawer completely out and ran
his hands around the back and bottom.

Without the slightest glance into the contents—for who
would be stupid enough to hide something there?—he slid
each drawer back into place before pulling out the next.

Nothing.

Dropping to his knees, he slid his hands over all the unex-
posed surfaces of the wood. Underneath, the bottom edges of
the sides, around the kneehole.

Nothing.

Without pausing, he turned to the wall behind the desk and
began neatly flipping paintings aside. He had just uncovered
an iron safe-box when he heard a small sound. Smoothly he
let the painting slip down and steadied it with his elbow as
he turned.

The door opened. Lavinia thrust herself inside as if pursued by wolves and shut it once more, leaning breathlessly against it.

"Will it do?"

"Will what do?" Simon nonchalantly moved forward to settle one hip on the massive desk.

"The desk," she panted. "Can we use it for the 'technique'?"

"Oh, yes, perfect. I was just searching for some ink."

Simon was forced to step back as Lavinia flung herself at the desk and pawed wildly through a drawer.

"Here!" She thrust an inkwell and brush into his hands, then hefted herself to sit on the polished ebony surface. A predatory snarl on her lips, she leaned closer and tugged at his cravat.

"Where do you want me?" she growled.

"Ah, here is good, for now." Damn, now what? Simon couldn't believe the speed with which she had gotten here. She must have run the entire way. He couldn't leave now that he was so close to success.

Hmm. How gullible was she while aroused? Reaching into his jacket for the packet of headache powder, he waved it before her until her glazed eyes focused on it.

"What is it?"

"Ah, my lady, it is a substance so secret that it has no name. Ground from the root of a plant found only in the highest reaches of Peru, it is gathered in moonlight by virgins and preserved in bowls made from the skulls of lechers."

Well, that was laying it on a bit thick. Hellfire, he was getting to be as much of a liar as Agatha. However, Lavinia was completely and utterly hooked. Now to reel her in.

"What is it for?" she breathed.

"A mere pinch in a glass of brandy will heighten erotic pleasure to an exquisite level. It—"

Flinging herself from her perch on the desk, Lavinia rushed across the study to a small side table on which stood a full decanter and glasses. She sloshed a glass brim full and returned to him, holding it out eagerly.

"Put it in!"

Delicately Simon undid a fold of the paper and tapped a tiny sprinkle of powder into the brandy.

"More," she demanded, and reached for it.

He held it out of her reach. "Ah, now, my lady. There lies the road to madness. Imagine yourself caught up in an unending orgasm, lost in the throes of ecstasy forever." He shook his head. "A fate worse than death, to be sure."

She didn't look sure at all. In fact, she looked quite ready to fling herself bodily into the pit of insane release. Simon shook a finger at her.

"Now, my lady, you must trust me in this. If after you have drunk your brandy, you do not feel the effects, we shall see about giving you a bit more."

She raised the glass and tossed back the brandy with a professional speed that made Simon blink. This might not be as easy as he had thought.

"There. Nothing. Give me more." This time she brought over the entire decanter. Filling her glass again, she held it out. Simon sprinkled the powder and watched the brandy disappear with breathtaking swiftness once again.

"Damn you, I feel nothing. Nothing at all." She glared at him suspiciously.

Simon shrugged. "I don't understand. You should be trembling on the floor by now, lost in wave after wave of rapture."

Her eyes bulged. "Wave after wave?"

"Positively. Perhaps the formula has lost some potency over time. I suppose it wouldn't hurt to give you a bit more."

He held out the packet over her glass. She snatched it from him and dumped the contents, watching the powder sink with a satisfied smirk. She backed away from him, swirling her brandy.

"Sorry, love. I don't feel much like star—sharing." She blinked, then shook her head and giggled. "Waves and waves. Oh my."

She flung the contents of the glass down her throat. For a moment she stood, head thrown back and eyes closed, swaying.

Excellent. Any moment she should pass out.

When she lowered her head and opened her eyes, Simon was surprised. What fortitude! Most men would be lost by now. When she focused on him, he felt wary.

"I feel it, now. I feel the pleasure." She danced toward him slowly. "Touch me. Tear my gown from my body!"

Reaching up, she grasped her neckline with both hands and yanked. With a rip the seams gave and her breasts spilled out. Swaying before him, she closed her eyes. "Touch me."

"Ah, I will, in just a moment. First, ah, first the ink!" Stepping around her, being sure to stay out of her reach, Simon grabbed for the inkwell and brush.

She was quicker than he thought. With a growl, she flung her arms around his neck and her legs around his waist, pressing his face to her bosom.

Under the unexpected burden, Simon staggered back. When the backs of his knees came in contact with the sofa behind him, he had no choice but to fall with her on top of him.

She straddled him now.

"I want to touch you. Take this off!" She tugged at his shirt.

Simon played for time. Surely the brandy would take effect soon? "All right, now. I don't want you to tear anything. Let me remove it." She swayed above him, giggling while he reluctantly undid his cravat and shirt studs.

"Oh, I like your chest. Do you like mine?"

She stroked her hands lightly up her body, teasing her own nipples, then slid her hands up her neck and plunged her fingers through her hair, pulling it loose. She stretched her arms above her head, arching her back seductively.

"Take me," she demanded huskily.

And then fell over, completely crocked.

Chapter Eight

Agatha smiled at her partner and curtsied low. When another fellow approached her for the next set, she pleaded exhaustion and slipped away.

It wasn't a fib at all, for she was full weary of being ogled and manhandled. She felt as though her figure led them to think she relished such attention. Rarely had she dealt with such disrespect.

Apparently there were two sides to this freedom coin.

And Simon had played his part all too well. She had spent the first part of the evening watching his every move, watching him laugh with the men and flirt with the ladies.

She'd had to force herself to stop so that she could do her own investigating into any rumors of the Griffin's true identity—which abounded. But through the last few hours she had tried to keep an eye on Simon.

So had many of the other women in attendance. Agatha quite feared she had created a monster in Mortimer Applequist. A flirting, charming monster wearing Simon's handsome face.

Where was he now? Agatha searched the ballroom from her perch on the third stair. There were many men with dark hair, some tall, some not, but there was no one with Simon's particular catlike grace.

He wasn't dancing. He wasn't gaming. The call to go in to supper was half an hour off.

Inasmuch as she had found all that she had come for, there was no reason to stay any longer. Besides, she thought it best if Simon left before supper. She wasn't at all confident of his newly acquired table manners.

Could he have gone into the gardens? She couldn't think why he would. Only couples seemed to be using the torch-lit graveled paths that wound away into the greenery. What in the world could one see in the garden at night, anyway?

Still, perhaps she ought to check. She started down the extravagant stairs to the ballroom floor, for the large open doors to the gardens were on the other side of the enormous room.

At that moment, her attention was caught by two figures who sidestepped her with absent nods and exited into the hall. The two gentlemen bypassed the gaming room and moved down the gallery, turning a corner that led back into the house.

If she wasn't mistaken, one of them was Lord Winchell himself.

Was there a smoking room set up deeper in the house? She hadn't been told of one, but if it was a gentlemen's chamber, there was no reason why she would have been.

Following the men at a slight distance, she could hear Winchell's words to his companion.

"If you'll join me in my study, I can show you the plans I've had drawn up for the new hospital wing. I think you'll see that my ideas are far superior—"

"Oh, I say, Winchell! Is this the painting you told me about? What a magnificent work! What detail . . ."

Art was fine enough in its place, but Agatha needed to find Simon. If Winchell was only going to his study, it wasn't likely that Simon would be joining him there as well.

She was about to turn back when she saw something glinting on the floor at her feet.

A cuff stud. Idly she picked it up and turned it in her fingers. Gold, inset with lapis.

Dear heaven, it was one of Simon's! She had chosen it herself because the stone so perfectly matched his eyes. What purpose could a chimneysweep have in skulking about in the halls of Winchell's house? Ignoring the tiny voice that reminded her that she herself was skulking, Agatha fumed.

He was going to get them both in trouble. If he was caught and ruined his charade, she'd be revealed as well.

She hadn't come this far to be thrown from her course by an ill-trained rascal like Simon. Keeping to the shadows of the wide passage, Agatha eased around the two men who were avidly debating the merits of the artist.

With her back to the wall, ready to smile and plead lack of direction, Agatha moved to the nearest doorway. Pressing the door handle, she thrust her head in and looked quickly about. Nothing.

The next room revealed only chill darkness as well. Sliding her feet and moving slowly to minimize the rustling of her skirts the way she used to do to sneak past her governess, Agatha slipped into the subsequent embrasure.

She knew the moment she saw candlelight through the first crack of the doorway that she had found Simon. Casting a glance back down the passage, she checked on Lord Winchell.

Blast! He was headed her way! Only his absorption in his conversation kept him from spying her immediately. Agatha slipped into the room.

She had taken a breath to warn Simon when she realized three things simultaneously.

First, the richly paneled room with the gigantic desk was certainly Lord Winchell's study. Second, the half-dressed woman sprawled upon the sofa was assuredly Lord Winchell's wife.

And third, the half-dressed man opening Lord Winchell's wall safe was undeniably her Simon.

Simon turned at the slight sound behind him, thinking that Lavinia was rousing. His heart sank when he saw Agatha's wide, betrayed gaze.

He opened his mouth to say something, anything to remove that look of suspicion from her brown eyes. Before he could cover his presence there, she burst into action.

With a flying leap, she wrapped her hands around the arm of the sofa. Grunting, she swiveled it a quarter-turn to face the fire. Then in a quick motion she flung a lap quilt from its perch upon the back to conceal what was still visible of Lady Winchell's sprawling limbs.

After, she turned to him and threw herself into his arms while thrusting one hand behind his neck to pull his mouth down to hers.

Rigid with surprise at first, it only took an instant for Simon to kiss her back. He pressed his lips against her tightly closed ones, tickling the seam of her mouth with his tongue.

She almost pulled away, then pressed into him with renewed force. Her full breasts softened to his naked chest in precisely the way he had dreamed.

Forgetting his mission, forgetting the fact that they stood in a stranger's study, in a stranger's house, Simon gave in to the siren call of her softness.

He wrapped one arm about her waist and pulled her to him, raising her to her tiptoes in his need to feel her body next to his. With his other hand, he shoved his fingers into her hair and pressed her mouth closer still for his ravishment.

Her lips parted slightly in surprise and he touched again lightly with his tongue, encouraging her to open to him. Why wouldn't she kiss him deeply, the way he ached for her to?

The door opened.

"I must show you this, Bingly—Great Scott!"

"I say—isn't that Applequist?"

Simon froze with Agatha in his arms. Ah. Not a fit of amour, then.

She must have known Winchell was on his way in and had flung herself at him to cover his undressed state. Even while his mind blessed her quick thinking, his body protested her lack of true intent.

"Oh!" Agatha pulled her mouth from his to gaze at Winchell in very believable shock and alarm.

"Oh, I say—isn't that *Mrs.* Applequist?"

"Ah, yes, well . . . newlyweds, you know, Bingly," mumbled Winchell, obviously torn between amusement and embarrassment himself. "What say we give them a moment to compose themselves, eh?"

He pushed the fellow out of the doorway. "Have you seen my new watercolors? I've discovered the most talented chap. . . ."

The door swung slowly behind them, and Simon relaxed his grip on Agatha, relief filling his lungs with blessed air.

Then Winchell stuck his head back in.

"Five minutes, Applequist. And for God's sake, man, put your shirt on." Then the door was shut in truth.

Agatha pressed her face into his bare chest, apparently unable to conceal her laughter. At least, Simon thought it was laughter. He was feeling a bit giddy himself.

But when Agatha pulled away, he saw only accusation in her angry eyes.

"You're a thief! A common parlor thief!"

"Agatha, we've only got a few moments. Can we fling epithets later?"

"No, I rather think I'd like to fling them now. How could you endanger my purpose so carelessly? I could be sent back to—" She halted, mouth still open.

Simon was desperately curious. "Where? Sent back to where?"

She shut her mouth with a click. "Never you mind. What are we going to do with Lady Winchell? We can't simply leave her there, all . . . What did you do to her?"

"Me? Not a thing. She merely drank a bit too much brandy."

"Brandy melts one's clothing off, does it?"

Chuckling despite her scornful glower, Simon nodded. "It has been known to on occasion."

"We cannot leave her here. He's bound to realize that she was in here all along, and then I will have kissed you for nothing."

Simon stiffened. "Pardon me. I'd no idea it was such a sacrifice."

"Oh, you know what I mean. Grab her arms."

Together they got Lavinia back on her feet, if one could call swaying like a badly set Maypole standing upright. Her head hung off her shoulders like a dead woman's, and Simon wondered absently if she had killed herself with her greed.

He didn't much care, one way or another, except that for her husband to find her when he returned would be inconvenient in the extreme.

"There is a dark sitting room next to this one. You hold her—no, I'll hold her up while you check the hall."

Simon turned his portion of Lavinia's weight over to Agatha and obeyed without protest, all the while adding up the events of the last few moments.

Agatha was quite the little professional, wasn't she? Cool as seawater, this one. Simon reminded himself that he was dealing with a woman who had likely seen it all and done her share of it.

Most important, she had revealed that she had a mission of her own, perhaps more than simply finding her lover.

Where was it she was in danger of being sent? Gaol? The Colonies?

There was no one in sight in the hall, and they managed to get Lavinia into the next sitting room and arrange her to look as though she had been drinking alone.

Simon grouped the filched decanter and single glass in a messy spill at her feet while Agatha did her best to repair the lady's torn bodice.

"I suppose she did this herself, as well?" Agatha shot him an acid look as she used her own lace to hide the worst of the damage.

"Most assuredly." Simon blinked innocently at her while he reassembled himself. He was missing a cuff stud. Oh, well, he'd just have to tuck it into his coat sleeve and hope it—

The lost stud gleamed in Agatha's pink palm, held before his nose.

"I believe you lost this. In the hall outside."

"Ah, I was wondering how you found me. That was quick thinking."

"That was unbridled terror," she shot back.

She took a last look around the room, then glanced at the clock on the mantel. "Three and a half minutes. Plenty of time left to hear your explanation."

"Not quite. I never did get to finish up in there."

Agatha went truly ashen. "You don't dare!"

With a wink and a tip of an imaginary hat, Simon dared. She came after him, tugging at his arm at the door to Winchell's study. "Don't do this, Simon. You don't have to do this."

"It'll only take a moment, love. You stand here and tap the door if Winchell comes back early."

"I'll not assist this! You will not go back—"

Simon shut the door on her objections, leaving her fuming on the other side.

Quickly Agatha turned to face the empty hallway, trying to assume a nonchalant pose against the door. Inside, however, she was anything but calm.

Her heart was pounding like a racing horse, and she knew it wasn't because of their close call. Simon's mouth on hers had been something of a revelation. She could still feel the shocking intimacy of his tongue sweeping across her mouth and the way that her breasts had tingled and tightened against his hard chest.

She'd only gripped his wide bare shoulders for a moment, but the heated rippling of his muscles against her palms still lingered, making her want to tighten her fists to keep him in her hands.

She desired Simon. Somehow, she'd managed to keep the fact from herself for an entire week. Oh, she'd been aware of some attraction, but not this pulsating ache in her belly and below that made her want to pull him down on Winchell's sofa for another round.

This was a complication that bore more reflection. Later. When she wasn't in imminent danger of being publicly exposed. And perhaps after she was no longer panting to be half-naked in Simon's arms.

Like Lavinia. Anger coiled through Agatha at the image in her mind. Ah, yes. It was quite astonishing how pure fury could erase the smoldering embers of arousal. That was something she'd take care to remember in the future.

Inside Winchell's study, Simon had returned to the wall safe. Thank goodness Winchell had been too distracted by the disturbed lovers to see that the painting that concealed his safe hung askew because the safe door itself was wide open.

With quick, sensitive fingers, Simon sorted through the documents and stacks of cash that filled the small square box.

There was nothing conclusive inside. Some rather sensitive documents, yes, but nothing that Winchell shouldn't have in his possession, considering his standing in the War Office. It was a bit surprising to find them stored at his residence, but perhaps the man took his work home with him.

Finally satisfied with what he did and did not find, Simon shut the heavy iron door and fiddled the lock back into action with his picks.

Straighten the picture here, shove the sofa back there, and, with a last glance about the room, the job was done. Not well and not without erecting some entirely new obstacles, but done just the same.

Now on to the hardest part. Convincing Agatha not to decry him for a "common parlor thief."

What nonsense. He was anything but common.

It was difficult leaving the party. Agatha tried her best not to blush while giving her regrets to Lord Winchell, but his grandfatherly reproof made her realize what a picture she must have made, wrapped in Simon's arms.

Simon, the rat, remained cool and relaxed, making his little bow of regret and the excuse of her—her!—headache as if the man had never seen a thing.

The one bright side was that their early departure would be entirely forgotten when his lordship discovered why his lady wife would not be joining everyone for supper. If only they managed to depart first!

The slight wait as their carriage was brought around was likely only minutes, but to a nervous Agatha it seemed like hours. Simon merely leaned nonchalantly against the wall, hands in pockets, looking sublimely unconcerned.

Well, simply wait. Once she got him into the privacy of the carriage, he'd find himself plenty concerned!

It had occurred to her in the last few minutes that if Simon was thief, not chimneysweep, then he'd had nefarious reasons for being in her house in the first place! The rat-sneak had been going to rob *her*!

He hadn't in the end, she was positive. She'd brought nothing of real value from Appleby. Even the silver had come with the rented house, and she'd had no complaints of anything missing from Pearson, who would surely have noticed.

So Simon had not stolen, but he had lied.

She could call a constable on him right now for what he had done at Winchell's. She wouldn't, of course, but she enjoyed the thought immensely in her ire.

She should threaten him with it at least, it was no more than he deserved for tricking her this way. Threatening him with exposure would teach him—

She became very still as the next thoughts began to ravel through her mind.

Would the threat of exposure keep Simon in line? Would it be enough to ensure his cooperation in something vastly more dangerous than posing as the harmless Mortimer?

The most important thing that Agatha had discovered tonight—other than the surprising appeal of Simon's kiss, which she was not quite ready to think about—was that the hospital had nothing on the social scene when it came to news and rumor. She had learned more tonight about the war against Napoleon than she had in weeks tending the wounded boys.

She would continue her work there, of course. The need

for what little comfort she could bring them was enough to merit it. But in the evenings, with Simon at her side, she might learn more than she had ever dreamed from the whispers and tattle that were like breath to these people.

In truth, there were nearly as many uniforms in that ballroom tonight as there were in the hospital. Officers, yet. Men in command, who might really know where a certain Captain Cunnington was even now.

Excitement rang through her tightened nerves like bell song. The last bit of information she had finessed from a doddering old general had made the entire night worthwhile.

"Oh, the Griffin!" he'd declared in his creaky voice. He'd blinked his rheumy eyes in indignation. "My, yes, of course I've heard of him, what with him being plastered all over the papers like he is."

Agatha had taken a deep breath, and the old fellow, who had truly enjoyed the way his decreased height had left his eyes level with her bodice, kept talking.

"I tell you if I were in charge, heads would roll about that security leak. These youngsters, no respect for the government, telling Crown business the way they do—"

"Not like you, good sir." She'd leaned closer and the old boy had practically fallen into her bosom. "I'll wager Napoleon himself couldn't drag the Griffin's identity out of a man like you."

"Not Napoleon, nor good King George himself!" he declared stoutly. Then he blinked. "That is, if I knew . . ."

Another blasted dead end. Agatha had sighed and prepared to disentangle herself from the general's wiry grasp as the dance ended.

". . . for certain."

With that, Agatha was back in the match, luring her gentleman back onto the floor for another waltz. Flattery, breathless attention, and a great deal of cleavage finally wrung his theory from him.

It seemed there was a certain reclusive gentleman . . . a lord, no less. A man of mystery who left the country for weeks at a time, then arrived back in town without fanfare or warning. A man who kept his mouth shut and his eyes sharp. A man with friends in *very* high places—this last was uttered with more than a dash of resentment.

If that wasn't the veritable description of a spy, Agatha didn't know what was. And she knew his name.

Now, she had only to gain entry to his inner circle, then somehow become invited to his home, and—and what?

Ask him if he were the Griffin? The futility of her plan made her slump. A royal spy would no more share information with her than he would any other gossip-mongering lady of Society.

No, what she needed was something more inspired, something—

The carriage came around, and young Harry jumped down to open the door. Simon stepped up to hand her in, but she pulled away from him. She didn't want him near her after he'd endangered her mission with his thieving—

The answer came to her with a triumphant rush of delight. Oh, she could not have planned anything more perfect if she had tried.

He wouldn't like it, she was fairly sure. Still, she would not be denied. It wasn't as though she would ever truly turn him in.

It was no worse than when Jamie had threatened to tell Papa about that unfortunate incident with the harvest bonfire and the gunpowder. She'd been forced to muck out after Jamie's palfrey for weeks in order to gain his word that he would blame it on their favorite scapegoat, the imaginary Mortimer Applequist.

In the end, she'd escaped detection and had only to sit through another one of her father's lectures about avoiding undesirable comrades. Poor Papa, to the end he had believed in the ubiquitous Mortimer.

Simon flipped up his tails and sat across from Agatha, reflexively giving the roof a double tap with his fist to signal the driver that they were ready. His mind was entirely on the luscious little problem that sat across from him.

Agatha was going to take delicate handling from here on

out. She was obviously angry at him. One could tell by the brilliant smile on her—

Simon checked again. Yes, she was smiling joyously at him, as if he were the answer to her every prayer.

Oh, hell. This could not be good.

"Absolutely not."

She only smiled wider. "Oh, yes, I rather think so."

"I won't do it."

"You don't even know what it is yet."

"If it is bad enough for you to be charming me instead of raging at me, it is something I want no part of."

"Please don't play the righteous and simple man of honor, Simon. If I wished, I could turn you in to the magistrate directly. You just rifled through both Lord Winchell's study and Lord Winchell's wife."

There was no denying that. Damn. Simon the Chimneysweep was dead, by his own hand yet. Time for Simon the Master Thief to come to the surface.

"Yes, you are quite correct. I am not a man of honor. I am a man of opportunity."

Her eyes narrowed. "Which I have provided for you, tenfold. You would never have free entry into a house like Winchell's without the training I gave you."

You used me. She didn't have to say it out loud. The thought was plain to see on her abruptly unsmiling face.

He could hardly deny her accusation without bringing up far worse offenses. If she knew that the past week had been nothing but a farce, Simon really couldn't predict her outrage.

If there was one thing Simon knew about women, it was that they were all violently allergic to liars, even if they told the occasional falsehood themselves.

Time to point her toward safer ground.

"What precisely do you have in mind?" he asked, knowing he was going to be very sorry he had.

"I want you to do that again." She waved a hand to indicate the Winchells' house in their wake.

"You want me to tickle Lord Winchell's . . . safe again?"

"Not Lord Winchell's safe, nor Lord Winchell's wife."

Did he detect a slightly possessive snarl in her tone? Oh, yes. How gratifying. Still, it was quite beside the topic.

"I will arrange to be invited to a house, and you will accompany me as Mortimer, as you did tonight. But the only mischief will be done at my direction." She gave him a stern look that was surprisingly impressive on her sweetly rounded face.

"Then whose safe will I be tickling?"

"Lord Etheridge's safe."

"Why do you want to steal from Lord Etheridge?"

"I don't want to steal from him. The very idea." She actually had the nerve to look offended. "I suppose there's no harm in telling you. It's not as though you'll go running to the authorities. I only want to find out how he is connected to Jamie."

"I apologize. You've lost me once more."

"Please learn to pay attention. I am looking for the Griffin. Lord Etheridge keeps a house, but rarely uses it. He comes and goes, and no one knows where. He avoids the social whirl, but for a few select friends, all of whom hold government posts. He is an obvious suspect." She sat back, her expression smug.

"Bloody hell!" He was stunned. Lord Etheridge *was* a perfect suspect. After all, the man was on Simon's own list, among others. If not for the short-handed condition of his team, Etheridge would already have been thoroughly investigated.

Still, it had taken some time before his own sources had ferreted out any suspicious activity by Etheridge.

Damn, but she was good.

She regarded him as if not sure how much he needed to know. At any other time he might have found this amusing, but he was too busy wondering how she had discovered in one night what he and his operatives had taken weeks to uncover.

"If this man is the Griffin, then he has been in touch with Jamie. Lord Etheridge likely knows where he is at this very moment."

She was wrong. Wrong about the Griffin, wrong about James. Unfortunately, he couldn't tell her so. All he could do was try to talk her out of her hideously dangerous plan.

If he couldn't, she was likely to get her pretty little carcass tied into a brick-filled sack and thrown into the Thames.

Agatha waited, but Simon wasn't answering, only sitting there watching her in the half-light that came from the lanterns bobbing from the sides of the carriage. Suddenly Agatha was very weary.

Weary of the lies, weary of the strain of not knowing Jamie's fate, weary of dancing with men who stepped on her toes.

Well, she could do something about the last, at least. Bending, she flipped off her silken slippers and took one set of her toes in each hand. Rubbing gently, she sighed with relief.

Her feet felt like stomped grapes. So many men had trod on her toes tonight, from lords to generals. Pity that none of them had been Simon. At least he had made it fun while he made mush of her toes.

Dancing was the last place for silk slippers. Better to wear the sturdy workshoes of a farm woman on the dance floor.

The image made her smile. Wouldn't that start talk? Green satin and hobnails. She looked up at Simon, ready to share the joke, but froze at the animal glaze to his eyes.

Simon was on fire. Was she teasing him apurpose? Did she have any idea that when she leaned that way, he could see her entire bosom?

The spark that had been kindled by her revealing gown and stoked by her quick-minded kiss suddenly flared into a white-hot inferno. He could hardly think over the roaring in his ears.

"Where is your lace?" God, was that his voice? He sounded hoarse and dangerous, even to himself.

"In Lady Winchell's bodice."

Her lace . . . they'd left it behind. A tiny fragment of his mind worried over that betraying bit of evidence, but the larger part led him to relive his little charade earlier.

Only this time, it wasn't Lavinia's gaunt body under his

ministrations. No, he wanted to replay it on Agatha's abundance. The wet brush swirling, warming . . . drawing designs that enhanced the shape and bounty of her curves.

Agatha, ripe and lush, naked and willing, painted like a primitive goddess for his worship—

"So will you?"

She leaned forward earnestly, and Simon saw the rosy circle of one nipple edge above the fabric. Her bodice was off-center, twisted from her efforts earlier. The heat within him flared out of control.

"Oh, yess. . . ."

When she sat up straight and clasped her hands together in delight, he realized that he had spoken out loud.

A bucket of icy realization doused his pulsating lust.

Oh, bloody hell.

She had done it to him again.

Pure hatred momentarily warred with blind want, then won. He could see her for what she was again, a manipulative player of games, a lady without morals or virtue, except that of being a very, very good liar.

She had taken him in twice with her beautiful body, made him no more than a mindless tool to her hand. He thought he might happily kill her for taking away his famous control.

But then again, what had he really promised? To attempt Lord Etheridge's safe, but only if she could get them into the house.

As the gentleman in question was not a social sort, was in fact damn near a recluse, this seemed as unlikely an event as Agatha's supposed brush with honest matrimony. It would likely never come up, then, so no harm in it.

He roused from his thoughts long enough to grunt a response to Agatha's happy chattering, though not to listen to her outlandish plans for convincing Lord Etheridge to include them in his nonexistent social calendar.

No, Simon's thoughts traveled over Lord Etheridge in an entirely different vein. A man of mystery indeed. A spy, was he? It was entirely possible.

However, the reclusive fellow was no spy for the Crown.

Simon would surely know if he was, although he could hardly tell Agatha that.

Not that she would likely believe him. Believe that Simon, her rascally chimneysweep-thief whom she had raised from a life of petty larceny on the streets of London, was none other than a royal spymaster himself?

No, it was better for her to believe the worst of him than to learn the truth. He could not afford for her to discover that her beloved James was the target of his mission. One of his own men gone rogue whom Simon must find before he could further betray his country.

There would be no public trial, for that would only compromise the anonymity of the Liar's Club. Regrettably, it was all up to Simon to find James.

Find, single-handedly try and judge, and if necessary . . . Execute.

No, he didn't think Agatha would like that one, not at all.

Chapter Nine

James Cunnington was floating, dreaming, lost in the trap of his own imagination. Behind him was the comfortable fog of unconsciousness. Before him rose the visage of a snake. It danced before him, swaying upright over its own coils.

"Jamessss."

Nasty things, snakes. Repulsive, yet fascinating.

"James? Who is Mortimer Applequist? I know I've heard you say his name. Who is he?"

The tongue flicked out and in, and the snake said his name again.

"James? Answer the question. Who is Mortimer Applequist?"

No one.

"Answer me, James. Who is he?"

Hadn't he just answered the damned slimy thing? In his dreamland, he wrapped his fingers around the snake's throat and squeezed.

But the voice continued. "Who is it? Tell me, James."

He wanted to be left alone. He needed to think. Something was very wrong here, but he just couldn't think what it could be. If the bloody snake would just go away, maybe he could gather his thoughts.

"S'no one," he muttered.

"No one? What do you mean?"

Thick-headed bugger. "No one. An alias. Don't wan' get caught, s'blame it on Mort'mer."

"An alias. Whose alias? Yours?"

Sometimes. Sometimes it was Agatha's. In the end, even the staff had used Mortimer as a scapegoat a few times. His mathematician father had fallen for it, too lost in his grief and his studies to be aware that there was no such person. He'd blink at them and remind them to watch the company they kept, to stay away from that dreadful Applequist boy. James and Agatha would nod solemnly and agree.

Agatha. There was something there he should remember as well. If only the damned snake would let him be . . .

He reached for the cloudy abyss, turning his back on the serpent. The voice kept speaking, but more dimly now. James slipped back into his insensible void, no longer listening.

Simon trotted down the stairs bright and early the morning after his close call at Winchell's, despite a night of pacing and thinking. He expected to see Agatha perusing the news-sheets over her eggs as usual.

Instead, she was already dressed to go out, standing in the front hall examining her post. There was a great deal of it. Apparently the Applequists had made quite the social splash last evening at the Winchells'.

There was an impressive pile on the salver, full of heavy paper and ornate embossing that he could see from where he stood. He imagined most women would be swooning with pleasure over such bounty.

Agatha, contrary creature that she was, paid it no attention at all. She had no shallow pretensions to raising her status in Society, he had to give her that. But was that really a rec-ommendation of her values or merely a sign of her profes-sionalism?

Instead, she was engrossed in the reading of a letter of several pages, written on ordinary foolscap. Simon itched to read whatever put such a frown between her sable brows.

He simply knew it would reveal something about her secrets. Perhaps a clue toward her lover's whereabouts. Or something that would give him the lever he needed to make her reveal all she knew of James Cunnington's activities over the last six months.

She looked up from her letter. "Oh, good morning. Pearson has breakfast ready for you." She looked down again distractedly. "If you'll excuse me, I really must answer this. . . ."

With that, she turned and walked away from him, entering the little front parlor and shutting the door. She was going to pen a reply now, with her hat pinned to her hair and her short coat already buttoned?

It must be urgent, and therefore interesting. Perhaps he could get a hint from her when she came out. Better yet, perhaps she'd leave the letter behind. Pretending idle curiosity, Simon strolled to the hall table and flipped through the invitations massed there.

Nothing from Etheridge, of course. Life was never that simple. Still, Simon was impressed by the range of hostesses interested in entertaining the Applequists. From a colonel's wife to a countess, with many a member of Parliament in between.

Agatha had truly worked the marks last night. Admiration laced his thoughts as he remembered watching her operate. He'd seen her dance with every gentleman soldier in the place. And he had seen those gentlemen losing all discretion when faced with her . . . ah, obvious charms.

The two of them had operated like a well-oiled machine, and Simon remembered how much he had once enjoyed working with a partner. He and Jackham had been just as unstoppable, once upon a midnight.

Mortimer had done his share, of course, before disappearing into the back hallways of the house. Boasting, charming the ladies, and all around being as putrid a fellow as any spoiled gentleman could be.

He had fit right in.

Simon shook his head. What a useless existence. How could any man with a backbone and smidgen of brains tolerate it?

The parlor door opened and Agatha hurried out. He opened his mouth to question her, but she was across the hall and out the front door before he could even speak, busily tucking a letter into her reticule.

If he didn't know better, he'd think she hadn't even seen him.

Pearson opened the door to the breakfast room and raised an inquiring brow at Simon.

"Will you be wanting Cook to hold your breakfast, sir?"

The smells wafting from behind Pearson were nearly enough to bring Simon to his knees, but who knew when Agatha would return? He ought not to let this chance go by.

"I'll be just a moment, Pearson." He turned away, then hesitated. Turning back, he couldn't resist asking, "Is it coddled eggs today?"

"Yes, sir. And bacon."

Damn. He'd better hurry then. As he let himself into the parlor, he wondered if it would be possible to steal away Agatha's cook when all this was over.

In the meantime, he would be sure not to miss any meals.

The blue-papered parlor was bright with sunlight. Agatha had obviously not wanted to take the time to light a lamp and had pulled back the heavy draperies to let in light from the windows instead.

Taking a deep breath, Simon realized that he could detect her scent, that warm sweet air that followed her everywhere she went.

Resolutely he pushed down his body's instant response. He wasn't normally the sort to let his erection rule his will or his brain.

There was a stack of stationery still lying on the little corner desk, and she had left her ink uncapped. Her hurry was undoubtedly fortunate for him. Had she a firm script or a delicate one?

Simon held the top sheet of paper atilt of the sunlight streaming in through the window. Ah, a firm hand indeed.

He carried the sheet to the cold fireplace. Pearson's dedication was evident in the pristine condition of the grate, despite its having been used recently.

No matter. He reached up the flue and scrubbed his fingertips against the firebrick. He pulled them back and eyed the black soot covering his hand. Excellent.

Turning the paper over on the hearth with his clean hand, he carefully brushed his sooty fingers across the reverse indentations of Agatha's curling penmanship.

The faintly raised letters took the soot and formed clearly, albeit backward. It was clear that he had in his hand only the last page of Agatha's reply, for it began midsentence and ended with a greatly enlarged "In loving reply, A."

Loving reply? Simon's eyes narrowed. Could she have written to James himself? Was her supposed mission as false as her use of "Mrs." before her name?

Or perhaps she had been honest with him until now, but had finally received communication from the elusive James Cunnington.

He would watch her, he decided. Closely.

Of course, not as closely as he'd like to. . . .

Voices in the hallway outside Agatha's parlor brought Simon abruptly back to himself. Now was not the time to be distracted by the winsome lady's voluptuous charms. No, he'd not let his purpose be obscured by his lust again.

She was hiding something. And now he held one of her secrets in his hand. The reversed script was tight and florid, likely difficult to read in proper ink, impossible in smudged soot.

He needed a mirror. Hurriedly departing the parlor, he could only give a wistful sniff to his breakfast before loping up the stairs to his room.

As Agatha removed her short coat and tied on one of the aprons kept in the utilitarian cloakroom reserved for the volunteers, she tried to force the letter from her mind. All the way to the hospital, it had weighed like a stone in her reticule.

She'd had to bring it with her today, for she'd not had

time to find a suitable hiding place for it. Perhaps she was being silly, but she could take no chances that someone would read it and inform Lord Fistingham of her whereabouts.

Although she knew that his lordship was rarely in town, she had been dismayed to learn how tightly knit the nobility was in London. Likely half the people she had met at the supper dance last night knew Lord Fistingham in some capacity. And now they knew her as well.

As much as she liked her new staff, it wouldn't do to forget that servants gossiped, although she doubted any might actually mean her harm. It was simply best that she keep her own counsel and hide any evidence of Agatha Cunnington safely away.

His lordship was becoming more suspicious by the day, according to her housekeeper's letter.

> I don't know how much longer I can deceive him, Miss Agatha. He comes nearly every day with his son, and waits for you sometimes for hours. I've told him you were berry-picking, though nothing's ripe yet. I've told him you were visiting Miss Bloom, and the next day he informed me that Miss Bloom told him you had not visited her for weeks. He is becoming most suspicious.

There wasn't much that Agatha could do from London, except find Jamie as soon as possible. In the meantime, she'd given Mrs. Bell what instruction she could.

She shuddered, as if she'd felt Repulsive Reggie's touch from afar.

Infinitely preferable to think of Simon. Last night's kiss, while no more than a ruse, still had set her heart to pounding every time she'd thought of it. His lips had been warm and encouraging without being demanding. He'd liked kissing her, she was fairly sure.

And she'd liked kissing him, far too well for her own peace of mind. Agatha licked her lips, fancying she could still detect the faintest trace of cinnamon. For a moment she was back in the dim study, pressing herself tightly to a half-naked Simon. . . .

Two ladies Agatha didn't know well entered the cloak-room, causing her to realize she'd been standing there for some moments, reliving that kiss.

How foolish. As if she had nothing more urgent on her mind. She'd best keep her attention on her business.

She left the cloakroom and made her way to the first-floor ward. The smells of illness and healing pulled her mind away from her own troubled thoughts at last.

Having been away for the past week working with Simon, she had forgotten how being here affected her. There was an air about those who worked here. A constant expression of mingled hope and despair, for the Chelsea Hospital was partly a place of miracles, partly a chamber of horrors.

So many, so young. She hardly considered herself old, but the boys who filled the beds and rooms and hallways of the hospital seemed like children to her.

Until one looked into their eyes. Some kept their pain at bay with jokes and charm, some retreated into a silent world of their own, faces to the wall.

Yet in all their eyes she could see the horror of fire and death and suffering, like shadows that would live within them forever.

She carried the basin of steaming cloths from bed to bed. Farther down the ward, Clara Simpson, a young widow Agatha recalled as being a relative of Mrs. Trapp, was feeding a silent, motionless boy with a spoon, whispering encouragement even while tears fell down her cheeks.

Agatha looked away from Clara's naked emotion. All the women who worked in the hospital, volunteers and nurses alike, understood the pain of hopeless cases but never spoke of it to one another. It was as if by acknowledging death out loud, they would invite it in.

"Ah, the fairest ray of the sun has found me at last!" No gloom dimmed the vibrant masculine voice behind her.

Agatha's smile was real when she turned toward the

speaker. Collis Tremayne was her favorite patient, and not only because of his well-spoken charm.

Collis had once dreamed of being a musician. That had been before he had donned a uniform and gone to war. Before the battle that had caused the shattering of one arm.

Rumor had it that he'd been destined to lose it entirely, but a sharp-eyed physician, sick of the piles of amputated limbs at his feet, had noticed that the young soldier's left hand was still warm with blood flow and still flinched when pricked.

"Let him keep it," the doctor had declared. "Likely it will be as useless as a log, but he'll still be whole." Then he'd sewn up the wounds and bound the arm tightly in a splint, matching the pieces of bone as well as he was able.

When Collis had woken from the shock of surgery and transport here in this ward, Agatha had seen the loss in his eyes at the realization that his left arm had been rendered little more than an ornament to balance the right.

He had lain in silence for a while, blinking rapidly, gaze fixed on the ceiling. Then, with a tiny smile quirking his lips, he had looked up at her and said, "That tears it. I'll have to learn the drum now."

And he had. When next she'd seen him, he'd been sitting up in bed with a new drum in his lap, the sort that marchers carried on parade.

To the encouragement—and sometimes complaints—from his ward mates, Collis had learned to play the drum one-handed, the nimble fingers of his right hand controlling both drumsticks with great precision.

Now, he tipped his twin drumsticks to her in a sort of salute. When he couldn't play, he spent every moment twirling the sticks between his fingers, ever compelled to gain more control.

"Good morning, Collis." Agatha couldn't resist teasing him. "You had best watch out, spinning those things in the air. Private Soames has sworn to burn them if you fly one into his nose again."

"Soames is a philistine. He has no appreciation of the fine

art of percussion." Collis leaned toward her. "I've missed you, sweet angel." He looked about them, then whispered, "The cards, did you bring them?"

"Collis, I already own your house, your cattle, and your first-born child. Haven't you had enough?"

"I suppose." He dropped back onto the pillows in disappointment. "I likely wouldn't win today, either. But won't you just shuffle the deck for me? Watching you is like seeing an artist at work."

Agatha sat on the edge of his cot and balanced her basin on her knees. "Fine. I'll shuffle for you. Then you'll leave off? No begging for another chance?"

"Not a word."

She gave him a doubtful glance, but he only returned her an innocent smile. Agatha reached into her dress pocket and pulled out a small deck of cards.

Collis sat back with a smile, and a few of the surrounding patients craned their necks to get a good look.

What was the male fascination with cards? Jamie had always loved card tricks and had taught her a few when they were young. While she waited between his rare visits home, she had practiced them and learned more, until she had surpassed the teacher, much to his glee.

Next, she cut the cards into two decks, spread her hands wide, and sent them sailing toward one another to land in a tidy little pile on Collis's knees.

He shut his eyes in rapture. "What a woman. Say you'll marry me. I'm leaving today. This is your last chance to say yes, sweet angel."

Agatha cocked her head at him. "Will you never stop? I've told you, I'm quite married already." The lie was getting easier to tell all the time. Was it a matter of practice, or did her feelings for Simon have something to do with it?

"Run away with me, then. I'll take you to Polynesia, where he'll never find us. We'll live on sunlight and honey, and have ten children to raise as our own native tribe."

"Oh, dear. That sounds exhausting." She returned his saucy smile. "Where will you go, when you leave here?" He'd told her once before that he had no parents or siblings now.

"My Uncle Dalton is taking me in. Oddly enough, he didn't like the idea of my future career, playing with the orchestra at Drury Lane."

"Not a fan of the theatre, is he?"

Collis gave her a sideways look. "Not of that sort of theatre, I think."

Agatha had no idea what he meant but only nodded sagely. There was so much about life in London that escaped her, but she pretended experience rather than endure questions about where she was from.

"Collis, I'm surprised at you, mentioning such a tawdry subject before a lady," a new voice rumbled from behind her.

Agatha turned so quickly at the deep voice that the basin threatened to slide off her lap. She grabbed for it hastily.

Instead of grasping the cheap tin rim, her own fingers wrapped around several larger warm ones. Agatha's gaze flew up, but she saw little but the outline of the tall man bending over her against the light from the high arched windows.

Collis chuckled. "Uncle Dalton, I'd like to present Mrs. Applequist, who I'm sure would like to stand if you would kindly stop looming over her."

Casting her patient a quelling glare, Agatha pulled the basin from Uncle Dalton's grasp and shoved it at Collis.

"Here. Stay out of trouble," she muttered.

Then she rose as gracefully as she was able with the tall gentleman standing so close. Even at her full height, her eyes were only level with his cravat, which was practically all she could see.

"How lovely to meet you, Uncle Dalton's cravat," she said dryly.

Collis snorted at that, but Agatha didn't want to encourage him, so she merely waited politely until the great oaf got the message and stepped back.

"I apologize, Mrs. Applequist. How clumsy of me." The broad chest before her retreated, and Agatha could finally look into his face.

She blinked. Well, they certainly grew them handsome in

London, didn't they? She was positive that most women would find the man before her absolutely devastating, although he seemed to lack the impact upon her senses that Simon had.

Still, there was no denying the appeal of a set of broad shoulders and a finely carved jaw. And those eyes, as silver as a wolf's. Really, quite a bundle of masculine appeal. Of course, handsome was as handsome did.

And this handsome was being a tiny bit rude.

She held out her hand. "Why, Uncle Dalton, we meet at last. Your cravat has told me so much about you!"

That finally broke the stern cast of his features, and a deep chuckle rose from his chest. He bowed over her hand, and when he came up, a half-smile had taken his mouth hostage.

"Great Scott, Mrs. Applequist! He smiled! Quickly, inform the press!"

"Thank you, Collis, I think we've had enough of that." Uncle Dalton's voice was mild, but Collis stopped just the same. Agatha was impressed.

In the meantime, how was she to remove her hand from Uncle Dalton's warm grasp? He didn't seem aware that he was still holding it while perusing her with his icy gaze.

"It is Montmorency, actually. Dalton Montmorency. As much as I'd love to welcome you to the family, Mrs. Applequist, I'm afraid that having a great lout like Collis call me Uncle is all that I can bear."

Ah, that's how he did it. It worked very well indeed. With one sentence, he had made her feel very gauche and foolish for teasing such an obviously powerful and impressive stranger. She pulled her hand away, no longer caring if it seemed rude.

"You have such a commanding manner, sir. I really must practice it." She had been in control of her own life for some time now and had found that she liked not answering to anyone. To be reprimanded like a child made her feel rather prickly.

"Now look what you've done, Uncle. She isn't smiling any longer." Collis fell back onto his pillows and raised his good arm over his eyes weakly. "I swan I feel faint. Perhaps I cannot come home after all," he said with the lisping accents of a fragile lady.

Agatha fought the smile, but she couldn't help it. "Oh, get up, you silly quiz."

"So you've become fond of my nephew, Mrs. Applequist. I see that you do not wear mourning." Dalton Montmorency's voice was silkily insinuating. "How long has it been since your husband passed?"

"Not long, surely, for he was just fine over breakfast," retorted Agatha as she took the basin back from Collis. "Oh!" She turned and put one fist on her hip, smiling widely at Mr. Montmorency. "You mistook me for a widow. Did you think I was gunning for Collis?"

By the surprise on his face, he most assuredly had thought so. Behind her, Collis was crowing in triumph.

"Uncle, I do believe you have finally met your match. Too bad she is married. If I cannot have her for my bride, she would have made a most entertaining auntie."

"Oh, shut it, Collis," said Agatha and Mr. Montmorency simultaneously. Then they caught each other's eyes and laughed.

Now that the issue of her marital status was out of the way, Mr. Montmorency seemed to unbend. As he spoke to Collis about the arrangements he had made, Agatha could see the genuine affection he had for his rapscallion nephew.

Montmorency was also much younger than first she'd thought. When the stern lines of his face relaxed, she realized that he was likely no older than Simon. Collis must be an older sister's child, to be within ten years or so of his uncle.

"I must get back to my duties, gentlemen. I'm glad you are going home, Collis, but I admit that I will miss you greatly." She bent to plant a kiss on his cheek.

He smiled up at her. "You must come to see us, sweet angel. Uncle and I will invite you and Mr. Applequist soon, won't we, Uncle?"

"Collis, I would enjoy nothing more, but I think Mr. Applequist might dislike you calling his wife by such pet names. . . ."

Agatha left them arguing, this time wearing a genuine smile on her face for her next patient.

Chapter Ten

Simon strode quickly into the Liar's Club, sparing only a nod for Stubbs at the door. Passing through the main club room, he noted that his customers were none of them early risers, for the tables and chairs were entirely empty.

Thankful that he needn't assume Mortimer's personality as well as his wardrobe, Simon passed beyond the servants' door and through the kitchens, into the real Liar's Club.

Nodding at three of his men gathered around a map spread out upon a table and another who sat making out his report, Simon continued into the office that was nominally his, but was actually occupied by Jackham.

Simon's real office was not gained through any but the most secret of means. Only a scarce few knew the entry. Unfortunately, James Cunnington was one of them.

His own lack of judgment buffeting him once again, Simon threw his hat and coat harder than he had meant to, toppling Jackham's hat stand with a clatter.

Jackham looked up, surprised. Simon narrowed his eyes at his old friend and manager in warning. The last thing he wanted to hear about today was the loss of his signature self-control.

"Ah, hello, Simon," Jackham said carefully.

"Anything new?"

"We gained six new marks—ah, members—after the

snake charmer performed. Kurt says that the price of lamb has gone up and he wants another lad for the scullery. Oh, and that little fellow Feebles stopped by, said he had a tip for you."

Simon only nodded, but inside he'd come to full alert. Feebles was the man he had put on James's case. The only man whom Simon had informed of his search at all.

The wily pickpocket was the one who had ferreted out the information about the bank account and was currently assigned to keep an eye on certain establishments for any man who matched James's description.

Affecting boredom, Simon threw himself down on the old, comfortable sofa Jackham kept in the office. "Did he say where he'd be?"

"He said he'd be working the street out front today. I told him fine, as long as he kept his mitts out of our gents' pockets. I'd rather keep all that lovely money in the club."

Jackham sounded faintly disapproving, as if pickpockets were not on the same social level as former upper-class burglars like himself.

Simon had to agree that on the surface, Feebles looked like a mighty poor specimen, all bones and mismatched apparel as he was.

"I suppose I'd better sort him out, then. I shouldn't think I'll be too long."

Simon forced himself to amble to the front door, when in fact he wanted to chase Feebles down at a run. He clapped the terribly flattered Stubbs on the shoulder. "Have you seen Feebles in the last hour or so?"

"Oh, yessir. He were working that corner earlier, then he mentioned he were going to give the next block a try." Stubbs gestured to his right.

Simon thanked him and strolled easily down the street, nodding and tipping his hat to other pedestrians. Soon he came upon Feebles leaning nonchalantly on the corner lamppost, his eyes casing the marks walking by.

"Having a good day?"

Feebles shrugged, a bit shamefaced. "Just workin' the fingers nimble, Mister Rain. Not keepin' anything."

"What have you got for me?"

"Been down to the Chelsea Hospital this morning. Didn't see Mr. Cunnington anywhere, but Ren Porter is in the third-floor ward, and he don't look good."

"Porter? Damn." Simon hadn't even known Porter was in trouble. His last report had come in good time, and his next wasn't due until tomorrow. "What happened? What did he say?"

"That's the thing, sir. He didn't say nothing. Head wound, and a bad 'un. He ain't woke up, and they don't think he ever will."

Sick remorse swept Simon. Another good man sent to his doom.

"Do they know who he is?"

"No, sir, and I didn't say a word. They call him John Day, there. Tell you the truth, I hardly recognized him. If it weren't for that curly hair of his, his own mother wouldn't know him."

"All right. I'll see to him being claimed, and find out what they know."

There were some rooms that his men used on occasion in town. Ren could be looked after there. He would have the best nursing money could buy, and perhaps by some miracle, Simon wouldn't have another soul on his conscience.

Simon turned away with a nod to Feebles, but the little thief called him back. "There's another thing, sir. That woman you was askin' about, the one using Cunnington's bank account?"

Simon turned swiftly. "What do you know?"

Feebles blinked at Simon's ferocity. "Nothin' much, Mister Rain. Just that I heard her being introduced to someone in the first-floor ward this very mornin'. She's there all the time. Seen her myself. I just didn't know her name 'til today."

"Mrs. Applequist? At the hospital?" What could be the point?. . . Of course. She was looking for James, just as he was. Yet another example of her cleverness.

"Thank you, Feebles. Good work."

"Yessir. I'll be gettin' back to you if I find anything more."

"Yes, do that." Absently Simon gave him a wave and turned down the street.

Not back to the club, then. The hospital, where he must face a living dead man and silently beg his forgiveness. The idea that he would be seeing Agatha there made it both worse and better.

Simon stopped, then shook his head and walked on. He didn't really want to examine that thought just now.

Once he arrived at the hospital, Simon strode confidently in as if he were on official business. No one so much as glanced his way as he followed the direction given by Feebles until he stood at the bedside of "John Day."

"Oh, Ren. You don't look good at all," he whispered.

Indeed, the young man did not. He lay in the bed with that deep stillness that might be mistaken for death but for the faint movement of his chest.

It was a miracle that Feebles had recognized Porter at all. With his face battered to a mass of swellings and bruises, and his distinctive curly hair nearly hidden by the great swathing of gauze around his head, Ren Porter looked nothing like himself.

Simon examined the chart hanging on the end of the bed. There wasn't a great deal of hope for the unconscious John Day, that was obvious.

Ren had been found outside a tavern on the outskirts of London, near the docks. He'd been added to a convoy of wounded coming off the ships by a local physician who'd felt the anonymous young man needed more help than he could give.

Simon had no doubt that the quality of Ren's clothing had something to do with that assessment. Porter had been posing as a disillusioned young gent who was down on his luck, in the hopes of drawing the eye of whoever was recruiting for the French intelligence.

Or so Simon had assumed they were. He certainly was, on the other side of the Channel.

Somehow, and Simon had a sickening feeling he knew, it

seemed that Ren's cover had been compromised and retalia-
tion had been swift and well-nigh fatal.

The chart blurred slightly. Simon closed his eyes. He'd not
let Ren Porter go so easily. The man would get better care in
Simon's hands than in this overcrowded ward.

Ren had no family to speak of, only a distant cousin who
lived in the country. Rumor around the club had it that he'd
been courting a London girl, a little blonde with more figure
than sense.

Simon seriously doubted the engagement—even had there
truly been a formal one—would last long. *If* Ren lived, there
was no telling what condition he would be in, mentally or
physically.

The nurses and doctors did their best, but Simon could see
how overwhelmed they were. Everywhere in the building,
men and women in street clothes moved among the wounded.
Volunteers, without skills or knowledge, offered what help
they could.

Simon rehung the chart, then put his hand on Ren's shoulder in promise. "I'll be back for you."

The administrator's offices were downstairs, but Simon
took a moment to scan the rest of the wounded for any more
familiar faces. As he paused in the door of one of the great
vaulted rooms that made up the wards, he spotted Agatha.

She sat on the edge of a young man's cot, laughing and
playing cards. There was a great deal of room for her on the
bed, for the fellow's legs were entirely gone.

"Got you again, Seamus," he heard her say.

"You've the luck of the fairies with you, Mrs. A." The
black-haired young man gave her a tired grin.

Simon observed that fellow had the look of fever about
him, the greenish pallor of his skin contrasting with the flush
of his cheeks. Likely sepsis was setting in. The poor boy was
doomed, for few men survived such drastic amputation and
the inevitable infection.

"Well, the fairies and I have taken enough of your money
today, Seamus." She tucked a deck of cards into her apron
pocket.

"See there? Just like a nixie, not giving a fellow the chance to win it back," he said.

"You'll have to wait another day to do that."

Leaning forward, Agatha pressed her hand to Seamus's forehead. "Your fever is back. If you don't lie down and rest now, I'll tell Nurse on you."

Laughing weakly, he held up both hands. "No, not that! I'll rest now, I promise."

Awkward and off-balance with so much of his body gone, the lad required Agatha's help to lie down. Still grinning slightly, he lay back upon his pillows and closed his eyes.

Simon watched as the teasing grin left Agatha's face. Blinking quickly, she tucked the young man's covers about him and rose quietly from the bed.

As she turned away, he saw her brush at her eyes and take a deep breath.

Then she smiled brightly and turned to the next bed, where another young soldier eagerly awaited her visit.

Simon stepped back from the entry and leaned against the wall of the corridor. This was not at all what he'd expected to find. He'd assumed Agatha merely checked the wards. He'd never thought to see her like this.

Such a simple thing it was, to laugh and tease and play cards with wounded men. One would think anyone could do it. But not everyone did. He himself had never thought to come here merely to spend time with the shattered boys who had given so much for England.

He had scarcely been able to stay at Ren's bedside for a quarter of an hour. How was Agatha able to spend hours with one wounded man after another? To be cheerful and teasing in the face of their ruined lives? In the face of death itself?

And perhaps more important—why?

He was going to have to seriously reevaluate his conclusions regarding Agatha's motives.

She was obviously loyal to James. Yet she was also here, giving of her time and spirit to the soldiers of England.

What he had seen in that ward was not the act of a French collaborator. The woman who had turned away to hide her tears could no more aid the enemy than he himself would.

So who was the real Agatha? The wild mistress James had described? The faultless professional whom Simon had seen in action? Or this gentle woman, giving of herself in the face of death and grief?

The letter he'd deciphered this morning only lent credence to her innocence, even while it raised new questions.

The final page had held instructions to "dear Mrs. Bell" about how to further evade the questions of "Lord Fistingham":

Tell him that I've gone to take a cure in Kendal. Be careful not to let on that I've left Lancashire or he'll know immediately that I've come to London. I'm sure to have word of James soon.

Lancashire. James hailed from Lancashire, although he'd not lived there for years. It seemed this affair went further back than Simon had originally thought.

And who was Lord Fistingham? Another paramour? A competitor for her affections? Perhaps one she was keeping on a string in case James was not to be found?

No, that he could not believe. Her affection for James was real; he'd wager his life on it. No mere business arrangement there. At least on her side of it.

James had made his lack of true feeling quite clear. Had he arranged for Agatha to leave her home in the country in order to keep her conveniently close in London? To be used at will, without regard for the pain he might cause her?

Anger sparked through Simon at this further sign of James's bad character. James had fooled him well. Likely he had fooled Agatha even more so.

If she was innocent of treason, she would not be the first woman to give her loyalty to the wrong man. The real question was: Which way would she choose when she did learn the truth? Her lover or her country?

Slowly he turned to make the arrangements for Ren's release from the hospital. Someone had much to answer for in Porter's case.

Simon was fairly sure he knew who it was.

James Cunnington rolled over on his malodorous pallet and blinked at the morning light peeking through the planks of the wall before his nose. At least, he thought it was morning.

It wasn't often that he was able to will himself free of the drugged fog he was kept in. But when he could, he tried to take in as many of the details of his surroundings as possible.

He knew that he was on a ship, probably a fishing ketch by the smell and the curve of the side. It wasn't new, for it creaked with the lift of every wave and the planks were warped, even the seaward ones.

There was one crack wide enough that he could press his eye to it and see a bare inch of the outside world. Not much to see but somewhat comforting nonetheless. At least he was above the waterline.

He knew that they were in a port, for he could sometimes hear horses' hooves in the distance, but that it was little used, for his sea-facing peephole had never revealed another ship passing on the open sea. No filthy Thames dock, this.

He knew the ship was run by Frenchmen, for he could hear them shouting at one another and cursing him when they fed him or beat him. He'd learned an astonishing number of new curses, but he doubted he'd ever have the opportunity to use them.

He knew that a man could survive quite well on bread so elderly it was almost solid mold and bitter water that tasted of dead fish and rust. He knew that being tied wrists to ankles, never allowed to fully straighten his body, was likely the worst torture ever committed upon a tall man.

He knew that rough-twisted rope didn't stretch, but skin did tear. He knew that teeth were no help at all against sea-hardened hemp. He knew that he was going to die in the end.

He knew that he was slowly and inevitably being reduced from well-fed, civilized man to murderous animal, one likely to turn on the next person to walk into his tiny cell.

That fact, he found perfectly acceptable.

The hollow sound of footsteps echoed outside his short and narrow door. Breakfast time. Of course it was his only meal of the day, but it amused him to observe the niceties.

James let his head fall back on the pallet, feigning stupor, not that he was ever far from it. But if he kept quiet, the fellow who brought his meal would likely leave after delivering only a contemptuous kick or three.

Sure enough, the burly man whom James had mentally nicknamed Bull tossed his bread to the floor next to the flat straw pallet, put down the bucket with a wasteful slosh, and aimed a vicious kick to James's side.

"Wake up! Wake! Eh, lazy English!"

James kept watch through carefully lidded eyes, not quite willing to trust that the man wouldn't kick him in the privates this time. But all sense of self-preservation vanished when the lout turned away to reveal a sheaf of news sheets protruding from his back pocket.

News! He might learn all sorts of useful things from a local news-sheet. His location, the date, accounts of the war effort . . .

He had to have it. But how?

Well, the Lazy English would wake up, for starters. With a groan, James rolled groggily to the floor, then attempted to get his feet beneath him.

It was alarming how little of the weakness was feigned. If he didn't get out of here soon, he might never be able to escape.

The Frenchman turned and grunted, raising a foot to kick him back down again. Bent over as he was, it was fairly easy for James to grab the raised foot as if for support and pull the heavy man down with him.

As they fell, Bull gave a great shout. Damn, that would bring the rest of them running.

It took a few tries to wrest the paper from the man's pocket without letting on what he was after. Finally, the rolled sheets fell to the floor. With a shove of his bound feet, James kicked them under his pallet as the two of them rolled across the floor.

Then he let Bull shove him off and fell unresisting into the hands of the rest of his captors, now piling angrily into the tiny cabin. They began to pass him from one to the other, cursing him in gutter French and taking out their frustrations on his stumbling, useless self.

Even as he began to black out, James was making note that there were six men in all. Hell. It looked as though this beating was going to take a while.

He only hoped he would remember why he'd earned it when they were done.

Agatha finished her check of the second-floor ward and started down the wide marble stairs to the ground-level vestibule. There were several new men on both the third and second floors, but none of them were Jamie and none of them knew Jamie.

She had also checked the list of casualties posted on the front door of the hospital as she had come in this morning and, as usual, had held her breath until she had seen that Jamie was not on the list of the dead.

She took the last few stairs at a bit of a run, eager to get out into the fresh air, gray though the day might be.

"Agatha!"

Pulled from her charge for the door by a familiar voice, Agatha skidded to a halt. Blast those slick marble floors, anyway. She ended up still standing, but with her arms stuck out like a windmill.

"Dear me, Agatha. Such a hoyden you can be."

Lavinia. Oh, simply lovely. The silken tones dripped poison, like the fangs of a viper. How appropriate.

Agatha fought a snicker as she turned to face the woman who had tried to seduce Simon last night. She almost lost what little control she had when Lavinia bared her teeth in a friendly smile and revealed sharply pointed eyeteeth.

Instead, Agatha managed a wide smile of her own. "Oh,

hello, Lady Winchell! I'm glad to see that you have recovered so quickly."

Lavinia's eyes narrowed suspiciously. "I wasn't aware that you knew that I had fallen ill last night."

Oh, blast. Agatha realized that she herself had supposedly left the party before she could have known that anything was amiss with her hostess.

"Ah . . . when we couldn't find you to make our regrets, I thought you must have had the headache and retired early."

"Hmm. As you say."

Lavinia considered her for another moment, and Agatha concentrated on projecting monumental idiocy. Apparently, the lady accepted the act, for she subtly relaxed.

"Have you been doing your bedpan duty so early, Agatha?"

Amused condescension was better than suspicion, of course, but vastly more irritating. Agatha kept her simpleton's smile in place and nodded earnestly.

"Oh, yes, my lady. Have you come to visit today as well?"

"Doubtful. I came to speak to the administrator about the Prince Regent's upcoming Royal Appearance at the hospital."

"The Prince Regent?"

"Surely you recall the ruler of our dear empire? Odious fellow," she added with supreme scorn. "Quite the most brainless man I've ever met. If not for the Prime Minister, England would fall to France in a heartbeat."

Yet her eyes gleamed, leading Agatha to think that Lady Winchell was very delighted indeed to be in the thick of planning for such exalted company.

"Lady Winchell! And my own darling wife. How delightful to run across you both."

Agatha jerked her gaze to her left to see Simon bearing down on them both with his Mortimer smile on. Blasted idiot!

"Lady Winchell, you are looking fine this morning. We were so sorry to miss you when we made our departure last eve."

Simon was at his Mortimer-smarmiest, Agatha could see.

She wanted to kick him soundly in the pants for running such a risk but was forced to paste a delighted smile on her face instead.

"Si—Mortimer! Darling, what are you doing here?" She tried to signal him with her eyes to get out, but he only took her hand and tucked it into his arm, turning to smile once more at Lavinia.

Lady Winchell's gaze shot sparks, but her smile was better than Agatha's. Oh, yes, Lavinia remembered well enough, Agatha realized, she simply wasn't letting on. Weren't they all a delightful bunch of liars?

"Mr. Applequist. How nice to see you again so soon. I am quite recovered, thank you. In fact, I look forward to our next evening together. Perhaps the two of you might come for a card party next week?"

"Oh, I don't play cards, Lady Winchell, but-thank-you-anyway," blurted Agatha.

Lavinia turned her chill gaze upon her, and the resemblance to a viper crossed Agatha's mind once more. Only this time she wasn't at all inclined to laugh.

"Of course you don't, Agatha. How silly of me. Well, I wouldn't want you to be uncomfortable in a sophisticated gathering. We'll have to think of something more . . . *rural* to do."

"Capital idea, my lady," Simon said pompously. "We'll look forward to your invitation."

"I'm sure, Mr. Applequist, I'm sure."

With her icy smile still in place, Lavinia turned and strolled gracefully into the hospital.

Agatha wrenched her hand from Simon's grip, leaning close to hiss at him. "Blast it, Simon, what did you think you were doing?"

"I thought I was saving you from being skewered by the rapier of her ire." He chuckled and gave her a jocular glance.

"Oh, would you drop Mortimer for a moment? I was handling her perfectly well. She doesn't know that I know, so I had the upper hand with her not knowing that I know."

"Unbelievable. I actually understood that." Simon flashed

his own sideways grin at her, and Agatha felt the familiar tug in her midriff. And slightly lower.

Why did he have to be so appealing? Why must the only man she had ever truly been attracted to have to be a thief and a scoundrel?

It was maddening. And completely inappropriate. Maybe she ought to take Collis up on his offer after all. They would have to negotiate over the ten children, of course.

She sighed. First she had to find Jamie. Then she would run away with Simon—er, Collis.

"What brings you here?"

"I came to . . . see you, of course. And take you out for the afternoon, if you'd like."

Pure joy burst through Agatha at the thought. A drive in the afternoon with Simon, like an ordinary couple. Eagerly Agatha grabbed Simon's hand and nearly dragged him from the building.

"Are we going to drive in Hyde Park? I haven't been there yet." Tucking her hand into the crook of his arm, this time quite willingly, Agatha felt the weight of her mission slip from her shoulders with more than a little bit of guilt.

But just for a while, just for one afternoon, she wanted to be a girl on an outing with her fellow, on the varied and fascinating streets of London.

Surely Jamie wouldn't begrudge her that.

Outside, Agatha saw that Simon had retained one of the small two-passenger hackneys that filled the streets of London.

"Why didn't you bring Harry? He loves to drive."

He didn't look at her. "Oh, I didn't know how long we'd be out. It didn't seem useful to have him waiting all day for us."

"I see," although she really didn't.

Simon handed her into the carriage, then settled in beside her. The two of them were quite tucked up together on the single seat and very private.

The day was damp, and Agatha told herself that was why she leaned ever so slightly into Simon's warmth. Truth be told, from the moment he'd climbed in with her she had detected the scent of cinnamon and her mouth had gone dry with wanting.

She tried to distract herself with chatter. "We will be very busy if we accept even half of the invitations we received today. I don't know that musicales are quite the thing. I'd prefer to be where I may converse with the male guests. Perhaps we should stick to dances and dinner parties. Many more opportunities there."

"Agatha, might we pass one afternoon in normal conversation?"

"Well, then, perhaps we should talk about our plan—"

"Dear lady, I think we should talk about anything but."

It was marvelous, how his new manners now seemed so ingrained in him. He had helped her into the carriage like a gentleman born, and his speech was beyond her expectations.

Taken from its nasal Cockney tone, his voice was deep, and rumbling enough to give her a tingle in her toes. She could happily listen to him all day.

"Well, then, what shall we talk about? Will you tell me more about your mother and the market at Covent Garden?"

"As today is Market Day, why don't I show you Covent Garden?"

"Indeed? Oh, I should love to see it!"

"Then see it you shall." He leaned his head out of the window and gave direction to the driver.

Chapter Eleven

The market was everything she had thought it would be. So many people and wares, in such a variety that she had never seen.

The square was huge and divided into a veritable maze by all the rows of stalls and wagons displaying any and every sort of fruit and vegetable possible.

There was more, of course. Among the bright displays of produce, there were flower vendors and ribbon sellers. There was a fellow with cages full of cats and one with multicolored birds.

"Do you think they might set up too near one another someday?" she asked Simon with interest. He looked at her oddly. Oh, well. It was an amusing thought.

Simon paid far too much for a bouquet of violets from a tattered woman standing before the church that faced the square. Agatha couldn't help the flutter in her heart when he turned and presented them to her with a courtly bow.

As they walked away, she glanced over her shoulder to see the woman clutching the coins in her hand and staring after them as if Simon had just saved her very life. Judging from the number of thin children clustered about the flower seller's skirts, Agatha had to wonder if perhaps he had.

A generous thief. How perfectly Simon.

He stopped again. Agatha followed the direction of his

gaze, but saw only a child, a soot-blackened little fellow who sat on the ground, dozing against the wheel of a vendor's cart, apparently too weary to eat the bruised apple he had obtained.

Agatha looked up at Simon. He didn't seem touched so much as taken aback.

"What?" she asked him softly. "What do you see that I don't?"

"Myself." The word came so quietly, she scarcely heard it.

She looked back at the boy, at the brushes and rags that he had carefully entwined with his legs to prevent theft of them while he rested. On closer inspection she could see under the soot to the gaunt hollows in his cheeks and the deep shadows beneath his closed eyes.

"Are you truly a chimneysweep then?"

"I was." He seemed to shake off the spell of memory to glance at her. "I'd not fit now, you know."

Agatha looked back down at the child. At Appleby, the local sweep was a prosperous man whose many sons, large and small, helped with the family business. There was no comparison of those laughing children to this thin, exhausted boy.

"Is it very hard?"

Simon shrugged. "It's grueling work, but I'm sure he feels he's lucky to have it."

Still, the memories swamped him. The tight flue, the choking soot, the pace of chimney after chimney, some so hot the bricks would leave blisters on his hands, some so cold with disuse his bones would ache. The endless climbing until he could scarcely stand at the end of the day. The hollow hunger when his masters had decided not to pay him for some imagined flaw in his work.

Lost in recollection, he was barely aware of Agatha leaving his side. Then he realized that she bent over the sleeping lad, gently touching his shoulder.

The boy blinked up at her in confusion. Simon could only imagine his thoughts. Most ladies would flick their skirts from his vicinity, but never kneel and touch him. In her cream velvet spencer and matching bonnet, Agatha must look like an angel to the little sweep. Simon rather thought she did himself.

She took the lad's grimy hand between her own with not a thought for the condition of her gloves. Simon thought he saw folded paper pass into the child's hand. It must have been pound notes, for the little lad's blue eyes grew large with disbelief, although he was careful not to look down or in any way betray what he had in his grasp.

Still, Simon thought it likely that the boy would be ducking into the nearest dark corner very shortly to examine his prize.

Agatha smiled encouragingly at the boy, who gazed back at her with near worship. *Yet another conquest,* mused Simon. She did rather collect them with her ready kindness.

She returned to Simon's side. "Shall we buy something? My appetite is quite invigorated by all this attractive produce. Perhaps some of those lovely greens to have with our dinner?"

She turned to the lettuce vendor, but Simon stopped her with a hand to her arm. "Why did you do that?"

Her soft brown eyes shifted away. "Because when I looked back at him, I saw you as well."

He let her go then, unwilling to let her see how her simple answer had touched him. As he watched her spirited haggling with the vendor as if she'd not just given ten times the amount away without a thought, he had to admit finally to himself that the main cause of his growing distaste for his former friend was less anger over James's probable betrayal and more anger over James's treatment of this singular woman.

They walked on together, Agatha commenting on things that Simon had stopped noticing years ago, and Simon providing explanations to her endless curiosity.

Simon bought her a bit of honeycomb from the beekeeper, and Agatha shared it with him. He made her laugh when he shuddered at its sweetness.

Still, for her, the taste brought back Appleby and summer

in the orchards, and the apple-blossom honey that she'd had on her toast every morning of her life.

Her heart stung from homesickness, although the last thing she wished to do was return right now to place herself in unfriendly hands. There was so much to see and experience in London.

And there was Simon.

Simon was surprised by his own reaction to being back at the market. He'd not been back since his youth, for fear of reliving his guilt and pain.

But although so much was the same, the same sounds and smells and sights of his childhood, he didn't recognize a soul. Well, it had been twenty years, and the life of a street merchant was a short and hard one.

Yet now he felt himself relax inside, as if this were a place where no one expected anything from him.

These folk worried about war, to be sure. But fighting on the Peninsula was a distant thing next to feeding themselves and their families for the next week until Market Day came round again.

Perhaps that was what he needed, to focus upon the immediate, short-term goal. Getting to the root of Agatha's secrets would be a good start.

"Tell me about where you grew up, Agatha."

"If you'll tell me about how you came to be a thief."

Her retort was swift, and she smiled as she said it, but Simon knew she was serious. He'd get nothing from her without sharing himself first. "Very well."

"I agree. You tell me your story, and I shall tell you mine." She stuck out her hand to shake on it.

Simon smiled. "A deal in Covent Garden is never sealed unless the hagglers spit into their palms first."

"Ew." She looked at her palm as if wondering if it would ever be the same afterward, then raised her hopeful gaze to his. "Must we?"

"No, we may pass on that this once." He shook her hand firmly. "But this deal is binding, nonetheless."

She nodded, and they turned to make their way onward through the labyrinth of stalls and carts.

"Very well, then. I saved a rich man's son from kidnapping, and he rewarded me by—"

He almost said "sending me to school" but stopped himself at the last moment.

"—by teaching me everything he knew about locks, and safety boxes, and making my way through the tightest fortification."

Agatha seemed a bit doubtful. "That was a reward?"

"It was for a boy who kept starvation at bay by spending his days climbing chimneys and his nights sleeping in alleys."

"What about your mother? Where was she?"

His mother had been closing the door on her child, desperate to feed them both, but not desperate enough to entertain her "visitors" in front of her son.

He could still see the shame in her eyes as she pressed a copper into his hand for his next several meals and pushed him from their grimy room night after night. And it still made him ache.

"My mother was . . . lost to me by then."

Agatha's gentle hand on his arm pulled him from that memory. "I'm sorry, Simon. I lost my mother when I was young. I know the pain never truly leaves you."

Simon shook his head, a quick, fierce rejection. He didn't want her mistaken sympathy. "She was not dead yet. Not then. Not until I—" He looked away for a moment. "I think perhaps she wished it, sometimes, but she kept up the fight nonetheless. I'm sure she thought that someday it would be over, that she would no longer have to whore for her survival and mine."

He waited for her scorn. It did not come. Her eyes were as gentle as a doe's. Loneliness spiked through him, accompanied by a sudden craving for her warmth. Why couldn't this woman be someone different?

An ordinary sort, without secrets. A woman without ties to a man who was fast becoming Simon's enemy.

Agatha was watching his face. Simon looked away. "Where was your father?"

He looked at her carefully and decided to take a chance. It was a calculated chance, not an effort to reveal his true self to her. Of course not.

"More to the point, *who* was my father? As a boy, I imagined all sorts of men were my father. Gentlemen, lords, even the King himself."

She said nothing, but neither did she show distaste. He continued.

"But my mother never had custom from any but the lowest of men, if they had the coin. Rat catchers, ragmen, the goose boy. That was the source from which I most likely sprang."

"Simon? Why were—"

"Your turn," he said roughly.

"Oh. All right." She walked beside him in silence for a moment.

Was she preparing to lie to him some more?

"I have lived always in the country, until I came to London for Jamie. My home is a beautiful place. Especially in the spring, when the apple blossoms make such a perfume one becomes almost drunken on it. Then, just before summer, the petals fall, and for a few magical days, it snows flowers."

Simon smiled at the fancy. She looked at him a bit warily.

"You find that silly and notional, but it's quite true. When I was young, I used to gather the petals into a pile, just as we did with leaves in the autumn, only smaller of course."

She smiled into the distance. "Just enough for one small girl to fling herself into and be buried in pink snow."

Simon couldn't help it. He was charmed by the vision of tiny, chubby Agatha leaping into the flowers. "Were you always such a creature?"

She glanced at him, one brow raised. "What do you mean?"

"Running wild in the country as free as a fawn."

She nodded. "Oh, yes, for a while. Then, when I realized that I wasn't safe at all, I stayed properly close to home."

"Why weren't you safe?"

"Repulsive Reggie is the son of a neighboring lor—land-owner. He's a horrid man and he was a horrid boy." She walked in silence for a moment. "He caught me alone once when I was a child. I couldn't have been more than eleven, so he would have been about seventeen."

Simon didn't want to hear this. He didn't want to know that the little girl of his vision had not had a life that was all apple blossoms.

"I was running wild, just as you said. Staying out in the orchards all day, swimming in the brook in my knickers."

Her pace slowed, and Simon found himself pulled nearer by the way her voice dropped to a whisper. She was looking down at her hands, toying with the orange he had bought for her.

"I didn't realize he had been watching me. Following me, possibly for weeks. I was very young, but I appeared . . . well, older, you understand? I wasn't tall, but I was quite mature."

Sick dread began to twine like poisonous vines in Simon's gut. A child-woman, still lost in a child's world while a man watched her with lust in his black heart.

"Did he know your true age?"

She seemed startled that he spoke but nodded. "Of course. We've known each other all our lives."

The bastard. If Simon let her continue with her story, he was very much afraid he'd have to kill someone. Someone named Reggie.

"Be that as it may, he cornered me one day in the ruins. We've an old castle there—well, not really. It's simply the shell of an old manor, but I used to think of it as a castle. I played there often. He knew I'd be there eventually, I suppose."

She abruptly handed him the orange and turned to look at a display of dried figs. Simon looked down at the sticky fruit in his hand. She had thoroughly mangled it as she had told her story, although her tone had been almost casual.

Agatha returned with a packet of the figs, seemingly quite repaired. Should he ask her to continue? He had no right, but he thought if he didn't learn the truth, no matter how terrible, he might never rest again.

But she continued on her own.

"He sprang upon me, and pushed me to the ground. Then he tore my bodice. . . . He was so much larger there wasn't a thing I could do. He held me helpless as he . . . touched me."

She paused to tuck the figs into her reticule. When she turned back to him, she was a bit pale but calm.

"It must have only lasted a few moments, but it seemed like hours. He would have gone further, I think, but my screams frightened him. I can be very loud when I choose to be. And Reggie always was a coward."

She fell silent then, and they walked on. It was as if there was a circle of privacy around them even as they moved through the crowd.

Simon was quiet as well, but his was an enraged silence. The child, assaulted and betrayed, had grown into a woman who was still being used and dishonored.

Simon had always thought that James had agreed with his stance on prostitution. Yet here was evidence to the contrary. A woman, kept by James for pleasure, whom he had made clear he had little feeling for.

"You don't have to marry a woman, Simon. You don't even have to love one."

Yet Agatha loved James. It was in the gentle way she called him Jamie. The way she focused her considerable determination on finding him.

Was James really any better than Reggie?

Agatha turned to him, her smile a bit shy. "I never told anyone before, not even Jamie. I don't know why I'm telling you. Perhaps it is because I think you know something about people like Reggie."

Simon met her gaze and nodded. There was no denying it, so he didn't bother.

Satisfied, Agatha continued walking. "I never felt truly safe again, although it is better since I came to London. The world had become a darker place for me."

She took a deep breath. "There is foulness walking this

earth. When this foulness touches you, it changes you. You lose something precious. If you are strong, you may gain wisdom as well, but mostly, you simply lose."

It was as if she'd read a page from his past. Simon felt a twinge of something that felt suspiciously like gratitude. A man wasn't supposed to put these things into words. A man was meant to soldier on.

For the first time, he saw that a woman might have her own strength, in that she wasn't afraid to speak her heart.

And sometimes, his.

Agatha couldn't believe that she had told Simon about Repulsive Reggie in the open marketplace. It was mortifying to think that she might have been overheard.

But then, Simon had found it necessary to lean quite close to her, so perhaps she need not be embarrassed.

As far as Simon knowing, she was not uncomfortable with that at all. It seemed right that he should know.

When he'd asked her to share her story with him, she'd been prepared to lie. It was a little worrisome, how she lied so easily now.

Then when he had told her about his mother, the stark pain that had shone from his eyes for that one moment had made her want to give something back to him.

A truth for a truth.

"Are you ready to go home, Agatha?"

A misty rain had begun to fall on the market and Agatha watched those vendors not fortunate enough to work under permanent shelter scurry to cover their wares against the wet. Simon was smiling at her. And Repulsive Reggie was far, far away.

Agatha smiled back. "Are you ready to talk about our plan?"

That white lightning smile crossed his face, the one that sent shivers up her spine and into her hair. Then she went entirely warm when he took her hand in his, fingers entwined.

"Very well, Agatha. We will discuss our plan in the carriage."

Every intelligent idea had flown from her head the moment he touched her, and all she could think was how much she wanted to kiss him again, this time in truth.

Her heart was growing somewhat attached, she feared. She resolved that she would think of Simon as she did Jamie. A brother, someone on whom she could depend, someone she could trust.

Not someone she could fall in love with.

The next morning, as they formed their plan in the blue parlor, Simon found out precisely what he had gotten himself into. Agatha had strategic abilities that some generals lacked and more than enough nerve to carry them out.

As usual, she was at her most attractive when she was using that surgically sharp mind of hers. At the moment, she sat on the floor next to where he sprawled in his customary chair. She was essentially ignoring him.

He hated that.

She was surrounded by a circle of opened invitations, with a calendar on her lap, writing in a notebook that contained the occupations and social connections of most of London's elite.

Even he had to admit that her information was excellent, if limited. When he remembered to think at all.

Her hair was down, pulled back into a simple braid that made him remember the way she wore it while she slept. She was clad for comfort, in an old flowered dress with a full skirt that didn't quite cover her white-stockinged ankles when she sat tailor-fashion.

He tried not to notice the free and delightful movement of her breasts under the muslin that proved she had abandoned her corset as well.

He wanted to take her hand and pull her down on the carpet with him, then roll around down there for the rest of the day. He blinked and cleared his throat.

Business.

"How did you come by those dossiers?"

She barely glanced at him, lost in concentration, twisting the end of her quill. "What's a dossier?"

If Simon weren't half-convinced that they would end up on opposite sides, he'd be in love. A woman with the mind of a master spy, the role-playing ability of a stage actress, and the body to make a man believe anything—

If only she would not choose the treasonous James, what he could do with a woman like her in his organization.

"A dossier is a file of information about someone, full of official and unofficial facts, gossip, et cetera."

He had finally gained her full attention. She was gazing at him with a puzzled but impressed expression. Somewhat belatedly, he realized that reciting definitions wasn't precisely in character.

"Button told me," he blurted desperately.

"Oh." She seemed to ponder this for a moment. "Perhaps we ought to bring Button in on this. He knows so much already, and there is no one like a valet for golden gossip."

"Really? How do you know?" Digging, always digging.

"Oh, James had one, before he joined the army."

Had Agatha known James that long? Or was this something that James had simply shared with her?

Damn, he wished he could simply question her for an hour, to hear every word James had ever told her, words that might tell him things she didn't even know that she knew.

An hour, a bright light, and a dose of opiate . . .

No, he wouldn't stoop to violating women, no matter how desperate he was for information.

And he was getting desperate. Something was brewing with the enemy, he could feel it like an itch under his skin.

A hunch was what people called it when the mind put information together in an inexplicable way, a way that didn't seem likely or possible. Most didn't trust it.

But he knew better. His information was very good, and usually he could reason things out consciously. But some-

times the facts came together in a feeling that he had learned
to rely on over the years.

Something was most definitely afoot. He was very much
afraid that he had work to do.

However, Agatha wanted to go housebreaking.

"I think I have our first victim. An adviser to the Prime
Minister. If we can get into Lord Maywell's study, he may
very well have information we can use to prove that Etheridge
is the Griffin."

Always the bloody Griffin. "Not to mention the famous
Maywell rubies."

Agatha scowled at him. "Simon, you are not to take a
thing. I must insist. You'll endanger everything I've worked
so hard for."

"Why?"

"Because if you get caught, it may come out that we aren't
married and—"

"No, I mean why work so hard to find James? Perhaps he
left you willingly. Perhaps he has decamped and is living high
somewhere, not thinking of you at all."

She tilted her head and studied him for a moment. "I suppose I shouldn't expect you to understand. You've been alone
for so long. James would never desert me. And I shall never
abandon him."

It bothered him, all that strength and loyalty directed to
another man. Especially one who was seeming more guilty
by the hour.

He wished she had less faith in James.

And more faith in him.

Agatha rose from her seat on the carpet and rang the bell-
pull for the butler. Pearson appeared as if she'd rubbed his
magical lamp.

"Pearson, would you kindly ask Button to join us?"

Simon had to admire how Pearson could invest such
wealth of meaning in one raised brow. When the butler left,
Agatha turned her head to grin at Simon over her shoulder.

"Do you think they teach that in butler school?"

Simon nodded. "The right brow is for disapproval."

Agatha returned to sit on the floor before him. "What is the left brow for?"

"Severe disapproval."

She nodded. "And both brows?"

"You don't want to know."

Pearson returned, opening the door of the parlor and intoning, "Mr. Button is here to see you, madam." When he spied his lady employer's unseemly sprawl on the floor, he raised his left brow nearly to his hairline.

Both Simon and Agatha broke into snickers, sending Pearson away with an offended sniff.

Button was obviously uncomfortable. He stood before them with hands twisted together, growing paler by the moment.

Agatha was all concern. "Button, whatever is the matter?"

Simon glanced at her dryly. "He thinks you've called him down to sack him, Agatha."

"That's nonsense. I'm not sacking you, Button. I'm promoting you, and I shall grant you a raise in pay as well."

Simon thought Button might faint with relief.

"Pr-promoting me?" The little valet whipped out a lacy handkerchief the size of a pillowcase to mop his brow. "Oh my. I was so worried—"

"Well, you have nothing to worry about. You're the finest valet in town, and a veritable lockbox of confidentiality." Agatha stood and urged Button to a seat. "Poor dear, you're overcome. Let me have some tea brought in for you."

"Oh, no, madam. I'm fine now. It was just the thought of having to find another position. . . ."

Button spared a moment for a theatrical shudder. "I'd never find another master with Mr. Rain's physique, or your taste and generosity, madam. My talents would never again have such a palette to work with."

"And you shine, Button, you truly shine. Why, everyone says that Mortimer Applequist is the absolute glass of fashion."

Button turned to peer at Simon in tearful adoration. "I know. He does me such credit. Not a speck of padding needed in the shoulders of his coat, and the way his tails fall—heaven, sheer heaven."

"Why, Button, you sound like a tailor."

The little fellow turned back to Agatha, fluttering his handkerchief. "Oh, thank you, madam. It is my dream to someday have my own exclusive sartory on Bond Street."

Simon sent Agatha a get-on-with-it look and she answered him with a just-a-moment flick of her eyelids.

"Button, you deserve nothing less. However, I do hope you'll remain with me for a while, as I've a special mission for you."

"A—a mission, madam? For me?"

Button appeared absolutely thrilled. Oh, hell. Not another amateur with delusions of glory.

"I know that you know everything about everyone in London."

"Well, only everyone who is anyone," demurred Button.

"Precisely. I need your information, Button." Agatha handed him her notebook. "Here are the people on my list. I want you to write down every detail you can think of, no matter how small."

She took Button's other hand in hers and pressed it down onto the notebook with great ceremony. "I cannot tell you any more than this, for your own safety. If you wish to withdraw, now is the time to speak."

Simon rolled his eyes. That was spreading it a bit thick, wasn't it? Button, however, was completely gulled, to judge by the smitten look on his puckish face.

"No, madam. I'll carry my mission through, you shall see."

"Thank you, Button. I knew I could count on you." Agatha leaned forward and kissed him on one cheek, then the other, as if she were sending him into battle that very morning.

Button rose, and Simon could swear the little chap stood three inches taller.

"I shall return when I have completed it, madam," he said formally. Then he paused. "I may need more paper than this."

Agatha nodded serenely. "I shall have Pearson deliver it to your quarters himself."

A twinkle of mischief pierced Button's solemnity. "He'll hate that."

Agatha smiled. "I know."

Chortling, Button bowed to Simon and Agatha. He left nearly strutting with pride.

When the door shut, Simon began a slow, sarcastic applause. "Encore! Encore!" he called.

Agatha wrinkled her nose at him. "Oh, shut it, Simon. I made him happy." She returned to her pile of invitations and sorted Lord Maywell's out of the mass. "This one's tonight. Do you think I might wear my green gown twice in one week?"

"How would I know? I'm no bloody valet," he growled.

She sat back on her heels and looked at him. "Why are you so grumpy?"

"Well, it seems like I've done a bit more for you than Button, and all I get is 'shut it, Simon.'"

"Poor little Simon." Cooing mockingly, Agatha rose to her knees and leaned on the arm of his chair. "Does he want a kiss, too?"

She was teasing, pouting her lips in an exaggerated kiss.

On impulse, Simon bent his head and pressed his lips to hers.

Chapter Twelve

Oh, the *hunger*.

Hot need hit Agatha like a flash flood, sweeping over her, stealing her breath, then left her dissolving in a pool of want.

Her lips were open, and so were his. His mouth was hot and wet and she could feel his tongue sweep across her teeth. He sucked her lower lip between his teeth and bit gently.

Her mind and her recent resolution to treat him as a brother melted clean away. All she knew was his hot mouth. When he gently gripped her braid, she let the weight of his hand pull her head back to expose her neck to his seeking lips and teeth and tongue.

Submitting to Simon's mouth was the easiest thing she had ever done.

His hand in her hair turned to fingers softly combing out her braid. The other became a warm palm cupping her breast. The heat of it seeped through the fabric of her bodice and melted her last resolve.

She pressed her hands against the arm of the chair and dug the toes of her slippers into the carpet, trying to get closer to him. She wanted to feel him against her, the way she had felt him in Winchell's study.

Then Simon slid from the chair to kneel with her on the floor. His hand left her breast to wrap around her waist and pull her close.

Yes. That was what she ached for, to feel his hardness against her softness.

Yet it wasn't enough. Irritably she pushed his coat from his shoulders. He shrugged it off one arm at a time, never releasing her completely. A wonderful skill, that.

Now she had access to his hard arms and chest, and her hands roamed over him possessively. Her Simon.

Hers.

Then she was on her back, the piles of invitations crackling beneath her. Above, Simon lay half upon her, his knee pressing intimately between her thighs. It was strange to feel him there, strange to open her knees just a bit more to allow him in.

Somewhat surprisingly, she felt no fear. This was no attack.

This was Simon.

She slid her fingers into his thick black hair and brought his mouth back to hers. Lips clung and tongues clashed, all of it feeding the hunger that welled endlessly inside of her. It was as though she wanted to eat him alive, to take him within her. She couldn't get enough.

Simon was lost in the softness of her. She lay beneath him, willingly sharing her lushness. His lungs were full of her scent, his mouth with her taste. He couldn't believe the silkiness of her skin.

Urgent. Throbbing. He filled his hands with her breasts and hungered to take her nipples into his mouth. He pressed his erection against her soft hip and ached to drive himself within her.

Her arms were wrapped about him, holding him close as she gave so generously. Her hands kneaded his shoulders and she writhed restlessly beneath him.

"Simon . . . please . . ."

Oh, yes. He moved above her, lodging himself in the cradle of her hips. Through her dress he could feel the heat of her center, and his erection throbbed in response.

"Please . . . stop."

Stop? The word was meaningless for a moment. Then, he

realized that her writhing hadn't been restlessness but resistance.

He pulled away slightly. She was gazing over his shoulder, her face crimson.

Behind him, he heard Pearson clear his throat. Oh, hell. Slowly, Simon turned to look over his shoulder. Pearson stood in the open doorway of the parlor, his gaze firmly on the horizon.

Both eyebrows had nearly disappeared into his hairline.

Simon shot a frantic look at Agatha, but she was no help at all. She destroyed his control with a red-faced giggle. They both dissolved into laughter.

"Madam, there is a Mrs. Trapp and her daughters here to see you," Pearson said over their laughter.

Simon couldn't answer. He rolled away from Agatha and lay on the carpet, one arm crossed over his eyes, laughing helplessly.

Agatha managed to catch her breath to say, "Thank you, Pearson. Will you tell Mrs. Trapp that I will be available in just a moment?" She only hiccupped once.

The door closed, and he could hear the hurried rustling of paper. Agatha was clearing up the mess. He rose and began to help. Perhaps it would take his mind off his aching groin.

Agatha was very carefully not looking at him. This was going to take some thought. He had complicated things considerably, but hopefully not irreparably.

He really ought to be grateful for the interruption. It had kept him from making a classic error. He had almost forgotten the first rule of survival in his business.

Don't get involved.

James Cunnington rubbed his eyes again and stared at the news-sheet with great concentration, forcing his eyes to focus. His vision wasn't much better, but he could make out the letters today.

He hadn't had the memory of filching the papers beaten

out of him as he had feared, but the recollection hadn't done him much good for the past three days.

When he'd finally awoken with his body aching and his head throbbing so badly he hardly dared breathe, his vision had been too blurred to make any sense of the writing at all.

He gritted his teeth and willed himself to focus. The writing swam before him, making him dizzy, then abruptly snapped into clarity.

W...H...E...N. When.

English.

James sagged back onto his pallet, his relief so great that it momentarily washed away the pain in his head.

The news-sheet was in English. Which meant he wasn't in France or Portugal, but home all along. If he did manage to escape the ship, he'd be able to find help from any solid British fisherman or farmer on the way to London.

For the first time, he began to hope he might really make it out alive.

Returning to a sitting position propped against the side of the ship, James examined the papers in the crack of daylight afforded him there.

They were a varied bunch. A page from a local farmer's bureau, which put him near a village on the coast that he believed lay somewhat west of London.

A sheet from a fashion journal. And, amazingly, three pages from the London *Times*.

Real news! James pressed close to his light source and forced his eyes to work together. The account of a battle won made his heart race, the list of dead made him want to rip the ship apart with his bare hands. He read every word of the sheets he held in his hands.

They weren't consecutive, just a jumble of pages, most likely kept by Bull for privy paper. James doubted the burly thug could read in his own language, much less English.

James read the fashion page and the agricultural sheet as well, starved as he was for news and the sight of his own language. Then he read everything again. And again.

It wasn't until the third time through that something caught his eye. Just a name mentioned in a society column, the one thing he was least interested in.

Who of the nobility was seen where, what they were wearing, and who they did and did not speak to.

There it was. Applequist.

". . . and spent much of their evening speaking to Mr. and Mrs. Mortimer Applequist of Carriage Square."

Mortimer Applequist? There couldn't really be such a person, could there? It was so unlikely. No, it must be Agatha. But who was playing Mortimer? Had Agatha married while he was gone?

She wouldn't. He couldn't imagine her going through with something so monumental without his presence or knowledge. She would wait for him to come home, he knew she would. Unless she was convinced he was dead.

But if that were true, she'd never make up a Mortimer and parade him around London.

No. James was forced to believe that his conniving little sister had done so for this very purpose. A signal for him to come home.

Well, he was on his way. Just as soon as he could figure out how.

Oddly enough, his mind was quite clear now. As far as he could tell, no drugs clouded his thinking for the first time since his capture.

Had his captors stopped bothering, figuring him too badly beaten now to be a problem?

James looked around his personal little hell. His water bucket stood where Bull had left it last night. His bread crusts continued to molder where they lay, for his loosened teeth hurt far too much to tear into the stale—

The bread.

Could it be the bread? He'd always suspected the water, for it tasted so foul and bitter. The bread he had striven not to taste at all. The flavor of the mold was so sickening that it had put him off fancy cheeses forevermore.

So, the bread was drugged somehow. He seriously doubted that his captors baked it specially for him, then let it rot for effect. They probably dusted it with some powder, which he'd hardly notice over the varied blotches on the crust.

Well, he now had his mind and will back, along with the beginnings of a plan for escape. Avoid the food entirely and drink only the water he needed to live.

He'd not have long, for without the sustenance of the bread he'd be dangerously weak within days.

Time for some hard thinking. James hid the papers and fell limply back down on his pallet, appearing for all the world a beaten and broken man.

But inside, the professional was back on the job.

Another ballroom, another escapade. Another toe-crunching dance with a man in uniform. After four such evenings, Agatha knew the drill by heart.

She smiled at the stout general with whom she waltzed, took a deep breath to draw her host's attention to her bosom, and raised three fingers behind the man's back to signal Simon.

Within moments she saw the footmen who were serving the guests begin to gather at the exits of the ballroom, then disappear toward the kitchens.

She wondered what Simon had done this time. During the last three evenings, she had been astonished and sometimes appalled at the lengths he would go to provide a distraction.

As long as he wasn't secretly setting loose a bagful of rats again. Agatha had hardly been able to sleep last night for thinking of her poor hostess, who had been embarrassed beyond belief by the rat streaking through her dining room in the midst of dinner.

Simon had promised no more vermin, but Agatha didn't entirely trust him. Honestly, men had no idea what a woman went through to put on an event. Agatha had been sure to spread the rumor of a prank played on last night's dinner party, for she would hate for anyone to think that there really were rats in that household.

The general was speaking, and Agatha tried very hard to

listen. She had already pumped him for information about Jamie and had led him to speak an opinion on the subject of the famous Griffin. Unfortunately, her digging had given him the impression that she wished to hear all his war stories.

Chronologically.

In detail.

With accompanying blast noises.

Agatha certainly hoped Jamie knew what she sacrificed for him. He was going to owe her forever after tonight.

The waltz ended. Agatha pleaded exhaustion and thirst, which spurred her general into battle to fight for a glass of champagne to save her.

As soon as he had disappeared in the crowd, Agatha made a run for it. Simon was taking too long. Usually he was in and out of the safe-boxes in a flash, with no one the wiser for it.

Simon was a talented thief, but she feared he was also a bit reckless. If he continued in his current path, he was going to get himself into terrible trouble.

And now she had made it possible for him to gain welcome in the finest homes. No petty pilfering here, but some of the finest jewelry and art collections in England. Temptation indeed.

He was on a dangerous path, and it was all her doing.

Well, perhaps not all.

Agatha had smiled and dodged her way through the crowd to the front of the ballroom. Now she climbed the stairs to the main floor of her general's grand house.

She wasn't the only lady traversing the halls, for the powder room was on this floor. There was a great deal of giggling traffic, and a certain amount of edgy shuffling of feet from impatient swains.

Consulting the map in her head, Agatha continued past the powder room and smoothly turned a corner. This hall was deserted but for an amorously engaged couple.

Agatha crossed her arms and put on her best outraged duenna expression. She cleared her throat.

The youngsters sprang apart, red-faced and gasping. Agatha remembered her own interrupted rolling-on-the-floor kiss with Simon and bit back a laugh.

"The two of you should be ashamed. I shan't inform your families," she said sternly, "but I shall expect better behavior in the future."

"Yes, ma'am!"

"Oh, yes! Thank you, madam."

The couple clasped hands and ran for the ballroom. As they left, Agatha heard them whisper to each other.

"Was that your chaperone?"

"No! I thought it must be someone from your family. . . ."

There was no danger that those two would ever come forward about seeing Agatha loose in the house. That secret was as good as kept.

As she continued quickly to where she knew the study was located, thanks to Button, Agatha pondered Simon's own little secret.

She had wanted to ask him about it tonight, but the plan had taken every moment to prepare for. And really, how was she supposed to question him?

"By the way, Simon, I noticed that you disappear nearly every day without telling me where you are going and without answering my questions when you return."

Thanks to Button's connections among the servant populace, Agatha had a memorized map of the house in her head. She counted doors until she was sure she had found the study, then gave a quick three-two-one tap on the polished wood.

The door opened swiftly, and a hand thrust out, grabbing her elbow and yanking her into the darkness.

"Really, Simon," she muttered, rubbing her arm. "You have such a flair for the dramatic."

A warm hand pressed over her mouth, giving her a start. Before it could frighten her, it was gone.

A voice whispered warmly in her ear, "Shut it, darling. We have company."

Simon's body pressed closely to her back as he maneuvered her through the darkness to where a glimmer of light appeared under another door.

It was terribly difficult to keep one's mind on housebreaking when one's body was on fire. Simon's breath was warm on her neck, and his grasp on her shoulders reminded her of the kiss in her parlor.

Having Simon pressed to her back was very nearly as exciting as having him pressed to her front.

"Here." It was a soundless whisper in her ear, and Simon pushed on her shoulders until she knelt before the keyhole.

Agatha put her eye to the small circle of light and saw that she must not be in the study, for the study plainly was the next room.

Then she heard rustling and footsteps and angled her head to see to the left a bit.

A man stood, examining a sheaf of papers by the light of a candle. He was very tall, and his back was broad. He was dressed for evening, as far as she could see, and his hair was dark.

"It's Etheridge," came Simon's voice like a feather in her ear.

Agatha eagerly pressed closer to the keyhole, willing Lord Etheridge to turn around.

With a disgruntled huff, the figure in the study straightened the papers in his hand and turned.

Agatha jumped and almost fell from her crouch. Simon pulled her tightly against him.

"What? What did you see?"

Agatha pointed, although of course Simon couldn't see her gesture in the dark. "Lord Etheridge . . ."

"What?"

"Lord Etheridge is Uncle Dalton."

"Are you telling me you've had entry to Etheridge's all along?"

They were back at Carriage Square, having made their escape from the anteroom of the study without detection and made their regrets to their harried hostess, who was dealing with a flock of swallows that had somehow swept into her kitchens.

Agatha sat penitently on the sofa in the parlor, nervously toying with a small tasseled pillow in her lap. Simon was pacing before her, anger boiling within him.

When he thought of all the ridiculous chances he'd taken this week, although he had found some interesting documents. Yet the exertion he had gone to—well, some of it had been rather fun.

"I didn't know he was Lord Etheridge, I told you. Collis called him Uncle Dalton, and Uncle Dalton introduced himself as Dalton Montmorency. Good lord, Simon. I don't have the peerage *memorized,* you know."

Simon did. All his operatives did.

But Agatha wasn't an operative. He was finally sure of it.

He glared at her, as if it were her fault that she wasn't. She was stroking the tassels in long, slow movements, petting the velvet and silk almost as if—

Simon shook his head. He'd wasted a week on her foolishness.

"So do you think Uncle Dalton is the Griffin?" Agatha asked.

"Stop calling him Uncle Dalton, for heaven's sake. He's not your uncle. He's no older than me."

Agatha shrugged, playing idly with an especially long, thick tassel. The way her fingers stroked down the length of it made his ears pound.

"Well, technically, you are old enough to be my uncle, if my mother were your older sister."

Simon bent over her and snatched the pillow from her grasp. *"I'm not your bloody uncle!"*

Agatha jumped up and stood in his path. "Fine! You're not my bloody uncle! Dalton Montmorency is not my bloody uncle!" She glared at him, fists on her hips. "I asked if you think Dalton Montmorency is the bloody Griffin!"

Simon glared back at her. *"No."*

Agatha grumbled and dropped her hands, returning to sit

on the sofa. "Oh, why am I asking you? I know more about the Griffin than you do."

Now that hurt. That truly hurt. Here he was, a bloody expert on the bloody Griffin, and she didn't believe a word.

Simon rubbed his face. What did he care what she believed? He was losing his mind. *She* was losing it for him.

"Look, Aggie—"

"Don't call me that. James calls me that. You'll have to come up with your own pet name."

"I don't want to call you pet names," growled Simon. "I want to engrave them on your headstone!"

Agatha eyed him reproachfully. "Honestly, Simon. I know you haven't been at this sort of thing for very long, but you really must acquire a bit of self-restraint."

She stood, then clasped her hands behind her back. This had the unfortunate effect of decreasing the flow of blood to Simon's brain, for the movement thrust her magnificent breasts virtually under his nose.

Oh, he wanted to bury her all right. He wanted to cover her with his body and take his time driving her as mad as he was becoming.

"I'm going to bed."

Simon shut his eyes in surrender. She couldn't be so ignorant that she didn't know what she did to him. In this field, he had to accede to the master.

"Very well, Agatha. You go to bed. I'm going out."

He stalked past her, leaving behind his coat and hat, and slammed the front door behind him. He wouldn't be going to bed for quite a while, if the state of his erection meant anything.

It wasn't until he was a hundred yards down the walk that he realized he still clutched the small tasseled pillow in his fist.

Her sweet and citrusy scent rose from the velvet. God, was he never free of her? Simon was tempted to toss the bloody thing into the gutter.

Instead, he lifted it to his nose and wondered if Pearson would miss it if he kept it.

Chapter Thirteen

The starvation had worked. James Cunnington was now as clear-headed as he could be without a few good meals inside him.

He remained very still upon his pallet, which led his captors to believe him so weakened that they ceased bothering him at all. Apparently, he'd become a very boring fellow.

He'd been able to drink his fill every day, but he continued to avoid the bread. He rode the thin edge of starvation, he knew. There was now a sort of dreamy clarity to everything, his mind at once sharp and yet detached.

He was able to consider his escape from all logical points, calculating the probabilities of his death coolly. He wasn't suicidal, simply supremely uninvolved. The goal was to get out alive, but he had no fear, no anxiety about failure.

After due consideration, he had decided that taking on the vicious Bull was unlikely to work. He couldn't battle him while tied, and hadn't even when he was stronger.

Once he had thrown out plans wild and unlikely, it seemed that the best thing would be to remove a few planks from one of the inner walls of his little cell. If he was in luck, he'd find himself in another cabin or hold that might not be locked up tight.

The trick was how to do it without causing so much noise that he'd be investigated immediately.

And perhaps more to the point, how was he to remove the
planks at all? The ship was old and in sorry disrepair, but he
wasn't in any better shape himself. Unless he could come
upon some sort of lever, he'd be faced with pulling the bloody
ship apart with his fingernails.

The only things in his cabin were his pallet, made from
moldy sailcloth stuffed with even moldier straw, and his water
container. The sorry dented pail had no handle at all, which
he might have used to force the nails from their planks.

Still, there was something about the pail that teased his
brain. He picked it up in his bound hands to examine it more
closely. Suppose . . .

Abruptly he dashed the contents to the floor and crawled
to the partition with the worst warpage. Holding the pail by
the bottom, he managed to wedge the rim under one corner
of a plank. Perhaps it would work as a sort of grapple hook.

He pulled on the outer edge of the rim, only really able to
lean his weight away while he held on with a shaking grip.
The plank shifted finally but gave a loud squeal of protest.

Too loud. He halted the experiment for the moment.

When he released the pail, he noticed that the raw edge of
the tin had scratched his palm. It probably stung, but he was
too distanced from his body to care.

What interested him was the sharp metal. He sat on his
pallet with his back to the door. Should someone come, he'd
be thrust away and his activity concealed. Gripping the pail
between his knees, he dragged the ropes that bound his hands
across the rim again and again.

After several minutes, he inspected his work. A number of
small strands within the thick rope were shredded. It wasn't
much, but it was far more than he'd ever managed with his
teeth.

A rumble of thunder penetrated past the creaking and
sloshing sounds of the old fishing boat. He began again,
working steadily. Cutting through was going to take hours.

No matter. He had the time. He had the means. And from
the sound of things, nature was going to provide the opportunity.

What he needed was a distraction, preferably something loud, to keep his captors too busy to hear or care about their prisoner's doings.

What he needed was a storm.

Another rumble came, louder this time. James smiled grimly and set to work on his bonds.

Simon hadn't come home last night.

Of course, Agatha hadn't sat up waiting for him. She had quite properly gone straight to bed. True, she had slept with her door slightly open and one ear aimed at Simon's room even in her restless sleep, but that did not count as waiting *up* for someone.

When she had finally risen it had been past nine. Assuming she had missed his entry and that he would be past impatient waiting for her to come down, she had hurried her toilette.

Simon had not appeared at the table, nor had he come home by the time she had taken her tea. By then she had been completely dying to see him, for included in today's post had been something very special.

An invitation to an informal dinner at Etheridge House for tomorrow night.

She had posted an immediate acceptance, of course, although the late notice of the invitation had earned a dark glare at the richly monogrammed paper. Dalton Montmorency was certainly sure of himself. Wasn't that just like a man?

Agatha had been enormously satisfied with this outcome until one thought had occurred to her.

If tomorrow night revealed Lord Etheridge as the Griffin— and somehow she managed to convince him to tell her where to find Jamie—then she would have no reason to hold Simon to his agreement.

She wanted Jamie home safe.

Yet she also wanted Simon to stay with her.

Forever.

That was the thought that had her pacing the house in Carriage Square. She had argued with herself until the sun began to drop in the sky. Here she was still, repudiating her feelings to the empty room.

Oh, blast. Who was she trying to convince? She was a complete goner, and there was no denying it. This was what all the stories were about, this feeling of being one-half of something larger than oneself. Of being bereft when one's other half was gone.

True, she hadn't known him long, but she knew that they were a perfect partnership. She knew that when she was with him, she was understood.

From the moment she'd first seen him, she had been captivated. First by his appearance, it was true. Indeed, what was all that masculine perfection for, if not to attract?

But the man within was what kept her enthralled. She'd seen handsome men before, enough to know that the outside didn't always reflect a superior inside. Yet Simon had been with her in this house for weeks and had never pressed unfair advantage. Even Nellie had reported nothing but gentlemanly behavior when discreetly questioned.

Simon was a thief, the product of a past she couldn't even imagine. The difference in their classes should make him the last man she should want. Yet wasn't the definition of a gentleman a man with honor and strength enough that he would never take advantage of those weaker than himself?

If so, then Simon was most assuredly a gentleman and Repulsive Reggie was not.

Besides, Agatha cared very little about the opinions of others. Where had those mysterious others been when she and Jamie had been virtually deserted to raise themselves?

If she wanted Simon over any other man, then why shouldn't she have him? Resolve strengthened her desire into determination.

Great lot of good it would do her. Here she sat, inescapably mad about him, and where was he? Out all night, no doubt housebreaking and putting himself in unbearable danger.

The truth was that there was no need for him to steal. She had more than enough money for the both of them. How

could she let him know she not only could make him a good
wife, but was an heiress to boot?

Goodness, the only reason that she didn't have beaux lining up on the street was that Jamie had decided they ought
not to put it about.

Still, a little voice murmured in her mind, if Jamie was so
concerned about her making a good marriage, why had he
never brought her to London? . . .

Nonsense. In time he would have, she was sure. He simply
hadn't wanted her to become bait for some fortune hunter.

Some money-mad bounder who only cared for profit—

Oh, dear. Perhaps she ought not to put quite so much temptation before Simon.

She understood that her beloved thief was only striving to
secure himself against ever returning to his boyhood poverty,
but she wasn't entirely sure that Jamie would.

If she could get some sort of avowal of Simon's feelings
before he ever learned of her wealth, then she would know
that he truly cared for her. Oh, wouldn't she just love to hear
the words from his lips. . . .

An idea began to grow from that seed of longing.

If Simon confessed his feelings thinking her nothing but
an ordinary woman, and if Agatha herself was ever so slightly
compromised before Jamie came home . . . well, that would
sort matters out quite nicely, wouldn't it? Even Lord Fistingham would be stymied by that little detail.

The kiss in the parlor wouldn't count as being compromised. Not if Jamie truly objected to Simon, as he most likely
would. Reggie certainly wouldn't let a mere kiss from another
man get in the way of his plotting.

No, nothing would do but a most serious tarnishing. And
it had better be tonight, for she could not count on keeping
her hold on him once they had broken Lord Etheridge's safe.

Tonight.

Her breath came a bit faster then. Memories of Simon's
lips and hands rose in her mind, and her body heated.

Oh my. She could not *wait*.

She would yield her virginity to Simon, and when he declared his feelings, she would tell him the happy news.

Agatha smiled. She couldn't wait to see Simon's face when he learned what she was worth.

She turned from the front parlor window and began to pace the room once more. What did one wear to a seduction, anyway?

It wasn't until late morning that daylight seeped past the clouds and between the surrounding buildings to shine through the window of Jackham's office. Simon rolled from Jackham's sofa and stretched.

The sounds of a body growing older filled the room. Disgusted, Simon shook out his arms and shoulders and rubbed his face.

He should have gone to his own house. After all, he'd gone to much expense to purchase it and make sure it was comfortable, if rather monastically furnished. But the painful contrast between that silent stately home and Agatha's warm and welcoming little house had made spending the night at the bustling club seem like a viable alternative.

Of course, his back didn't seem to agree. One bloody night out of a comfortable bed. He was getting soft, was all.

And maybe just a tiny bit . . . seasoned. He must admit, he hadn't had those creaks and pops when he'd been younger.

Fifteen years on the job took it out of a fellow. At least he still had his career. Younger men than he had burned themselves up under the pressure.

Simon hadn't burned up, because he had long ago learned to be ice.

Cold logic and hard facts kept him to the course, until there was room for nothing else.

Still, it wouldn't hurt to begin looking for another successor, now that James was out of the running.

The loss of James hurt, in both the loss of a man he called friend and the loss of something he hadn't realized he held so dear. His faith in his ability to read someone, to know the good men from the bad.

Simon chilled the pain and drove it deep, and turned his mind back to the problem at hand.

The reality was, however, that there was no one else in the organization now with the proper view.

He needed someone who could see the shifting threads within the knot, who knew when to pull this one, when to ease that one, yet never lost sight of the entire tangle.

The job required a very singular vision. And at the moment, Simon knew of no one else who could do it.

There was time, of course. Years to train another, as he had been trained to take over for the Old Man. Simon wasn't leaving the center of his web for a long time yet. There was time to bring up another young fellow, if he could find one. He had years.

For a moment, Simon longed to set down his burden. What life might he have led without it? The comfort of a loving wife, the joy of sons and daughters, a life without secrets?

A life in the light of day?

He shook off the fantasy. Rubbish. If not for his own mentor, the Old Man, he'd most likely never have lived to his thirteenth birthday, much less had a life of comfort and familial warmth.

Simon shook out his crumpled jacket and donned it. For a moment, he contemplated braving Kurt's kitchen for a roll, then decided he'd be better off cajoling a meal from Agatha's cook.

He rubbed his face. He'd handled Agatha badly the night before. He should have charmed her, not baited her. He should be at her side now, charming her for all he was worth.

It was time to get to the bottom of that woman's secrets, even if it meant going to the extreme and seducing her loyalty away from James.

He was halfway there already, judging from that kiss in her parlor.

Halfway to damnation, whispered his conscience.

Halfway to ecstasy, whispered his lust.

With a growl, Simon grabbed his hat and strode from the club. The possibility of having Agatha naked and willing by midnight was more than a plan of action. It was a dream come true, there was no denying it.

Every ache in his body disappeared at the mental image of Agatha in his arms, Agatha in his bed. Need pounded through him, scorching lust with a raw edge of loneliness.

He halted just outside the door of the club and leaned gratefully against the cold iron of the nearest lamppost. He took several deep breaths to clear his head.

The air outside was hardly fresh, but it was full of real scents and noises. The clattering of coach and wagon wheels, the clopping of horses, the ever-present sooty smell of his beloved London.

This was real. This was the world he lived in, the world he needed to protect. His city, his homeland. His role, to deal with the grit and grime of wartime and espionage.

The mission. Focus on the mission.

Find James Cunnington and take him down, by whatever means necessary. Stop a dangerous intelligence leak and protect his country.

Unfortunate that he was fond of the man, but entirely irrelevant. Unfortunate that he was captivated by his target's mistress, but also irrelevant.

Simon felt himself steady, felt himself grow flinty and cold inside once more, as if the iron of the lamppost were flowing through his palm and replacing the hot blood incited by Agatha's charms.

He had a mission. This time, he wouldn't forget it.

Once her decision had been made to seduce Simon, Agatha found that she was suddenly no longer in a hurry for him to return. She needed every spare minute she could manage.

First, she ordered the linens freshened in both their chambers, for she wasn't entirely sure where the night would end. Then she took a bath, hiding beneath the water until she remembered her tendency to prune. At which time she promptly erupted from the lather calling for Nellie.

Sitting in her bedchamber wrapped in a satin wrapper and

a cloud of lemon verbena *eau de toilette*, Agatha decided to organize her thoughts.

She pulled a sheet of foolscap to her and uncorked her inkwell.

First, invite Simon to her room. No. Too spider-and-the-fly. She would go to his room.

When? Immediately after he retired? The stroke of midnight?

Heavens, how complicated seduction was. It was a wonder the human race continued at all.

Agatha chewed the end of her quill for a moment. She must decide. Very well, then. His room, as soon as Button had left him for the night.

She heard the chime of the clock in the hall. The day had nearly passed already, and Simon was nowhere to be seen. What if she had used up her favorite bath scent for nothing?

Just as she was truly beginning to panic, she heard Simon's familiar tread in the hall and the rumbling of his voice. She hopped up to press her ear to the door.

"If Mrs. Applequist is having supper in her room, then I'll do the same. No, I don't think I'll be joining her. You can bring up the food, Button, but then I want my privacy."

She heard Button respond, but his higher tones didn't travel as well. Simon's door opened and then closed.

Agatha sat back, nervously toying with the sash of her wrapper. The time was only just eight. Her own early supper sat congealed on the table in the corner. She had been quite unable to eat.

Shortly Simon would be alone in his room for the night. Alone, relaxed, and ready for bed.

A warm tingle went through her at the thought. Then a cold wash of utter fear. What if she went about it all wrong?

She was country-bred and had been involved in keeping sheep for as long as she could recall. When a ewe was ready and a ram was ready, they simply acted. Surely people did not need lessons on this subject, either?

Agatha heard Button arrive with Simon's supper. A few moments later, she heard Button leave again.

Determined to wait until Simon had eaten, Agatha began pacing again. After all, one should digest one's food entirely before embarking on . . . physical activity.

The thought shook her resolve and she sank to a seat on her mattress. She didn't have to do this. It still was not too late to back out of her plan—

And lose Simon. Lose her beautiful thief and never see his breathtaking smile again. Never again feel his laugh vibrate through her body or taste the faint flavor of cinnamon on his lips.

Never again experience that unrivaled sense of union that fed her parched soul.

Her resolve suddenly renewed, Agatha stood. *That* was simply not an option.

She took a deep breath, then strode calmly to the door and stepped into the hall.

As Simon never went into any fray without a strategy, he was going to take tonight to form his plan.

Unfortunately, he couldn't think of a thing that would convince Agatha that she should abandon James for him.

The James that Simon had known, and the man that Agatha believed she knew, was altogether a finer candidate for her affections.

James was a wealthy man and an educated one. Although Simon was secure financially and was now well-read, there was no denying his low birth.

James was a gentleman and could move freely among the finest of society. Then again, as a gentleman, James would never marry a ladybird like Agatha, but only break her heart.

Simon would . . . no, he could not marry her, either. Not to someday put her in danger as his bride.

Then again, James was not here, and Simon was.

She'd be better off with him. He understood her and he understood what it was like to live in the world between the low and the high.

He could do it for his country and save her from herself

at the same time. But he wouldn't keep her, paying for her wares. No, he'd buy this house for her and make it a gift.

Then give her the choice. It wouldn't be wrong if she came to him as an independent woman, would it? A knowledgeable, experienced woman, who made her decision freely?

Would it be so wrong, to have something warm for himself after all these years? To take pleasure in Agatha's hot, sweet flesh and giving nature?

She wouldn't be his whore. She would be his woman, his partner, wife in all but name.

He was fairly confident that he could maneuver his way into her bed, and from there he was sure he could maneuver his way into her heart. She would be better off.

Wouldn't she?

Simon turned away from his mostly intact supper tray and stood to pace restlessly around the room.

Everything here belonged to another man. The books and dressing table items belonged to James, the clothes to Mortimer. There was nothing of Simon but a tiny sack of cinnamon drops tossed carelessly on the washstand.

As it should be.

Simon perused the books on the shelves once more. These had never been a surprise to him, for he had known that James had a fascination with Daniel Defoe. Every one of the Liars went through it at some point.

Who was this man, this king of liars? A writer, a poet, everyone knew this. Not all of them knew that he had also been a master intelligencer.

Had he been a man of great emotion or a man of cold logic? Artist or artificer?

The questions haunted them all as they struggled with the eternal conflict between being a man and being a spy.

Simon chose *Moll Flanders* from a shelf and hefted the weight of it in his hands. His own burning question had always been . . . where had the man found the time?

Idly he lifted the cover to flip through some of his favorite passages. On the flyleaf, he found an inscription in a familiar sturdy script.

For Jamie,
Beloved kindred spirit
A

Kindred spirit. Ice wedged itself deeply into Simon's gut. How could he sink so low that he would divide her from the man she loved?

Thinking furiously, he sat in the chair before the fire without even realizing he had moved, still holding the open book before his unseeing eyes.

He couldn't do it. He couldn't be the next man to lie and deceive her faithful heart. Not for himself and not for his country.

Not and remain the man he had worked so hard to become. So that was that. He was finished here.

He could only hope the Liars weren't finished as well.

Chapter Fourteen

Agatha tapped a stuttering tattoo on Simon's door with trembling knuckles. Heavens, she sounded like a woodpecker.

"Come."

His deep voice was even lower than usual. Agatha took firm hold of her nerves and slipped into the room.

Simon sat before the fire with a book open in his hands. He was still nominally dressed, although his shirt was undone and his hair mussed.

For a moment his face seemed grief-stricken in the half-light of the fire. Agatha stopped when a tiny spark of unease unexpectedly flared within her. Then he smiled slightly, and the feeling was gone.

Just a trick of the light, then.

She smiled back at him. He was so perfect. He was just the sort of man who would never let her walk all over him yet never ignore her for more interesting pursuits.

And he was beautiful. Agatha could feel herself breathing faster at the mere sight of him in his loose white shirt and snug black breeches.

He didn't stand as she approached, but leaned back in the armchair and stretched his long legs out before him. She had seen him nearly naked once. She knew what lay beneath his fine clothes.

She couldn't wait to see him naked again. Completely.

He hadn't spoken yet, but only looked at her with his head slightly tilted, as if waiting for her to explain herself.

Considering she stood before him in her wrapper, with a dark and silent house about them, she thought she was making things rather clear.

Still, he was a man, albeit a perfect one. Perhaps a hint.

"I've made a decision."

He shut the book and laid it on a side table, then looked back at her with his hands loosely clasped over his flat stomach.

Still not a word.

"I want to sleep in your bed." After she'd blurted that out, sheer frozen embarrassment was all that kept her standing there.

That got his attention finally. He sat up straight, pulling his legs from their beguiling stretch and bracing his hands on the arms of the chair as if to stand. But he didn't.

He watched her carefully. "I assume you are not saying that you wish to switch chambers with me."

"No."

"Ah."

Something flashed in his cobalt eyes, something like triumph mingled with regret. Surely it was only the fire flickering in their midnight depths.

"Well, then." She stepped closer to him, almost standing between his feet.

He didn't move. Dark eyes traveled from her hem to her hair, but his hands remained on the chair arms.

Fear of rejection and humiliation coursed through her for the first time. Yet he wasn't refusing her. And if the evidence straining his trousers was any indication, he wasn't going to do so anytime soon.

Apparently, she was simply going to have to show him what to do. Feeling suddenly powerful in a new and tingling manner, Agatha smiled.

She moved to stand directly between his knees, and he leaned back a bit in response, still watching her. Agatha could see the smooth skin of his chest gleaming within the undone placket of his shirt.

She wanted to see more. She wanted to see those square shoulders again, wanted to touch his skin to feel the way the muscles rippled beneath it.

As if it belonged to someone else, her hand reached out and slipped beneath the white linen. His body jerked the slightest bit when her cool fingers found his warm flesh, and Agatha's sense of power grew.

Simon was not as calm as he strove to appear. When her fingers stroked over his skin, his heart had leaped like a stag. Even now, with the faint tracing of her fingertips the only contact between them, he could feel his breath coming faster.

She gathered a handful of his shirtfront, then tugged lightly. He leaned forward at her bidding. When she bent over him to gather the tails of his shirt in her hands to pull it off, he closed his eyes and breathed her in.

Lemon and flowers and lust. He was almost paralyzed by the contrast. He was being seduced. Should he push her away? Should he overcome her tantalizing pace with his own urgency? Should he take control?

Her hands caressed his shoulders and slid slowly down his bare chest. She was so bold, yet she would not look into his eyes. She was staring at him as if she had never truly seen a man's body before.

Her lips were parted, and she chewed one in concentration as she moved her hands over every inch of his chest. No wonder James hadn't been able to get enough of her.

It was very seductive, this way she had of making a man feel as though he was the most amazing thing she had ever seen.

Her hands met the waist of his trousers at last. She lowered herself to kneel before him. One by one, very slowly, she undid each button with great attention.

Simon was so hard by then that he sprang from the confines of his trousers with a vengeance, to rise before her eyes.

Her only reaction was utter stillness but for the rise of her arched brows.

Oh my. Agatha couldn't think past that. Oh my, oh my.

It would never work. Never, never, not in a thousand lifetimes was it going to fit.

Perhaps people were not like sheep after all.

Deciding to attend to that amazing detail a bit later, Agatha tore her gaze away. She sat back on her heels and turned her attention to pulling Simon's boots and hose from him.

When he was naked but for his trousers, she looked back. He was yet so very large.

Yet still Simon sat watching her. Not touching her, not responding in any other way. Beginning to doubt herself, Agatha wondered if she ought to leave right now.

He must have seen it in her face, for he abruptly leaned forward and took her face between his hands. She felt the warmth of his palms seep all through her body, she was so starved for his touch.

He tilted her head back and gazed into her eyes. His expression was stern and hungry at once. "Agatha, how far are you prepared to take this?"

What? "Good Lord, Simon. Must I draw you a bloody map?"

His lips twitched into a reluctant smile. "No, I think I know where we are headed."

Then he pulled her mouth to his.

If Simon thought he was on fire before, it was nothing to what he felt when Agatha threw herself into the kiss. Her arms twined about his neck, and she rose on her knees to press herself fervently into him.

She opened her lips and kissed him as hard as he kissed her. When they finally broke for air, she let her head fall back and surrendered to his mouth completely.

The mission was gone, burnt from his consciousness by the fire of his craving. There was only Agatha, soft and fierce, pliant and willful.

And eager. So gloriously, fantastically eager.

When he moved her wrapper aside to continue to feast on her neck, she yanked it off one shoulder with impatience.

When he slid from the chair to tumble her on the rug

before the fire, she rolled with him until she lay above him, pressing herself closer still.

Simon's lips moved over her throat and down her neck to her shoulder. Icy molten shivers rippled through her.

The wrapper slid from her torso at Simon's urging. He held her by the waist and pressed her away from him to see her better, looking up at her with glazed admiration.

"Beautiful . . ."

The only thing concealing her breasts was the thin batiste of her chemise. Agatha raised her chin, unashamed to be exposed before him. He wasn't looking at her like a thing, like a walking bosom.

He wanted her the way she wanted him.

Entirely.

She took her hands from his chest and raised them to the neckline of her chemise where it clung half off her shoulders. Never taking her eyes from his, she slipped it down, baring her breasts for him.

Amazingly, he raised his gaze to hers.

"May I?"

Her deepest heart stumbled and fell into his hands, right then and there. To be asked so respectfully, not stolen from . . .

"Please." She closed her eyes and let her head fall back. The room whirled and then she lay beneath him, splayed on the rug, revealed by the firelight to his gaze and his touch.

He rose above her, gently trapping her thighs between his own, and simply looked at her. Then his fingertips drifted over and around both breasts at once, making her skin tingle and the tips tighten unbearably.

Agatha stretched her arms above her head, granting willing passage to his exploring hands. When his warm palms cupped and raised her, the heat went directly to her own center, and she felt herself tense and throb.

Simon bent over her to take her nipple into his mouth, and Agatha jerked in surprise. Her astonishment was quickly overwhelmed by the pleasure shivering through her. How had he known it would please her?

How was she to know what would please him? For suddenly his happiness was very important to her.

Then a thought occurred that wiped out her pleasure and her purpose. She had based her decision to come here tonight on the certainty that Simon would want to marry her afterward.

What if that wasn't what he wanted at all?

What if he had other goals? Things that had nothing to do with her? She had manipulated him all along, and tonight was no exception. How could she do this to him if she loved him?

Self-disgust roiled through her. She pushed Simon back and rolled away.

"I'm sorry."

His face darkened. "What is this game?"

"Not a game, Simon. I am not toying with you, I promise. I have been, somewhat, but not now."

"What are you talking about?"

"Oh, Simon, I'm sorry. I'm sorry I hired you, sorry I blackmailed you. Sorry I came to you like this rather than tell you the truth."

"The truth." His tone was flat, and his face revealed nothing in the glow of the fire.

"Yes. You deserve to know the truth, so that you may decide for yourself."

"And what is the truth?"

It came out on a breath. "That I . . . I love you, Simon."

His expression didn't change. If anything, he withdrew even further. "You love me."

"Yes. I love you and I want to be with you forever. I came to you tonight to force your hand, but I cannot go through with it. I love you enough that I want you to be happy."

"Happy."

"Stop that. Stop answering me with my own words. I love you, and I want you to love me back. But that is for you to decide, not me."

"Yes, I'd rather thought so."

Now she saw that his eyes burned in his calm mask, afire

with something that gave her shivers and gleaming hope. "So do you?" she asked.

Simon lifted a hand and ran his knuckles across her cheek, so gently it made her want to weep.

"What about James?"

She tilted her head and smiled ruefully. "I cannot lie and say that he'll be happy about it. But I think he'll recover."

Slowly, Simon bent his head toward hers, looking into her eyes all the while. Then as he softly touched his lips to hers, she closed her eyes to feel every moment of his tender kiss.

So soft, so light, a promise of a kiss.

He drew back and Agatha opened her eyes to see his become dark with emotion.

"I love you, Simon."

Then he pulled her close, wrapping his arms around her tightly, her head tucked beneath his chin.

Simon could scarcely breathe. *She loved him.* Raw emotion coursed through him. He tipped back her head and devoured her mouth with his. He wanted to claim her, to make her his—body and soul.

Primitive need took the fore, and he tugged the silken wrapper from her and tossed it across the room. Her delicate chemise followed suit, with his trousers fast behind it.

She was a dream come true, and he had dreams enough to feed a lifetime of caressing her. The things he wanted to do to her—*for* her—blazed through his mind in a single heated vision. Touch her *here*. She gasped in response. Kiss her *there*. A small cry escaped her lips, urging him on.

She was naked and she was *his*. He took possession with his mouth and hands, spurred on by her joyful sounds of pleasure.

Simon was everywhere. Agatha's mind spun, strung on a web of his making. His hands were rough and gentle at once, caressing her, pulling sensations from her body that she hadn't known existed.

His large roughened hands drove her gently, implacably mad, delving between her thighs, stroking swiftly across her cleft. Then she felt his caresses upon her neck and cheeks, as he held her face still for deep, long, drugging kisses that stole more of her sanity away.

His body was hard and hot under her own stroking, grasping hands. She was adrift in a burning sea, lost in him. The feel of him, the taste of him, the scent of him was all she knew in her surrender.

Simon was both humbled and transported. "So passionate," he whispered wonderingly into her skin. "So honest." When he lowered his mouth to taste her sweet folds, she opened trustingly to his kiss upon her thighs.

The taste of her in Simon's mouth was nectar, and the sound of her escalating cries was music. Kissing his way back up her body, he felt as though he lay in the arms of a goddess, and she was as eager as he, reaching for him with emotion shining from her eyes.

She loved him. Whatever her past, whatever her previous loyalties, she loved him and he drank of her love like a man parched by the desert.

He pressed her to the floor beneath him, her generous curves glowing like pearl against the jewel tones of the carpet. Willingly she parted her thighs at his urging.

She was so sweet, so hot and ready for him. He wrapped her in his arms and plunged deeply into her.

She yelped, a brief cry of surprise.

He froze, icy disbelief warring with burning need. A virgin? She couldn't be. He gripped her shoulders tightly, holding her still while he tried to pull himself back from the brink.

If only she would not move—

Agatha twisted her body, pushing her hips against him in protest. Simon's orgasm exploded, and he growled helplessly into her soft neck as his body betrayed him. His shaft jerked within her and she gasped softly with each pulsation.

Breathless and blinded, Simon could only hold her tightly. It was finally when the fog of release cleared that the reality of what they had done, what *he* had done, became abruptly obvious.

Lifting himself upon his elbows, he stroked her tangled

hair back from her face. Her soft doe eyes were wide and unsure, all passion erased.

"Did I hurt you, sweeting?"

She blinked rapidly for a moment, then spoke. "Not . . . hurt, but—"

"But hurt." He'd been in such a damned hurry to make her his, he hadn't bothered to test her readiness. Surely he would have discovered her virginity then.

With a soft kiss to her lips, he gently disengaged from her to rise from the floor. A small washstand supplied a dampened cloth and a moment to think. When he returned to their place before the fire, he gently tended her body.

After he had tossed the cloth back in the general direction of the washstand, he pulled her discarded wrapper around her. Lifting her in his arms, he sat in the chair by the fire with her in his lap.

"There is no other lover."

It had not been a question, but Agatha answered, "No, of course not. Why ever would you think so?"

Who the hell was she, then, if not James's mistress? Why would she be searching—

Just then there came a distant pounding. Someone was at the door of the house, demanding entry at a very late hour. Concern bit through Simon's preoccupation.

His men knew where he was. Could there be a problem at the club? With one of his men?

Simon set Agatha on her feet and dropped a quick kiss on her brow.

"We aren't finished here. I'll be back directly."

He pulled on his breeches and left the room. From the top of the stairs, he could see Pearson answering the door in his dressing gown and slippers.

The butler had only opened the door slightly and apparently was in the midst of refusing entry to someone. Then he was flung backward when a man burst in from the rain outside.

A man so thin he looked as though his skin were stretched over nothing but bone. A man so beaten and weak that he could scarcely remain upright once his momentum was halted. "Aggie!" he cried hoarsely.

Simon hardly recognized his old friend.

"James!" Agatha's breathless cry came from behind him.

Simon watched as Agatha ran past him down the stairs and threw herself into James's arms. James held her tightly, leaning on her in his weakness. The two of them stood wrapped together in the circle of light from Pearson's candle, leaving Simon in the darkness just beyond.

The pain was rather astonishing. And yet what had he thought, that she would stand with him while they gently explained the facts to James?

And what would he say? "Good to see you, old friend. I stole your woman. And by the way, you're under arrest for treason. I'm probably going to have to kill you."

James held Agatha close for a moment, then set her back to look into her face. His eyes widened when he took in her obvious state, fresh from her lover's bed.

"Aggie? What is this?"

Ah, his cue. Simon strolled down the last few steps.

"Hello, James."

"Simon? What are you doing here?" Then James saw Simon's matching state, and his sunken eyes grew murderous.

"You bounder! *What have you done to my sister?*"

Sister? Oh, no.

The vastness of his mistake came home to Simon in a surge of awe at his own stupidity.

Bloody, bloody *hell*.

He, Simon Rain, had just ruined the sister of the Griffin.

Chapter Fifteen

The sound of Jamie's voice saying Simon's name cut through Agatha's joy. She pulled herself from Jamie's embrace and looked from one man to the other, her smile fading.

"Jamie? I don't understand. How do you know Simon?"

Her brother shot her a horrified glance, then turned roughly to Simon. "You're *covert*? With my *sister*?"

Jamie took a lurching step forward to swing his fist at Simon, but his legs gave out beneath him. Simon caught him as he sagged.

Agatha looked to Simon. "What is he talking about? What does that mean, covert?"

Simon said nothing, but his eyes were dark as they met hers.

James answered for him, his voice hoarse and shaking with rage. "It means he's on the job, the blackguard. It means that while he was with you, he was *working* you."

Agatha shook her head. "No, Jamie. I discovered that Simon was a thief days ago. I know you aren't happy about us, but—"

"I'm not a thief, Agatha." Simon reached one hand toward her, then let it fall. "I'm an intelligence agent. I came here to apprehend your brother."

Apprehend? Agatha looked at the both of them. "I want to know what is going on. But Jamie is obviously ill. He needs to be in a bed, and a physician must be called."

"No!"

The refusal came from both men simultaneously. Then Jamie shook his head. "No, Aggie, not yet. I think perhaps the two of you had best start explaining this to me. Now."

Pearson stepped up, regal as ever in his dressing gown. "Shall I bring you some refreshment, madam? Perhaps something soothing for Mr.—" He indicated Jamie.

"Yes, Pearson. I think my brother could use some broth and perhaps some bread."

"And a blanket," added James. "And a place to sit."

"Yes," Agatha said stiffly. "We'll use the parlor."

Simon helped James to the sofa, then turned to bring up the fire. James was in terrible condition, and Agatha put aside her own uncertainties to make him comfortable.

A bleary-eyed Harry came with a pile of blankets, and Agatha wrapped Jamie in the soft wool as he lay propped up on the sofa.

Pearson returned with tea and steaming broth. Agatha occupied herself for several moments helping Jamie drink the broth with his shaking hands.

Simon turned from the fire and came to sit on the arm of a chair, watching them both.

Agatha couldn't bear to look at Simon. She refused to believe it. It wasn't true. It couldn't be. In a moment, she was sure that Simon would explain that, yes, he had perhaps been looking for James and, yes, he had perhaps not been entirely truthful, but yes, he did love her, just as he'd said he did.

But he had never actually said it, had he?

Soon James stopped shivering and pushed the last of the broth away. Agatha had no excuse to avoid speaking to either of them. She stood and pulled her wrapper tightly around her.

"Simon, why were you looking for Jamie?"

James spoke up. "I'm not surprised he was, Aggie. After all, I haven't reported in for weeks."

"Reported in?"

"Simon and I work together, Aggie."

She flinched at Simon's name. He stood within feet of her,

but she couldn't look at him. The sick feeling was growing worse, fighting back her happiness at Jamie's return.

James continued. "I was captured by the French one night after I left my . . . a lady's home. There were several of them, and I was soon taken down. The next thing I remembered, I woke in the hold of a small ship. They kept me insensible much of the time—"

"Oh, Jamie," breathed Agatha. "How horrible."

He patted her hand absently, looking worriedly at Simon. "What I'd really like to know is why Simon chose to conceal his search from you."

"I didn't know you had a sister, James. A little fact you managed to keep out of your files. I made quite a different assumption when I decided to investigate Agatha."

"But why did you investigate me? What do I have to do with anything?" She finally turned to meet Simon's gaze.

"You spent the money in his account for this house. I came to see who you were and what you knew."

"Why?"

"Because I suspect James of being a double agent and a traitor."

"What??" Agatha and James turned in unison.

Simon gazed back into matching brown eyes. Dear God, he was blind as well as stupid. How could he not have seen the resemblance?

"The facts are irrefutable. A leak about the Griffin's activities went public. James disappeared. A large amount of money was deposited into his bank account at about the same time my men began having their covers compromised. Agatha moved in and began to use that money freely."

Agatha frowned. "That was *my* money, Simon. I took it from the estate account when I left Appleby."

Simon shook his head. "It was a great deal of money, Agatha. Far too much to be yours—"

She only tilted her head and gazed at him. Simon began to get the sneaking suspicion that he was wrong about this as well.

James broke in urgently. "Simon, you said identities were

compromised. What did you mean?" In his eyes Simon could see the depth of James's fear.

"Some dead. Some just too badly wounded to work. All told, we lost twelve men off active duty."

"I wondered . . ." James said quietly. "I had such dreams while I was insensible. Endless questioning by a serpent who wouldn't let me rest. Still, I'd hoped I had let nothing important out."

He passed a shaking hand over his eyes. "It was the only thing that kept me sane."

Doubt replaced the near certainty in Simon's mind as he considered his old friend. His voice grim but devoid of anger, Simon said, "Ren Porter even now lies on the edge of death. Only you could have given the French the information that ruined his cover."

James flinched as if he had been struck. Guilt twisted his hollowed features. "Oh, God, Simon. Oh, dear God. I wish they'd killed me first," he whispered.

His anguish seemed quite real, and his condition certainly reinforced his story.

James was innocent. Relief swept Simon as he realized that it would not be necessary to take steps against James after all. But now the larger problem loomed. What to do with him?

Even Simon had to answer to someone. The Royal Four would not be interested in Simon's instincts. They were going to require concrete proof. "There will be an investigation into your story, James. Until then, you had best keep to house arrest. I'm sorry, but until your innocence is proven, I cannot allow you your freedom."

James nodded slowly. "No more than I deserve. 'Tis an improvement over my last prison. I won't be up and about for a while, in any event."

He lay back on the cushions, his eyes tormented, lost in his guilt and regret.

Simon turned to Agatha. This was not an explanation he was looking forward to giving. Taking her hand, he led her from the parlor.

She followed to stand before him in the chill entry hall, her arms folded tightly about her thin wrapper. Her eyes were wide and betrayed. She waited for him to speak with the obvious mingled hope and fear of a woman who didn't know if she wanted to know the truth or not.

Simon wanted to pull her close and warm her. He did nothing. "I came here to find him. I found you. I thought you were his mistress, and that you knew more than you let on. I even wondered if you were a collaborator yourself."

She grew paler as he spoke. "And these past weeks?"

"Your ruse was . . . convenient to my own search. I was hoping to uncover something, some document or letter that would point me to James."

She moistened her lips. "And tonight?"

Simon wanted to lie, to tell her that tonight had nothing to do with his case. But the time for lies was over.

"I decided to find out if I could seduce the truth from you. But then, I—" Simon stopped. Then he what? Then he had changed his mind? Then he had wanted her for herself?

It didn't matter if he had. She was a gentleman's sister, a lady, and far above the likes of him.

And he was a spy, a danger to anyone whom he was fool enough to care for.

Agatha hadn't moved an inch, but she was suddenly miles from his reach. She raised her chin and met his gaze with severe composure.

"I see. You were simply doing your duty."

She turned and walked slowly to the front door. "Pearson," she called, "please assist Mr. Rain with his coat. He is leaving forthwith."

Then she opened the door, letting the cold outside air flow over Simon, chilling him deeply.

"Good-bye, Mr. Rain."

She was as cool as winter sleet. Her frozen manner made Simon ache with regret. His own stupid fault. He had tried to steal her warmth for himself, and now it was lost to them both.

Agatha left the door standing open as Pearson approached

with Simon's coat. With quiet dignity, she turned and reentered the parlor, shutting the door between them.

Simon left the house in Carriage Square, striding down the steps and turning down the walk with automatic precision.

He wasn't seeing the late-night street, or the way the lamplight was cast into glowing spheres of fog, or anything at all but the icy look of pain in Agatha's eyes.

He was shaken, both by the magnitude of his regret and by the sheer monumental error he had committed over the past weeks.

He had been wrong about everything. Every bloody conclusion he had reached about Agatha had been entirely in error.

What kind of spymaster was he, that he could be so deluded by his own assumptions? Blind. Stupid. And deeply, deeply ashamed.

He had enacted many a sin in his life, but he had never broken anyone's heart. Until now.

Turning blindly down another corner, Simon stumbled into a group of carousing young Corinthians. Sidestepping them, he turned and watched them stagger down the walk, jostling one another and casting lewd aspersions on one another's manhood.

Shaking his head, Simon looked around him. He'd wandered into a street where he knew there existed several exclusive men's clubs for the fashionable set.

Again, not his world. He had no business in this place of shallow amusements, any more than he did in Agatha's house. His business was to defend the Crown and apprehend anyone who threatened it.

It was a lonely business. He wondered why he'd never realized that before. He was a secret entity, one who did not exist in any record. A phantom man, without friends or family. A man with only one purpose on this earth.

Very well then. Back to business.

Several minutes later, Simon slipped from the dark of the

alley along the garden wall of a house located in a respectable but not fashionably visible part of town.

With a quick look about, he grasped the top of the wall and pulled himself swiftly over.

The hedges were overgrown all around the perimeter of the yard, providing even more cover from prying eyes. He slipped through the dark garden, avoiding the gravel path with its betraying crunch.

Unlike many houses, this one bore a sturdy lock on the kitchen door. Simon didn't even pause to toy with it, although he knew he could pick it if he chose.

Instead, he made his way to where the decorative brick-work that delineated the corners of the house provided a simple ladder. Using only the tips of his fingers and the edge of his shoes, Simon quickly and silently clambered up to the third level of windows.

Reaching for the window nearest him, he flicked it open with one outstretched hand. With one fluid motion, he grasped the sill and flipped neatly into the room.

The valet standing at the bureau whirled around to face him, clutching one hand to his heart in surprise.

"Oy, sir, I hates it when you does that!"

Simon pulled off his jacket and tossed it to the man. "Sorry, Denny. You know I can't resist." He tugged at his loosely tied neckcloth and threw it on top of the jacket.

"Well, you might've let me know where you was. Ain't been half-worried about you, sir."

"Yes, Denny. I know. I'm sorry."

Denny wasn't the genius with a cravat that Button was, but then, he hadn't had Button's advantages, either. Barely eighteen, the poor little ex-bagman was still rather unsure of his position as majordomo and tended to fret overmuch.

"I've been taking care of business. Something local, as you must know, since you have sent me a good twenty messages at the club in the last two weeks."

Denny sniffed but stopped his nagging. Sometimes Simon wondered who served whom. Keeping servants was half caring for them and half being mothered by them.

Still, he used this Spartan house so rarely that Denny managed to take care of it well enough on his own, hiring out day work for the grounds and the housekeeping.

He ought to sell the place, for it was more headache than home. It hadn't half the warmth of the house on Carriage Square.

And never would, for Agatha would never step foot within its walls. But then where would he put his finds, his strays from the street, such as Denny?

Stubbs was one of his found treasures, as was Feebles. The pickpocket had been more than worth the bribe Simon had been forced to pay to free him from being transported. There was such a blinding need for good information acquisition that Simon wished he had a full staff of pickpockets with Feebles's skill.

Denny tended to his duties silently, with only the occasional theatrical sniff to remind Simon of his sins.

Simon reached for patience. "Denny, it's very late. Why don't you go on to bed? I'll be needing you bright and early tomorrow."

That cheered the fellow, and a smile almost creased his doleful face. "Yessir. I'll be up with the milk wagon then."

"You do that. Good night."

When he was finally alone with his regrets, Simon didn't go to bed. Instead, he pulled a chair close to the fire, seeking a little of the warmth he had lost.

It had taken him a while to see past his surprise and understand precisely what Agatha had done. A young woman, a lady, forced to fabricate a husband in order to have the freedom to search for her lost brother. Rather heroic, really.

And her actions tonight. She had believed herself in love. With Simon Rain. Thief, former chimneysweep, and bastard son of a Cheapside whore.

Well, she wasn't in love any longer, he'd wager. Not after what he had done.

He had taken her virginity, then promptly betrayed her heart.

It had not been well done, either. In his ignorance and lust, he had hurt her more than necessary. The memory of her wide eyes haunted him, making him flinch every time he thought of her.

He had simply been so . . . shocked. Shocked at her, shocked at himself. He didn't like knowing he was the kind of man who wouldn't stop, who could lose control of his mind to his body's need.

And was it only your body's need?

He shook off the thought. Of course it had been. Agatha was a heavenly armful, a real delight, with her ardent abandon and sweet flesh. Any man might let his senses take over with a woman such as she.

Any man but him. He was the master of control, the surgeon, occasionally even the cold instrument itself. There was no room in his dark world for the sweetness and warmth of Agatha.

He was the Magician, called so by his men for his ability to know precisely what the enemy was about to do and where to send a man and what assignment to give him.

And early on, it had been given him for his uncanny ability to make things disappear. Including himself.

A man of the shadows. Always between worlds, walking in the eclipse between what was legal and what was necessary, for the good of his country.

The same class-conscious citizens of which would never accept him as one of their own.

As if he would even be allowed to try. Should he choose between being a trumped-up bastard chimneysweep trying to pass himself off in good society, or being an overeducated street rat who would forever be highly suspect among his fellow commoners?

Or remain invisible, where he might do some good and where his life might have some meaning.

Not much of a choice really. More of a destiny. It was only too bad that his destiny included mind-bending solitude.

It had never truly bothered him before, but he wasn't enough of a liar to pretend that he didn't know why it bothered him now.

He couldn't deny it any longer. He wanted more. He wanted warmth and heat and heart.

And passion.

During the last few weeks he had been guilty of more than one lapse of judgment. He had underestimated Agatha, time and again. And he had underestimated passion. Passion had sneaked up on him like an alleyway thief, club upraised.

From the moment she'd collided with him in her hallway, he'd been entranced by her. Completely captivated. Utterly and totally besotted.

Passion. He'd never seen it coming.

Now he didn't want to live without it.

He wanted Agatha. And a lifetime in her arms.

Pity he would never be able to let himself have it.

"I wanted him to marry me."

Agatha turned from the parlor window as if the morning light hurt her reddened eyes. James watched her as he lay recovering on the sofa, his forgotten breakfast tray still on his lap. Her pallor and quiet pain alarmed him. His Aggie was never quiet.

"Marry you? Why?"

"I'm in love with him."

Jamie grimaced. Damnation. What a situation. "Are you sure? You've only known him a few weeks."

Agatha raised her gaze to his. "You've known him for years. You tell me. Is there any reason why I shouldn't be in love with him?"

There was no denying that Simon was the finest man he had ever known. James currently might want to kill him, but he couldn't disparage him.

"He was playing a role," he couldn't help reminding her. "Perhaps you are simply infatuated with the role."

Agatha looked down at her hands. "I did nothing all night but wonder about that. It isn't a nice thought, to know that you may be in love with someone who doesn't truly exist."

She turned to pace the room. That was better. Aggie in motion he could handle.

"Then again, I'm not sure," she said. "I think that there was much of him in that role. Perhaps it was the man he used to be, or almost was, but it was him, all the same."

James ran his hand through his hair. "What do you want to do? It's possible I can force him to marry you."

A spark of indignation lit her dull eyes briefly. "Is he that against me as a wife? If he needs so much convincing, then I don't want him."

James felt obliged to defend Simon on that score. "It isn't that, Aggie. For Simon to marry would mean the end of his post, the end of his career. He's said it many times, and I believe him. He reasons that if he were to marry, his wife and family might someday be used against him."

He could see the realization dawn on her face and continued. "Don't you see? In his position, he might someday have to choose between his loved ones and his country—"

She finished it for him. "And he is a patriot. He would force himself to choose England, to choose the greater good. Then he would blame himself for abandoning his family for the rest of his life."

"Yes." He considered her for a moment. "I'm glad you understand, Aggie. You've grown up a great deal in the last month, haven't you?"

She sat on the sofa near his knees and tucked up one slippered foot beneath her. For a moment she regarded him sadly. "I've been growing up for years, Jamie. You simply haven't been there to see it."

James did not reply. There was no defense of his abandonment of her. He had told himself that writing letters showed his devotion. He had promised himself that he would visit, just as soon as things settled down, as soon as he finished the next mission. . . .

The truth was that he loved his work. He loved the risk and the intrigue. He was the master of sabotage in the Liar's Club. The mighty Griffin, who moved with the stealth of a lion and struck with the accuracy of an eagle, the man called upon in one desperate scenario after another.

And he simply hadn't wanted to miss a moment of it.

As if she could read his thoughts, Agatha shook her head in bemusement. "To think you were the Griffin all along."

James tried to lighten the mood. "What? You don't think your older brother could be a blade at the throat of Napoleon?"

She snorted. "Don't get full of yourself around me, James Cunnington. I've seen you in your winter drawers."

He raised one fist and struck a haughty pose. "The Griffin does not wear drawers! The Griffin is not human enough to need drawers!"

"Baggy drawers yet. Baggy and gray with washing," mused Agatha. "I wonder if the Voice of Society would be interested in knowing about that?"

"Watch it, Aggravation. You're not too big to tickle."

"I am so."

James moved as if to prove his point. Though it was a weak gesture, Agatha jumped up with her hands held in front of her in defense.

"Fine! Whatever you say, O Master Griffin, sir."

Glad that he had been able to lift the sadness in her eyes, if even for a moment, James took one of her outstretched hands in his and settled back against his cushions.

"I'm glad to be home again."

"You aren't home yet."

He tilted his head, smiling at her. "Appleby is just a house and some trees. You are my family."

Abruptly her slight smile crumpled into tears. James pulled her close. She curled up on top of his quilt, face tucked into his neck.

He should never have left her so long. If he had been a better brother, none of this would have happened. She would not have come to London unprotected, she would not have been ruined. . . .

"Agatha, we need to talk about your future. How many people know that Simon was not really Mortimer Applequist?"

She sniffled, then shrugged. "No one."

"Not even your servants?" This was excellent news.

"No. Pearson might have his suspicions after last night, but he'd never utter a word. The rest of the world believes wholeheartedly. Simon was very convincing once I—" She stopped, pressing her lips together.

James eyed her carefully. "What is it?"

Agatha flushed angrily. "I just realized. He never needed etiquette lessons at all, did he?"

James almost laughed out loud. "Simon? Oh, lord, no. He could pass as a gentleman in any ballroom—"

That had apparently not been the best way to put that, for Agatha's anger began to flare higher.

"That—that rat!" She grabbed a pillow from the sofa and flung it at the wall. "I took his hand in mine to show him how to hold a *fork*! That sneak! That unbelievable . . . rat . . . sneak . . . *bastard*!"

James blinked. "He told you that?"

"If I ever see that man again, I'll *kill* him! Even if I don't see him again, I shall kill him!" Another pillow struck the wall, and a painting teetered. Agatha glared at the sofa. "There's a pillow missing."

Then she slumped onto the cushions once more. "I made Mortimer up," she muttered. "I can unmake him just as easily. . . ."

"Aggie, pay attention. Did Simon tell you that he was a bastard?"

"What? Yes, of course. He told me all about his mother, and sleeping in alleyways. . . ." She turned to look at him, becoming pale. "Did he make that up as well?"

"No, Aggie, he didn't." Dear God, he had told her about his *mother*? Even James had never heard those details.

That could only mean one thing.

For the first and only time in all the years James had known him . . .

Simon was in love.

Chapter Sixteen

After sitting with Jamie most of the day, Agatha had persuaded him to return to his bed for an early night. Now she paced restlessly in her own bedchamber, ignoring her own bed entirely, despite the fact that she had told Jamie she was tired as well and ready to retire.

Her anger threatened to overwhelm her, yet she clung to the strength it gave her, feeding it with thoughts of Simon's lies.

For Simon couldn't marry her, and she couldn't rightly force him to. If he'd fought marriage for any other reason than service to his country, she might have found some way to combat his decision.

For truth be told, she would do just about anything to have him. Lie, cheat, steal to have him, and to hell with her already severely endangered soul.

But he was too important to England, too devoted to his people.

What mortal woman could compete with that? What worthy woman would want to?

And to be honest, could she bear a lifetime of being second in his heart? She had no illusions of her own selflessness.

She would grow to hate it, and the hatred would grow and the love would shrink, until she'd loathe the very sight of his sheets of figures and equations—

No . . . that was Papa's mathematics she was thinking of.

Were Papa and Simon the same? Had she made the fatal mistake of falling in love with a man who could give her no more than indifferent attention and absent-minded affection?

Good lord, she'd be mad to do that!

And yet, there was no denying that she had done precisely that. And would do it again.

If Simon so much as crooked his finger at her, she would gladly throw her life away on those scraps of him that were left when his grand purpose was done.

And it would destroy her. Already, she was filled with self-loathing that she could resent her own homeland for taking him from her.

Why couldn't she have fallen in love with a simple man? Someone cheerful and uncomplicated, like young Collis Tremayne?

Absently she realized that she'd forgotten about the much-sought-after invitation to Etheridge House. She should be there now, she and Mortimer both.

Of course, Mortimer wouldn't be making any more parties. He was dead, as was any chance of her living happily ever after with Simon.

Dead . . .

Of course.

Quickly, she went to her little escritoire and pulled a sheet of foolscap from the drawer. If she hurried, she could send Harry immediately, and still get it into tomorrow's issue.

She only wished she could be present to see Simon's face.

Simon was in no mood to be patient the next morning as he struggled to make his way against the tide of traffic. He'd made a later start than usual this morning, after spending many sleepless hours lost in thoughts of Agatha.

The walks were crowded with pedestrians, and the streets were completely locked with carriages and carts. The teeming populace of London was on its morning rounds.

Simon growled as he was shouldered by yet another person walking the opposite direction.

"Sorry, guv'nor," said a familiar voice.

Quickly, Simon glanced over his shoulder to see the slouching figure of Feebles slipping away through the crowd. Simon didn't slow his pace, or react in any obvious way, but his hand slid to the inner breast pocket of his jacket.

His fingers met the crackle of paper. Paper that had not been there when he'd left his house shortly before.

Walking with the same impatient stride, Simon passed through the entrance of the Liar's Club without a glance at its Gothic facade.

Immediately he could feel himself relax. Here he was a respected leader, not a bastard chimneysweep, not a lowborn man who had ruined a lady.

Damn her for toying with his mind, for making him remember and acknowledge the man he had tried to leave behind years ago. He had dredged it all up for her, shown her the lowest side of himself . . .

And still she had said she loved him.

Simon pushed her away, from his thoughts and from his heart. He was more than that here.

He was the Magician.

Feeling much more the thing now, Simon strode through to the kitchen. Already steamy with the day's baking, the kitchen was warm and welcoming.

Simon snatched a fresh-baked roll from the pan cooling on the massive scarred table in the center of the room. Kurt turned with a swift growl, but the roll was already stuffed in Simon's cheek and his hands were empty.

Simon even managed his usual irreverent salute as he left the kitchen for Jackham's office.

The old fellow wasn't about yet—Jackham's aching bones didn't rise from bed as well these days—but Simon didn't mind. He had some reading to do.

He settled onto Jackham's spring-ridden old sofa and pulled Feebles's gift from his pocket.

It was today's news, folded to display a page of Announcements. Someone had married, or birthed a child, or died. Someone of interest to the Liar's Club.

Simon scanned the names, trailing one finger down the page. When he found it, his mouth actually dropped open for a moment. Then his jaw clenched tight with anger, along with his fist. The paper in his hand was reduced to a crumpled ball.

Someone had died all right.

He had.

Agatha had killed off Mortimer Applequist.

"That rat didn't deserve to live!"

"I know, but, Aggie—"

James rubbed his face with both hands. Not a good sign. He only did that when he was about to lose his patience. Agatha firmed herself against his disapproval. No one would tell her what to do with her life. Not even her beloved brother.

He took a deep breath and smiled at her across the small table in his room where they shared breakfast. Agatha narrowed her eyes and pointed an egg-laden fork at him.

"Don't charm me, Jamie. It won't work."

"I only wish you had consulted me before running off to the news with this outrageous story. Declaring a man dead who is all too obviously still breathing is bad enough. But to claim . . . what was it again?"

He glanced down at the news-sheet in his hands and quoted, " 'Mr. Applequist met his end yesterday evening in a tragic incident with his masculine unmentionables. Apparently he was strangled to his death—' "

Agatha toyed with her fork. Perhaps she had gone a bit too far. But it had seemed such a lovely vengeance at the time. "He ought to be strangled for telling me such lies!"

"But, Aggie, to call such attention to yourself? You aren't in any shape to stand up to scrutiny right now. Should it be discovered that your marriage was a sham and that you have been living with a man for weeks unmarried, you'll be past ruined!"

"I see no reason why I should be revealed now. I shall simply be the Widow Applequist, and have even more freedom than before."

"But you have no license, no legal proof at all."

"Pish-posh, Jamie. Do you go up to all widows of your acquaintance and demand legal proof? Of course not, because people believe what they are told."

"Because they can't believe anyone would be so twist-minded to lie about such a thing! It's wrong!"

"Oh, are you lecturing me on my morals now, Mr. Spy? Your *life* is a lie, just as Simon's is! You told me you were a soldier. You even carried a captain's uniform in your trunk!"

"How do you know what I carried in my trunk?"

"Because I looked, of course! Honestly, Jamie, can you be so naive?"

He appeared hurt by that. Agatha calmed her temper with an effort. "I know that you are worried about me. But all is well. I am the Widow Applequist. I'm not supposed to be a maiden."

"Even widows must watch their reputations, Aggie."

"Well, then it is a good thing my dear brother is in residence to act as my chaperon, isn't it?"

"About that . . . I don't think anyone should know that I'm here. Whoever I escaped from may still be looking for me. You could be in danger if I'm discovered."

"Oh." That did put a different light on things. "Well, no matter. I may receive a few callers in the next several days, but there shouldn't be much fuss."

However, there was a great deal of fuss. No sooner had the noon hour struck but flocks of tearful ladies descended upon the house in Carriage Square.

Jamie had been trapped upstairs all afternoon, and Pearson had warned Agatha that Cook was all but in tears over the run on refreshments.

Agatha whispered to him to let cost be no object and to fetch a likely scullery maid from an agency to help in the kitchen. She wasn't sure, but she thought she caught a glimmer of approval in his dry gaze.

Then she was forced to return to her tearfully fascinated guests. The ladies were clustered around the tea tray as she reentered the parlor, but their whispers carried well across the room.

"Strangled by his unmentionables! Do you think he was trying to do something . . . unusual?"

"Well, he was an exotic sort, wasn't he? All that traveling, you know. Perhaps he picked up some bizarre . . . proclivity?"

Agatha wished mightily that she had restrained herself while writing that news account. It had given her great vengeful satisfaction at the time, but now she realized what Jamie meant by calling attention to herself.

An accident while cleaning his pistol, a fall down the stairs, or even a simple trampling—anything would have been more forgettable.

Agatha strode into the hushed titters with her head high. She had no need to fake her pallor or her reddened eyes, for she had spent the last two days alternately raging and weeping.

Indeed, she fed her anger, for without it she would have dissolved into a worthless puddle of tears. Simon had much to answer for, but the one thing that she most hated him for was the fact that she couldn't hate him at all.

Despite the titillated gleam in her visitors' eyes, Agatha welcomed their sympathy. She had suffered a loss, after all. She had lost her heart.

So she tried to remain serene in the face of their fascination, nodding at their condolences and ignoring their veiled attempts to extract the gruesome details.

In truth, she toyed with the idea of embellishing upon her tale. How deeply could she embarrass Simon with this story?

But in the next wave of visitors was a young woman whom Agatha recognized. She was Clara Simpson, the widowed sister-in-law of Mrs. Trapp. Her black dress signified her own mourning and her sympathy was very real.

"I know you want us all to go," Clara said in a low voice.

"I remember precisely how I felt. But when we do, the silence will be so very . . . loud. Please send for me if you wish someone to fill the silence. I won't tell you that 'only the good die young' and that you should immediately turn your life over to your nearest male relative."

Agatha was moved and somewhat shamed by Clara's simple and sincere sympathy. In the face of real grief, Agatha's little fib seemed suddenly rather nasty and cheap.

It was wrong, just as Jamie had said.

Unable to look Clara in the eye, Agatha glanced away to see Pearson moving past the parlor to the front door. Oh, blast. Not more visitors.

A moment later, Pearson appeared at the door of the parlor. Agatha was astonished to see that he'd gone completely ashen.

"M-madam, Mr. A—"

Simon slid past the petrified butler with a quick movement and stood before the room with a slight smile on his face.

Mrs. Trapp screamed and fainted dead away. The other ladies shrieked or fanned the shriekers, depending on their dispositions.

Pearson raised his voice above the mayhem, his stutter gone. "Mr. Applequist, madam."

"But—but he's *dead*!"

Agatha dropped her hand from Clara's and rose, glaring at Simon. Her heart was racing. From anger. Only anger.

"Ladies! Ladies, please!" She raised her hands. "This is my husband's brother. His twin brother." She shot Simon another killing look. "*Ethelbert* Applequist."

The ladies sighed with relief.

Loudly and in unison.

Agatha wanted to roll her eyes at such dramatics, but she kept her gaze firmly on Simon, daring him to say her nay.

She saw his lips move slightly. *Ethelbert?*

"Yes, Ethelbert," confirmed Agatha, "come to pay his respects before he leaves on an *extended* tour of the Americas."

Again, the gathered ladies sighed as one, with the notable exception of the sensible Mrs. Simpson. Agatha could see herself quite liking the woman, were they meeting under other circumstances. True circumstances.

But would someone such as that wish to be friends with a liar?

As Simon bowed to each lady in turn, they twittered in obvious enjoyment of his novelty and charm.

"To think there is another man just like your Mortimer, dear Agatha."

Agatha could scarcely keep from snarling. "Not so very like, in my opinion. Mortimer was entirely more handsome and appealing."

"Oh . . . ah, of course." The lady fled to the other side of the room and joined the fascinated group seated there like an audience in the theatre. Perhaps Pearson ought to sell tickets.

"More handsome, dear sister? You wound me."

Of course he had heard her.

"Don't you have some spying to do?" she hissed at him under her breath. "I believe I hear Napoleon knocking at your door this very moment. You do have a door, do you not?"

He bowed slightly. "I do. A very nice door, on a house in a very respectable neighborhood."

"How nice for you. Please go there. Now."

"I'd rather stay. You and I need to talk."

"I don't think so. Likely nothing would come out of your mouth but lies anyway."

"I'm sorry, Agatha. I was only—"

"Doing your duty. Lord, spare me from a dutiful man. I declare I've had my fill."

The ladies were watching them both, avidly trying to hear every whispered word. Agatha wished them all gone, the women and Simon, too.

Agatha thought furiously, trying to fabricate some excuse, some way to force him from the house.

But her creativity failed her, and all she could think was how difficult it all was. Balancing the weight of all the lies she had woven around herself, until she couldn't sleep nights for the anticipation of it all falling on her head.

Abruptly she felt trapped. The room and the people within it seemed to be closing in on her, pressing upon her chest and stealing her breath clean away.

Chapter Seventeen

Simon must have seen it on her face, for he stepped forward to support her with one warm hand on her arm.

"I think my dear sister has had enough visiting for the day. If you ladies will excuse us . . ."

The ladies responded with a bustle of leave-taking, still casting fascinated glances at Simon. Mrs. Simpson left Agatha with a brief squeeze of her hand. "Do call on me, Mrs. Applequist, or send for me if you'd like a little quiet company."

Agatha struggled to smile at them all, then realized that in her pose as widow she needn't put on a cheerful face. It was a relief to merely nod in reply to the well-wishes until the room was empty and all the ladies were gone.

Then Simon steered her to the kitchen and sat her at the table. Cook, her face dusted with floury panic, rushed to fetch madam some tea. The kitchen was warm and very quiet after the endless chatter of her guests. There was only the sound of pots bubbling on the stove and the soft crackle of the fire in the hearth.

"Drink," Simon ordered, pressing the hot china cup into her shaking hands. "You look exhausted. You haven't slept, I gather."

Agatha shut her eyes, for she couldn't bear to look at his handsome face so near, and drank deeply. The tea scalded her tongue a bit, but the heat loosened the tightness in her chest and allowed her to breathe easily once more.

Then she set the cup aside and laid her head down on her crossed arms. She would not look at him. She would not reach for him or beg him to hold her close against his warmth and strength.

He never loved me. He never loved me.

I love him.

How could she be so weak? So girlishly sentimental?

"How supremely annoying," she muttered into the table.

"I know you didn't expect me to return."

"Actually, I rather thought you might. I'm annoyed with something else entirely." Agatha gently banged her forehead on the scrubbed-to-satin wood. It didn't knock him from her mind.

"You expected me?"

"Oh, yes. One doesn't scrape off a leech that easily."

"Ah." It was a quiet sound, but she knew she'd hurt him. It hurt her to hurt him.

"I apologize. That was nasty of me. I seem to be growing nastier by the moment." She took a deep breath and sat up. Then she opened her eyes.

He looked rather terrible. Good. Why should she be the only one who was unhappy?

"I see you've already found something black to wear."

"Simon, I was two years in mourning for Papa. Practically all I own are black gowns."

"I still don't understand why it had to be Death By Drawers."

"I was—am—very angry at you. You weren't here, so I took it out on Mortimer."

He gazed at her for a long moment. "Have you any idea how peculiar that sounds?"

"Simon, I invented peculiar," Agatha said wearily. "I thought you knew."

He grinned, that swift and deadly slash of white. Did he never smile for longer than a fraction of a second?

She couldn't think about his smile, couldn't sit here and

wish more than anything that she could spend her lifetime making him smile.

"So pray tell, why are you here? If you're concerned that my brother has escaped you, Jamie is still in residence, recovering very well from his ordeal."

"I never thought anything but."

"Well, if you aren't here to guard Jamie—"

"I came to see you."

Blast. Why did her betraying heart have to leap at his words? She narrowed her eyes at him.

"I'm growing annoyed again."

"Agatha, we have to address what happened. What I did to you—"

"What *you* did to *me*? Unbelievable. Who undressed you? I did. For that matter, who undressed me? *I* did! I knew precisely what I was doing!" She tried to glare at him, but her vision was just a bit blurred. "I simply thought I was doing it with someone else."

"So did I."

True. He'd thought her a woman of low virtue, a ladybird who spent her lover's money freely and took strange men into her home. For the first time, Agatha realized how she must have seemed to him.

So many things that she had said and done had only reinforced his impression. It was almost as if she had lied without intention.

"I know. But I never said I was a mistress. I thought you knew that Jamie was my brother."

He sat there, tracing a design on the table in her slopped tea. "I see. But the fact remains that I ruined you."

"Ruined me? You forget, I was a married woman. I am now a widow. It would seem odd to the next man if I were still virgin."

His head lifted abruptly and he fixed his gaze on her. She'd never known blue eyes could burn so hot.

"What next man?"

He needn't act so surprised, as if she could not find another man if she wished. "I'll have you know I have a standing offer of marriage."

"From whom?" The words were shot from his lips like bullets.

Agatha leaned back a bit in her chair. This was a new Simon. Suddenly she could very easily see him leading a band of spies and assassins.

She didn't want to answer the question. She'd only mentioned the standing offer to bait him. Now she wasn't sure she wanted this particular beast released.

"Agatha?"

She sighed. "Reginald."

"Reginald who?"

"Reginald Peasley, my neighbor to the west of Appleby."

"Repulsive Reggie?"

The slight slopping became a flood of tea on the table when Simon jolted her cup awry as he sprang to his feet.

"You can *not*—I won't allow—"

Agatha only gazed up at him. "There is nothing you could do to stop me, Simon. I am of age, and may marry where I wish."

He twitched at that, and Agatha got the impression of darkness barely held in check. Pain arced through her at his possessiveness. What did it matter who she married? They both knew it would not be him.

She desperately wanted him to leave now.

"Do you really want to know why I killed Mortimer? To set you free. Jamie explained who you are. I *cannot* marry you even should you ask, for you are too vital to the security of England. I will not rob her of you, dear as you are to me."

The weariness returned and settled between her shoulders and into her brain, booming like cannon fire. She rose shakily to face him, leaning her fingertips on the table for support.

"Don't worry. I'll not marry Reggie, either, though Jamie might wish me to. He'd like to keep me close to Appleby, I think, and he doesn't . . . he doesn't know."

She walked past him, balancing her aching head carefully on her shoulders. At the swinging doors she turned. "Not that it matters really, but I'll have no dearth of beaux once I let on how wealthy I am. Perhaps I'll pick one of them."

"But James—"

"Jamie was given Appleby, of course. He's welcome to it, for I seem to have had my fill of sheep and apples. It was a lovely place to be a child, but I'm not a child. London is more to my taste now."

She managed a brief smile. "However, I was given half the funds. I believe it now rounds out to about twenty thousand pounds. So please, feel free to let any obligation die with Mortimer. I don't need either of you any longer."

James shifted restlessly in his bed and put down the book he was reading. Although his current prison was a comfortable one, he could see that it was only a matter of time before he was going to want to escape from it as well.

Here it was, mid-afternoon, yet he had been put to bed like a weanling. Agatha had even come in a few moments ago and tucked him in!

He had protested under the guise of teasing, but she'd been in no mood for it. He'd asked if she wanted to stay and play a hand of cards, but she'd declined, claiming the headache.

He could hardly blame her for that. The hen chatter from her callers had resounded all the way upstairs. James had the distinct feeling that Agatha was regretting her rash vengeance, but she'd never admit it.

The tap on the door was a welcome relief from his boredom, and James gladly called out for the visitor to come in.

Simon was the last person he'd expected to see.

"You're looking much improved, James."

"For a traitor, you mean."

With a raised brow, Simon reminded him that there had been every reason to suspect him.

"Come now, Simon. You *know* me."

"I wanted to trust you, but I also wanted to find out how so many of our identities were uncovered."

The knife of guilt went deep, and James had to look away. "How many were lost?"

"James, it's not—"

But it was. He'd been careless. He hadn't bothered to hide his path, or to take alternate routes every evening to see his mistress. As if his lust had been a separate thing from his life as an operative.

He'd been a fool. Too busy thinking about the woman he had just left to be aware of being followed. Too sotted with wine and erotic delights to fight them off when they'd attacked from the shadows. *"How many?"*

"Five, if you count Ren Porter."

"Why wouldn't you count him?"

"Head injury. There's no telling if he'll ever open his eyes. And if he does, we don't know if he'll be himself, or just another brain-shot veteran."

"God. Poor Ren."

"We've never had all the men we've needed. We've certainly never had enough specialists. We're now down to two pickpockets, one knife man, four scouts, three rooftop men, and one saboteur, without you."

"And I'm a bloody partridge in a pear tree, stuck under house arrest."

"The irony is that the club is bringing in more profit than ever. We could afford to support many more missions, had we only the men to cover them."

"That's perfect. For once we've no need to beg funds from the War Office, and we cannot even use it."

"It's all thanks to Jackham really. He simply can't help making money, for himself and all of us."

Simon set one hip on the arm of the chair by the fire. "Quite different from when I first began. Did I ever tell you that the first few missions I ran for the Old Man fell under the classification of 'Acquisitions'?"

"No, what—you're joking! You funded the club with housebreaking?"

"Only from the most deserving, I assure you. We kept a file of the sinners and the charlatans, and we never completely cleaned anyone out. Not of anything they'd have been willing to report, at any rate."

James laughed, then he sobered once more. "You came to talk about Agatha, didn't you?"

"I came to talk about everything. I'll need your full report, as much as you can remember of what you were asked under the opiates. As well as what you learned on your escape."

Simon stood and walked to stand before the fire. He gazed down at the carpet, his face turned so James could not see his expression.

"And about Agatha," prompted James.

"Yes. About Agatha." Simon's voice was flat.

"You've done a terrible thing to her, Simon."

Simon turned, his face dark with anger. "Do you think I don't know that?"

"We've never used the tactic of seduction before. You said that it was unreliable. That there were better ways, that the seducer often became the seduced."

"I still feel that way."

"Then what happened?"

Simon gave a rueful bark of laughter. "You said it yourself. The seducer became seduced."

James couldn't help his surprise. He'd never dreamed it would be this easy. "You admit it then? You're attached to her?"

"Madly."

"But that's wonderful! She's mad for you as well."

"James, she knows I cannot marry. She refused me before I ever asked."

James knew he would have to tread carefully here. "Simon, I've never been entirely convinced of your reasoning on this. A man needn't walk away from a life of his own to still be loyal to his country."

"You may marry if you wish. All the Liars may. It is a decision that every man must make for himself. I made my decision years ago."

"But why?"

"James, you are my friend. But even friends must toe a line. Don't overstep."

James scowled. "Well, you bloody well overstepped with my sister! I know why you did what you did, but make no mistake, Simon. I am not happy about it."

"Yes, I did overstep. I thought she was a woman without boundaries, a woman that I could have without tying her to daily danger as my wife. Family ties are the ties that kill, at least in our profession."

James was horrified. "Then she is already in danger because she is my sister."

"Of course. You must have known that all along, James. Else why did you never mention her, even to me? Why did you leave her isolated in the country, safe at Appleby?"

It was true. James had not done it consciously, but he had most certainly kept his own counsel on the subject of Agatha.

"Great lot of good that did me. If I'd told you, none of this would have happened."

"True. But as always, that could apply to a myriad of small actions. Had you never joined the Liars, had you never taken that last mission . . . One could go on for hours. What's done is done, James."

"Yes. The question is, what do we do next?"

"I've decided that Agatha needs protection. You're in no condition yet, and I've already achieved an acceptable cover as Mortimer's brother."

James grinned. "So I've heard, *Ethelbert*."

Simon grimaced. "She has a lawless streak, your sister."

"Oh, yes. A rather wide one."

"The fact is, James, I'm moving back here to Carriage Square. Indefinitely."

"In this house? What about Agatha's reputation? Don't you think you've done enough damage? Even a widow cannot reside with only her brother-in-law, not at her age."

"Until the day Agatha says 'I will' to another man, she is mine to protect. And I can't very well protect her from half-way across the city, can I?" His tone was remote, as if it was simply business.

James still had doubts. It was a risk. "Wouldn't she be safer back in Appleby?"

Standing with his hands braced on the mantel, Simon seemed to hesitate. "She doesn't think so." Simon turned back. "I'll lie low. The outside world will never know I'm staying on, any more than they know that you are here. I'll be in evidence when callers come, and I'll leave very obviously every evening."

James narrowed his eyes. "You simply like climbing walls."

Simon smiled. "That I do. But with the two of us here, she'll be as safe as anyone is in London. I can accompany her if she goes out, and when you are better, we can trade the night watch."

James folded his arms. "Oh, I'll be watching you come nightfall, Simon. Never fear."

"I've no intention of carrying on with Agatha, James," Simon said stiffly.

"I'm sure. But I'll keep my eyes open, just the same."

Let Simon spout that rot about "killing ties" after living with Agatha for a while. If he was not mistaken, his sister still wanted Simon, and what Agatha wanted, Agatha usually got. James eyed his friend, debating whether he should warn him.

No. He wasn't quite over his anger. Let the bounder suffer.

Chapter Eighteen

The next morning, Agatha sat alone in the breakfast room and toyed with her eggs. Loss of appetite was not at all usual for her. Another reason to be angry with Simon. He'd put her off her feed completely, and while she had the finest cook in London, too.

She forced herself to eat a bit, for she didn't want to hurt Sarah's feelings. But the last bite turned to sand in her mouth when Simon sauntered into the breakfast room, his hair still damp from his morning ablutions, his hands busily adjusting the sleeves of his coat.

"Good morning, pigeon."

Her throat was too dry to swallow and the sand had turned to gravel in her mouth. Finally, she choked it down.

"What—"

"Eat up, pidge, your eggs are turning cold."

"Did you stay here last night?" She had meant to shout, but her voice scarcely managed a horrified whisper.

"Oh, yes. I've quite moved back in. The rear bedchamber is a bit small, but I'll share Button with James, so there's no need to put my own valet up as well."

He filled his plate from the sideboard and took the chair opposite her. When he took his first bite of eggs and made that all too familiar sound deep in his throat, the pain broke Agatha's paralysis.

She shoved her chair violently away from the table, putting distance between them. "What are you *doing* here?"

"I'm guarding you."

"Me? I've done nothing wrong."

"I'm safeguarding you, against whoever kidnapped James."

"Don't be ridiculous. There's no connection between James Cunnington and Agatha Applequist."

"I made one. Others might as well."

There was no denying that. She tried another tack. "Well, I won't have it. I'm perfectly safe in this house. And if I'm not, I'll hire guards of my own."

"Will you be sure they're not working for the opposition? Your servants are loyal, but new staff in the house won't necessarily be."

Agatha cast about for any possible argument. "You'll ruin my reputation!"

"As if you gave a fig about that."

Blast. He knew her too well.

"And I've covered that contingency," he said. "I'll play the attentive brother-in-law by day, then make the appearance of leaving for the night. Then I'll return covertly, and no one will be the wiser."

"Jamie won't allow it!"

"Sorry, pidge, he's already seen the logic of it."

"Why are you calling me that?"

"Pigeon? Well, you said I should come up with my own pet name for you. Don't you like pigeon?"

"No, I most certainly don't." She struggled to keep her voice cold. He would not charm her.

He raised an eyebrow. "Pity. I thought it suited you quite well."

"Not a bit of it. Pigeons are common and rather nasty."

"I find them endearing, and very pretty in their own way."

He would not melt her anger; she would not allow it. It was the only thing holding her spine erect.

"A pet name is out of the question. You have no place giving me one."

He stretched lazily, leaning back in his chair. "I'll just keep at it then. I'm sure to find the right one eventually. Perhaps 'pumpkin.'"

It was no use. "Simon, if you must stay here, would you—"

"What?"

"Would you please try very hard not to . . ."

"Not to?"

She looked away, defeated. "Not to make it hurt so much," she whispered.

He didn't respond. She made herself look back at him.

All the teasing was gone. His eyes reflected the torture that she herself was feeling. "I apologize, Agatha. I thought I was."

She fought the pain, and the tears that threatened, but was about to lose the battle when James came into the room.

"Ah, Simon, I'd hoped to beat you to table this morning to explain."

Gratefully, Agatha tore her gaze from Simon's. "Jamie, what are you doing out of bed?"

"Saving my brain from curdling with boredom. I can rest just as easily downstairs as upstairs."

"And it's easier to cadge sweets from Sarah Cook," contributed Simon.

James grimaced. "I see I'm found out already." He turned to Agatha. "Are you all right about this, Aggie?"

"I don't know that I am," she said quietly, "but I don't see that I have much choice in the matter."

"I imagine that you'd prefer that I stay far away from you," Simon said, "but that simply cannot be. I'll receive your callers with you, and I'll escort you when you leave the house."

"Oh, lovely. Good lord, Simon, why don't you simply pull out my hair strand by strand? Why should torture be so subtle?"

"I'm not trying to hurt you, Agatha. I must protect you. Please understand." His tone was soft, but implacable as well.

The blasted thing of it was, she did understand. Just as he'd put his mark on her, she'd put her own on him. He might not love her, but he felt responsible for her.

Well, strike "honorable" off the list of things she'd been wrong about. He was undeniably honorable, putting her as high among his priorities as was possible in this situation.

Of course, should some national emergency occur, she was sure he'd be gone in a flash. She had learned long ago that when a man had a grand purpose in life, emotional ties faded to insignificance.

She'd merely have to bear it until something came up that was more important to him than she was. In her experience, such things never took long.

Pearson appeared in the doorway.

"Madam, two gentlemen are here to call on you. Shall I tell them to come back at a more appropriate hour?"

Agatha gladly seized on the chance to leave the table. "No, Pearson. Now is fine. Who is it?"

"A Master Collis Tremayne and his uncle, Lord Etheridge."

"Collis?"

She left with a smile lighting her face, startling Simon. How long had it been that he had seen Agatha smile? Not since that night—

Who the hell was Collis Tremayne to make her smile? A young man, she'd told him. One of her patients. And what the bloody hell was Etheridge doing here?

Throwing down his napkin as if he were issuing a challenge, Simon rose to follow Agatha from the breakfast room.

As he strode purposefully toward the hall he heard James laughing behind him.

The guests were waiting in the front parlor. Simon managed to catch up to Agatha before she so much as touched the knob, so they both heard the voices arguing within.

Agatha paused, as if unsure of whether or not to interrupt. Simon held up a hand, signaling to wait. She drew back her hand immediately, and Simon was reminded of what a superior partner she had made.

If only she weren't who she was. . . .

"Collis, aside from the fact that you've nothing to offer

her but your prospects of an inheritance from me, you are too young for her."

"Codswallop. I daresay she's not a moment past twenty."

Agatha leaned close to whisper in Simon's ear, "I think I'm fonder of him than ever, for I'm every day of twenty-five."

That she was fond of the pup was the last thing that Simon wanted to hear. With the possible exception of the next thing he heard.

"If anyone is to marry her, I shall. I'm of a maturity to be a good husband, and I've considerably more to offer."

"Oh my," Agatha whispered gleefully. "I told you beaux would flock to my door."

Simon lifted his lip in a quiet snarl at her satisfied tone.

Collis raised his voice in protest. "But you spent the entire morning trying to dissuade me from marrying her!"

"Because it is extremely improper to speak to her about such a thing when Mr. Applequist is scarcely cold in his grave."

"I know that. But she is widowed, with no family that I know of. Who knows what condition her finances are in? I only want her to know that she has options. Women are fond of options, I've found."

"In all your vast experience, Collis? Well, now she'll have yet another option. Me."

"But why? You've only met her the once."

"She's quite suitable. I don't want a fluttering debutante, but an adult. And I like her. She's uncommonly sensible. I'd think you'd be pushing her on me, Collis. After all, if I marry and have an heir of my own, then you'll be free to pursue your music."

"And I'll feel proper sorry for the poor little sod if you do. Bloody tyrant."

Once again, Simon's lip threatened to curl. "Listen to them in there, arguing over who will rescue the damsel-in-distress."

Agatha sighed dramatically. "I'm a damsel. How thrilling. I've always wanted to be a damsel."

"Fine," Simon said, his voice a hiss. "You're a damsel. It's easier to remember than 'pumpkin,' anyway."

She narrowed her eyes at him. "No."

"No what, damsel?"

She closed her eyes and shook her head. "To think I ever tried to manipulate you. What a fool I am."

Simon turned to her. "You are not—"

His swift denial was cut off when the door before them was pulled open. Dalton Montmorency stood eyeing them both with one brow raised.

"Mrs. A!"

Collis rushed forward to take Agatha's hand. Simon tensed when he thought the lad might embrace her, but Collis only led her to sit on her own sofa. Simon rolled his eyes. As if she didn't know perfectly well where it was.

Unfortunately, Agatha seemed charmed by Collis's attentions. "Collis, you came to see me after all. How are you feeling?"

"Never better, Mrs. A, don't worry about me. I'm more concerned about you. When I read of Mr. A's accident, I wanted to come straightaway."

Etheridge gave a nod of apology. "It was I who kept him at home, Mrs. Applequist. His doctor said a few days more bed rest. I felt it was important enough to abide by."

"As well you should, my lord. Collis, you are a terrible patient." She smiled fondly at the boy, and Simon almost growled.

"I know." The lad's smile was unrepentant, and Simon had to admit that he was a likable sort. He'd treat Agatha well, but he was too easily ordered about. She'd charge right over him.

Lord Etheridge bowed over her hand. "My condolences, dear lady." He straightened and shot a measuring glance at Simon. "And are you a member of the bereaved family as well, sir?"

"I beg your pardon. Lord Etheridge, Collis, may I present my late husband's brother . . . Ethelbert Applequist." Agatha winced a bit as she said the name she had given him.

Simon despised the name, but his loathing for it gained new depths when a flash of amusement gleamed in Etheridge's damnable eyes.

On the surface, this man was perfect for Agatha. He was wealthy, titled, stalwart enough to resist her when she had one of her harebrained notions, and reliable enough to care for her properly all the days of her life.

Simon had never hated anyone more.

The visit didn't last much longer, much to Simon's relief. Agatha very prettily deflected Collis's protestations of affection and thanked Lord Etheridge politely for his businesslike offer, but told them both that she needed more time before she was ready to plan her future.

The sadness in her eyes when she spoke was all too real, and Simon beat back another surge of guilt. This was precisely why he had never pursued emotional ties. Someone was always going to be hurt.

When the two men had left, after Simon received another probing look from Etheridge, Simon followed Agatha back into the parlor.

"Why didn't you turn that pup down flat?"

"Why should I?"

"Oh, come on. You'd trample him in a week and you know it."

"Well, I'd not trample Dalton. He's no pup."

Simon's jaw fell open. "You can't be serious. Not him!"

"Why not?" Defiance and hurt flashed in her eyes. She had never looked more beautiful to him.

She tossed her head like a stubborn horse. "I like him. He seems stuffy at first, but underneath I think he's rather fun. Perhaps he's just what I need, considering he isn't the Griffin after all."

Meaning Etheridge wasn't a man such as Simon was, a man who couldn't afford to divide his loyalties. She was entirely right, but still Simon steamed at the thought of her belonging to another man.

"Then who is he, and why was he in Maywell's study?"

"Perhaps he had a perfectly good reason."

"What reason could he have?"

"Well, you were there, and you had good reason. Or so I thought at the time."

An uneasy silence fell. It always came back to that between them. Motives.

"Agatha, I never would have—"

She held up her hand. "Stop. I know. My apologies again. You had an excellent reason for everything you did. Your duty."

Simon stepped closer and ran his knuckles down her cheek. "Not everything was out of duty, damsel. Not everything."

Then, before the tear that trembled on her lashes could fall, he turned and left, cursing himself for a bloody coward.

The remainder of the day brought incessant callers. The tiresome Trapps came again, although Agatha was glad to see the interesting Mrs. Simpson was with them.

Once Mrs. Trapp's attempts to gain more gory details about Mortimer's demise had failed, the lady reverted to her true love. Gossip.

Agatha let her ramble on, thankful that the inquisition was over. Simon survived only another ten minutes before he fled the room. Yet another thing to be grateful for.

Best of all, the longer Mrs. Trapp stayed and dominated the conversation, the less Agatha needed to speak at all.

So she nodded now and again and expressed proper sounds of amazement and disbelief at the appropriate places, and the afternoon soon began to take on an unreal quality.

Perhaps she was in Hell. Hell might very well be a parlor full of ladies whom one had lied to, and the infernal atonement was to be forced to continue the sham forever. Oh, yes, a veritable tableau of perdition.

It did not help that the room was perfumed with the many bouquets of flowers she had received from the men and nurses at the hospital. The sweet scent of guilt . . .

A familiar name came up, and Agatha seized upon it before her wild notions could make her break into frantic giggles.

"Have you known Lady Winchell long, Mrs. Trapp?"

"Oh, no, dear. Not personally. She came onto the board about the time you began volunteering. Although I've heard of her for years, you understand. Not much gets by me."

Mrs. Trapp wiggled deeper into her seat cushion, and Agatha recognized the signs that a particularly choice piece of information was on its way.

"Well, you'd not know this, dear, for you're new to town, but Lavinia Winchell is . . ."

The lady leaned forward and looked to each side, as if to look out for eavesdroppers. Agatha stifled a hysterical giggle, for the parlor was chockablock with ladies, who had all gone silent and leaned forward as well.

"French."

Agatha stared at her. "But so many people are, Mrs. Trapp. There was such a flood of them emigrating during the Terror."

"True, true. But it does account for those airs, you know. Good English stock has no need of such pretty ways."

The woman spoke as if all English ladies were corn-fed and pastured, chewing their cud. The fact that the fashionable set slavishly copied the French whenever possible, in style and in social graces, seemed to have escaped her entirely.

Of course, the Trapp daughters were rather bovine, with their square faces and large, bland eyes. At the moment, both young women blinked slowly at Agatha, jaws moving from side to side while they downed another pair of cakes.

Another giggle was working its way up Agatha's throat, and she cast desperately about for a lifeline.

"Your daughters are so . . . appealing, Mrs. Trapp. Have you considered possible matches for them?"

Mrs. Trapp swelled with pride. "Indeed, Mrs. Applequist. With all the overtures we've had for them both, my husband and I are contemplating providing another season for them. One must allow the most options possible for one's children."

Then a look of smug horror crossed the lady's face and she turned to Agatha in apology. "I'm so sorry, dear. I forgot that you'll never know the miracle of children of your own."

The pain was instantaneous. It shot to Agatha's heart like an icy spear and lodged there, spreading the chill outward. *Children of her own.*

Mrs. Trapp continued, carrying on about the shortage of young men in the marriage mart now that so many had been lost in the war, but Agatha had stopped listening.

It was true. She would never have a child, for despite her pose of independence to Simon and James, she knew that she could never marry anyone but the man she had given her heart to.

The man who didn't—couldn't—want her for his wife.

For her, there would be no sons with sky blue eyes and thick black hair. No laughing daughters to jump into the heaps of pink petals at Appleby.

Agatha turned away from the chattering lady, longing to flee to some haven from the ache that grew inside her. She found one in the level gaze of Mrs. Simpson.

"Beatrice Trapp is a fool," Clara said quietly, "but she doesn't mean to be unkind."

"I know," Agatha said. She felt as though a band around her heart would not let it beat properly. "It is only that it had not occurred to me—"

She stopped, shaking her head.

Mrs. Simpson took her hand in both of hers. "Perhaps all hope is not lost? There is a chance, perhaps, that Mr. Applequist has left something of himself behind?"

Perhaps. Agatha had not considered it at all, not even before that one magical night, or after it, in the mess of anger and pain.

There was a chance . . .

And there could be more.

She could ensure that Simon left something behind when duty stole him finally away.

Determination filled her heart, and the constriction around it eased somewhat. She had given her hopes of love and marriage to the voracious flames of duty, but she need not feed her hopes of motherhood to it as well.

Her window of opportunity was small. If she could become pregnant in the next few weeks, the child would simply seem to be a blessing, the only part of her dear departed husband that remained.

She could take her child back to Appleby, and no one would be the wiser. Not even Simon. She could make up a tale of quick wartime marriage to tell the village. That sort of thing happened all the time. If Jamie backed her story—and she was sure he would—no one would dare to doubt it.

New strength brought her head up.

Mrs. Simpson eyed her approvingly. "Hold on to that hope awhile. Let it give you strength." Then she stepped back and said more loudly, "You are a bit pale, Mrs. Applequist. Ladies, I think we've comforted her enough for one day."

As if a net full of birds had been cut, the ladies fled the room, happy to leave the pall of mourning behind them and continue their gossip elsewhere. Mrs. Simpson was the last to leave, and Agatha impulsively put out her hand.

"Thank you. You've helped me more than you know."

The lady seemed delighted, and Agatha felt another queasy wash of regret for her deception. She was fast becoming sick of this lying.

But she had one more act of treachery to perform. She must seduce Simon yet again.

Chapter Nineteen

Upstairs, Simon had been prying as much information out of James as he could. He made James repeat the story again and again, start to finish, finish to start.

James was familiar enough with this form of debriefing, but the strain was beginning to tell. Even from where he sat in the chair by the fire, Simon could see that James had gone pale and slumped against his pillows.

"I don't know, Simon! I can't remember mentioning any other names, but then, I can't remember mentioning any in the first place!"

"Think, James! I can't send another man out until I know how much the Liars have been compromised."

There came a knock on James's door, and Agatha entered with a tea tray. "The callers have all gone for the day. I thought you might need something to eat."

She eyed James severely, although Simon noticed that she did not cast so much as a glance at him. That was odd. He'd thought they had resolved some of their tension earlier today.

"Sorry, Aggie, but we don't have time to eat. Unless His Mightiness will allow it?"

"Don't be snide, James. Simon doesn't like this any more than you do." She placed the tray across James's lap.

Simon was glad to see that it held two cups and enough of Sarah Cook's delights for both men. There was some comfort in Agatha's unwillingness to let him starve.

James picked up his tea after she poured for him. "Aggie, I want to think of something else for a while. Tell me what's new at Appleby."

"Well, the lambing was very successful this year, and we received top price for those that we sold at the meat market. The shearing was uneventful, and the wool is even now being baled." She sat comfortably next to James and clasped her hands over one knee as she recited. "There was little frost damage in orchards this year, so I hope for a good crop of apples—"

Jamie grinned and poked her in the arm with one finger. "You sound as if you run the place instead of Mott," he teased.

Agatha looked at her brother strangely. "Mr. Mott died a year before Papa did. Did he never tell you?"

Frankly confused, James shook his head. "No, it never came up. Who has been managing the estate?"

Agatha drew her brows together. "Why . . . I have. I've been making regular reports to you."

James actually paled. "I thought you were just catching me up on the news. I had no idea you were playing at running things."

"Playing?" Agatha stood, her tone growing cold. "*Playing,* you say. I'll have you know I've been in complete control of Appleby for nearly four years."

Simon tensed. *No, James. Don't say it.*

James did. "Dear God. Do I have anything left?"

Agatha flinched. Simon knew James could not have hurt her more if he had struck her.

"When the new trees mature, you'll have three times the acreage under harvest than you did before. Your flocks have nearly doubled every year. Your cottages are in excellent repair, and your house is well kept. I wish you much enjoyment of it all."

Spine straight, she turned and strode from the room. Simon shook his head at James, who stared after his sister.

"I daresay you could not have handled that worse."

James whistled softly. "Three times the acreage, she said. I'll be the largest apple producer in Lancashire," he marveled.

"You hurt her."

"Aggie? Oh, I doubt it." James shrugged. "She'll get over it soon enough, if I did. Never one to hold a grudge, that's my sister." He was popping one of Cook's little cakes into his mouth when Agatha opened the door and stalked to his bedside.

"You need broth to regain your strength. Drink this, every drop." She set a deep bowl on the tray. Then she left again with starchy dignity.

"Managing sort, isn't she?" James said carelessly.

For the first time, Simon realized what the Liar's Club had cost Agatha, long before he'd even met her. What had it been like for her, to be left by everyone she should have been able to depend upon? Suddenly angry, he rounded on James. "You should never have left her with all that on her shoulders. She was little more than a girl."

Surprised, James choked down a mouthful in order to defend himself. "She did all right."

"She should have been dancing, going to parties, flirting with young men. Where were you when she needed you?"

"Working for you!"

"You told me you had no other responsibilities, no other commitments."

"I thought it was all taken care of."

"You chose to think so because it suited you," Simon said scornfully. "Even now, you treat her like a pet, when she saved everything you own and tossed it back into your undeserving lap."

James set aside his tray. He narrowed his eyes at Simon. "Let's talk about undeserving. You've ruined her, and you're leaving her with no future at all."

The truth hit Simon like a blow. He jerked in response and turned away, unsettled. "You know I cannot marry," he said in an undertone.

James gazed at him steadily. "No, I know you *choose* not to marry."

Simon worked his jaw. "You don't know anything."

"Then pray, enlighten me."

The old pain came back in an instant, and Simon paced restlessly before the fireplace. "I never told you about my mother."

"No. I knew she was not married to your father, but that is all."

"She was a tuppence whore in Covent Garden," Simon said bluntly. "When I went to work for the Old Man, I went on my first courier mission, carrying accounts of troop movements on Malta from the drop point to the club. I was so sure of myself. It never occurred to me that the transfer point had been compromised. I never once looked over my shoulder."

"I think we all feel a bit immortal on our first mission," James said quietly.

"But do you all race to brag to your mother the moment you complete it?"

He could see the horror cross James's face. "Oh, Simon, you didn't."

"I did. I made the drop well. Too well. The French agents must have thought I still carried the intelligence. I led them right to her. So damned cocksure I hadn't been followed. But I haven't told you the best part."

His voice almost failed him. "I left my courier pouch behind, quite by mistake. So busy counting out my pay to her, so busy being the one to save her from her life—"

"They thought she had something. Oh, God, Simon."

Simon drew a breath. "I missed my pouch after only a few blocks. I ran back, but I was too late. They'd beaten her so severely that she was like a broken bloody doll. She only lived a few moments, just long enough for me to discover what I had done. She died, right there in my arms." His voice dropped to a whisper. "By my hands."

James didn't say anything for a few moments. Grateful, Simon sank into the chair by the fire and pressed his palms into his eyes. When he had his control back, he opened his eyes to see the carpet at his feet.

Memory swept him of making love to Agatha on that rug.

God, he was an idiot. He wanted that carpet in his room. Wanted to keep just one good thing from all this.

"But, Simon . . . you aren't sixteen anymore. You're a professional. You're the Magician."

Simon sat back, letting his head fall back against the chair. "James, do you have any idea what our enemies would do to get their hands on the wife of the Magician? Being close to me is more dangerous than ever. Do you want her to die?"

James raised his chin, glaring tightly at Simon. "No, I want her to live. I want her to live a life without shame and censure."

"Her story has held. Even you thought she was wed. No one has censured her."

"Let us hope our luck continues."

"Indeed." Simon rose. "You're recovering well enough. Feebles is taking the street watch. I need to go out for a bit. And tomorrow I'll need to return to the club for the morning. I'll check on Ren while I'm out and let you know how he's doing."

He left James alone then, moodily picking at his food. There was a little matter of a certain mysterious suitor that Simon wanted to clear up.

Etheridge's town house was very fine and very large. Simon watched from the roof of the unoccupied house next door. He could see the rear of the place was as well kept as the front, and that the servants who came and went had none of the furtive attitude of the overworked and downtrodden.

The man was more than just wealthy, as Simon's reports indicated. Dalton Montmorency was the perfect gentleman. His wealth lay solidly in the Bank of England instead of in some bookmaker's pockets. His education was no farce paid for by family connections but was recorded as earnest scholarly pursuits. He took his seat in the House of Lords with serious dedication, promoting a far-sighted liberalism and concern for the less fortunate.

His servants were deathly loyal and astonishingly close-mouthed. He entertained rarely and had no apparent family other than the irreverent Collis. While fine, his wardrobe and accoutrements were neither ostentatious nor dandified.

There was no record of a mistress or of an extremely pious nature. Neither sinner nor saint.

The perfect gentleman indeed. In Simon's book, such perfection was so unlikely as to be a cover for more sinister things. No man could be so evenhanded, so refined, so unblemished.

Of course, Simon was investigating his lordship this evening solely for the purposes of the Liar's Club. A man such as this bore watching, for he had gone into Maywell's study like a true professional and left not a trace of his presence.

The fact that Etheridge had expressed interest in Agatha had nothing to do with tonight's little expedition. Except, of course, that Agatha seemed to return a certain amount of the gentleman's regard.

Simon banked the slow burn that resulted from that thought. He would uncover Etheridge tonight, and there would be no further danger of Agatha becoming involved with someone unscrupulous.

He shifted his weight to the balls of his feet, preparing to walk the rope between the houses. Here in this wealthy neighborhood, the homes were nearly as large as country manors and as far from one another as the properties afforded.

As the neighborhood settled into late-night silence, and the lighted windows were long winked into darkness, Simon prepared to make his entry.

His two ropes were strung tautly across the gap, completely invisible in the dark. Earlier, Simon had sent his grapple across to Etheridge's roof to catch on the slated gable nearest him.

The best time to do that sort of thing was early in the evening, when the servants who lodged in the attic rooms had not yet retired.

Simon favored the blue wash of dusk for this work, for the inevitable rising fog and the uncertainty of light hid the most obvious of activities.

But for the actual rooftop work, the deepest night served best. Simon liked the quiet crossing, even the familiar bite of the rope through the bottoms of his soft-soled shoes. He'd missed the silence of his specially crafted gummed shoes on the slates and the muffled *snick* of a lock releasing to his picks.

Simon crossed the space on his double ropes, feet walking the lower, hands hanging from the upper. He was quick about it. If he was seen, as unlikely as that was in his dark, tight-fitting clothing on a dark night, the observer would not look back swiftly enough to catch him twice.

Padding across the slates with silent competence, Simon reached the far side of the house from where his rope was strung. He slipped easily down the stone walls to the second level. Then a quick heel-dangling stroll along the slight ledge that people insisted on decorating their homes with, bless them.

The window was locked, of course. There had been nothing in Feebles's report to indicate that Etheridge was a fool. It was a very fine lock, entirely suitable to the wealth likely held within.

Fortunately, Simon had mastered this particular lock when he was not yet shaving. In less than a minute, he was inside the silent room, letting his senses expand to fit the space.

A house the size of Etheridge's was actually easier to work than a smaller one such as Agatha's. A quick rifling through the study wouldn't be audible from the bedchambers of such a vast place as this.

The night was damned dark, and now Simon didn't even have the city glow reflected from the low-hanging clouds to see by.

There was no help for it. He'd have to light a candle. He only hoped enough coals remained in the fireplace to start a flame. Striking flint would take far too long.

He began to dig the brimstone match and candle stub from his pocket but halted.

There was someone in the room. Simon hadn't heard a

thing, nor had he smelled anything but books and ink and leather.

Still he knew. He wasn't alone.

Simon had taken one step back toward the window when a scrape sounded and the glare of a flame seared his night-expanded vision.

"Mr. Applequist. How kind of you to stop by. Or should I say 'Mr. Rain'?"

If Agatha hadn't known better, she would have thought that Simon stayed out late purposely to vex her. Here she was, waiting to seduce him again, and he was gone.

Again.

Honestly, men and their lack of timing!

She threw down her cards in the middle of her turn and left the table.

"Oh, dear, and you were winning, too," Jamie drawled. "What's he done this time?"

"He's late."

"Well, he isn't in short pants, Agatha. I believe he is able to handle himself out there in the big bad world. If he survives it, he may even go out in the morning as well."

Still upset by his lack of faith in her, Agatha didn't answer James. She was in no mood for teasing and banter tonight.

Tonight would mark her real descent into immorality, by her own standards. All her conniving, all her manipulations to find Jamie, amounted to nothing when compared to what she was about to do.

She was going to steal a child.

She didn't bother to rationalize it to herself. Those days were done. There was nothing noble and altruistic about seducing Simon for a child. She was serving no interests but her own.

He'd hate her for it if he ever found out. Jamie would have to be sworn to secrecy forever, something that would likely drive a further wedge between the two men. Agatha accepted responsibility for that as well.

She would take her child back to Appleby and spend her days dutifully producing wool and cider to support them all. What had only days before seemed a prison sentence amounted now to the only penance she was able to pay for the crime she was about to commit.

It would be worth every day of lanolin in her hair and apple peels in her shoes.

If only the blasted man would come home.

Simon lounged on a luxurious velvet chair and swirled a crystal snifter full of rather amazing brandy in one hand. He was warm and dry and would have considered it all the height of comfort under other circumstances.

However, it was a bit difficult to relax with a pistol pointed at one's head.

Dalton Montmorency also lounged. His feet were up on his massive mahogany desk and a matching brandy glass hung negligently from the fingers of his left hand.

His right hand held the gleaming weapon that ruined Simon's peace of mind. Even when Dalton tipped his head back for the final taste of his brandy, his aim didn't waver.

The glass was set on the desk with a careless clink, and Simon winced, even though he ought to be more concerned for himself than for the priceless crystal.

Still, the thief in him could not help cataloging the street value of the contents of Etheridge House. Compared to Dalton, even James was a grubbing shepherd. Where had all that lovely money come from? Treason could be a very profitable business, if one went about it properly.

"Please, finish your drink so that we may begin our conversation." Dalton waved the gun in a gesture of encouragement.

Simon shrugged and tossed back his own brandy, only pausing for a moment to regretfully let the last of it slide down his throat. Well, if he was going to die, at least Etheridge was letting him go in style.

Etheridge raised a brow. "All done? Well, why don't we

start with an explanation of why you crept through my study window in the middle of the night?"

"I certainly would be a fool to do it in the middle of the day, wouldn't I?"

"You're a fool to do it at all, Mr. Rain."

"Rain? Who is he?"

"He is you, the sometimes Mortimer and/or Ethelbert Applequist, and let us not forget Simon Montague Raines, the proprietor of a little place called the Liar's Club."

Simon didn't react visibly, but he was stunned that his cover had been so easily broken. As far as he knew, today was the first time Etheridge had laid eyes on him. How could he have cut through the layers of disguise so quickly?

"What do you know of the Liar's Club?"

"I know everything about the Liar's Club, Mr. Rain. I am one of the men who, along with the Prime Minister, decide what use to put that gang of misfits to in the service of His Majesty."

Simon's mouth fell open. "You're the Cobra."

Now it was Dalton's turn to be surprised. "You've redeemed yourself considerably with that leap of intuition, Simon. I'm happy to see that you are an intelligent man after all. How did you know? Even I have not yet been made privy to the identities of the other three."

Simon shook his head. "I have complete dossiers on the Royal Four, and have for years. I know what they eat, and drink, and who they cry out for in their sleep. When Spencer Perceval was assassinated earlier this year and Lord Liverpool was made Prime Minister in his place, I knew there would be another member selected to fill in for Liverpool eventually."

"Your informants must be slipping, for I've been fully invested since Perceval took his final breath."

It was his damned manpower shortage at fault yet again. "The lack is mine, my lord. The Liars are all the finest in their specialties."

"I am not entirely certain the Liars are anything but what their name implies. Lord Liverpool isn't at all sure you merit the freedom granted your predecessor, and I need not tell you that the Prime Minister's approval is necessary to the continued existence of your organization. It took you months to track down your leak, losing several men in the process, and in the end, the man shows up at your very door."

Dalton narrowed his eyes. "Whereupon you failed to report his capture and placed him on house arrest on his own recognizance."

Simon nodded. "That explains the pistol, then. You think I've gone over."

"Sir, I trust no one, with the possible exception of Lord Liverpool. Not even the other Three. For all I know, you could be on official assignment right now."

Simon grinned. "What? The mighty Lord Etheridge fears assassination by one of his fellows? Tell me it isn't true."

"Power can be an ugly thing in the hands of the wrong men. I am loyal to His Majesty, and to the Prince Regent. I work for England, not for my own enrichment. This can be hard for some men to understand."

"It seems we are on the same side." Simon spread his hands. "And all this?"

"Inherited, mostly, increased with a few investments of my own." Etheridge shrugged. "I am used to suspicion as to my holdings, Simon. It is all quite the usual."

"The way you lit that match was not usual."

Etheridge held up a small wooden box, smiling slightly. "This is quite interesting, I must agree. Something that a friend of mine has been working on. He calls them Lucifer matches. One scrapes the sulfur head of the match against sandpaper, and it miraculously lights itself."

Simon felt an instant acquisitive lust for the things. What freedom such an invention would give the Liars! "I must have some. Where might I get a supply?"

"Oh, I doubt he is in production just yet."

"He will produce for me and my Liars," Simon said with certainty.

With a raised eyebrow, Etheridge considered the small case in his hand. "I see. These would be quite invaluable to you and your men." He tossed the box to Simon, who greedily plucked it from the air and tucked it into his pocket.

"My thanks."

"A trifle."

Indeed, a trifle for this man. A tingle of resentment ran through Simon. "So, you are a wealthy, eligible, powerful patriot." How putrid could the fellow be? "And you want to marry Agatha Applequist."

"Agatha Cunnington, to be precise."

"Ah, yes. Of course you would know about her family ties. I'm surprised you would consider a match with the sister of my primary security leak."

"As far as I have been able to ascertain, Miss Cunnington is entirely blameless in the whole affair."

"She is. Her only flaw is a tendency to manage things. She thought she could discover her brother's whereabouts on her own."

"Why didn't you discourage her from such a dangerous act? How could you allow her to put herself in such jeopardy?"

Simon darkened but did not reply. It would serve the pompous bastard right if he did marry Agatha. Simon gave Etheridge one week before he would be as stunned and bemuddled as Simon himself.

"More to the point, Simon, why are you here if not to clear the way for the ambitions of one of my colleagues?"

"I was investigating you as a possible spy," Simon said. "You've a very suspicious way of life, my lord. Positively reclusive. And all those journeys abroad? Not very subtle of you." He sat back with his hands clasped over his abdomen, watching his captor narrowly. "You were a spy, weren't you? An independent operative."

This time Etheridge was the one to redden. "That's preposterous," he sputtered. "I have shipping interests! And I don't socialize because I despise silly people and their idle chatter—"

He halted at Simon's grin and grimaced. He set the pistol down on the desk with more respect than he had the glass.

"You don't know how I envy you, Simon. I've missed the

fieldwork terribly since I took over for Lord Liverpool. Now it is all politics and court intrigue."

"I'd hate every minute of it," Simon said with feeling. "Is that why you were in Maywell's study? Because you missed the fieldwork?"

"Bloody hell. You are as good as Liverpool claimed. How did you know that?"

"I was right behind you." Simon snickered. "So was Agatha."

The front legs of Etheridge's chair made sudden contact with the floor as he sat up straight in surprise. "*She* does sneakwork?"

"A finer partner I've never had. She's the most creative liar and the most spontaneous confidence artist I've ever had the pleasure of being finessed by. For days even I thought she was a professional."

Etheridge pursed his lips in admiration. "And all tied up in that pretty little package, too." He cast Simon a measuring look. "Who are you to Miss Cunnington, really?"

Her worst nightmare. Simon had to look away. "A friend." Then he shot Etheridge a warning glare. "One who would be highly upset to see her hurt."

Etheridge nodded. "A friend. Yet you lived with her for weeks unchaperoned. And she is so very beddable."

With the speed of a bullet, Simon was across the room, over the desk, and at Etheridge's throat. His voice was a deadly hiss. "Lord or no, I will rip your foul tongue from your head if you ever belittle her that way again."

Etheridge managed a nod and raised both hands to show his agreement. When Simon released him, he rubbed his throat calmly.

"You've answered my question. I wanted to know your true feelings for the lady. I think you've expressed them quite well."

"Manipulative bastard," Simon muttered.

"Aren't we all?"

The hell of it was, he was right.

Chapter Twenty

The clock struck nine. The servants cleared away the dishes from Agatha's lonely breakfast. Her restless thoughts had kept her up so late that she'd missed Simon already this morning, and she'd not wanted to disturb James's rest simply to provide herself with company.

"What would you like Cook to serve your guests today, madam?" Pearson stood before her.

Oh, blast. Another day of callers to get through. Agatha pondered the thought of claiming illness to avoid them.

"The usual, I suppose, Pearson. They seem to like it very well." She sighed. "Or perhaps we should prepare something less appetizing. Chocolate-covered snails, perhaps?"

"Are you asking my opinion, madam?"

"Oh, heavens, no, Pearson. I can hear the disapproval dripping from your very voice."

"Indeed, madam."

Agatha closed her eyes. "Can you make it all stop for a day, Pearson? I simply need to catch my breath."

"Yes, madam. I shall inform God."

Agatha jerked her head up, but Pearson had gone. Had that been humor? From *Pearson*?

"Good lord, the world is coming to an end," she muttered.

"That's a pity, for I was going to take you out for an ice."

Simon strolled casually into the breakfast room, bringing with him the fresh spring air from outside.

Suddenly the day was brighter, strung with light and joy. She'd missed him, silly fool that she was. She ought to be eager to put her plan into play, but for the moment she was simply content to be in the same room with the man she loved.

She smiled wistfully. "Out? I can't go out, I have callers coming."

"All the more reason to go, if you ask my opinion. It's a lovely day. The sun is shining and the sky is clear. I say, go out."

Agatha's smile widened, thinking of the child's game. "Simon Says, 'Go out for an ice.'"

He leaned one hip upon the table. "Indeed. You must always do what Simon Says."

Agatha jumped up. "I'll be ready in two minutes." She left the room, then thrust her head back through the door. "Did I ever tell you how much I like raspberry?"

Simon had never had the urge to eat a raspberry-flavored ice before, but suddenly it seemed that if he didn't have just one taste, just one sweet drop, he would expire on the spot.

Of course, it might have been the fact that said little pink drop was just then tracing its way down Agatha's chin and was threatening to fall to her bosom.

Simon decided then and there that if it did fall, he was throwing caution and career to the four winds and following it down.

Wild visions of Agatha's magnificent breasts smeared in sweet pink syrup ambushed him, and he grabbed the edge of the table tightly. His trousers were fit to split, and if he wasn't mistaken, he was beginning to pant.

Fortunately for all concerned, Agatha absently caught the drip in question with her handkerchief, keeping her attention on her ice all the while.

It was a terrible thing for a man's career to hang on the

flick of a hankie. He really needed to do something about this situation. He would think on it seriously.

Later.

At the moment, it was all he could do to keep responding in an intelligent manner while watching Agatha take sensual delight in a frozen concoction of sugar and ice and raspberry juice. Her tongue swirled round and round the pile of shaved ice in its card holder until she pulled it back between her pinked lips to savor the sugary treat.

God save him, for he was surely going to die. Suddenly he was very thankful that they'd taken a secluded table where Agatha could throw back her heavy widow's veil. Perhaps no one would notice the tenting of his trousers from where he sat.

"Whatever are you thinking of? You have the oddest look on your face."

With a jerk, Simon came back to himself to watch Agatha pat her lips daintily with the damned hankie, having finished the very last lick of her ice.

"You've scarcely touched yours."

He followed the path of her finger pointing to his own melted dish of lemon-scented syrup. He'd ordered an ice? Good lord, he hated the stuff.

Except for raspberry ice. He thought he could possibly become very fond of raspberry ice.

"Agatha, would you please excuse me for a moment?" Without waiting for a reply, Simon pushed back his silly little chair and fled the Italian ice parlor at a near run.

Agatha leaned back in her chair, pushing her finished treat away. If she was to be perfectly honest with herself, and she had vowed she would be, she must admit that she had just done her best to drive Simon wild with lust.

She almost hadn't. They had been having a lovely time on the drive and had been very comfortable with each other, as they used to be.

It hadn't seemed the time to pursue her plan, and she'd been happy for a brief moment free of pretense and deceit.

Until she had remembered how short a time she had to secure his child.

Well, she certainly had him thinking in that direction now. He'd tease and laugh no more this afternoon, but she'd wager he'd think of her all the more.

Simon was gone for several minutes. Agatha spent them eyeing his lemon ice. Regretfully, she decided that her hips did not need the extra padding and let the attendant take it away.

She was just beginning to become curious when Simon returned and gave her a cool smile before he took his seat once more.

"Is everything quite all right?"

"Of course." His cool smile remained, but it didn't reach his eyes. "Everything is fine."

It was truly beginning to get on her last nerve, that smile. Daring him to remain indifferent to her, she leaned forward on her elbows. Blast good manners, anyway. She was on a mission.

Reaching out with one hand, she stroked his coat sleeve. "I've always admired how well you look in blue. It brings out the color of your eyes."

Simon didn't respond beyond a polite nod, but she noticed that his throat bobbed forcefully. Excellent. She leaned slightly closer and dropped her voice.

"Simon? Do you know what I like you best in?"

He leaned closer to hear her and made a polite noise of inquiry, keeping that blasted cool indifference upon his face.

She slid her fingers down to stroke his wrist beneath his cuff. "I like you best in . . . me," she whispered.

He jumped as if she'd slapped him. No longer indifferent, she could see. His jaw was clenching furiously, and his eyes flashed darkly.

"Stop this immediately," he growled.

"Why? I've decided that I'd very much like to discuss what happened that night."

"Agatha—"

"There's no need to go all prudish now, Simon. If you

were willing to do what we did, you should be willing to speak of it."

"I—"

"One does have to wonder at your motives, it is true. But now that I understand you, I think there's all the more reason—"

"Agatha!"

His sharp remonstrance drew glances from the other patrons, and she noticed that his jaw tightened furiously. He grabbed her by the hand and towed her to the door and out to the street.

With one hand, he waved Harry forward with the carriage.

"Simon—"

"Go home, Agatha. I'll see you at supper."

Swiftly he bundled her into the carriage and signaled Harry to take her home. As the carriage clattered away, Agatha thrust her head from the window to see Simon turning away to walk down the street.

He didn't seem at all affected by her boldness. How disappointing. She'd thought that surely he would—

As she watched, Simon took a sharp detour, turning aside to plant his fist against a rubbish bin.

Agatha smiled and sat back onto the seat of the carriage. Perhaps not so indifferent, after all.

Agatha tied her wrapper with determined movements. The house was silent and dark. Some of the servants might still be up, but they wouldn't come to this part of the house unless rung for.

She hadn't seen Simon at supper after all. Jamie had pleaded weariness, so Agatha had taken her meal in her room once again.

It was time. She was going through with this.

She was fighting for her future child, and nothing would get in her way, not conscience, not nerves, not fear of Simon's rejection.

There wasn't much time left. No one would believe a

widow's child more than nine months after her husband's death. She wanted a baby, but not at the cost of her child being a known bastard.

She knew without asking that Simon would be very upset by her plan. His own childhood as an illegitimate had been so terrible. He would never forgive her for inflicting it on his child. She might lose him forever if he knew.

But then, she already had, hadn't she?

She leaned her head against her door for a moment, her hand on the knob. If she was to follow her new resolution not to lie to herself any longer, she must admit that her heart's longing to be with Simon again played a large part in her decision.

To see him all day, to speak with him, to sit across from him at meals was becoming more than she could bear. She was so unhappy that she thought she might throw back her head and scream from the pain of it.

Her bedchamber certainly had paid the price, for when she couldn't be sad anymore, she became angry.

Nellie hadn't said a word about the pillows ending the night across the room or the odd broken vase. Still, Agatha had noticed that the vase currently holding flowers on her night table was a cheap thing covered with irregular green glazing.

A veritable projectile waiting to happen.

But not tonight. No more helpless tears or childish rages. Tonight she would be in Simon's arms again.

Her hands had stilled their shaking and her breathing had evened. Agatha raised her head and opened her door.

She didn't knock on the door of the third bedchamber. Instead, she boldly walked in to find Simon lounging on his bed holding a book. This room was too small for a fireside sitting area, but it was all the warmer for it.

His eyes dark and unreadable, Simon slowly closed his book and sat up off the pillows.

"Agatha, you can't be here."

"Well, I am." Was that her voice, trembling and breathy?

"You must go."

She shook her head, not trusting her speech, and moved to untie her wrapper. If she could tempt him with her body, she might be able to make him forget his reservations.

In an instant, he was off the bed and standing before her. His hands closed over hers, stilling her in the act of undoing the knot. She closed her eyes and breathed him in. Cinnamon and warm, lovely man.

He stood close enough for her to feel the heat coming from his skin and she hungered to press herself close. He'd shed everything but his shirt and trousers. She could see his pulse pounding through his open collar and longed to press her lips against it.

"Don't send me away."

Blast. She sounded like a pleading child being sent to bed early. Then she damned her pride and tilted her head back to look into his beautiful eyes.

"Please, don't send me away. I miss you." She swallowed. All the way, now. "I want your touch."

A tremor went through him and his eyes darkened as he gazed down at her. Freeing one hand from his slackened grip, she raised her fingers to his face. Gently she traced the precious angles of his cheekbone and jaw.

She could only hope that her son would have those features, so that she might never go a day without seeing Simon in some small way.

Her heart hurt with her feelings for him. She couldn't hold the words in.

"I love you."

It was a mistake. She saw it as soon as the words left her lips. He had begun to lean toward her slightly, as if he couldn't help but kiss her. The words made him snap his head back as if she'd bitten him.

"You must go, damsel," he said grimly. "There's nothing for you here."

With one swift movement, he reached behind her to open the door, then he firmly thrust her out into the hall.

The door didn't slam—quite—but Agatha felt as though her heart had been trapped in the closing.

She'd obviously made a terrible error.

Next time she wouldn't stay so close to the door.

Simon leaned back against the door, one hand moving to rub away the tightness in his chest.

He'd been staring at the damn book for hours, seeing nothing but the memory of Agatha, naked on the rug, reaching for him with tenderness in her eyes.

And then as if he had conjured her from thin air she had appeared before him, offering herself and her love once more.

How much was a man to take? His hands still trembled from the sheer cost of tossing her from the room instead of onto his bed.

She had touched him, stroking his face with such tender longing that he had very nearly given in on the spot.

The thought crossed his mind that he could be with her again. She'd already been ruined and survived it, there was no worse he could do there. She knew and respected his duty, yet she chose to come to him herself.

Why shouldn't they snatch a moment of happiness from this unsolvable dilemma? She was an intelligent woman making a choice of her own free will, not some silly girl he had seduced.

Perhaps—

No.

He had sworn that he would never again endanger someone because of his position. If something happened to Agatha because of who he was, he would never be able to live with himself.

He rubbed his face and threw himself down on the bed, staring blindly up at the bed draperies. It was going to be a very long night.

Again. This time, she would use the advantage of surprise.

The clock in the hall chimed two in the morning as Agatha

silently opened Simon's door. She closed it behind her and crossed the room to the bed.

The fire still gave a glow, and she could see just well enough to make her heart speed up with the view.

Simon slept naked, with limbs outflung as if restless dreams kept him in motion all night. Even in relaxation, his chest and arms were roped in hard muscle that made delicious shadows and shapes by the dim firelight.

This time, her hands were sure as she untied her wrapper. The silk slid from her shoulders to puddle on the floor around her feet.

Now she was as naked as he. She reached to touch his shoulder. "Simon—"

He struck like a tiger, yanking her down so quickly her breath left her body in a gasp. Then she was pinned to the mattress by an arm across her throat and a knee in her stomach.

Oh, yes. He was definitely naked. The only thing between them was the tangled satin of the counterpane. She could feel his chest against hers and his breath on her face.

All of this would have been much more enjoyable had she herself been able to breathe.

Then the snarling predator above her focused on her face. "Agatha!"

He was off her as quickly as he'd been on her. Gratefully she inhaled as his powerful hands lifted her to her feet.

"Did I hurt you? Can you talk?"

A cough cleared the tightness in her throat. "I'm fine."

With a sharp exhalation of relief, Simon pulled her tightly to him, wrapping his arms around her.

Agatha relaxed into his hardness and his heat, wishing she could sink into his very skin. This was where she wanted to be. This was where she belonged.

Which was why she was so very surprised to find herself thrust firmly into the hall once more.

Unfortunately, this time she was quite thoroughly naked. As she scrambled for her room, she had only one thought.

This meant war.

. . .

Must he barricade the bloody door?

Simon paced desperately before the fire. His feet tangled in something silken. Her wrapper. He knelt swiftly and picked it up, prepared to throw it out after her damnably determined, adorably shapely, barely resistible rear as she ran back to her room.

His fist clenched in the soft fabric and her scent rose to him. Instead of tossing it through the door—or, better yet, into the coals—he raised it to his cheek.

Better he should keep it. Perhaps it would deter her from wandering about where she didn't belong.

So he went back to his cold bed, where the sheets now smelled ever so faintly of citrus and flowers. If he was lucky, he would dream of her and not wake too soon.

Chapter Twenty-one

The next morning, Agatha was dressed and downstairs before dawn. She leaned against the parlor wall, peeking into the front hall through the carefully narrow crack in the door.

She hadn't heard Simon come down yet, but he was leaving earlier every day for his mystery destination and she didn't want to miss him. He was going to hear her out this time, she swore it.

Her head tipped against the door frame quite on its own, and her eyelids trembled with the urge to close them. Behind her the sofa called her name. Its lure warred with the siren smell of bacon wafting from the breakfast room.

The conflict was almost the only thing that kept her awake.

The parlor door opened suddenly, and Agatha jerked upright. "I was only—!"

Pearson gazed inquiringly at her from his position just outside in the hall. "Will you be having breakfast now, madam?"

Agatha checked his eyebrows, but they were as level as could be. Apparently, skulking behind doors spying upon one's sham brother-in-law was perfectly acceptable.

"No breakfast for me yet, thank you. Has Mr. Applequist risen yet?"

"Yes, madam. Button went up not ten minutes ago."

"He rang for Button?"

"The master never rings for him in the morning, so Button has learned to anticipate him a bit."

This was apparently good form as well, for Pearson continued to keep his brows at sea level.

"Ah. Well, er, carry on, Pearson."

"Yes, madam." Pearson left, closing the door to the precise degree that it had stood before he had opened it.

Agatha returned to her vigil and was soon rewarded by the sound of Simon's familiar step on the stairs. He stopped just within her range of vision and gathered his hat and coat from Pearson.

He was wearing the blue coat that gave particular emphasis to his eyes. Agatha spared a moment to admire the picture of gentlemanly quality he made.

"Has Mrs. Applequist risen yet?"

"Mrs. Applequist has not yet sat down to breakfast."

One must admit, Pearson was good. It wasn't even a lie, strictly speaking.

Quickly Agatha slipped from the parlor. "Simon, I wish to speak to you."

He started and turned. "Agatha! Good lord, what are you doing about so early? I thought you'd—" He stopped and had the grace to flush a bit.

"You thought I'd have a nice lie-in after my little adventures last night?" She smiled sweetly at him.

He had grown to know her very well, for he backed away. "Now, damsel—"

"Simon Rain, you are a coward. A lily-livered, jelly-spined coward. You are not going to walk away from this conversation. You cannot thrust me naked from my own house."

Simon halted his backward sidle. "You are quite correct, damsel. It is time that we talked."

He gestured for her to precede him back into the parlor. She went, although she did watch from the corner of her eye to be sure he didn't make a break for his freedom.

She stopped and turned as he entered behind her. As he walked swiftly toward her, she opened her mouth to begin—

And he pulled her into his arms and swept his lips down

upon hers. Astonishment melted into joy as she gave in to his kiss. His hands pressed her hard to him, and his lips were demanding and fierce. It was an invasion of a kiss, and she was willingly conquered.

Her anger was gone and her knees were swiftly weakening when he finally raised his mouth from hers. She blinked up at him in dazed need as he dropped a swift peck upon her forehead.

Then he turned and strode from the house before she could blink.

Damn and blast. The thieving sneak.

Agatha rallied her senses and raced to follow him. She found Pearson waiting for her in the hall with her mantle and gloves.

"I thought perhaps you might wish a bit of breakfast after all, madam."

He serenely handed her a napkin-wrapped packet that smelled suspiciously like a bacon-egg-and-roll sandwich.

Agatha was delighted. "Pearson, if you weren't my grandfather's age, I'd marry you." She stood on tiptoe to peck his withered cheek.

"Yes, madam. I hear that a great deal."

"Why, Pearson! Was that a jest?"

"No, madam. Butlers are forbidden to jest. It is the law." He held the door open. "Mr. Applequist is now halfway down the block to your left, madam."

"Thank you, Pearson."

Quite encouraged with the thought of a new ally in her butler, Agatha set off behind Simon with a skip in her step and a mouthful of egg.

At first, Agatha's only intention was to chase after the rat-sneak-bastard and pin him down for a good neighbor-rousing row.

His stride was too long, however, and Agatha began to feel the effects of too much sedate city life. She decided to simply keep after him until he got to wherever he was going.

After several long blocks, he turned down a quiet street,

then climbed the steps of an unassuming little house. Agatha scurried to catch up.

He was admitted immediately and disappeared within. Agatha hesitated. She wanted to catch Simon, but if he was doing some shady spy activity, she didn't want to be responsible for his discovery.

Perhaps she'd best wait and see what was about first. Her burning curiosity had nothing to do with that decision, of course. Still, it was too bad she couldn't get a peek into the house. She eyed the windows on the ground floor, but the draperies were all drawn.

She would have done the same, if her private life were so visible from the street, but it made it very difficult to sneak.

A movement caught her eye. On the second floor, the window coverings were being pulled back by a very efficient-looking woman in a nurse's uniform. Quickly Agatha stepped within the shadow of the building.

The room was too high to see into and Agatha could hear nothing, for the window was still closed against the early-morning chill.

Blast. Well, he had to come out sooner or later.

She had just settled into a hopefully casual position next to the corner of the house when the front door opened. She ducked around the edging stones, then peered carefully back out. Wait a moment. Was she trying to catch him or not?

Catch him, of course. But if she didn't reveal herself, what fascinating Simon secrets might she find out?

Simon stood on the stoop with the nurse.

"I know you have high hopes, sir. I'll do my best with him."

"All I hope for is that he be himself again, Mrs. Neely."

"Poor lad. I've been saying his name to him every hour, just as you asked, and reading to him as well."

"I know, I couldn't ask for better care. Now we must simply wait."

"Yes, sir. Will you be coming back tomorrow?"

"I'll try."

Simon turned to go. His gaze flickered past Agatha's hiding place. She ducked back quickly. Had he seen her?

After a breathless moment, she looked again. Simon was several lengths down the block, walking with that particular feline grace of his.

With a sigh of relief, Agatha fell into step far behind him. Really, he was quite handsome from the rear. One of her favorite aspects, in fact. And it was a lovely day for a walk. Agatha set herself to enjoy her outing.

An hour later, she was no longer so enthused. Simon had led her a pretty race, up and down the streets of Mayfair and beyond.

She had no idea where she was, her feet were aching, and she was beginning to get very hungry. Pearson's delicious roll was a distant memory.

Now Simon was traveling through a merchants' district. Drapers and clothiers, mostly, with the occasional tempting restaurant. Determined, Agatha resisted. It wasn't easy.

The walks were becoming more crowded as the morning wore on, and Agatha began to have trouble keeping track of Simon's blue coat and black hat with its matching blue hatband.

Suddenly she could not see him at all. Where had he gone? Agatha risked discovery to climb a set of steps and scan the growing crowd.

Nothing. She had lost him again.

And this time she had lost herself as well.

Simon tucked several pound notes into the man's hand and shook it. Then he donned his new brown beaver hat, which went quite nicely with his new brown felt coat and set off toward the Liar's Club with a chuckle.

His pursuer was likely even now searching for his blue coat in the crowd. He knew he'd lost them this time. It had taken longer than he had thought. They had stuck to him like a parasite when he had tried to lose them through exhaustion, then confusion.

The coat change was the oldest trick in the book but one

of the best. The eye became accustomed to a certain thing,
such as a color, and began to follow the color alone. Change
the color, lose the tail.

He'd suspected a tail since he'd left Agatha's, for he'd
long ago developed an instinct for them. He was fairly sure
he knew who was responsible.

Damn, but Etheridge was a suspicious sort.

Whistling, Simon turned smartly into the club and clapped
a yawning Stubbs on the shoulder. Playing Ethelbert was giving him a lovely break from his usual morning climb.

"Morning, Mr. Ra—I mean, Mr. Applequist."

"Good morning, Stubbs. Out early today, aren't you? Is
Jackham about yet?"

"Yessir. He sent me out here to wait for you. He said it's
a doorman's job to stand by the door."

"Good man. What would we do without you?"

"Yessir. Thank you, sir."

Simon stepped into his club with fresh purpose today. He
had a new mission for some lucky Liar. It was time to get
the goods on Dalton Montmorency, the distinguished Lord
Etheridge and powerful member of the Royal Four, for the
man was still something of an unknown quotient.

Simon hated unknown quotients.

Agatha approached the doorway through which Simon had
disappeared. A young man of perhaps seventeen wearing
blue-and-silver livery waited by the door but made no motion
to open it for her.

There was no sign, not even the most discreet. The only
marking the double doors held at all was a stylized bird
carved on each. It had an outrageous tail whose shape rang
familiar in Agatha's mind.

"Oh! A lyrebird," she said out loud.

The boy turned to glance at the markings as well. "Is that
what it is, then? I thought it was only a pretty sort o' pheas-
ant." He turned back to her. "Do you need direction, miss?"

"I'd like to speak to Simon Rain," she said cautiously.

"You mean Mr. Jackham, don't you?"

"No, indeed I do mean Simon Rain."

He eyed her suspiciously. "What d'you want Mr. Rain for?"

Just then a gust blew the parting in her mantle wide and the young man's eyes focused on her figure.

"Blimey!" His smile became a bit familiar. "You must be come for a job. Why didn't you say so?" He leaned closer. "Is it better than the snake act?"

He seemed honestly interested. Well, there were only two possible answers to that question. Agatha gathered her cloak tighter and nodded gravely. "Significantly."

"Cor." He seemed breathless with wonder. He ogled her for a moment more, and Agatha could almost hear the gears clicking slowly into place. "I s'pose you want to talk to Mr. Rain, now."

"Yes, thank you."

With a rather courtly gesture, the young man opened the door for her and bowed her through it. He took her cloak with a sort of reverence and hung it on a row of gilded pegs. Then he cleared his throat.

"If you'll please wait here, I'll fetch the owner."

The owner? Not simply a chimneysweep-thief-spy, then.

Agatha had every intention of following him directly to Simon, but when she stuck her head through the door after the boy disappeared through it, she earned herself a growl from the largest man she had ever seen. He stood before a vast chopping block with a rather intimidating knife in one mighty fist and an even more intimidating glare in his eyes.

She backed out quickly, then irritably perused the room in which she had been left. There were tables of different types, some low and small, some larger and round, with chairs all around. Dining tables? No, cards.

A gaming hell? The room was large, with different areas delineated by the placement of furniture. Over there, a place for relaxation with large overstuffed chairs. On this side, game tables and billiards. On the far end of the long narrow room there was a raised dais framed by velvet curtains.

It was unmistakably a stage. Ah, the snake act. How did one perform an act with a snake?

" 'Scuse me, Mr. Jackham, Mr. Rain. There's a woman out front wants to speak to the owner." Stubbs leaned farther into the room, as if to impart a secret. "She's a right looker, sir. Built like a dream come true, if you take my meaning."

Jackham looked as if he willingly took Stubbs's meaning, but Simon held up one hand.

"Jackham, we've gone over this. No working girls in the club."

Stubbs shook his head. "Sorry, sir. I didn't tell you, she's got an act. Says it's 'sig-ni-fi-cant-ly' better than a snake act. Talks like a right toff, she does."

Jackham gazed pleadingly at Simon until he had to laugh. "Fine, then. See what she's got. But if you hire her, make sure she understands the house rules."

"Oh, I will." Jackham was out of his chair with more speed than Simon had seen in months. Apparently, a crippling limp was nothing compared to profit.

Waiting a moment to be sure Jackham wasn't coming right back, Simon stretched out his legs before him and crossed them at the ankle. A yawn caught him unaware.

He wasn't sleeping well, even on nights when Agatha wasn't sneaking into his room.

The old dreams came, as always. Dreams where he watched his men die, one by one, unable to help them, knowing he had sent them to their deaths.

Ren Porter was there as well. Eyes open but unseeing, he had reproached Simon in silence, a statue in the midst of his nightmare.

But he was long accustomed to those sleeping journeys of guilt. They'd been with him for years.

It was the damned erotic visions of Agatha that haunted him to wakefulness. The recurring theme was very simple. She came to him and he took her.

Again and again, night after night, in every way known to

man, and a few that he thought he might have made up from his own desperation.

Sometimes the act was rough and angry, his resentment at her power over him coming to the fore. Sometimes it was slow and languid, poignant enough to make him ache with loneliness when he awoke.

And he always awoke, damn it. Every damn time, just before he achieved his release. He'd be moving within her. She'd be crying out beneath him or above him, and he would be close, so damn close. . . .

Then he'd snap to consciousness with a painful wrench, throbbing and panting, and unfulfilled. Next came the hours of sleeplessness—aching, sweating alertness that sometimes lasted until dawn.

Any more of this torture and he'd soon find it difficult to walk.

He shook off the spell and the coming yawn and stood. After listening for the tread of footsteps in the hall for a moment, he placed his palm over a carved rosette on the mantel and pushed.

Beside him, a narrow slit appeared between the fireplace and the bookshelves. Stepping through quickly, Simon noted that he'd best not get too fond of Agatha's cook, or he'd never make it into the dusty passage that led to his office secreted in the attic above.

Feebles was just plain exasperated. He'd followed the lady for near two hours, only to end up outside the Liar's Club. He could have walked here in not more than half an hour.

He shambled up to Stubbs where the young doorman leaned against the wall.

"Women, eh?" Feebles shook his head in disgust.

"Don't I know it," Stubbs replied socially.

"Mr. Rain know she's in there?"

"O' course. Told him meself."

"All right then."

Feebles stuffed his hands back in his pockets and turned away.

" 'Keep your eye on the lady,' he says to me," he mimicked in Simon's tones. " 'The lady must be kept safe.' Ha! That lady knows her way around, all right."

The bloody Magician could have told him not to bother, could have told him they were playing some sort of catch-me-if-you-can game.

Grousing to himself, shuffling his feet, Feebles headed back to his post watching over the house on Carriage Square.

When the door from the kitchens opened, Agatha was thoroughly prepared to deflect Simon's anger about being followed with a few recriminations of her own.

The man who emerged proved to be a grizzled fellow with a pronounced limp, who eyed her as if she were a piece of fish displayed on the salt. Agatha shut her mouth with a snap and gazed back at him warily.

Had Simon sent him out in the hopes of frightening her away?

"Well, then, let's have a look at you." He twirled a finger in the air.

Deciding to keep her mouth shut until she knew what was about, Agatha spun obediently. When she returned to her position facing him, the fellow's expression was decidedly more approving.

"Is that all your own? No padding and such?"

Padding? The very idea! "I should say not!"

"No need to get all shirty about it. Man's got a right to know what he's dealing with."

To tell the truth, although the fellow seemed to like her looks, he didn't seem altogether stirred by them. Deciding that her virtue was in no immediate danger, Agatha relaxed. Besides, with that limp, she could easily outrun him if she chose.

Feeling better, she managed to smile at him. He blinked, then rubbed his hands together.

"Well, you're a pretty lass, just as Stubbs said. But I must warn you, house rules say no whoring. If that's what you're after, you can keep walking."

Whoring? *Whoring?* Her appalled silence must have spoken for her, for he nodded.

"Good, then. We understand each other. So, what have you got for me?"

Oh, dear. "Ah, well . . . what do you mean, precisely?"

"Good Lord, you do sound like a toff. Where'd you pick up that ladylike speech, m'girl?"

"Er, I've always been able to do it. You should hear me do the King."

His brow wrinkled. "Is that your act? Mimicking the mad King? Don't know if we've got much call for that sort of entertainment. . . ."

Suddenly it became clear to Agatha that this fellow thought she wanted to be hired to entertain. She opened her mouth to set him straight—then closed it.

What if she did manage to get hired on here? She'd like to see this place in operation and find out what Simon's role here was.

Her curiosity burned. She'd wondered about Simon's secret life, the one that kept him from her. Here was a chance to see it for herself.

Entertainment. Well, she couldn't possibly pass herself off as a singer, nor a musician. Her pianoforte lessons had come to a sudden halt at her mother's death. Her father had seemed to forget all about them, and Agatha had not reminded him.

She doubted very much if she knew any stories that would entertain a club full of gentlemen. They came here for drinking and cards and snake acts—

"Cards! I'm very good with cards."

The man scowled at her thoughtfully. "A dealer? Well, well, well. . . ."

Agatha hadn't thought about claiming to be a dealer. Did they actually hire someone to deal the cards? Why didn't the gentlemen simply take turns? Well, perhaps it kept things fair. . . .

"Oh, you want me to cheat for you!"

His eyes widened and for a moment she thought she'd offended him. But the twinkle of pure glee that entered those cold eyes told her that she'd found his weakness.

"Can you? Can you deal that well? Could you cheat the sorry sods?"

Could she cheat? Well, if there was one thing she was good at, it was cheating at cards. One didn't grow up in a primarily male household without gaining the upper hand in something.

"Would you like to try me out?"

The fellow had her at a table with a deck in her hand so quickly that the green felt blurred before her eyes.

"Vingt-et-un," he demanded.

She began to shuffle the cards. Deciding to show off a bit, she did it so quickly, the cards were a blur. Then again, sending them in an arc through the air from one hand to the other. That one was very impressive, of course, but it also gave her the chance to glimpse the undersides of the cards.

"Would you like a high card or a low one?"

"Give me a decent start, to get me betting, then make it bad."

She gave him an approving smile, for that was one of her favorite gambits as well. She dealt him a three, then hit him again, keeping track of the cards in her mind's eye, chatting all the while.

"Did you know that the inventor of the modern card deck originally intended them to be used for children only?" She had no idea if that was true, but the point was distraction, not education. "But when he gave them to the poor little tots, he found that they couldn't remember what all the cards were."

She leaned forward flirtatiously, and the fellow's eyebrows climbed a bit as he couldn't help sneaking a peek down her bodice. Heavens, men were so predictable.

While he was thusly occupied, she slipped him the very worst card possible from the bottom of her deck. He took it absently and added it to the others without glancing at it.

"How close are you to twenty-one, sir?"

He looked down. "Bloody hell!"

He spread the cards out on the felt. Agatha leaned to peer at them herself.

Hmm. Where in the world had that two come from? Obviously, she needed to practice. Still, it was a truly horrid batch in all. And he'd received it with a smile. Even now, he was having a hard time keeping his gaze on his terrible cards.

"Can you do it for a full table? Can you do it all night long? How about letting one fellow win for a bit, then letting the others catch up, then taking them all down at once?"

"Well, I shouldn't want to be too obvious. Perhaps after they've been in their cups for a bit?"

"Oh, you're a bright girl, you are. Do you have a bit of flash to wear? Something nice, that will give the place a touch of class. But low-cut, you know, take their minds off their cards?"

"Why, sir, I blush," she teased. "Are you telling me you weren't watching the cards the whole time?"

His face lit up. "That's the way! If you catch them looking, they'll never admit it, will they? Oh, you're a treasure." He stuck out his hand. "My name's Jackham. Welcome to the Liar's Club, Miss—"

Agatha's mind went a complete blank. Name, name, anyone's name—

"Nellie Berth!" She sent a mental apology to the little housemaid at Carriage Square. Surely it was a harmless loan.

"Well, Miss Berth, you're hired. Now, just so you'll know, the owner's got his standards. No whoring on the premises, like I said." He actually reddened a bit at that. "Not that I'm assuming anything, mind you. And not that your own time isn't your own, if you take my meaning. But while you're in the club, you're to be a lady at all times."

"I think I can manage," Agatha said dryly.

"Good girl. You can start tonight, but take it easy at first. Just keep the marks happy, and take a bit in here and there." He looked over his shoulder, then leaned closer. "Just one more thing."

Agatha leaned closer as well, although there wasn't a soul in the room with them.

"There'll be no cheating the boys in the back room. Not by the house, and not by you. Just you remember that. The marks stay out front, the Magician's boys stay in the back, and that's the way we like it."

Agatha nodded seriously, but her own gears were turning. The boys in the back room? Who was the Magician? Simon?

Good lord, the spy ring was concealed within a gaming hell? The Liar's Club. How absolutely twisted and divine.

As she donned her cloak and made her way to the street, waving politely at Mr. Jackham, Agatha realized that she had stumbled onto something that Simon did *not* want her to know.

Now, how was she to get home? Then she saw that the young doorman had returned to his post.

"Mr. Stubbs, might I trouble you to whistle down a hansom?"

The boy almost fell over his feet to do so for her. His piercing whistle rent the air, and a small carriage stopped almost immediately. She gave the driver her direction, then Stubbs handed her into her seat with reverence.

"I hopes you come back soon, miss."

Agatha smiled. "I shall be back this very eve."

"I'll spread the word, I will. If it ain't too bold, miss, could you tell me what you're wearin' tonight?"

It occurred to her that she had a truly serious problem. Oh, dear. What did a lady dealer in a gaming hell wear, anyway? "Something . . . um, tight?"

"Cor!" seemed all that he could manage at the prospect.

Agatha giggled as the carriage pulled away from the curb. It seemed she had another conquest. He was as enamored as Button, although for completely different reasons.

Button! Of course! If anyone could dress her for a night of employment in a gaming hell, Button could.

Chapter Twenty-two

"I don't understand, madam. A lady dealer in a gambling establishment? Why would you wish such a costume?"

Agatha sighed. She didn't think Button was being purposely obstructive, but he was wearing out her patience nonetheless.

"It's for . . . a bit of parlor theatre. A charade."

Button's eyes lit. Apparently she had stumbled upon his levering point.

"Theatre! Oh, madam, I know the very thing. Let me send to my friend at the theatre. I myself had my start as a dresser on Drury Lane, you know," he said modestly. "That isn't normally the thing to tell one's employer, of course, but I believe I can trust you, madam."

"Indeed." Agatha grinned. Her own little platoon simply got more interesting, didn't it? A chimneysweep-thief-spy, a jesting butler, and a costume-mad valet.

Worlds to conquer, oh my.

"I am all yours, Button. Have at."

That evening, Simon stretched at his desk, rolling his head to ease the kinks in his neck. The clock on the shelf said nine, but that couldn't be right, could it?

Oh, hell. Agatha would likely be pacing a hole through

the carpet by now. It was an oddly satisfying notion, the thought of someone waiting for him. Comforting. Of course, having her furious at him for his trick this morning wasn't part of that cozy little fantasy.

Deciding that he ought to squelch that notion within himself as soon as possible, Simon decided not to go home.

At this point of the night Jackham was most likely on the floor watching the marks spend their money. Simon decided to risk the office entry.

He wasn't in the mood to go through the window and walk the narrow ledge to the secret entry over the kitchens. It was far too wet out tonight.

Making his way soundlessly through the dark passage to his exit by the fireplace, Simon listened. Not a sound came from the other side of the wall.

He eased the slot open just a fraction of an inch, then froze. There was light in Jackham's office. Miserly Jackham never burned oil if he wasn't using it.

But this wasn't a lamp. The light was dim and flickering. Like a candle.

Jackham didn't use candles. He considered them wasteful and dangerous. So who was in Jackham's office?

The candle went out.

In a flash, Simon was out of his passage, crouching low and ready to strike.

He listened for any rustling or breathing that would tell him where the intruder was. Then he straightened. Damn. He'd missed whoever it had been.

He moved swiftly and silently to the door. The candle had likely been blown out as they left, for the scent of beeswax and burnt wick was strongest near the door.

Then another scent twined its way through the air. A floral perfume with a lemony undertone. An aroma he knew very well.

Agatha?

Simon bolted from the dark room without a thought to being seen. He followed his nose down the short hallway to the Liar's Chamber, where the real work was done.

She wasn't there, but her scent lingered among the tobacco smoke, and her obvious presence lingered in the bemused smiles of his Liars.

Cherchez la femme. Too bloody right.

How had she gotten in? What filthy, lying, manipulative trick could she have pulled to have infiltrated his world?

Simon continued, dashing through the kitchen where he glared at the silly grin on the face of Kurt the Cook—who wasn't called that because he was a chef, but because he was the deadliest knife man in England.

She had charmed *Kurt*?

Good lord. Was she insane?

Simon paused before he entered the gaming room. He never made appearances there, for he didn't want to be known. It was doubly dangerous now, for some of the over-privileged young men who frequented his club had been among his new circle as Mortimer and Ethelbert.

Well, Ethelbert it was then. Simon straightened his coat and smoothed it. He was still dressed for day, but that wasn't as bad form as showing up wrinkled. He tilted his hat arrogantly upon his head and strode through the kitchen doors.

No one noticed. They were all gathered around the Vingt-et-un table, three men thick. As not that many could play at once, there was either a superb winning streak going on or some other distraction.

Quickly he moved to the door to hand his hat to Stubbs.

"Mr. R—"

"Applequist, Stubbs, Applequist. Where is she?"

"Oh, Miss Berth?"

"Who?"

"Nellie Berth, our new dealer. Didn't Mr. Jackham tell you, sir? It's a good idea, ain't it? A woman dealer's nearly as good as whores, when she looks like that one."

Simon realized it was the name of Agatha's maid. At least the little lunatic had the presence of mind to use an alias.

But the risk she was running was enormous. These men were some of the same ones she had been dining and dancing with for weeks. Surely someone was going to remember her.

Then he drew up to the table, at least as close as he was able. He was tall enough to see over the heads of the others.

Simon felt as if someone had punched him in the stomach.

For at the table before him, painted and plumed, dressed in elegant but very daring feathers and silk, flirting with thirty men at once, was the very essence of a successful woman of the demimonde. A radiant, painted creature. A creature for fantasy and passion.

A creature for hire.

He stood tall and waited for her teasing gaze to wander up. She leaned toward the player who was winning, sent him a slow smile, and stroked the edge of her deck carelessly down her throat.

The man almost fell down that magnificent bosom, he ogled so. Simon had the almost irresistible urge to smack the back of the man's head. In the meantime, Simon was fairly sure that Agatha had slipped a card from the bottom of the deck.

Cheating. Why was he not surprised?

Then she saw him. She started ever so slightly. It was difficult to tell under the paint, but Simon thought she paled a bit. She should be very concerned, for he was quite positive that he had never been so coldly furious in his life.

Then she boldly winked at him and returned to her game.

"Ah, sir." Jackham was at his elbow. "I see you've discovered our newest treasure. Care for a game?"

Jackham was being careful. He'd never seen Simon on the floor before and obviously didn't know quite what to do about it.

"The name's Ethelbert Applequist, my good man," Simon drawled, never taking his eyes off Agatha. "She's very ... interesting. Wherever did you find her?"

"Showed up this afternoon, just after—about the same time as the owner. My doorman came in to tell me he had another act for us."

Bloody hell. She'd been the one following him all along. He'd underestimated her yet again.

"So what was this lady doing in your office, sir?" Simon kept his voice quiet.

"Oh, fetching a fresh deck. A player had bent a card."

Simon couldn't even castigate Jackham for his gullibility. Not when he himself had fallen for her charms again and again.

Jackham continued to gaze at Agatha with a besotted grin, as if he couldn't decide whether to pat her on the head or hire her for a night. They were all goners—Jackham, Stubbs, Kurt.

Simon wanted to drag her out of the club by the hair. He wanted to drop her into the river, but he rather thought his own men might string him up before they'd allow it.

Well, her circle of protectors wouldn't be there forever. Sooner or later, he was going to get her alone.

And then he was going to make her regret her little adventure.

The night had both dragged and flown by after Simon had come to her table. The look on his handsome face had been almost terrifying, until she had decided he was teasing her.

At least, she hoped he'd been teasing her. How angry could he be, really? After all, she had only followed him.

And lied to get in.

And dressed herself up as a soiled dove. Albeit a very expensive one.

Too late, she remembered Jamie's reaction one day long ago. She had followed him to his secret hideout in a giant tree by the brook. He'd been furious to see her, giggling and teasing him, and his fury had lasted for weeks.

It seemed that the appeal of a secret place was in its secrecy. When someone else knew about it, and knew they could find you there at any time, the joy was gone.

Like the ruins, forever lost to her by Reginald's presence for just an hour.

But Simon wasn't a child. This wasn't a secret castle.

Many people came here every day. It couldn't possibly be considered the same.

Could it?

The last of the players had finally left—she couldn't find it in her heart to call those dear boys "marks"—and Jackham had counted up the house take with unrelenting glee. Apparently, honest money wasn't quite as lovely as cheated money.

Agatha was exhausted. Her face hurt from smiling so, and the torturous corset that Button had laced her into was cutting deeply into her flesh. She wanted to leave, but Jackham had told her the owner wanted to talk to her.

Well, she wanted to talk to him as well.

Stubbs was roaming through the gaming room, yawning and sweeping the floor with dubious aptitude. Finally, he gave up and joined Kurt to clean up in the kitchen.

Agatha wandered over to the stage. Stubbs had finally described the snake act. Now she had a mental image of a scantily dressed woman dancing with a giant snake draped over her outstretched arms like a garland. Oh, surely not.

She was tapping one finger on her lips, considering the possibilities, when Simon approached her. She glanced over her shoulder at him, then turned back to the stage.

"I wonder," she mused, "was it a very large snake?"

"Oh, yes," Simon answered easily. "At least ten feet long. I'd have thought the poor woman could hardly lift it." He smiled at the memory, and Agatha wanted to hit him. "It was really quite a show."

"I'll be sure to stop by next time." Aware that she was snarling, Agatha smoothed her temper.

"Nearly as enjoyable as the one you put on tonight. Tell me, did it once occur to you that you might be recognized as the Widow Applequist?"

"*You* scarcely recognized me, yet you've seen considerably more of me than they have." That hadn't come out quite the way she had meant it to. She turned to face him, chin high. "So you have another secret."

"So you followed me. You're very good at tailing."

"Oh, Simon, you didn't really think that coat change was

going to work, did you? No one's passed that one over on me since I was six. I know to watch the person, not the clothing."

"So you had an early start in your unconventional education."

"As did you. Chimneysweep, thief, spy. Now you run a gaming hell."

"Ah, own, actually. Jackham does the running for me. And it's not a gaming hell, it's a gentlemen's club."

"Indeed. The Liar's Club. In that case, all men must qualify for membership."

"If it were that easy, I'm sure many women would join as well."

Dangerous territory. Time to change the subject. "In your position, wouldn't it be awkward to run afoul of the law?"

He shrugged. "There is nothing illegal about cards and spirits." He gave her a wicked smile. "Or dancing with snakes."

"No," Agatha said, eyeing him thoughtfully. "All women dance with snakes sooner or later, do they not?"

He slapped his hand over his chest. "Ouch! A direct hit."

Then he stepped closer and she could see the fierce light in his eyes. Ah. She'd ruined his tree house, after all.

"I'm sorry I spoiled your little spy club for you, Simon. I never dreamed you took such boyish delight in secrets."

"Is that why you think I'm angry, because you spoiled my secret?"

"Of course. It's rather childish of you, in my opin—"

Simon lost his renowned control at that. He reached for her, grasping her shoulders to pull her closer. "You are unbelievable! You disobey orders and escape safety, wander the streets of London alone, dress up as a courtesan, and parade yourself in front of thirty men who might recognize you at any moment—risking that pretty little neck in what I can only see as an impulsive stunt—and *you think I'm angry about my 'little secret'*?" He couldn't believe it. She'd actually reduced him to yelling.

"Oh . . . that," she muttered.

Simon desperately reined in his temper. "Precisely *that*. What in the bloody hell did you think you were doing?"

Slowly Agatha raised a brow and placed her hands on her hips. "Don't take that tone with me, Simon Rain. I am my own woman, remember?"

"You are your own worst enemy, you thoughtless little maniac!"

"You have no right to issue orders to me. You aren't my husband! You aren't my brother, or my father, or even my lover, as you made so clear last night!"

She was right. He was a cipher, nothing but a trumped-up Cheapside street rat infected with danger all around him. He was no one to her at all.

He absolutely couldn't bear to hear her say it.

With a single step forward, he grasped her shoulders to pull her close and stop her words with his mouth.

She was sweet and hot and everything he had ever wanted. With answering passion she pressed against him, but it was not close enough.

He maneuvered her back a few steps until he brought her up against the billiard table. Slipping his hands down to her buttocks, he squeezed those luscious hillocks for one self-indulgent moment before lifting her to sit on the edge of the frame.

She was higher now, high enough for him to dive headfirst into her bosom the way every man in the club had been dying to all night.

He couldn't keep his hands still. Her neck, her shoulders, the exposed tops of her breasts drove him mad with their softness. She was a fantasy creature of silken-wrapped stubbornness, and he couldn't get enough.

Her hands were fisted in his hair, and the impassioned tugging was sweet pain. Heat and softness and breathless moans of need were all he was aware of.

Until Jackham walked in.

"Here, you! I told you no whoring on the premises," he barked.

Simon jerked his mouth from Agatha's in dismay.

"Ah—sorry, sir, didn't see it was you." Flustered, Jackham turned on his heel and left them alone.

Agatha giggled, soaring on the joy of having Simon in her arms again. The look on Mr. Jackham's face had rivaled Pearson's for trenchant disapproval.

She raised one hand to stroke Simon's face. "Now where were we?"

But the damage was done. Simon gathered the tatters of his self-control and took a step away from temptation. "I'm sorry, damsel. That was unforgivable of me."

Agatha puffed a sigh of exasperation. "Simon, the only thing I object to is the fact that you aren't kissing me any longer."

The cold resolution in his eyes surprised her. Obviously, she was simply going to have to prove to him that between the two of them were no boundaries, but only love.

But he wouldn't listen. He lifted her down to her feet and silently adjusted her neckline with all the passion of a nursemaid. Then he walked to the door to gather her wrap and tell Stubbs to call a hack.

The streets were nearly silent so late in the night, and they were home in a very short time. Simon helped her from the carriage into the dripping night and silently walked her to the door.

Pearson said not a word as he took their outerwear, but Agatha thought she could see sympathy in his piercing eyes.

"Wash that paint off your face and go to bed, damsel."

"I think we should talk about what—"

"We should not talk about it. We should forget it ever happened. It will never happen again."

The words were too painful. "Don't say never, Simon. Please," she whispered.

"Agatha, we have no future."

She nodded. "I understand that. I only ask for the present with you. What we began the night Jamie came home, we have never finished. You taught me what passion was that night, Simon."

He shook his head, a quick violent motion. "I only taught you pain."

"I was curious about that, I admit. What was all the fuss and fury about? So I asked Sarah Cook, and she explained that it won't be like that again."

"It won't happen at all."

"That isn't fair, you realize. I shall go all my life wondering what should have been, in your arms."

Is that what would happen? He had taken from her and given nothing. Did he owe to her the real pleasure they could have shared?

Hell. She was in his head, twisting his thoughts again. "I know what I'm doing, Agatha."

She tilted her head, narrowing her eyes at him. "I don't think you know any such thing. I think you are a coward, Simon Rain. Well, I'm not. And I'm not done with this."

"You are for tonight." He pointed to the stairs. "Up. *Now.* I've first watch, so there's no use sneaking into my room this night."

She gazed at him in silence for a moment, then turned to climb the stairs. With a sick relief, Simon walked to the parlor.

After building a small fire against the chill, he flopped into a chair and stared morosely at the flames. He was a worthless coward indeed, because in spite of the danger he might put her in, all he really wanted was to follow her up those stairs and into her bed.

Her room was cold and damp in the deepest hour of the morning, for she'd left her windows wide. She'd hoped the early ringing of the tower bells would rouse her, and they had.

Shivering, she pulled her wrapper around her. Nellie must have returned it after finding it in Simon's room. What did the servants think of all this, with identical twin masters and a mysterious brother coming home in the night?

They probably quite rightly thought it all the most hideous

blarney. She only hoped they'd keep their opinions to themselves.

There were no servants about to see her make yet another journey down the hall to the third bedchamber. There was no light, but Agatha moved confidently in the darkness.

Simon may think her impulsive, but she had planned ahead enough to clear the hall of impediments the day before she began night maneuvers.

She'd oiled the hinges of Simon's door as well as her own, and stashed a spare wrapper in a cupboard just outside it. She didn't relish another nude dash to her room, thank you very much.

Simon had been up late and was likely sleeping deeply. She was sure she had covered every possible contingency. There would never be a better opportunity.

His room was as dark as the hall, but she had taken a moment while Button prepared her costume to count the steps it required to move from the doorway to Simon's bedside.

Counting silently, she finished just as the bedskirt brushed her ankles. With slow, controlled movements, she dropped her wrapper to the floor and lifted the counterpane.

The mattress rustled slightly as she inched her way beneath the covers. She could hear Simon's breathing just inches away. Hopefully her feet were not so cold that he'd wake before she reached her goal.

Success. His body was burning against her air-cooled skin, and for just a moment she held still, allowing herself to warm and soften to his heat like candle wax held too close to the fire.

Then she made her move.

Ever so slowly, she stroked her fingertips from one outflung manly wrist down to the tender inside of one elbow. His skin was smooth, with a different texture from her own.

Touching him was all new somehow. Perhaps because the dark enveloped them, making her senses focus on even this slight contact. Perhaps because he was oblivious to her attentions, not watching her every move with a hungry gaze as he had the first time.

Gaining courage as Simon continued to sleep on, Agatha began to trace the muscular hills and dales of his shoulder and chest.

So hard. So different from her.

His warmth spread to her and she carefully snuggled closer. Laying her head gingerly on his shoulder, she pressed her palm over the rippled contours and the patch of wiry hair that crested his chest from flat male nipple to nipple.

Her heart pounded in delicious anxiety. It was somehow illicitly thrilling to stroke him unawares. There was a word for such things.

Erotic.

She'd never truly understood that word before. Probably because she wasn't supposed to know it at all. But this dance of caresses and darkness was undeniably erotic.

If only she could see him as well. She daren't light a candle, and she did not want to stop, so she pulled from her mind the indelible memory of the first time they had met.

Ready for his bath that day, he had seemed the finest possible picture of a man. He had taken her very breath away even then.

Now she knew the soul inside her Simon, the strength and the selflessness, the past pain and heroic loneliness. Indeed, the dazzling outside of him seemed the only fitting wrapping for the man inside.

She moved still closer, pressing her bare breasts to his ribs and trapping one hard leg under her thigh.

He moved then, but without the striking intensity of last night. This time, he shifted his leg lazily under hers until her inner thigh pressed upward into most interesting territory.

He was rigid beneath her knee. Agatha's eyes widened and she bit her lip. There was no point in becoming faint-hearted now.

Her hand slid down past his stomach, trailing down a subtle path of hair until her fingers contacted another growth of springy fleece.

Oh my. Interesting territory indeed. She hesitated. Should she take him into her hand? She knew nothing about a man's organ, despite her previous intimate acquaintance with Simon's. What would he like her to do next?

Chapter Twenty-three

Simon was floating in a fantasy of warmth and wicked pleasure. It was his best Naked Agatha dream yet. He could even detect her scent and feel the softness of her nest against his hip as she snuggled close.

He turned into her silken haven and wrapped her in his arms. Her lovely breasts melted against his chest except for the rigid jewels of her nipples.

Long fragrant tresses fell against his cheeks as he pulled her up over him to bring her mouth to his. She tasted of tea and honey and Agatha.

Rolling to his back, he felt her soft thighs embrace his hips. He wanted to plunge himself within her, to find her sanctuary of gentleness and warmth. He slid his hands from her waist to cup her luscious rear and—

He really *was* cupping her luscious rear!

Agatha was a little disappointed when Simon froze beneath her, his hands going hard on her bottom.

"Agatha, what are you doing here?"

His voice was thick with lust and confusion. If she was to be fair, she should back off now and try to convince him with her words that they should be together.

But her own escalated arousal desperately cried out for more. And words hadn't worked very well before.

With a mere tilt of her hips, she slid his thick shaft into position, poised at the verge of her cleft.

"Agatha—"

She stopped his protest with an open kiss, thrusting her tongue in to battle his in a hot sortie. His objection died away. His hands tightened on her flesh and he gave a roll of his hips that told her he would dispute no more.

Prepared for the pain, Agatha drove herself down on him in one fatal plunge.

Pleasure exploded through her, driving the breath from her lungs in an astonished gasp. Oh, *again*.

Instinctively she rose on her knees, then impaled herself upon him once more. The excitement burst over her again, and this time Simon groaned aloud with it as well.

With his hands urging her on, Agatha set a steady pace of rising and falling that soon took on a life of its own.

Her body was a wild thing, spurred by animal need, while her mind was lost, tossed by the waves of exquisite sensation. Her entire consciousness centered about that one point of delicious friction. Swiftly she rose high, leaving him until they almost parted. Slowly she descended, savoring every inch of him until he filled her deeply, cleaving her with sweet aching pleasure.

She began to move faster, driven by the growing craving within her. Suddenly Simon cried out beneath her, arching his body and bucking deeply into her.

He swelled and throbbed inside her, expanding her with a last erotic spasm. A wordless sound of ecstasy was ripped from her own throat as she shattered into a thousand bright shards of rapture.

When he had control of himself again, Simon eased his fierce grip on Agatha's bottom. He hoped he hadn't left marks on her skin, for he had not been in command of his actions in the slightest.

She lay panting upon him, her hair trailing down his neck, her hands gripping his shoulders.

"Shh," he soothed, although he could scarcely breathe himself. She shuddered still, trembling from the power of her orgasm. "You'll be all right in a moment," he whispered.

"What—what was that?"

Her astonishment made him want to laugh, but he didn't wish to mock her innocence.

Morning was about to break, and silvery light had begun to seep into the room. She'd timed her attack perfectly. He'd always been a morning man.

"That was the usual result of making love," he told her.

She raised her head and blinked at him through the damp strands of her hair.

"*That* happens to everyone?"

"Well, honestly . . . no. Not to everyone." Not to him, either, not like this. He'd been dazed by the strength of it.

Of course, it had been a long time for him.

Less than a week, whispered reality.

She'd sprung it on him, he argued. He'd been taken by surprise.

Admit it. In your life you've never before given yourself body and soul.

"Oh, very well," he muttered.

Agatha rolled to his side, leaving one arm and one leg draped over him. Her skin clung to his damply, and her sweet womanly scent was intoxicating, mingled with that of their lovemaking.

He liked it a great deal.

"What did you say?" She'd regained her breath, but still lay limply against him, skin to skin.

Her unconscious lack of modesty was appealing in its innocence. He was nude—therefore, so was she. There was no prim show of covering up what he had already seen and touched.

For all her skill at lying, she was as honest a woman as he'd ever known. No halves for Agatha. Only full-strength loyalty and devotion would do.

"I can't give you any tomorrows," he blurted.

"I know," she whispered.

He felt her lips press to his shoulder. She was reassuring *him*. His throat tightened.

"You are the most peculiar creature, Agatha."

"Is that bad? Or is it another way of saying I'm unique?"

"Oh, unique does not begin to cover it." He realized that he was stroking her hair and almost stopped. But he continued. God, he was so tired of resisting her. So bloody damned tired of fighting his heart.

Gently he rolled with her until she lay on her back, looking up at him. Tracing her beloved features with his fingertips, he gazed down on her solemnly.

"I want to be with you for as long as is allowed us," he said. "When our time is done, we must both walk away."

She nodded, her eyes filling.

"No tears now and no tears later. Can you do that, damsel? Can you let me go when the time comes?"

"I know I cannot compete with her." Her soft voice was resigned.

"Who?"

"England."

"Oh, sweetness, it isn't that I love her more than you. But you are strong. You can get on without me. She cannot."

Her eyes went wide, her expression stunned.

"Agatha? What is it?"

"You love me?"

He had never told her. Too afraid, too cowardly to say the words. If he told her, he might not be able to let her go.

He opened his mouth, but she brushed her fingertips across his lips, silencing him.

"No. Perhaps it is best if you don't."

She freed both hands and held his face between her soft palms, gazing up at him.

"But *I* am free to speak my heart. I love you."

She was braver than he. He looked away. "Love is a great risk, Agatha."

"You are not a risk."

"How can you know that?"

"You came back."

"Only to leave you again."

She shook her head. "Being torn from me is not the same as leaving me."

He kissed each eye in turn, feeling and tasting the faint trace of tears. "I'm glad I returned to you. Although I shouldn't be dishonoring you this way."

She snorted. "Simon, I practically ravished you."

He grinned. "I know. I feel so cheap."

"There is nothing cheap about you." She reached up to stroke his damp hair from his brow. "Darling man, you deserve the finest of this world."

He didn't say anything for a moment. Then he rolled back to lie beside her, staring up at the canopy.

"I really am merely a bastard chimneysweep, you know."

"Yes, I know."

And the hell of it was, he knew she truly didn't care. So he told her everything. Everything he hadn't told before, to anyone.

He told her how he grew up, often cold and usually hungry. How his mother had barely fended for her own survival. How she had sent him out on his own, unable to face his growing understanding of how she earned her way.

As a boy, he'd become a chimneysweep to support himself, but the pay was small, when he was paid at all. He'd spent many a cold night wandering the streets in his efforts to stay warm.

When he'd strayed into a wealthier neighborhood one evening to poke through their rubbish, he'd climbed nimbly to a rooftop to crouch next to a wide chimney for warmth. After he had slept for a time, a noise had awoken him and he'd spied something odd going on at a neighboring house.

He'd crept closer and heard a heatedly whispered discussion of who would be going off the roof to fetch the little boy from the nursery, the third window from the left.

Realizing that there was a kidnapping in progress, Simon almost decided that it wasn't any of his business. Then he'd thought about the little boy and how the child's life was so good, so warm and full of food and love, and how easily it could turn into a life such as his own.

So slipping down his own roof edge, he'd jumped from one ledge to the next, ledges that would never have supported an adult. He'd slipped into a neighboring room and seen the sleeping nursemaid.

He'd tried to wake her, but she was sleeping unnaturally deeply. Creeping into the child's room, he'd woken the little boy and kept him from being frightened by pretending to have come to play hide-and-go-seek with him.

He'd challenged the five-year-old with all the scorn of an older child that he could not stay totally quiet and hidden. The sturdy little fellow had declared that he could so hide quietly, and he could prove it.

Simon had heard the man working at the window and had swiftly stuffed the boy into a trunk in the nursemaid's room.

Then he had run screaming down the hall, "Fire! Fire!" until he had roused the house.

At first, they had not believed his story. When they'd discovered that the little boy was indeed missing, Simon had feared for his own safety for a moment. Especially when he'd shown them the trunk and it was empty.

They were all around, threatening him, then each other, so loudly that they hadn't noticed the little boy coming between their legs to reach Simon until the child had loudly stated that he wasn't an idiot, and that he wasn't likely to hide where the seeker put him, was he?

Then came a yell from outside. The entire company looked out the window to see the broken body of a man lying in the street, a man who must have slipped on the icy ledge when he'd heard the outcry of "Fire!" from inside the house.

Impressed by the young chimneysweep's wit and presence of mind, the master of the house had taken Simon from the streets and put him in school.

And when Nathaniel, the boy whom Simon had rescued, rejected his father's path and turned to a life of less responsible pursuits, the father took an interest in Simon and brought him into the family business.

For the Old Man had been the spymaster of a royal network of intelligence. At first, he had used Simon simply as a courier, then as reconnaissance—and a bit of acquisition when needed—then more deeply undercover.

Finally, Simon had taken his place as spymaster of a group of thieves and scouts called the Liar's Club.

Agatha listened, entranced by the tale and the way Simon's voice took on a wry fondness when he spoke of his mentor.

"You loved him as a father."

"Perhaps. I was very alone after the death of my mother. But he did not love me. I was a tool of his creation. A weapon to aim at the enemies of England. What happened to the man in me was not his concern."

She was uncomfortably aware that she had thought much the same thing about him in the beginning. A tool to hone for her purpose of finding James.

Why should James and his happiness be of more importance than that of the simple chimneysweep she had first thought Simon to be? She had never thought of herself as a snob. It was humbling to find the flaw within herself.

"You loved him. And you love the Liars."

"Perhaps, but I don't love what they have cost me."

"What have they cost you?"

He gazed at her, his eyes full of dark depths. "You. A life with you, out in the open. You would have no protection as my wife."

"Would I not be protected by the Crown?"

He shook his head as he twisted a strand of her hair around one finger. "We Liars are expendable, like kites. To be cut from our strings should we fly too deeply into the storm."

Agatha rolled to her stomach to face him fully. "I wish I could be a Liar."

A smile lifted one corner of his mouth. "You're a lady."

"I'm a woman."

"Too bloody right. But you were meant for better things than what I could give you."

Agatha snorted. "What do you see me someday as? Another Lady Winchell? All scrawny fashion sense and cynicism? Betraying my husband under his very nose? Throwing endless boring parties attended by useless boring people?"

"Well, when you put it like that, I don't know how you can resist the prospect." He tugged her closer and she came, bonelessly adapting her body to his. He loved the way they fit together. "I thought you said you liked London."

"I like you. I like the excitement of working with you. I even like the club. But the idea of being some gentleman's ornament leaves me cold."

He hated it, but he had to say it. "Etheridge wouldn't treat you that way."

She lifted her head and stared at him. Then she pressed her lips to his shoulder again—and bit him.

He retaliated with a tickle attack on her ribs that left her giggling helplessly, her head hanging off the bed, hands weakly fending him off.

When he'd pulled her back into his arms, she used his chest to dry the tears that laughter had left on her face.

"Simon, do me the favor of staying out of my love life. If I want to marry someday, I'll do the choosing."

"But you will marry, won't you?"

She gave a frustrated feline growl. "Simon, leave it. My future is quite secure. You've no need to worry."

"You shouldn't be alone. You were made to be loved."

She was still for a moment. Then she whispered softly, "That may very well be the nicest thing anyone has ever said to me."

He held her in silence after that, as they listened to the city awakening outside. The servants would be stirring downstairs by now. Agatha knew she should go back to her room.

She should, yet she stayed, thinking about their pasts and how they had come from such different worlds to meet here on Carriage Square.

And what were they now? Lovers, with the future an uneasy subject between them.

"You should go," he said finally.

"Definitely."

"One kiss," he demanded.

Carefully, aware of the fragility of what they had begun this night, they kissed.

Simon ached to keep her there. To close out the world and stay in bed for days, drinking her in.

The power and the potential of what might lay before them both humbled him and devastated him that it could never be. As he ran both hands down her neck and over her shoulders, he made a silent vow to her that she would always know how beautiful and precious she was when he made love to her.

Then she was gone, slipping away with a smile that made him hurt inside. And he was alone.

Of course.

That morning, the tension over the breakfast table was thick. Simon was very aware of Agatha seated at the end of the table, but he couldn't look at her for fear of betraying his need to steal her away to someplace safe and very, very private.

When James entered late and plopped into the chair opposite him with an insouciant, "Good morning," Simon's frayed temper snapped.

"Finally up, layabed? What sloth. I can't believe I ever thought you were qualified to take over the club."

James stopped with a forkful of eggs an inch from his open mouth. "What did I do?"

Simon sat back and folded his arms. "You let her out of the house yesterday."

James shrugged defensively. "She was gone before I woke. Hell, she was gone before the sun awoke."

Agatha broke in, her expression apologetic. "I'm sorry I worried you, Jamie—"

"I wasn't worried. Pearson told me she was with you, Simon."

"But she wasn't *with* me. She was tailing me."

Agatha made an exasperated noise. "Am I not here?"

Simon didn't look at her.

James grinned. "She's good, isn't she?"

"Not good enough to keep herself out of danger."

"I must not be here. How annoying." Agatha put down her fork.

"There's no need to get your knickers in a twist, Simon. Feebles was right behind her."

Agatha leaned forward. "What? What's a Feebles?"

Simon ignored her question. "Feebles is a courier, not a bodyguard."

"He's pretty good with a knife in a pinch."

"Street fighting. He'd go down quickly against trained men."

Agatha was looking from one man to the other in confusion. "Wait, do you mean to say that someone was following *me*?"

James had lost his smile and was eyeing Simon narrowly. "Any of us could go down against trained men, Simon. Even you."

"The point is, James, that you didn't keep her—"

A piercing whistle cut the air, and both men turned in surprise. Agatha removed her two fingers from her mouth and smiled sweetly.

"Hello. I am Agatha Cunnington, and this is my house. If you must pretend I don't exist, you may go elsewhere to have this discussion. *Without* my cook." Her smile turned slightly feral. "Is that perfectly clear?"

"Of course, Agatha."

"Sorry, Aggie."

"Thank you. Now, I would like to know why I was followed by a Feebles."

James shrugged. "He's a Liar, assigned to watch the house. I thought you knew."

"How would I know that? Do I pluck knowledge from the thin air like a mystic?"

She turned to Simon. Her gaze was fond, but annoyed all the same. "Simon, is there anything else I should know?"

"Feebles is the day man. Kurt is night watch."

"Kurt? The lovely cook from the club?"

James sputtered. "You took her to the club?"

Simon tilted his head and eyed James for a moment. "My dear fellow, your sister not only followed me to the club, she gained entry without my knowledge, then persuaded Jackham to give her a job *and* the keys to his office."

Awestruck, James turned to his sister. "You didn't?"

Instead of showing any sign of remorse, Agatha looked positively smug. "I did."

A look of profound admiration crossed James's face. "Damn." He leaned closer to Agatha and whispered, "What did Simon do?"

"He kissed me."

Simon closed his eyes and dropped his face into his hands. Hell. "Agatha, why do you never lie when you should?"

James sniffed. "Aggie would never lie to me, would you, Aggie?"

"Not unless I had a very good reason," she assured him, patting his hand.

Suddenly James did not seem quite so confident. Simon decided to save him. "James, today we are going over every moment of the evening when you were captured."

Apparently breakfast no longer appealed to his friend, for James slowly put down his fork. "I rather thought we had."

"Not the way we are going to today."

Agatha nodded. "Very good. I want to hear this as well."

James turned a peculiar shade of red. "Aggie! There were some very personal events that day. Things you shouldn't hear."

"Oh, you mean the fact that you spent six hours with your mistress that evening? Honestly, James, what in the world were you at for six entire hours? I happen to know it doesn't take nearly that long. Does it, Simon?"

Simon choked on his eggs. This time it was his turn to redden and look away from James's stunned gaze.

"Ah, well . . . perhaps James is correct, Agatha. There's no need for you to sit in on our discussion. It isn't likely—"

"You don't think I'll be of any use, do you?" Agatha folded her napkin carefully by her plate. "Very well then. I suppose I might take Dalton up on his offer of a drive."

Bloody hell. Bloody Dalton and his bloody offers.

Agatha continued dreamily. "He is such good company. And his carriage is enclosed, so I needn't worry about wearing a heavy black veil all day—"

"I think we'll be needing your perspective after all, Agatha." Deliberately casual, Simon kept his eyes on his plate. Still, he caught a movement at the edge of his vision that looked suspiciously like Agatha's elbow hitting James's ribs.

"Er . . . right!" James agreed. "Absolutely. Perspective, the very thing."

Chapter Twenty-four

Throughout that afternoon Pearson kept all callers away and kept a steady supply of tea and cakes running to the parlor. Simon had spread a map out on the table, and the three of them traced every second of that fateful night.

Agatha was pleased to prove to be of some help, knowing James well enough to ask pointed questions about his habits. Thanks to her, James was able to recall that before he had visited his mistress, he had stopped at a confectioner's for his lady love's favorite bon-bon.

"Is this her house, Jamie?" Agatha pointed to a small side street on the map.

"No, it belongs to a friend of hers. She is married, so we took care to be discreet."

Disturbed, Agatha looked away. An affair with a married lady seemed so tawdry. Agatha was not sure she liked knowing that her idolized brother had the flaws of a normal man.

Simon stood and stretched. "Chocolates are all very well and good, but what I'd like to know is how the Voice of Society knew so much about your activities."

"Voice of Society?" James looked up from the map. "What are you talking about, Simon?"

"You know, Jamie, that gossip note that runs in the paper. The Voice of Society regularly reported on the activities of the Griffin."

"I'll be damned. Is that how all that got out? But no one truly believes that rot, do they?"

Agatha put her hands on her hips. "Jamie, when will you learn not to scoff at any source of information?"

Hoping for reinforcement, James looked at Simon, but Simon only grinned. "She took the words out of my mouth, I'm afraid."

James shrugged. "Vinnie adores that codswallop, but I've never read it."

Agatha perked up. She'd been waiting all day to learn the name of the mysterious lover. "Who's Vinnie?"

"Someone I know."

"Your mistress," Agatha guessed.

"Well, she isn't a real mistress. I didn't keep her or anything. She is merely a married woman with time on her hands."

Vinnie. *Oh, no.* Certain knowledge sent a shock through Agatha. "Lavinia."

"What?"

"Lady Winchell is your lover."

"Well, yes. You needn't go all missish on me, Aggie," James said defensively.

"But don't you see? Lavinia could be working for the French!"

The two men blinked at her. She spread her hands in her urgency. "Now it all makes sense. Lavinia knew where you'd be that night. She was suspicious of me from the start. Did you ever speak to her of me?"

"I told her a few boyhood stories, but I've always been very careful never to give anyone your name or your location. She couldn't have known about you. You're jumping to conclusions."

"But she tried to seduce Simon!"

A knowing expression crossed James's face, and he shook his head indulgently. "I see it now. You cannot let petty jealousies cloud your thinking. This is serious business. Honestly, Aggie, I'd have thought better of your logic."

Infuriated, Agatha lashed back. "Honestly, James, I'd have thought better of your taste."

Frowning, James leaned back. "See here, Lavinia's not an operative. She's selfish and shallow and far too interested in fashion and gossip to care about politics."

Agatha made an appeal to Simon. "You see it, don't you?"

Simon was eyeing her doubtfully. "It seems very circumstantial, Agatha. But I'll have someone check out her history if it will make you feel better."

A verbal pat on the head. She wanted to scream out loud with frustration. "I know that James thinks of me as perpetually twelve years old, but I'd have thought that you would have some trust in my intuition, Simon."

"I believe in hunches—*if* one is operating under good information."

"What better information do you need than the fact that every time we turn around, Lavinia is there?"

"It could be many things. Coincidence. A taste for meddling. Even perhaps attraction . . ."

He didn't finish, but she saw the glance he exchanged with James. Blasted male ego. "Oh, *of course*," she said snidely. "You are so irresistible that any woman would be insane to care about something as tedious as treason while you are in the same room."

"Watch out, Simon. This could get ugly," muttered James, who was carefully backing away.

Agatha ignored her brother. She had Simon in her sights and moved in on him.

"Let me understand you. Lavinia cannot be an operative for the French because she's a woman, and because she finds you attractive. I, on the other hand, was not only a suspected traitor, but a whore! Now, how can that be, Simon? How is it that Lavinia merits your support, while I only invited investigation?"

Simon stared at her as she advanced. "Agatha—damsel—what's gotten into you?"

"Don't you 'damsel' me, Simon Rain! Was it because I didn't strip you naked in the study on first acquaintance? Or perhaps it was that I am not so elegant and refined?"

"Don't answer, Simon. There's no way out of that one!" warned James.

Agatha turned her head to eye her brother malevolently. "Get out."

James saluted her, then turned to Simon. "It's been nice knowing you."

His expression puzzled, Simon watched as James let the door shut behind him. "I do believe he meant that literally."

"He did. I'm sure you'll wish you had followed him."

He flashed a smile at her. "Are you trying to intimidate me, damsel?"

"No, of course not." She came closer and placed both hands on his chest.

Then she pushed, hard.

Simon landed half-sprawled on the sofa. Swearing in surprise, he quickly moved to stand. She pressed him back, finally resorting to straddling his lap to fix him to his seat.

With great precision, she said, "I want you to answer me, Simon. Why was I so questionable while Lavinia is so above suspicion?"

Agatha pressed both hands to his shoulders, pinning him in place for her inquisition. He was going to answer her once and for all. She opened her mouth to badger him again.

Then she felt it.

He was growing hard beneath her. She could feel him stiffening and expanding until he pressed directly against her cleft.

The hunger swept through her, and she felt herself throb in response. She froze there, wanting to undulate upon him, wanting to press his mouth to her breasts until she hardened against his tongue the way he hardened against her dampening center.

But this was not the safe darkness of night. This was not the secluded curtained world of his bed. And Agatha didn't know what to do with the sweeping tide of hunger that made her hands shake and her sex pulsate with need.

She gazed helplessly into his blue eyes, which had darkened with his own lust. She wanted him. Now. Not tonight, after a day of assumed indifference and heated glances.

Now. Here on the sofa, velvet be damned. With the door unlocked and the daylight streaming through the uncovered windows. Hard and fast—and immediately.

Simon felt the shift in her pose, and what was already hard became harder. Her skirts flowed over his legs like a private screen, and her breasts thrust forward at chin level. All he need do was release himself, and he could take her here, in the middle of the afternoon, with the rest of the household mere feet away.

It excited him deeply, and he knew he ought to wonder at himself, but the ache in his throbbing erection wasn't letting him think much at all.

When she eased forward to grind softly against him and kiss him with tender longing, he thought he might burst on the spot. Her mouth was soft and a little hesitant. He restrained his urge to kiss her blind and allowed her to set the depth of the kiss.

She grew more daring. Her tongue darted into his mouth in the way that he had taught her, and he felt a rush of triumph that he was the first to earn a kiss like this from her. Then he forgot ego as she pressed more fervently to him and the sweet boldness of her passion left him breathless for more.

His hands slid beneath the froth of petticoats to find the ripe flesh of her thighs. She wore no drawers, a habit he promptly decided to approve of. At the touch of his hands, she gasped.

He slid warm palms upward to clasp her bottom and watched as the desire grew in her gaze. Then he dipped his fingers into the tempting crevice of her bottom, slipping them forward until he felt her dew on his fingertips.

"What were you saying?" he whispered as he slid one finger deeper.

Agatha squirmed, but he tightened his grip on her, filling his hands with sweet womanly flesh.

"I truly . . . want to know . . ." She faded, her head falling back as she arched her back to ease his penetration.

She was liquid heat in his hands, and he took full advantage. Almost harshly, he drove two fingers deep within her. She arched against him in response, and he could feel by the way she melted bonelessly into his rough caress that she liked it very much indeed.

He pulled his other hand from beneath the veil of her skirts to satisfy his need to see her breasts. She was ivory-skinned, and he ached to see her nipples glow pink in the brilliance of daylight.

Urgently he tugged down the cap sleeves of her morning gown until the neckline hung from the rigid points of her breasts. Then he yanked it to her waist even as he drove his fingers into her once more.

She arched willingly into him again, offering her luscious flesh so sweetly that it made him ache in more ways than one. That she would give to him so trustingly, so generously, was more than he could ever deserve.

He wrapped his arm about her waist and devoured her sweet offering, sucking and nipping her tender flesh while using his other hand to return the gift of pleasure to her.

Agatha was dimly aware that she was next to naked in the parlor, with Simon's hands and mouth upon her while she threaded her fingers through his black hair to urge him closer. She was even more vaguely appalled at her own wanton ability not to care.

"Tell me what you want," he growled into her breasts, his breath hot on her skin. "Say the words."

"I want you inside me," she gasped. He drove his fingers deeper in response, making her quiver. But it wasn't enough. "I want *you*."

"In time," he murmured. "First I want to watch you come apart. Simon says, fly for me."

Agatha whimpered as he began to touch her in rapid stroking motions that sent ecstasy splintering through her.

With gasping sighs, she rode his probing fingers until she could stand no more. He seemed to sense that, and the pressure changed. Suddenly his slippery fingertips moved forward, caressing somewhere else entirely.

She remembered his mouth upon her there, tasting her, nibbling and flickering over her, and the memory combined with the new rougher sensations was enough to send her over the edge.

She cried out, then clapped a hand over her own mouth as she helplessly continued to spasm with pleasure.

"Oh, God, damsel—oh, God, I have to—" Dimly she felt his hands return to fumble between them and used the last of her conscious will to pull away slightly to allow him to release his erection.

Each brush of his knuckles against her threatened to set her off again. She leaned her face against his neck, trying to gather her wits and her strength.

But it was no use. When he at last drove into her with an animal growl of triumph, she felt the wave sweep her up once more.

Simon thrust forcefully into her slippery heat. Then he withdrew until he barely held his position at her cleft.

"Oh, please. . . ." She quivered above him. "Simon . . . I need . . . please . . ."

Simon grasped her bottom hard and drove upward, forcing a cry from her lips. She shuddered in his hands as he pierced her again and again.

His woman. *His.*

She was such a sight above him, such a vision of abandon in the daylight. His own eruption began building. He took a hard pink nipple in his mouth and sucked deeply. In reaction, Agatha jolted violently upon him, then began to tremble anew.

When he felt her spasm around him, he'd not the control to hold out any longer. Burying his face into her breasts, he groaned aloud from the sheer shuddering power of his release.

She collapsed upon him, sagging in his grasp. He kept her there, only shifting enough to lean back against the cushions with her in his arms, still wrapped quivering around him.

He'd never seen a woman orgasm so powerfully, without reservation or self-conscious restraint. It was uniquely Agatha, although he had to admit to a certain exhausted pride in his own role.

She finally began to breathe more easily upon him. With one finger, he tipped back her chin to see her face.

"Are you still with me?"

She nodded, taking one last ragged breath. "I may be dead soon, but not yet."

"Why would you be dead?"

"Because it grows better every time. And if it grows better than *that,* I shall surely die."

"That good?"

"Yes, that good, as you very well know." She wriggled to lie beside him, her legs still draped over his. "You still haven't answered my question. And now I have another."

"Why am I not surprised?" He stroked a lock of her mussed hair from her face, although she was astonishingly unrumpled from what they had just done. In fact, she was lovelier than ever.

Her skin glowed with satiation, and her sweet lips were further swollen and pinked. Never had her brown eyes been brighter or her gaze gentler.

"Not merely pretty," he murmured. "I can't believe I ever thought you so."

She wrinkled her nose and shook her head. "Oh, I'm well enough, I suppose. But I'm no Lavinia."

He could tell that she was not merely fishing for reassurance. She honestly believed it. He obviously had not been doing his job. A man who couldn't make his woman feel beautiful was neglecting his function. Simon only wished he had the rest of his life to do it properly.

He took her face in both palms and made her raise her gaze to his. "Do you still want to know why I suspected you in the beginning?"

She nodded, watching him with wide eyes.

"This is why—this way that you make me feel by simply breathing the same air that I breathe. I couldn't believe it was real. I'd never been so susceptible to a woman before, and I couldn't believe it was not some artifice, some spell you wove apurpose."

She blinked at him. "But I'm so ordinary—"

He kissed the thought right out of her mind. When he raised his head, she'd apparently forgotten what she had been about to say. He smiled.

"You are a most extraordinary woman, damsel. And I intend to make sure that you remember that." He tucked her against him once more. "Now what was the other question?"

"Oh, yes. My other question is . . . Do you think James is coming back to finish your session?"

With horror, Simon realized where and when they were. "Oh, God, Agatha, I'm sorry." He sat them both up and began tugging her bodice up once more.

She helped him while regarding him with a smile. "Why are you sorry? I'm the one who sat upon you."

"True. However, as much as I enjoy being sat upon, I fear we must be more discreet." He put himself back in order as well.

"That will be difficult, for I cannot look at you without wanting you within me."

Her simple honesty took his breath away. He gazed into the warmth of those long-lashed brown eyes and wished he could keep her forever.

Then she toppled the moment by grimacing and squirming off the sofa. "But I never suspected it was all so very . . . messy."

He laughed. "I'm afraid it is rather basic in nature—"

There was a discreet tap on the door. When Agatha raised her voice to answer, Simon had to admire her nonchalant tone. Then Pearson appeared in the doorway.

"Madam, there are two gentlemen here to see you."

"Oh, hell, not bloody Etheridge again," muttered Simon.

"No, sir. It is a Lord Fistingham and—"

Pearson was shoved rudely aside and two men entered the room. One was older and shorter, with a balding head and a round girth.

The other was tall and would have been called devastat-

ingly good-looking by any definition. Golden-haired and possessed of a physique to make women drool, he strolled
cockily into the parlor. He waved a folded news-sheet tri-
umphantly at Agatha.

"Ha!" the fellow said. "I knew it was you, Agatha. You
didn't know that we get the London papers at Fistingham, did
you?"

He tossed the paper down on the side table and posed
before Agatha with his chin thrust out aggressively. "Did you
think that I wouldn't remember the many tricks you and your
brother played on me, then blamed on your imaginary Mortimer Applequist?"

"Reggie?" Agatha said faintly.

Simon stared. This was Repulsive Reggie?

Agatha turned toward Simon, instinctively reaching toward
him for help. It took only the tiny flash of fear in Agatha's
eyes to send his fury to its zenith.

He struck so quickly that all Agatha saw was a blur. One
moment, Simon was standing beside her. The next, with a
roar and a crashing impact, he had Reggie pinned to the
wood-paneled wall, hands about his throat.

"What's this? Stop that!" Lord Fistingham raised his walking stick to break it over Simon's head.

Agatha stepped quickly beneath it and snatched it before
he realized what she was about. "My apologies, my lord, but
I cannot allow you to strike him."

Then she turned to the purpling Reggie. "Reginald, may I
introduce Simon Rain? I fear he has an unfavorable view of
you."

"Why?" demanded his lordship. "I say, let him go before
I call the magistrate!" He turned to Agatha. "What have you
been telling this man?"

"The truth, I'm afraid," she replied. She tapped Simon on
the shoulder. "Darling, please let Reggie go. His lordship is
going to make a terrible fuss if you kill his heir."

"No," Simon growled. He gave Reggie's neck an extra
wrench. "Not until he's dead."

"What the bloody hell is going on in here?"

Agatha turned to see a fascinated audience of servants in the doorway. Armed servants. Sarah Cook brandished a giant rolling pin, while Pearson carried a fire-iron.

And there stood James, who held a pistol in one hand.

Lord Fistingham gasped. "James!"

Even Reggie managed to turn his head in Simon's grip. At the sight of James, Reggie's eyes widened in astonishment. The fight went out of him then, and he hung limply from Simon's hands.

"Fistingham? Reggie? What are you two doing here?" James looked from one man to the other. Then he seemed to notice Simon's murderous intentions. "Ah, Simon? Reggie surely deserves whatever you think he does, but would you mind killing him later? I'm truly curious now. I'd like an explanation."

Agatha stepped back as Simon reluctantly liberated Reggie, and the five of them stood in an uneasy circle in the center of the room.

Lord Fistingham seemed unable to believe his eyes. He kept looking wonderingly at James and shaking his head. "It's over," he mumbled. "It's all over."

James looked at Agatha. "Do you have any idea what he's speaking of?"

"I rather think he's disappointed that you are alive, for that means he cannot force me to marry Reggie."

"Marry Reggie? I should bloody well hope not! Not after what he did to you, the bounder!" James shot Reggie a venomous glare.

Agatha's mouth dropped open. "You knew?"

"Of course I knew. Mott knew, the servants knew, we all knew, except for Papa, because he didn't want to know. Why do you think you never went anywhere alone after that? Why do you think he never dared get close enough to touch your hand after that day? I beat the living hell out of him, that's why."

Agatha stared at her brother's face, marveling at his white-hot anger. He'd been there for her after all.

She turned to Reggie. "That's why you thought you could

compromise me into marriage, isn't it? Because you thought Jamie was gone and there was finally no one to stop you."

Reggie paled, looking from Simon to James. "I don't know what she's told you—but she pursued me! Women are always pursuing me—"

Simon moved again, but it was James's fist that smashed into Reggie's face and left him slumped groggily on the floor. They all stood and gazed at Reggie, James rubbing his fist with his other hand.

Even Lord Fistingham seemed disinclined to help his son. "Bloody twit," he muttered. "If he hadn't ruined his chance with the girl years ago, she would have been easy plucking for him. That face of his would have got her wedded up before she knew what was what."

Agatha could barely keep from sneering. "Your faith in my sense not withstanding, my lord, I've always hated your son. I'd never have been 'easy plucking.'"

Reggie shook his head. "Bitch unmanned me once already," he muttered. "And now this. I won't marry a sorry cow like her now, no matter how many notes *he* holds." He jerked his head toward James.

Agatha blinked. "You hold his IOUs?"

James nodded grimly. "Many of them. Enough to take Fistingham, what isn't entailed."

Lord Fistingham wheezed. "The pretty simpleton ran us out of every penny with his gambling. He had to marry you. It tied everything up so neatly. I'd have had possession of Appleby and its income, and we'd have wiped out any chance that you'd find those IOUs and call them in."

James angrily answered his lordship, but Agatha wasn't listening. She was too worried about Simon. He'd not taken his lethal glare off Reggie for a moment. From the way Simon held himself poised in predatory readiness she had the distinct impression that he was keeping himself on a very short, very weak leash.

"Jamie," she interrupted, "Simon still wants to kill something."

James looked at Simon. "Oh, hell. Simon? Simon, stand down!"

There was no response from Simon, not an easing of his stance, not a glance aside from his target. Reggie began to seem truly afraid.

"What's he doing? What's wrong with him?"

"He's fine, Reggie," replied Agatha. "I fear you are the one who is doomed." She glanced at James. "Simon has never by any chance . . . killed anyone, has he?"

James shrugged. "I've no idea. He never tells me anything." He carefully approached Simon but didn't touch him. "Simon, old man. You can't kill Reggie. I know he's a bad sort and needs killing, but this house is only rented, and Aggie will have to replace all the rugs and things if you get them bloodied up."

Logic wasn't working. Agatha stepped up. She put her hand gently on Simon's arm. He twitched beneath her touch but never looked away from Reggie, who was by now frankly cowering.

Stepping between the two men, Agatha slid her hand slowly up Simon's arm to his shoulder. She leaned in close.

"Do you know, I can still feel you inside me," she whispered to him. She trailed her fingers over his shoulder and stirred the hairs on the back of his neck. "I never think of Reggie or of fear anymore. I only think of you. Come back to me, Simon."

With a giant shudder, Simon finally tore his hunting-lion stare from Reggie. He closed his eyes, and when he opened them he was back.

Reggie whimpered and collapsed limply on the floor. "I want to go home," he whined.

Lord Fistingham was finally able to take a breath himself. He moved to leave and strode by Reggie, stopping to plant a swift kick in his son's pants as he passed. "Get up and get out while you can, you fool! Who knows when that madman will go off again?"

"Oh, Fistingham?" called James as the two men scrambled for the door. "Don't forget that little matter of the vowels.

I'm not happy that you tried to compromise my sister, not at all. I'm giving all my records of your debts to her as of today. Do keep that in mind, won't you?"

"Oh, thank you, James. That's a lovely thought." Agatha turned back to Simon. "You see, I now have them just where I want them."

Simon took a deep breath and gave her a strained half-smile. "Are you sure you wouldn't rather let Kurt have them for a moment?"

Agatha shook her head. "No. As entertaining as that sounds, I'd rather never spend another moment worrying about either of them."

Then she smiled sweetly. "But I'll be sure to tell every woman on the Fistingham estate to alert me if Reggie so much as pats a single bottom."

Simon let his rage go in a gust of laughter, then gathered her close in a tight hug.

"Ah—Ethelbert?" James indicated the watching servants with a nod.

Simon released Agatha and turned to Pearson. "I don't suppose all this could be forgotten?"

Pearson blinked serenely. "All what, sir?"

Harry pointed. "Him gone mad like a cat sighting a mouse, Uncle. And her calling him Simon, and that Reggie fellow—"

Agatha didn't see Pearson move, but suddenly Harry went red and gasped, "All what, sir?"

"Thank you, Harry." She smiled at her little Carriage Square family. "My thanks to all of you. I couldn't ask for a better band of friends."

Pearson actually blushed at that. He gave a stiff bow. "Madam." Then the audience was gone, leaving Agatha alone with James and Simon.

Agatha smiled, her ancient fear of Reggie snuffed like a candle. Then she saw the glower on James's face.

"Jamie, what is it? We handled Reggie beautifully. He'll never bother me again."

"No, Reggie won't." James's glare targeted Simon. "But what about you, Simon?"

Agatha put a hand to her hair. Blast it. James had noticed her mussed state. She'd truly fumbled her plan now, for she'd hoped she wouldn't have to suffer objection from James.

Simon only gazed calmly back at James. "I can make no such promise, my friend."

James stared at him, jaw working furiously. "Damn it, Simon! She's my little sister!"

Agatha moved closer to Simon. "James, please understand. I love you terribly, but I am little no longer. I know what I want."

"But, Agatha, you'll be ruined, ostracized, if you're discovered. I'm supposed to protect you from this very thing!"

"I know." She stepped softly to James and gently removed the pistol from his hand unnoticed. He gazed at her with anguish in his eyes. "Someday you'll understand."

James looked from one to the other, then shook his head. "If this is any example of the pain love will bring me, I don't want it."

His words struck Simon with a jolt. For he did want it, pain and all. He'd freely trade a lifetime of numb existence for one moment of Agatha's loving gaze, even if it was followed by the agony of leaving her.

The clock struck three in the hall, and Agatha started.

"Oh! I nearly forgot. There's a meeting of the volunteers at the hospital at four o'clock. I must change."

Simon reached to stop her as she bustled by him. "But they think you're in mourning. Surely they'll excuse you."

She furrowed her brow at him. "But I'm not really. And I refuse to use that as an excuse not to do my duty. Surely you of all people can understand that?"

Simon let her go, a half-smile on his face. Indeed he did understand. He turned to James. "I'll accompany her to the hospital. She'll be safe enough there. The place is nothing but soldiers as far as the eye can see. Then I've some business at the club. Anything you'd like for me to do for you while I'm out?"

James watched him with narrowed eyes. "Yes," he said. "Kindly drop dead."

Simon shook his head. "Sorry, old man. I can't do it, not even for you. We need each other, she and I, even if it only be for now."

"And I'm expected to stand aside while you shame my sister?"

"No. You cannot simply stand by. I understand that. I only hope someday you'll come to forgive me." With that, Simon left, feeling as though he'd just lost his best friend.

But then of course, he had.

Chapter Twenty-five

The hospital was bustling, but still many of the nurses and volunteers stopped to give Agatha their condolences. Her lies cut deeper into her, like bindings outgrown. As she slowly progressed to the cloakroom set aside for the volunteers, Agatha felt like a deceitful crow amongst the angels in her fraudulent mourning black.

Finally, she escaped into the blessed privacy of the cloakroom, only to discover Mrs. Trapp and her daughters were there before her.

"Ah, you've come to the meeting after all, Mrs. Applequist? I didn't expect you'd feel up to it."

"The war effort will not wait for me to finish mourning, Mrs. Trapp."

"True enough, true enough. Still, I rather thought you'd be busy with that houseguest of yours." The woman's eyes glittered with curiosity.

Houseguest? Had the prying biddy somehow learned that Simon remained in the house? "I'm sure I don't know what you mean."

"That brown-haired fellow I saw up on the landing the last time we called. Very handsome, he was, and so nicely dressed. Family, I assume?"

With horror, Agatha realized that James had been spotted.

And by the biggest gossip in London, too! "Ah, you mean my . . . cousin, ah, Merryl . . . pickle . . . dor."

"Pickledor? Would that be the Brighton Pickledors? Well, what do you know?" She nodded to one of her daughters. "Kitty was just saying to Lady Winchell how he had that Brighton look to him. You know, all bookish and thin, but good-looking as well."

Agatha's hands stilled, her cloak half off her shoulders. "Lady W-Winchell?" she choked out. "Wh-when did this occur?"

"Oh, just a moment ago. I'm sure you saw her. She left just before you came in. All in a rush she was, of a sudden."

"Oh, no, Mummy. It was at least ten minutes past," Kitty contradicted.

Agatha pulled her cloak back on, then whirled for the door. If she could catch Simon—

Harry and the carriage were long gone. Agatha paused on the walk for a moment. Should she hail a hansom and return home to warn Jamie? But Simon had impressed on her the need to remain safe inside the hospital.

Then she knew what to do. A boy on foot would likely be faster than a carriage. She'd send a messenger to the club and one back to the house as well. Satisfied with that solution, she turned to reenter the grand double doors of the hospital—

To find two very frightening individuals standing in her way.

"Best you don't let on, madam." The larger one spoke with a decidedly French accent. "We would not want to hurt such a little woman."

The two Frenchmen were dressed just well enough that they caused no comment as they each took one of her arms. Agatha cast around for help and saw a small tattered fellow watching her intensely. He seemed oddly familiar, as if she'd glimpsed him before.

Feebles? mouthed Agatha. The little man gave a swift short nod, then indicated a nearby carriage with a jerk of his head. Agatha looked ahead to see an ordinary hansom parked along the street.

Then she spied the trailing silken skirts of a pale green gown draping through the open door of the cab. In a moment, her suspicions were confirmed as Lavinia Winchell leaned out to smile in her direction.

"Agatha, darling! I'm so glad to see you made our appointment."

Agatha began to struggle then, for she had the sudden conviction that she would never see Simon or Jamie again if she entered that carriage.

She risked a glance at Feebles, who had followed them at a distance. He gave her a helpless look, but she could see that there was no way he could stop her abductors. Even had there been only one of them, he was simply no match.

Still, he would tell Simon. If he didn't foolishly risk himself to save her, as it seemed he was considering. For he had moved closer still.

"Oy there, guv'nor! Would ye be wantin' a bigger hack? Me mate's got a right nice rig, fit the four of ye better—"

Feebles's sales pitch was interrupted when one of the giants lifted a hand to his throat. The thug pinned Feebles to the side of the hack with one hand and proceeded to load Agatha into the carriage with the other.

"Get rid of that wretch," hissed Lavinia to her henchman.

"But why? He's done nothing to you," gasped Agatha. She leaned forward, but Lavinia sent her back into her seat with a vicious slap that made Agatha's ears ring.

Then she saw the pistol that was pointed directly at her heart. Helplessly she watched as, with one flick of his wrist, Lavinia's ruffian flung Feebles nearly ten feet. The man landed facedown on the street, in the path of any wheeled vehicle that came along.

The last Agatha saw as she was driven away was the poor little man in the tattered brown coat lying still as death on the cobbles, along with any chance of word reaching Simon in time.

Simon finally managed to get away from Jackham. Agatha was waiting for him at the hospital and all he could think about was getting her home. Now that they'd reached an understanding, he intended to spend every possible moment in her arms.

As he told Harry to return to the hospital, and settled back into the cushions, Simon could think of nothing he'd like better than to make an early night of it. His palms went damp to think what Agatha might dream up for that night.

Would she wait for him fully dressed, so that he could reveal her slowly, removing one piece of clothing at a time? Would she continue that delightful habit of hers—approaching him clad in nothing but a silken wrapper? Or would his enchanting little maniac devise something wholly new for their mutual enjoyment?

It occurred to him that perhaps it was time that he took the initiative in lovemaking. He smiled to himself. Then again, why not let her run things for a bit more? She so obviously enjoyed it, as did he.

Finally, he was back at the hospital. Letting his mounting desire speed him along, he rushed inside, expecting her to be waiting for him in the entrance hall.

What he saw instead was a bloodied Feebles struggling against a number of nurses and orderlies who were obviously trying to coax him to a treatment room.

"Let me go, ye rotters! I'm all right, so get your bleedin' paws off me!"

Agatha was nowhere to be seen. Sick fear began to twine its way into Simon's gut. In two strides, he was on the little group. He pulled two orderlies away by force, then grabbed Feebles by the collar and towed him free.

"Thanks, guv'nor. I've been tryin' to get to ye ever since I woke up."

"What happened? Where is Agatha?"

"She got took away in a carriage, sir. Right off the street. Happened so fast, I couldn't stop 'em. Giant blokes, they were." Feebles indicated the bloody gash on his head. "The littlest one did this to me with one hand."

"Did you recognize them? What about the carriage? Can you describe it?"

"The carriage were just a hack. The two blokes was Frenchies, I'm pretty sure. One of 'em said something to your lady."

French. It was everything, but it helped them not at all. "What else?"

"There was a lady in the carriage, sir. Posh sort. She'd been to the house to see your lady. You've seen her yourself, I think."

Dear God. Lavinia. Agatha had been right all along. If only he'd listened to her!

Simon shook off the thought. He needed to hurry. "Feebles, go to Miss Cunnington's house and gather everyone there, from James down to the cook. I'll head back to the club and start bringing in everyone who is in town. I fear we're going to need all the help we can get."

The afternoon light was fading as the carriage rumbled through the London streets. Lavinia sat silently, her only expression a cold smile of satisfaction as she continued to hold the pistol on Agatha.

Agatha was silent now as well, for she had exhausted every plea and threat she could think of to make Lavinia let her go. Now she only sat pressed to the door, as far from the thug at her side as possible, while a continuous stream of hopeless plans ran through her mind.

At one point, she realized that they were driving through Covent Garden. With a hot burst of grief, she remembered the day she and Simon strolled the length of the market.

Tears gathered in her eyes as she leaned closer to the window. If she thrust her head out just so, she would be able to see the very spot where—

A sickening impact struck her skull, and she was knocked to sprawl on the sticky floor of the hack.

"Stay down, you little fool. Do you think I'll chance someone seeing you?" Lavinia waggled the pistol at her, and Agatha realized that she had been struck with the iron barrel.

Lavinia turned to the one henchman who rode within the carriage with them. "Bind her well. And keep her down on the floor. It's where she belongs," Lavinia added with a sneer.

It was growing dusky by the time the carriage stopped, but there was enough light for Agatha to be alarmed by what she saw.

They were at the docks. Even this late, there were many men about, but even had she been able, Agatha wasn't sure she would have tried to enlist their help.

Some were merely tattered and unshaven, but most were burly and openly foul. They made Lavinia's thugs look like upstanding citizens.

Then Agatha was wrapped into her own cloak and tossed over the shoulder of the larger man. With her hood flopping over her face, leaving her with only a view of the ground, she couldn't be sure what route they traveled.

With the man's broad shoulder in her belly, it was all she could do to force each breath. All she knew was that they walked for a time over warped pier planks, in such bad repair that her captor had to step carefully for fear of putting his huge foot through a gap.

Then she was loaded—rather like a sack of goods—into a dinghy. Her hood flopped over her face completely then, and all she could do was listen as Lavinia snarled orders to her minions.

Agatha lay on her side in several inches of oily water, and most of her concentration was taken by holding her mouth and nose free of the wet. By the time the boat scraped against something larger, she had swallowed more of the bilge than she wanted to think about.

Rough hands hauled her up and over, then she was tossed onto someone's shoulder once again. She knew he then traversed some sort of steep stairway, for her head banged against every tread behind him.

"I believe I shall vomit now," she muttered faintly.

The fellow apparently understood more English than he spoke, for she was quickly dumped onto a hard, gritty surface.

"Thank you," she said politely. She wasn't being facetious, for she hadn't been so comfortable in hours.

She heard Lavinia complain, "Oh, for pity's sake." Then the hood was whisked away from Agatha's face and she was physically propped sitting against a wall.

She was in a small wooden room and, by the rocking motion beneath her, most definitely on a ship. Remembering Jamie's stories of his incarceration, Agatha wondered at this reuse of a known prison, until she realized that a boat made a wonderful dungeon, for it could be moved at will.

Lavinia stood before her, her features twisted in a sneer. Frankly, she looked most unattractive that way. Agatha wondered if she ought to tell her so.

"Well, why don't you speak now? No more pleas for your life?"

"I believe I've used the best ones already," replied Agatha.

"Look at you, sitting there as cool as frost. You truly think he'll come for you, don't you?"

Agatha could see no reason to deny it. "Indeed, he will."

"Ha! James Cunnington has never truly loved a woman in his life!"

James? Did Lavinia think what Simon had thought, that she was James's mistress? Then the bitterness in Lavinia's voice leaked through Agatha's surprise. "Is that what this is all about? You're angry because James wasn't in love with you?"

"Not for a moment, and if you were more intelligent, you would know that he never loved you, either. You can play games all year with that chimneysweep of yours, but you'll never make James jealous, because he'll never love you enough to care."

"Chimneysweep?" Agatha asked faintly.

Lavinia smirked. "Of course. I've had your house watched since first you rented it using James's account. My man saw a chimneysweep go in and never come out, and lo and behold—your previously nonexistent husband had come home. I must say you did a magnificent job with such raw material. I found him to be quite . . . entertaining."

Agatha would have laughed, but the seething hatred in Lavinia's voice was far too frightening. "But why were you watching me? What could I possibly be to you?"

"James told me some amusing stories of his youth, and in them he mentioned his favorite means of avoiding punishment. I never forgot Mortimer Applequist. Then when *Mrs.* Mortimer Applequist began to make withdrawals, I knew that another of James's lovers had been unearthed."

Simon had been right after all. He hadn't been the only one watching the bank. "How did you get access to James's account? Did he tell you?"

"Not willingly. I had to dose him first. I had some . . . expenses come due. It was something of an emergency."

The lady was a known gambler, and not a very good one. "So you drugged him to *rob* him?"

Lavinia smiled knowingly. "A man will drink anything if he thinks it's an aphrodisiac."

"Oh, Jamie, you silly sod," whispered Agatha to herself.

Then Lavinia's gaze hardened. "But there was so little money in the bank. I drugged him again to find out where he kept his other valuables, and that's when I stumbled across his secret life. I thought about blackmailing him, but why squeeze a poor man? Instead, I conceived a plan to sell my information to the Voice of Society."

With a swirl of mint-green silk, Lavinia began to pace the room. "That's when my countryman tracked me down and asked me to strike a blow for France."

Now she was claiming patriotism? Agatha couldn't let that one go by. "You mean—paid you to strike a blow."

"Indeed. Paid me well. They promised me a great deal more if I could discover the names and missions of the others. But James wouldn't talk, not even while drugged."

Lavinia spread her hands, indicating the boat. "So I decided to steal him away, somewhere I could keep him well dosed and wear him down. I'd already taken the money, you see. I had to get those names!"

"So you held him captive and questioned him?"

"At first I truly tried to get him to run away with me. But he wouldn't leave his tiresome post."

"You can't have truly expected him to."

"Why not? I'm beautiful. I'm skilled. I'm every man's dream, my mother made sure of that. And until James, no man has ever failed to give me precisely what I want."

"So this is a case of 'Hell hath no fury like a woman scorned'?" Agatha could scarcely keep the incredulous laughter from bubbling up. Was the woman nothing but a hackneyed jest? "Or will you admit that you simply wanted the money?"

Lavinia's face twisted in sudden rage. "What would you know about the pressures of living up to a certain level of Society? You think goats are good company!"

"Sheep, actually," corrected Agatha.

"Well, that suits you to the ground, doesn't it, little lamb?" Lavinia snorted. "And here you sit, as stupidly as one of your sheep, talking to the wolf."

"Well, I've nothing better to do whilst I wait for S—Jamie. For indeed, he does love me."

Her confidence seemed to be the last straw for Lavinia, for the woman strode forward to strike Agatha sharply across the cheek.

"Silly little fool! Do you believe everything you are told? Men will only use you if you don't use them first." Lavinia began to pace again, her features twisting sharply. "Do you know how I came to your precious England during the Terror? Tied into a sack and hidden inside a coil of rope on a stinking fishing vessel very much like this one. I was but five years old, but even then my mother feared what the *English* sailors would do to such a pretty child. And she was right. I poked a hole through the sacking for air, only to see my mother paying for her passage against her will."

Agatha shook her head. "No woman deserves that," she said quietly. "But to blame all the English for the actions of a few?"

"Few? Even after we arrived in London, there wasn't a man who saw my mother who didn't try to possess her. But she was smart and played them against one another, rising from the mistress of a shipowner to a merchant to a gentleman within a year, and then marriage. She taught me well how to get what I want from men. I landed a lord, did I not?"

Agatha looked around her. "You hid Jamie on this boat, like the one you and your mother crossed over on."

"A brilliant little whimsy, if I do say so myself. One with unexpected side benefits. Boats can be moved so easily, and no one need learn your business."

Agatha found Lavinia's careless attitude chilling. "Do you realize that five men are dead because of you?"

Lavinia seemed surprised. "They are?" A shadow passed over her face. "How remarkable. . . ." Then she recovered. "Well, it serves them right, English wretches. It's too bad that James isn't one of them. I thought he was dead, since my men reported seeing him go over the side during a storm."

"He almost was." Agatha hated to think of the danger Jamie had been in, swimming weakly through the high waves. "If it hadn't been for the tide . . ."

"Hmm. What a pity. Surely he remembers me questioning him."

Agatha wasn't about to disabuse her of this notion. "But why am I here? I don't know any names." *Please don't drug me, for I know more than I should.* Now she understood why Simon had tried to keep so much from her.

"Of course *you* don't. The very thought is laughable. This sort of thing requires *some* small scrap of intelligence. No, you are merely a diversion. Looking for you will keep James busy for hours. I knew he would be pursuing me the moment I learned he was hiding out in your house this afternoon. I can't afford the complication of having him looking for me, for I've a new and larger mission now. One that will buy my way back to Paris in style."

Agatha decided not to tell Lavinia that James believed her too shallow and silly to enact treason. Surely by now Simon and James knew that she'd been taken and realized that she'd been right about Lavinia.

Vindication of her theory would be much more satisfying

if she lived long enough to say, "I told you so."

"I truly don't understand you, Lady Winchell. Your mother was fighting for her survival. You are only interested in money and lust."

Lavinia whirled on her, eyes blazing with scorn. "You're wrong there, little farm girl. I am only interested in moneyed men, who are only interested in lust." She sneered. "Bah! Why do I bother to tell you this? You *trust* men. You're like an idiot child."

"Being trusting doesn't make one an idiot. The shame is on those who take advantage of trust."

Agatha gazed at the fuming Lavinia, her calm seeming to grow as the other woman's left her.

So this was where lies would take one. A life of bitterness and regret. There would never be a single clear moment of pure joy, for how could one trust anything enough to let it happen?

What about herself? Could she forgive herself for her own lies? Now, when her life seemed rather uncertain, she could scarcely remember her reasons at all. Why had she always felt such a need to flee the truth?

Perhaps honesty was a strength of its own.

Lavinia hissed like the viper she was and turned to leave. "I must get back. Gag her," she ordered her henchman. She turned to flare one more icy smile at Agatha. "James will be far too busy trying to rescue you to interfere with me. . . . I wish him luck. He'll need a net, I fear."

She contrived a tinkling laugh and gave the hulk nearest her a poke with her umbrella. "*Allons-y!* We have more important things to attend to. Once I do away with the old man, I may escape this horrid country forever."

Chapter Twenty-six

James leaned over the privy seat hole and sniffed. The stench made his eyes water. Excellent. Winchell didn't bother to ensure that his staff kept the privy sweet with lime, nor was the tiny wooden shed well ventilated.

This was one of James's favorite "distractions" to work in the field. Where there stood an army, there stood a hundred privies. Not a fatal outcome unfortunately, but it would have to do.

For despite the fact that he was breathlessly worried about Aggie, James was forced to admit the sense in Simon's plan.

"Lavinia panicked," Simon had reminded him. "She's running scared and making mistakes. Her abduction of Agatha may give us the only opening we'll have to search her possessions before she disappears forever. Our duty is to uncover the conspiracy. Don't forget that, James. You are a Liar first."

"Why not simply arrest the lot of them, Winchell too?"

"I don't think she's had a chance to complete what she has begun with her abduction of you. There must be some reason why she is still working in London after your escape. I want to know what that is. As long as Lavinia and her cohorts feel safe, we can hope that they will simply hold Agatha captive as they did you."

Duty warred with family loyalty once again. As much as he ached to search for his sister, he knew Simon was right.

So James satisfied himself with this particularly appropriate bit of sabotage and the knowledge that now, Simon would have sufficient time to search Lavinia's house for any information that would lead them to Agatha's rescue.

Working by feel in the darkness James felt in his satchel for the tin box of salt and opened it carefully on the plank next to the hole. Several feet of fine chain hung from each side of the sturdy box and James took a moment to lay the chains over his shoulder to dangle down his back.

Then he removed the lid from the small crock he carried in one gloved hand. Nestled within on a bed of ash, live coals glowed in the dimness. With a pair of small tongs, James transferred the coals quickly into the salt box. Immediately, the contents of the box began to put out an acrid odor.

"One," he whispered. He tossed the crock aside and swiftly lowered the salt box into the privy until it met the bottom.

"Two." The gas from the vaporizing salt would collide with the foul gases from the privy in a matter of seconds.

The box settled firmly and James released the chains.

"Three!" He leaped from the privy to take cover behind the alley gate.

Simon watched from the corner of the house as James threw himself out of the splintery wooden doorway to run for cover. There was a muffled *whump* and Simon felt the ground quiver beneath his feet. Then the Winchells' privy roof flew high into the air on a geyser of filth and flame.

It was spectacular. Smoking muck hung in the air for a moment, then spattered the grounds and garden in a solid sheet of greenish-brown. Simon heard James give an involuntary whoop of vengeful delight and grinned fiercely.

Then the smell hit him, and he hurriedly covered his face with the hood he carried with him. Even the scent of well-used damp wool within the mask was a welcome change from the odor without.

The doors opened and the household staff rushed out, only to halt in horror. The first of them slipped and staggered in the slime covering the ground, a few of them falling to land in the filth. The others flinched away from the hands reaching for help in rising.

Then the group of servants parted way for Lord Winchell. The man's mutton-chop whiskers quivered in disbelief as he stood blinking at his previously pristine grounds.

There was no sign of Lavinia. It was no more than Simon had expected. She was doubtless still seeing to securing Agatha somewhere. He had to believe that. It was the only thing that kept him focused.

Time to go to work. Simon turned away from the spectacle to make his way swiftly around the house. He'd already confirmed that a side window remained unlocked while James had set up his privy distraction. Now he didn't hesitate as he vaulted over the sill into the house.

He needn't be careful tonight, but speed was imperative. Still, he predicted it would be some time before any of Winchell's staff came upstairs to Lavinia's chamber.

This time, he passed by his lordship's study without a glance. His target lay upstairs, in the secret confines of a lady's boudoir.

Women had twisty minds. There was no telling where Lavinia hid her private papers. Surely not somewhere sensible like a desk or escritoire.

As he ascended the stairs like a shadow, he thought about Agatha's instinctive suspicion of Lavinia Winchell. He wished he could speak to her now to get a woman's perspective on this particular search.

Fury twisted within Simon. If only he had stayed with her. If only he'd—

He shook off the self-blame. Such activity would be pointless if he recovered her safely, and if he didn't, he'd have the rest of his damned existence to hate himself with thorough dedication.

Simon reached the bedchamber he felt sure was Lavinia's and stepped inside. The scent of the room confirmed his selection. The musky-powdery perfume that Lavinia favored made him think longingly of Agatha's refreshing scent.

He quickly lit the candle in his pocket, blessing Etheridge's gift as he did so. Then he examined the room. As he'd supposed, the spindly escritoire contained nothing but blank paper, ink, and pen nibs. There were no books in the room at all. Apparently, Lavinia was not a great reader. What a surprise.

Quickly Simon searched every drawer and shelf in the suite of rooms, including the vast wardrobe and the luxuriously appointed bathing chamber. He examined the contents of each, and the backs and bottoms. Nothing.

He slid his hands beneath the feather beds upon the grand frame. Nothing. He climbed upon the bed to examine the canopy and crawled beneath the bed to feel between every slat. Still nothing.

Simon felt helpless fear begin to erode his professional detachment. He'd been so sure that he would discover something here. That he would find his way to Agatha once again. Ferociously he quelled the spreading sense of loss that poisoned his ability to think.

He closed his eyes and concentrated, trying to think like Agatha would, using instinct and an understanding of human nature.

Lavinia was a suspicious, perhaps even paranoid, woman. A cunning creature, but without demonstrable intelligence. Her primary advantage lay in her apparent incredible unsuitability for intrigue. She simply wasn't the type.

She was more likely to gamble and shop her way into astonishing debt. She was a creature of tawdry passions, licentious as a mink. Impulsive, lazily cruel, and fond of low humor . . .

Simon opened his eyes and smiled grimly. He had it.

He strode confidently back into the necessary and lifted the seat of Lavinia's typically thronelike commode chair. No back garden privy for her. Then he pulled up the porcelain basin that sat within the seat.

There, in the hollow beneath the basin, lay a packet wrapped in oilskin.

"I've got you now, you viper," Simon whispered.

Though the cavity was somewhat damp, the packet was

quite dry inside, and Simon quickly scanned the contents. Letters from lovers, records of some rather astonishing gambling debts recently paid off in lump sums, and a grimy handwritten receipt for the purchase of "wun smal bote namd *Mary Klar*."

The boat James had been held captive on. The very vessel that Agatha might now be held on. The note was signed: "John Sway."

Another target for the hunt, then. Captains tended to keep track of their ladies of the sea, even when they didn't own them anymore.

Simon tucked the scrap into his breast pocket as he turned to go. Then he hesitated, eyeing the pile of love letters. Some of the most important pieces of intelligence came in the most unimpressive packages.

The first notes were varied, from painfully penned youthful anguish to sophisticated erotic wordplay. The lady did not seem to have any preference to either sort of lover at all.

Then, at the bottom of the stack of folded letters, he discovered one that began as insipid poetry on the first page, but then became abruptly businesslike on the second page.

References to payments and contacts were worded carefully, but Simon could recognize his own language when he saw it. The one paragraph that made no sense to him was a brief accounting of cloth yardage cut and bought. Simon shook his head. Codes were not his specialty, but he knew anything containing numbers likely contained dates and times as well.

He tucked the entire pile of letters into his jacket, on the chance that the others held information as well. As he left the bathing room, he glanced at the rosewood escritoire again. Lavinia was a decisive creature, who likely wrote in a strong hand. . . .

Quickly he took the stack of paper from the drawer and examined it page by page, slanting it against the candlelight.

Yes, there, on the third page. Definite curling script that dug deeply through to the back of the paper. Only a few lines, but perhaps, just perhaps . . .

Simon knelt on the hearth and performed the soot technique just as he had on Agatha's letter once before. *Please, God, don't let it be some silly social letter. . . .*

Fresh and clear, legible even in reverse, Simon read ". . . love, I shall be your bullet aimed at Prinny's brain. Yours forever, L."

The enormity of the plot shot through Simon in a bolt of pure lightning horror. The assassination of the Prince Regent would throw the British government into complete disarray for months, perhaps even years.

Yet such an attempt would be useless. Prince George was perhaps the most heavily guarded man in the world. Even in public appearances, it would take an army to get within a pistol shot of the man, not to mention that an assassin would never survive the attempt. Lavinia was a determined amateur, as evidenced by her foolish uncoded reply. But was she suicidal?

Could it be some other form of weapon? Lavinia used the word *bullet*, but that could be figurative. Either way, it was his duty to report this to His Royal Highness and his advisers immediately.

Once that was done, protection of the royals was not Simon's job, thank the fates. He wouldn't want to be the poor fellow faced with containing the Prince's excesses. Even the arrest of Lavinia would fall to the Royal Guard.

Simon's place right now was to find Agatha. Hopefully he would find the enemy operatives in the process, but frankly, he couldn't find it in him to care very much if he did. For the first time in his career, he had other priorities. God help him.

He blew out his candle and slipped from the room. Despite the desperate search that had taken place, the only evidence of his visit was the fast dissipating wisp of smoke.

Agatha finally realized both she and the ship had been deserted. Slimy fingers of fear began to work their way through her belly. Somehow she knew that neither Lavinia nor her cohorts were ever coming back.

She knew Simon and Jamie would be looking for her. But a small, ramshackle ship among hundreds, anchored in the sea of masts in the filthy docks? How in the world would they ever find her?

The gag was all too effective, muffling her loudest cry to something less than the creaking of the rigging above her. She thumped her heels for a time but soon exhausted any hope of being heard.

What she needed to do was free herself. Jamie had cut his bindings with the rim of a pail, but her captors had apparently learned better, for her wrists were tied tightly behind her back.

If she could make her way to the deck somehow, surely someone would see her.

This thought brought back the image of the unsavory denizens of the quay. Might she be putting herself in further danger if she was seen by the wrong sort?

It was a possibility, yet death by dehydration and starvation was a certainty if she remained hidden below.

Agatha rolled to her knees next to the splintery wall and managed to get to her feet by nearly standing on her head. She could do no more than tiny shuffling steps, scarcely an inch at a time. Her petticoats didn't make the effort any easier, for they hung ragged around her feet, impeding her even more.

Impatiently Agatha used her bound hands to pull up the rear of her skirts. By the simple pulling free of the tapes tying her petticoats in the back, she was able to drop them to the floor.

Kicking them off proved impossible, and she was forced to hop from the center of the billowed underskirts in awkward little bounds.

"I believe I look quite ridiculous," she muttered to herself around the gag. Still, this form of locomotion got her to the door.

If it was locked, her fate was inescapable. She turned and

sidled backward to the door pull. It was a crude affair, with no keyhole at all.

She tugged, and for a breathless moment she felt it stick. *Oh, please—please open.*

The door gave toward her suddenly, causing her to lose her balance. She pitched forward onto her face, quite unable to catch herself. Reflexively she flinched aside, narrowly missing landing on her nose.

Still, it was painful. After a moment, she took a breath. "Ow," she muttered, then wasted no more energy on the subject, despite the scrape on her cheekbone.

Roll to the wall, struggle to her feet, inch her way. The ship tossed her down a number of times, but she continued to repeat the process until she stood in the passage, looking up the steep staircase to the deck above.

Truly, it was more of a ladder than a staircase, and a broken one at that. Her knees went weak with frustration.

Turning, she sat gratefully on a narrow tread for a moment. She was frightened and weary, and her face and body throbbed from her many encounters with the floor. She didn't have the strength to face the climb.

Then again, she hadn't anything better to do.

Going up the ladder was easier than she'd first thought. She was able to use her hands to pull herself up backward, scooting on her bottom like a tot.

She was concentrating so thoroughly on her slow climb that she didn't realize she had reached the top of the companionway until a fresh breeze stung her abraded cheeks. The air smelled of fish and garbage and unwashed sailor.

It was lovely. She might still die on this wretched excuse for a ship, but at least she wouldn't die in the dark. Except, of course, that night was fast on its way.

The deck was piled with stinking netting, filthy clothing, and tangled rope. Seabirds flocked to the piles of refuse here and there among the litter. Lavinia's men were obviously bad housekeepers.

Irritated that she could not possibly make her shuffling way through all those obstacles, Agatha decided to stay where she was for the moment. She could see rescue coming from here, and she could also let herself slip back down the steps should danger approach.

She only hoped she'd be able to tell the difference.

James pulled Simon aside to one corner of the main gaming room of the Liar's Club. "It'll take hours to search the docks, perhaps even days. If I've read this coded letter properly, the dates match up with the Royal Appearance tomorrow. They want us out of the way for the Regent's tour of the Chelsea Hospital, I'll wager."

"It won't make any difference." Simon dismissed that concern with a restless shake of his head. "The Prince is well guarded."

James nodded, relieved. "Then we can turn our manpower to hunting Agatha."

"But it also sets a time limit on our search. If we don't find her before the attempt on the Prince, they'll have no reason to keep her alive afterwards. They may flee for their lives, cutting the dead weight."

Immediately Simon regretted his poor choice of words, at the images that rose in his own mind. He turned to face the motley gathering that filled the gaming room. Cooks and thieves, spies and servants. Pearson rubbed shoulders with Feebles, while Button murmured to Jackham in a low voice.

The clock on the mantel chimed ten bells into the low hum of conversation, silencing them all by the last ringing note.

"We've a long night before us, lads—sorry, Sarah Cook, and ladies. James's sister Agatha, who is known to some of you as Nellie Berth, has been taken by the opposition."

There were nods and angry mutters at this, and Simon was struck again at Agatha's ability to win the loyalty and affection of others.

"As James escaped from an old fishing boat moored off a small village west of here, and Winchell's servants confirmed that they had delivered supplies to the dock twice in the last two months, we are going to focus our search on the docks.

Hopefully, the enemy has not had time to flee local waters."

James moved to Simon's side. "We have reason to believe the boat is named the *Mary Klar,* formerly owned by a fellow named John Sway. Kurt, you and Stubbs comb the dockside taverns. Find Sway and determine if he has any idea where his boat may be now."

Kurt nodded grimly. Of course, Kurt was always grim. He and Stubbs stood, waiting to be dismissed.

Simon nodded. "Yes, go. Bring any new information back here."

Then they were gone, his deadliest man with one of his youngest. Simon suppressed the automatic worry that always rose at this moment. He couldn't afford to second-guess himself now.

"I need two men to work their way into the dockside registration offices. All boats must be registered with their destinations and their docking locations. The information will possibly be falsified, but that may tell us something as well."

Feebles stood. "Sounds like my kind of job, guv'nor."

"Excellent. Take someone with you to provide any needed distraction." Simon scanned his little army. Button straightened hopefully as Simon's gaze passed him. Simon nodded. "Yes, Button will accompany you. That theatre background of yours should come in handy here, Button."

"Yes, sir, Mr. Rain."

Feebles looked askance at his new partner but obviously wasn't going to debate Simon's choice. "Right, then. We'll be off. *Mary Klar,* you said?"

"Or anything remotely close. Shay isn't much for spelling."

They left. Soon others followed, as Simon assigned sections of the docks to search. In pairs and teams, they left the room until only Simon, James, and Sarah Cook remained.

"Aren't we going out, Simon?"

"Yes. We've enough evidence to move on Lavinia now. It's time for a little talk with the lady. James, let's go before Lavinia gets wind of the search and absconds. Sarah, can you make note of any new information that comes through that door?"

"I can feed a dinner party of two hundred, on time and hot. I think I can handle bein' your secretary." She waved a hand. "Go. Bring my madam home."

As he ran for the street accompanied by James, Simon had a terrible feeling that they were fast running out of time.

The boat was sinking. She was sure of it now.

An hour ago she had hoped it was her imagination. It was merely the river becoming rougher with the changing current. Only the darkness making her hear the sloshing of water from *inside* the vessel.

Now there was no denying it. Even the list and roll of the boat had become sluggish and heavy, slow to return to its upright position in the water. And the process seemed to be accelerating.

There would be no daybreak for this pathetic vessel. Or for its solitary passenger if she couldn't divine a way to untie her bonds. If she weren't bound, she might have a slight chance to float her way to rescue clinging to something buoyant.

A very slight chance.

Well, there was no help for it. She was going to have to find something sharp with which to cut her way free. Fortunately, the deck was rife with trash. Surely there was something broken in the mess.

Carefully Agatha swung her legs over the frame of the companionway. She had a bad moment when she thought she might slip through the opening and fall headfirst into the darkness below. She managed a panicked heave of her body and rolled onto the littered deck instead.

The moon was only half-full, but Agatha couldn't see where her hands were anyway. The best method of search turned out to be a backward scoot into the rubbish, while her bound hands searched each item frantically for a cutting edge.

It was quite the most revolting thing she had ever done.

What wasn't smeared with slime was stiffened with filth. Still, she kept on. She needed something sharp. Jamie had used the torn metal edge of a pail, but even that had taken him several hours.

Deep in her soul, Agatha was very much afraid that she hadn't that much time.

Chapter Twenty-seven

Simon and James were able to hail a cab directly out of the door, but that's where their luck ended. The rain ensured that everyone was driving their largest closed vehicles, and the streets were jammed at every junction.

When they finally pulled to a stop in front of Lord Winchell's house, Simon wondered rather desperately if he could not have run the distance faster.

"Careful, James," he cautioned as they climbed the steps. "And calm yourself. We don't want to be refused. Ask for his lordship first."

The severe fellow who answered the door led them to the very study where Simon and Agatha had seen much adventure. Lord Winchell sat at the fire, one foot bandaged and raised on a footstool before him, and a damp cloth raised to his forehead. From the look of the empty brandy decanter beside him, his lordship was on the outside of a considerable drunk.

The man blinked dully at them. "Applequist? Thought you were dead." He didn't seem much concerned by that. "I'd offer you gentlemen a brandy, but I seem to have drunk it all."

He removed the compress from his brow, and they could

see a sizable lumpish bruise. Winchell rang a bell that sat on the carpet beside him. The butler reappeared.

"More brandy, Pruitt! These men want brandy—"

Simon interrupted. "Lord Winchell, you should know that we are not here for a social visit. Could you please call your wife—"

"Got no wife," the man muttered.

"What?"

"Got no wife! Got no blunt, no horses, no wife."

"My lord, where is Lady Winchell?"

"No lady. Lord w' no lady . . ."

"Sir—"

"She left me!" Winchell roared, sitting up. "The little snake left me for a Frenchman, run off with her Frog Count." Abruptly he began to giggle. "A snake and a Frog. Snakes eat frogs, don't they? Well, he'll be sorry he hooked up with Vinnie, won't he?"

"Without a doubt," James said with feeling.

Winchell seemed to sharpen somewhat. "What do you want with Vinnie, eh? She doesn't need any more lovers. Got herself a slimy Frog."

"Has she left permanently? Did she take anything?"

Winchell snorted. "Just all her clothes, my best carriage horses, and every damned bauble she ever coaxed out of me. Took my mother's jewels, all the notes that were in my safe-box." He pointed to his foot, then his head. "Tried to prevent her. Still, I would've caught her if she hadn't bashed me with a pistol from my own gun cabinet."

He peered into his glass mournfully. "Didn't even know the slut had a key," he muttered into his snifter.

Simon didn't have the heart to tell the man that his wife wasn't only a slut, but a traitor as well. He looked at James. "I don't think we're going to get anywhere here. His lordship doesn't seem to be involved."

James shook his head slowly. "He'll be investigated anyway. Likely it'll ruin him."

As they left and reentered their hack to head back to the

Liar's Club, Simon could see that James sympathized with the man. Likely he was thinking of his own fall at the hands of Lavinia. "James . . ."

James held up a hand. "I should have been more careful, Simon. I was cocky, too convinced of my immortality. I fell right into her hands."

Simon nodded. "The investigation will be a tough road. You may never regain your post. But you should know . . . I would trust the Griffin with my life."

James smiled, a mere twist of his lips. "That means something, Magician. It means something indeed."

Then he seemed to forcefully shed those thoughts. "There's no tracing Lavinia now. Let us return to the club. I wonder what Kurt and Stubbs have discovered?"

Stubbs burst through the doors of the grimy tavern and collapsed onto a table, as if he scarcely had the strength to hold himself up by his grip on the splintery wood.

His hair clung damply to his forehead, and he breathed with desperate gulps. The tavern owner regarded him with brows raised in surprise.

"Who be chasin' ye, God or the Devil?"

Stubbs mopped his face with his begrimed sleeve. "The Devil himself, I swear it." He buried his face in his hands briefly. "You should have seen it. It was like Hell come to earth."

The others began to gather round in curiosity.

"What? What 'appened to you?"

Stubbs shook violently. "I was in a place just like this one, not two lanes south, havin' a pint with me mates. Just sittin' there, when suddenly in walks the biggest bloke you ever saw in your life. A bloody giant, I'm talkin'. The evil in his eye would kill a man, even without the knife in his fist."

"Knife?" blurted the tavern owner in alarm.

"More like a colossal butcher's blade. He raised it high—" Stubbs swept his arm up to demonstrate, and his audience ducked in unison. "*Swish, swoosh,* that knife moving like a great ax—and two blokes was dead. Blood went high as the rafters, spraying everyone there. And they never even touched him."

Stubbs shuddered and continued.

"Some went as to run out the back, but the rush and trample soon blocked the door. I was at the bottom of the pile, trapped under another bloke, but I could see it all." His voice dropped to a whisper and his audience shuffled closer.

"It was like killin' time at the piggery, I tell you. He'd pick a bloke up by his very hair and slice him from gullet to guts in one swipe. The floor was covered in slime and blood, and he just kept killin'. Hot blood splashed me face and I couldn't see! But I felt his great paw grab me—"

The tavern door slammed open, shaking the shabby building with the force of it. Nerves already strung tight by the gory tale, every man in the place jolted in alarm and swung to face the terrible apparition entering the door.

The fellow was so giant that he needed to duck nearly double to avoid the lintel. His shoulders were as broad as a plow horse, and his hair hung tangled over his eyes like that of a wild man.

And from his fist hung a great knife, no longer shiny— but now dripping red slowly to the floor.

No one breathed. No one had the air in their lungs to yell. The monster raised both massive arms and shook his fists high.

"Boo!" he roared.

Every man in the place ran for his life in a mad rush out the back. Every man, that is, but for Stubbs and the tavern owner. The tavern owner didn't move because Stubbs had him down on the floor and was sitting on him, tossing back a pint he'd snatched in the rush.

Stubbs burped delicately. "About bloody time you showed up, Kurt."

"Oh, shut it, boy. I was givin' 'em time to get good and scared. Didn't want to have to kill 'em all."

"Kill 'em all, that's a good one." Stubbs laughed uneasily, but Kurt didn't join in.

"Get off, now. I want to have a little talk with Mr. John Sway."

"You can't. He's done fainted away like a girl. No stomach to 'im, if you ask me."

Stubbs stood, but the tavern owner lay still on the floor. He poked the man with the toe of his boot. "Blimey, I think he's dead."

Kurt leaned over and eyed the downed man closely. Then he grunted. "Best not be. I'd have to kill him if he was."

That did the trick. John Sway moved, then climbed shakily to his feet. He stared at the two of them, eyes so wide the whites showed.

"Don't kill me! I ain't done a thing, I swear it!"

"Now, see. That's the trouble, ain't it?" Stubbs shook his head. "You ain't done a thing about them as bought that boat o' yours. I'll wager you've kept your eye on 'er, haven't you? You've seen what been going on."

Sway shook his head. "No! I haven't seen her in months, not since I sold her to that French bloke."

"What French bloke?"

" 'E was a skinny fellow, with a light voice and an even lighter way o' walkin', if you take my meaning."

Kurt glanced at Stubbs. "The Winchell hussy herself, you think?"

"Sounds like. So you sell this boat to a woman dressed up like a bloke, and then you never see it or hear about it again, eh?" Stubbs pushed Sway roughly in the chest and the man staggered backward. "Well, I know you're lying. You captains might give up the sea, but the sea'll never give you up. I'll wager you know just where she is, and who's on 'er right now."

Sway began to shake his head until Kurt growled and flexed his arms. The man's eyes fixed on the dripping knife, and the last shred of resistance seemed to leave him. He slumped onto one of the few benches not overturned in the scuffle.

"You're right, I kept an eye on her. She wasn't much of a boat, but she was the best I had. Me wife made me sell her and buy her brother out o' this stinking tavern. Now I'm nothing but a landlubbing alewife."

Stubbs rolled his eyes. "My 'eart bleeds for you. Now get on with it, or your 'eart's going to do a bit o' bleedin' as well!"

"I ain't seen her in a week or more, I tell you. First she'd come in once a month and pick up some supplies, just docking overnight. One o' the blokes aboard her come into the tavern, but he was a Frenchie fellow what didn't speak much English. He come in with Johnny Dobb, who runs a skiff through the port, picking up them that wants to come ashore.

"I asked Johnny what was about, and he told me that a crew of dirty Frenchies was on the *Marie Claire* an' that they was braggin' about some poor sod they had beaten near to death belowdecks. But I ain't heard or seen nothing of her since."

"*Marie Claire*? That's the name of the boat?" Stubbs glanced at Kurt, who nodded.

"Well, sure. Didn't you know that?" Sway eyed them suspiciously. "Who are you, anyway? Who sent you here?"

Stubbs ignored the question. "When she docked, where'd she tie up?"

"East India Dock for some reason. Must've had to pay a pretty pence to be let in over there. Didn't look the type to throw money away, that sailor. The light bloke, the one you say is a woman, must have paid a hefty bribe to use them there company docks."

"Anythin' else?"

"I did see somethin' today. Don't know if it means anything. . . ."

Kurt growled. The man swiftly continued.

"I seen that bloke, the Frenchie from the *Marie Claire*, walkin' down the quay with a bunch of his mates. All of 'em had their duffels on their backs, like they was leavin' the boat for good."

Stubbs looked at Kurt, who jerked his head toward the door. Stubbs nodded and turned back to Sway. "That's all we need to know for now, but we might be back. Best you remember who let you live, you bounder."

"Wait! You don't think they'd just leave her somewhere like that, do you? She's not the tightest against the water, you know. If she ain't bilged regular, she'll hove to for sure."

Kurt grunted. "The Magician will want to know that." Stubbs nodded. Ignoring the tavern keeper, Kurt and Stubbs left the dingy place to hurry for the club.

Stubbs grinned at his giant companion once they were out in the night. "You were a right nightmare come walkin' in there! How'd you fake the blood on the knife?"

Kurt didn't even glance at him. "What makes you think it's fake blood?"

Stubbs stopped in mid-stride, letting Kurt move ahead. When there was safe distance between them, Stubbs followed the big man. "Blimey, 'tis a good thing he's on our side," he muttered. "I think."

Feebles took one look at Button and swore. "Whose bloody side are you on?"

For Button was clad in a shining silk example of what short tyrannical French generals with delusions of grandeur were wearing that year. He waved his plumed hat at Feebles with glee.

"If I'm to provide distraction, I'll need the proper costume. Moreover, it was my favorite role until the revue closed. Ah, those glorious nights . . ."

"Right. Get on with it, then. They's a crowd before the offices, but it don't look like anyone's inside this late. You get 'em all lookin' your way, and I'll get into the files."

Button gestured grandly. "Lay on, Macduff!" Then he gasped, clapping one hand over his mouth. "Oh, dear! I've quoted the Scottish play! We're doomed for certain!"

"You'll be doomed if you don't get your shiny self down on that street to distract them as is still on the docks!" Feebles gave Button a friendly boost out of the hired hack, leaving the valet to dust fruitlessly at the boot print on the seat of his silk pants.

"Hmph! Philistine!"

Then Button was off. Feebles watched him strut down the way, attracting attention with every step. Of course, the fact that he was loudly conversing with an invisible "Josephine" about the offensive hygiene habits of the English might have had something to do with it.

"God help him, for he's goin' to die," muttered Feebles as he kept to the shadows on his way to the side of the dock registration offices. He'd never been here before, but offices was offices. File clerks were all the same, bless their borin' little hearts.

With a simple twist of his picks on the lock, he was in the rear door. A right joke it was, how everyone always spent their money on the front lock, when no right-minded thief would ever use the main door. The rear-door lock was usually some simple device that a child could open with a hat pin.

Once he was inside, Feebles lit himself a candle with his fancy new matches. He had a precious five left, for he'd earlier used three of them in sheer amazed experimentation.

Only the best for the Liars, but then, the Magician had always insisted on that. He even gave them good wax candles for sneakwork, as they didn't smoke or drip, and gave a lovely bright light.

Feebles had been following that advice for so long that it only took the hot-honey smell of beeswax to put him at full sneak attention.

A rumble of angry protest came from the street outside. He'd better hurry, afore Button got himself flayed by a fisherman's knife for his sorry behavior.

To Feebles's dismay, there was a single great drawer of "M" registries, packed so tightly with slips and forms that he could hardly pick one out without tearing it.

The rumble abruptly became a roar, and Feebles clearly heard cries of, "Hang Napoleon!"

Cursing fervently and with great imagination, Feebles yanked the entire laden drawer from its slot and hefted it to his shoulder. Then he was out into the alley and running for the hack still waiting outside.

The driver was standing and craning his neck to see what the crowd down the way was doing. He didn't so much as glance at Feebles's odd burden.

"Whot's all that down there, do you think?"

"Don't know." Feebles dropped the drawer onto the ratty seat cushion and ducked back out. "I'll find out and tell you."

He dashed to the edge of the angry mob and began elbowing and toe-stomping his way through. In the center, he found a rotten-vegetable-slimed Button bravely holding off the "enemy" with a tattered plume from his hat, which had disappeared.

"Off wi' zeir heads!" Button declared with an accent and an insolent sneer. "I shall have zee lot of you sent to zee guillotine!"

"Bloody hell," muttered Feebles. Then he sprang forward and grabbed Button by the scruff of his elegantly ruffled neck. "I've got 'im, lads! Get some rope and some tar and feathers, and we'll make a real peacock out of 'im!"

This met with a roar of approval, and half the mob scattered to find materials for their amusement. The other half remained to jeer at Button and to continue to decorate his costume with rotted produce.

They didn't seem to notice that Feebles was moving sideways out of the center of the action, for he continued to exhort them all to finer efforts.

"That's no good, lad! Get him in the gut with that one! Osh, you throw like a bloody girl!"

Then they were within yards of the hack. Feebles pointed back down the street and yelled, "Blimey, look what they've got!"

Button followed the direction of his finger and gave a fearful shriek. Unable to resist, the crowd before them turned to see.

The two men made a mad dash for their hack and flung themselves within. Button huddled on the floor while Feebles shouted up to the driver.

"Go, man, go! They're all barmy! Stark staring lunatics, escaped from Bedlam this very night! Drive, man!"

The startled hackney driver whipped his horse to a leap of speed, twisting the hack nearly on its side in the speed of his turn.

With a clatter of wheels and hooves, they sped down the cobbles, leaving the mob far behind them.

Feebles clung to the side grip with one hand and wrapped the other arm around the drawer, which threatened to bounce clear off the seat. Button lay gasping on the floor, curled into a ball.

In spite of his irritation, Feebles was a bit worried about the poor little fellow. He gently toed him with his boot.

"You all right, then? Button, you ain't gone and fainted, 'ave you?"

Then he heard it, over the clattering coach and all. The little loony was laughing!

"Oh, dear!" Button chortled as he wiped a tear from his eye. "Oh my! That was ever so much fun. I always did love an enthusiastic audience."

He hopped up to sit in the narrow space left by the drawer and began plucking the fruit peels from his costume. Peering down at the papers crammed within the box, he beamed in admiration. "Did you take *everything*, Mr. Feebles?"

"Well, himself said to get *Mary Klar* or anything like. These are the 'M' slips."

"Smashing job! Very efficient. There'll surely be something useful in this lot to help us find Miss Agatha."

"Bloody well hope so," muttered Feebles. "For I ain't got a good feelin' about the lady, indeed I don't."

Chapter Twenty-eight

The boat heaved slowly to one side, and this time it didn't swing back. Agatha was tumbled sideways onto the steeply slanted deck and awakened from the half-doze she had fallen into as she sawed slowly at her bonds with a shard of brown bottle.

Fear jolted through her. She was sliding down the planks, unable to prevent herself. She squirmed and flailed, trying to turn herself, or catch something, anything!

The mast caught her full in the back, cracking painfully against her bound arms and knocking the breath from her lungs. Still, she had stopped her slow fall into the dark water.

Carefully, she moved. If she could roll to her stomach so that the mast pressed her side, she could continue to work the shard of glass clutched in her right fist against the bonds on her left.

It was astonishing that she had been able to keep hold of it in her panic. Then again, without it, she might as well voluntarily dive into the cold river, for there would be no escape if she could not cut her way free.

She made the move without toppling from her uneasy perch, although now her head hung low, as did her legs. She felt as though she might crack clean in half.

Don't think. Cut.

She had been cutting for hours. The rope was thick and

she couldn't see what she was doing. She'd wasted a long time working on a loop that turned out to be nothing but the end piece that was already hanging free.

Experimentally she pulled her sore wrists against each other, trying the rope yet again. Was there some give after all? Could she be close to freedom?

Don't hope. Don't despair. Just bloody cut.

Simon paced the floor of the club, Sarah Cook's neatly printed list in his hand. His Liars had done well.

First, the *Mary Klar* was actually the *Marie Claire*. It had last been seen moored in the East India Dock, which was confirmed by the docking slip recovered from Feebles's files.

This meant that all the searchers could be pulled from the main docks and sent to concentrate on the ones belonging to the East India Company.

As small ancient fishing vessels weren't at all the Company's style, the *Marie Claire* should be relatively easy to spot there . . . if the East India Company Dock was not full to the brim with hundreds of their own vessels.

The other news was not so good. Not only had the *Marie Claire* been deserted by its crew, it also had a tendency to take on alarming amounts of water.

Simon was almost paralyzed by his fear for Agatha. The thought of her trapped below, alone in a sinking vessel—

The paper in his hand crumpled in his fist. *No.* He would not count her as lost until he held her lifeless body in his arms. Until then, she lived. And he would find her in time.

James entered the room, tossing his wet coat over a chair. "They've had no luck at the Company dock so far. I've set Stubbs up as contact there, everyone knows to where to find him for the latest reports." He eyed the crushed list in Simon's hand. "Anything yet?"

Simon shook his head. "Not since I spoke to you an hour ago."

"What about this Dobb character? He knew where the boat was."

"Weeks ago. He may have no idea where it is now. Still, we're keeping an eye out for him."

"It's almost dawn. She's been in their hands for more than sixteen hours. She could be anywhere by now." James ran both hands through his hair. "We need more men."

"We have her servants, my servants, and every one of the Liars searching the dock. There are simply too many ships out there, James."

"Small, grimy fishing boats named *Marie Claire*?"

"You'd be surprised," Simon said grimly.

"They were out fairly deep in the inlet where I escaped from them. Maybe we should restrict our search to those anchored outside the docks."

"Ships move. It's the whole point of them, after all."

"I know that," snarled James. "I simply—"

"Be easy. We'll find her."

James took a deep breath and asked, "Where are you going next?"

"To the East India Dock. I'm searching those anchored outside the docks."

James's head snapped up. "But you said—"

"Are you coming or not?"

James grabbed up his coat and raced Simon through the door.

The fog was clearing as the mass of men marched down the East India Dock, but still Simon imagined they formed an impressive sight stalking en masse through the trailing mist.

Hopefully they would be intimidating enough to inspire some of the permanent denizens of the wharf into cooperation. At this point, Simon didn't much care if the cooperation was prodded by a desire to help or the point of Kurt's knife.

They were at a standstill in the search. Dawn was imminent, which would make the hunt easier, but they'd lost the trail here in the tightly knit underworld of the Docklands. There were hundreds of ships in this section of the Thames alone, and not a helpful sailor among them.

"S-sir? You be lookin' for your lady?" The small voice came out of the darkness to his left.

Simon froze, holding up a hand to halt his fearsome troop. He turned and peered into the shadows. "Who is there?"

A figure stepped out, and for a moment Simon was sure it was an apparition, for even in the full light of James's lantern the creature was as dark as the night. Then a frightened pair of blue eyes blinked slowly at him from a soot-blackened face.

The double pang of familiarity struck deep into Simon. "You're the sweep from the market, aren't you?"

"Yes, me lord." The child's voice trembled, and Simon realized what a frightening crew of bandits the lot of them must look to him. Kurt alone would set most children to flight.

Simon shook his head and knelt to look the boy in the eye. "I'm no lord, boy. I myself was born within the sound of Bow bells, just as you were," he said gently.

The child blinked, sizing up Simon's clothes and manner. "You, sir? Out of Cheapside?"

"Indeed. So you've nothing to fear from one of your own, do you?"

The child shook his head slowly.

One of the men made an impatient noise, but Simon only waved him to silence without turning his attention away from the boy. "Now tell me, what do you know of my lady?"

"I seen her, drivin' through the Garden. She were ridin' in a hack, and lookin' out the window. She looked so sad, I started followin' along, watchin'. I don't know why. I just wanted to 'elp 'er, if I could."

The boy looked to Simon as if for explanation. Simon only nodded. "Yes, I know precisely what you mean."

"Then I seen it." The grimy face screwed into a scowl. "Someone hit her and knocked her down!"

Several of the Liars growled at that, and the boy nodded fiercely, growing bolder in his indignation. "That's right. She didn't come back up, not that I saw. I knew somethin' were wrong then for sure."

"Did you follow the hack?" The boy nodded. "All the way from Covent Garden?"

The child nodded again. It was an astonishing journey for such a little lad, who likely had never left his own square mile.

Simon was impressed. "What's your name, lad?"

"Robbie, sir."

"You're a good man, Robbie."

"'M only ten, sir."

If that were so, then he was a poorly grown ten years. Like plants lacking light and soil, children rarely thrived in the grime and stone of Cheapside.

"Wait a bit. Are you sayin' the wee tyke *walked* it?" Kurt pushed forward and hunkered down before the lad.

The child's eyes widened in alarm, and he glanced to Simon for reassurance. Simon smiled. "Don't fear him, lad. He looks bad, but he makes the best trifle on three continents."

"Trifle?" Remembered pleasure erased the fear on Robbie's face. "I tasted that oncet."

"Once?" boomed Kurt. "A brave man like yourself deserves trifle every Sunday!"

From the awed confusion on the pinched little face, such ecstasy was obviously beyond imagining, but the child now eyed Kurt with near worship. Simon gently reminded him of the subject at hand.

"So you followed them here?" he prompted.

"Yes, milor—yes, sir. I rode partway on the hind of a cart or two, when they was movin' too fast for me. When they got here, they took somethin' out of the hack all wrapped up. I think it was your lady." His eyes blinked rapidly. "She weren't movin', sir. Not a bit of it."

Simon pounded down his rising dread with sheer will. "Do you know where they took her?"

Robbie shook his head, and Simon's heart sank. Then the boy said, "But I knows who took them as had her, took them out and back. Dobb, they called 'im. He's down there," he said, pointing down a street traveling away from the quay, "Havin' a pint in that pub there."

Scarcely had the boy finished giving the direction before Simon and James were running full stretch toward the tavern. "Take the lad to Stubbs, Kurt!" Simon ordered over his shoulder. Then he focused all of his attention on assuring the cooperation of a certain Johnny Dobb.

The boat surged again and again in the current, and every time Agatha feared she'd not be able to maintain her awkward position draped across the tilted mast. And the only place to fall was into the filthy Thames.

She was facing down as she dangled over the mast, but she tried not to look at the encroaching black water. She felt a few more strands of the rope part from around her wrists, although her hands were now so numb that she couldn't be sure. She only hoped she wasn't doing too much damage to her wrists and palm with the shard of brown bottle glass she used.

The boat surged again, and she forgot about her wrists as she felt herself slipping. The deck tilted away as the mast finally touched the reaching water and the boat gave up any attempt of staying upright. Agatha jackknifed her body in desperation, but there was no stopping her feet-first slide down the grimy deck.

She kicked out, hoping to feel her foot catch on something—anything—

She felt her ankle strike something solid, but the brief contact only turned her slide into a sideways tumble, and she fell even faster.

Then her left elbow snagged violently on a large iron cleat, pausing her fall with a jerk that felt as though it wrenched her arm from its socket.

It wasn't enough to stop her, for the pull ripped the last of her bonds free. Her numbed hands could only flail in the air as she plunged into the icy Thames.

When the black water closed over her head, the cold was

almost enough to jolt a gasp from her lungs. She held on to her last bit of breath with all her might and thrashed her arms to take her back to the surface.

She'd been a good swimmer all her life, but never fully dressed with her ankles tied. By the time her head broke the surface, she was out of strength and out of air. Clumsily she tugged down her gag and took a desperate gasp.

The skirt of her gown was twisted tightly around her legs, and she realized dimly that her final roll had likely saved her life. Not only had it torn free her hands, but the yards of muslin had not swept over her head underwater. She'd never have been able to fight free of them in time.

Now, however, the fabric took on water and became incredibly heavy. Her legs could only kick in unison, for her feet were still bound.

The water rolled over her head again and again. It was all she could do to keep thrashing her mouth and nose clear afterward. She cried out for help again and again, but it seemed her voice had been returned to her too late.

The cold began stealing the feeling from her body, leaving only desperate fear behind. She was going to die. The river would take her down and she would never see Simon again.

Her head went under again, and this time the surface was simply too far to reach. She could see the silver light of morning gleaming above her through the swirling strands of her hair, but not all the will in the world could force her leaden body to return to the dawn.

The sail of Johnny Dobb's skiff was useless in the still air of daybreak. The five men Simon had chosen to accompany him out to the *Marie Claire* each manned an oar, including Dobb himself. Of course, it had taken the presence of James's pistol and Kurt's speculative gaze to inspire the man.

The skiff cut across the current with rather excellent speed, yet Simon could not help the sick dread within him. They should be able to see the mast of the *Marie Claire* by now, if Dobb had been accurate in his information.

There was no reason to expect him not to be. Information gained by strangulation was usually to be depended on. Even now, Dobb took a hand from his oar to rub resentfully at his bruised neck.

Simon had no sympathy at all. If he thought it would make the skiff move faster, he'd dump the sorry sod overboard himself.

"Where is it?" James stood awkwardly in the skiff to scan the lightening water ahead. "I don't see—oh, God, *no*!"

With a jolt of pure terror, Simon raised his eyes from his desperate rowing to see the stern of a small vessel upended in the water, like the rear of a diving goose.

"Agatha!" James's hoarse appeal was echoed by the cries of the seabirds in the otherwise eerily silent scene.

"Cor," breathed Johnny Dobb. "Sway weren't jokin' about the bilge."

Simon spared no breath crying Agatha's name but stood and began to tear off his coat and his boots as the skiff neared the wreck. When they were within yards of the sinking vessel, he kicked off into a hard dive, as deep as he could go.

James was less than a second behind him. Plunging deep with powerful kicks, they reached the wallowing boat in time to wrap their hands around a stay-line and follow it down to the gaping companionway.

The pearly light of morning did not filter through the small opening into the bowels of the little ship, but the planks had burst from the keel in several places. These gaps gave just enough light to keep up their hope of finding Agatha.

The inside was filled with debris freed of its lowly position on the floor to drift about the spaces within. They had to bat aside everything from tools to wooden casks drifting on the swirling eddies of the water invading the ship.

Simon saw a pocket of silvery air above him, trapped in an airtight corner. He swam to it and thrust his head up to take in any possible air.

There was only room to tilt his mouth and nose above water, so he took a few swift breaths and moved aside to allow James a lungful.

Simon was making his way into another cell-like chamber when he felt the vessel take a violent shift and roll. It would sink completely soon, too swiftly for escape. They must get out now if they were to survive themselves.

Simon turned and pushed James toward the companion-way. James shook his head, his anguish plain even in the distorted dimness. Then, when Simon shoved him again harder, James turned reluctantly to kick his way to the small square of brightness to their left.

Simon watched to make sure that James escaped, then turned back into the darkness. His lungs ached and his body grew numb, but he would not leave without her. The thought of abandoning her to the dark river was more than he could bear.

His love had killed her, and the least he could do now was take her home. Filling his lungs once more at the now-stale pocket of air, Simon returned to his grieving search.

When James's head broke the surface, the skiff was only feet away. Kurt bent to reach for his hand, but as he was pulled aboard, James noticed that the other men were watching something behind them.

"Ahoy, there!" came a cry over the water. James rolled over, still gasping for his breath, to see another small-boat making its way to the foundered fisher from the direction of a large schooner anchored some distance away.

James knew he ought to reply or ask for help in their search, but dots still spun dizzily before his eyes and grief further tightened his chest. He was grateful when Dobb stood to call out, "Man—er, woman overboard!"

The small-boat was gaining on them swiftly. Now James could plainly see the man standing in the bow, one foot raised to rest on the prow. The fellow brought his hands to his mouth once more.

"Another one?" he called.

"What?" James croaked. *Another?*

Agatha!

He rose, clinging to the sail rigging with his hands. "Aggie!"

A high cry came across the water, and for a moment James was sure it was only the weeping gulls above him. Then he plainly heard it, what he'd thought never to hear again.

"Jamie?"

His heart skidding with joy, James turned to share the moment with Simon.

But Simon was nowhere in sight.

James grabbed Kurt's massive arm. "Simon is still down there!"

She wasn't here. He'd searched every corner of the small vessel until he could no longer feel his arms and legs, and his bit of breathing air no longer sustained him.

He hung there now, suspended unmoving in the water with his nose just barely above. His lungs fought to take in more, and he knew the air in his little pocket had gone bad.

Pain washed through him, making the numbing ache of the cold seem trivial in comparison. He'd lost her, *killed* her, and the knowledge made him want to sink into the depths with the *Marie Claire*.

"*Simon!*"

He could hear her now, naming him craven.

"*Simon Rain, you are a coward. A lily-livered, jelly-spined coward. You are not going to walk away—*"

"No, damsel," he whispered. "I'm going to swim away."

"*—you are too vital to the security of England. I will not rob her of you, dear as you are to me.*"

"I can't go on to live without you." He was almost begging, but even as the words left him, he was breathing deeply to take the remaining air with him.

Simon let himself sink, then turned. He could see the shimmer of daylight through the companionway, like a door into Heaven. He stroked toward it, his limbs heavy and slow. He wondered numbly if he was going to make it.

Then the light disappeared from the square and Simon was

swept up in a massive eddy. As the water tossed him away from the portal, he realized that the ship was moving.

And the only way the ship could move was if it was finally sinking completely.

He almost gave up then, for his will was battling to force his lungs to breathe, and the numbness had reached his mind.

Simon!

Instinctively he followed her voice. She needed him. He must go. Slow, leaden stroke after stroke, he followed the musical, comforting call.

Then he was out of the darkness. The water danced with light. It streamed down from above in brilliant amber bars all around him. Simon wanted to go up. Up to the light, where Agatha awaited him.

Peace filled him, and he surged upward with new strength, ignoring the burning agony of his lungs and the deadened weight of his body. The dark threatened to pull him back, and indeed it almost did, but the lilting call continued.

Simon! Simon!

His head broke the surface, and he heard it once again.

"Simon!" came a voice raw and ugly with strain. It was the most beautiful voice he'd ever heard. "Here! Bring him into the boat! Simon!"

Through water-blurred eyes Simon could see rough hands reaching for him, but his frozen body could feel nothing but the final thud that landed him in the bottom of a wooden craft. Then an angel came, a bruised, scraped angel with dripping hair and a dripping nose, and she cradled his head in her lap and cried for him.

"Hello, damsel," he croaked. "So we're dead then?"

"No, darling," she whispered hoarsely. "I'm too vile to die, and you're too good."

"Not vile," he murmured as his sight dimmed with exhaustion. "Merely a bit peculiar. But I like you that way."

Chapter Twenty-nine

As she made her way down the main way of the schooner, Agatha balanced her tray with one hand. Her other arm still didn't feel quite right from the dreadful wrench she had taken when her bonds had snagged on the cleat.

In addition, her head was rather sore from her rescue. Apparently, all her dear saviors had been able to see was her hair streaming below them, so they'd pulled her up to the surface by it.

Still, she was warm in her borrowed sailor's finery—warm, dry, and alive. With the cooperative captain even now taking the schooner into dock, she would soon be home as well.

Humming quietly, she paused to open the door to the captain's quarters, smiling at two of her passing rescuers as she did so. They nodded glumly back.

The large, intimidating fellows had been quite disappointed to learn that she had a large, intimidating fellow of her own, along with an equally large and intimidating brother.

As she set the tray down next to the warming stove, Agatha decided that the best thing about being alive was that Simon was still alive as well.

She settled to the rug next him, quite comfortable in her sailcloth trousers, and handed him another mug of steaming broth. When his arm came about to encircle her, she relaxed wordlessly against his chest. He also wore a wool fisherman's jumper, only his didn't fall to his knees.

They stayed that way in grateful silence for a while. No teasing. No bantering. Just the blessed sound of his breathing matching hers.

Presently the door opened once more, and James entered. He stopped short when he saw them half-lounging on the rug together, then he shrugged.

"I don't care anymore. Be happy while you can. Only please try not to make her the talk of London, eh?"

"Is that your blessing, Jamie?" Agatha asked from the comforting circle of Simon's embrace.

"Blessing, sanction, permission—call it what you like. You never required it in the first place."

Agatha smiled, then winced and put a hand to her face when her lip split yet again.

Jamie leaned forward, his eyes widening. "I hadn't realized—they beat you!"

She blinked. "What? Oh, not really. I did most of that myself, I believe."

Jamie laughed, a helpless snort of relief. "I don't think I want to know."

Agatha snuggled back into her warm haven. Then she remembered. Sitting up, she twisted to face Simon. "I'd forgotten! Lavinia mentioned an assassination plot!"

Simon only nodded calmly. "Yes, we know. The Prince Regent is well protected for his appearance today."

Agatha drew her brows together. "The Prince? But she spoke of an old man."

James shook his head. "The message clearly used the phrase 'your bullet aimed at Prinny's brain.' "

Agatha frowned down at her tea. "Oh, truly? His brain? I was under the impression that Lavinia thinks Prince George doesn't have one. She believes the Prime Minister runs everything."

She looked up when only stunned silence met her words. Then Simon and James sat up and spoke as one.

"Lord Liverpool!"

The House of Lords was not scheduled to meet until noon, but it was already striking eleven when James, Simon, and Agatha piled into a hack at the dock.

There was no time to gather the Liars or to take Agatha home or even to send word ahead. As it was, Simon promised an outrageous sum to the cabdriver to see them to the front doors of Parliament before the half hour.

It was a wild ride, but Simon kept one arm tightly around Agatha to brace her and urged the driver on. Agatha was eventually convinced to simply close her eyes against the imminent dangers, for her yelps of dismay were disturbing the driver's concentration.

When they pulled up to Parliament with a clatter and jolt, Simon saw a familiar carriage stop farther up the block. Even as the three of them tumbled from the rented cab, unkempt and sailor-clad, Simon saw a polished shoe emerge from Liverpool's carriage. Out stepped Dalton Montmorency, who turned to ease the older Liverpool to the street. The smaller man seemed all the more narrow and bent next to Etheridge's size.

Hurriedly Simon looked all about, but his hack and Liverpool's carriage blocked his view. He sent his cabdriver to collect his ransom from Jackham at the club. "Get on, man; go!"

Liverpool's carriage was also pulling away, although more sedately. Simon ran ahead, scanning all around. There was nothing unusual—

His eye caught on the black gleam of gun metal. He halted abruptly to focus. "There—in that hack parked across the way! A pistol!"

James ran past him, straight to Liverpool. "You get the gun, I'll get his lordship."

Glancing back, Simon saw Agatha staying safely behind. He ran for the armed man in the carriage. Even as his feet hit the cobbles, however, he saw the barrel of the pistol take careful aim. As if his vision had become unnaturally sharp, he saw a gloved finger slowly tighten on the trigger—

He wasn't going to make it. Too late, too worn out. The pistol fired a split second before he grabbed the killer's arm and pulled it forward and down, neatly snapping the bone.

He knew as soon as he did so that it was Lavinia, even before her piercing shriek of pain split the air.

Then her cry was followed by another, one that cut him to his heart. Agatha's scream echoed in his heart long after the sound was cut off, but he could only spare a glance her way.

There was a crowd gathered across the street, but he couldn't see a thing. James was there. He would care for her. Simon had work to do.

The driver of Lavinia's hack was no cabbie. The big man who had sat so quietly a moment before in his seat now lunged at Simon with the lethal force of a bear. Simon managed to dodge the large knife in his attacker's hand once, but the next swipe caught his woolen vest, cutting a long hot slice across Simon's midriff.

It burned, but since his innards did not instantly spill to the cobbles, Simon ignored it. He knew he'd never take this fellow hand-to-hand, for he was obviously well trained.

Simon knelt swiftly to retrieve Lavinia's pistol, then stood to hold it pressed to the big man's heart. The fellow froze. "Sorry, I know it isn't very sporting of me, but I've had a very long day."

Then he fetched the giant a catastrophic kick to the groin, followed by a tap to the head with the pistol, and stepped out of the way as the big man fell.

Several of the guards from the hall reached them then, and Simon gladly left them to secure the conspirators. With one hand pressed to his side, he ran to where the crowd gathered around Agatha.

She knelt on the cobbles, covered in blood. Simon's heart almost stopped until he realized that the blood was James's, as was the still form she held in her arms.

"Oh, God," Simon breathed.

Beside him, a shaken Lord Liverpool was mopping his

brow with a scrap of linen. "Threw himself directly in front of me. I didn't even know what happened until the girl screamed." Then Liverpool noticed Simon for the first time. "What the hell are you doing here? Get out of sight!"

Simon struggled inwardly for a long moment. He was needed here. Agatha needed him.

Liverpool waved his walking stick. "Go on, man! You cannot be exposed now! We cannot afford for you to be at the center of a public brouhaha," he hissed.

Reluctantly Simon stepped back. It cost him deeply. He thought the world might hear it as his soul broke clean in half.

He didn't leave, however. He couldn't. So he clung to the outer fringes of the crowd to watch, like many another low-dressed fellow might. After a moment, a man scurried from the building carrying a physician's bag.

"A shoulder wound," the man declared after a quick examination. "He's bled badly, but he'll survive."

Simon closed his eyes in profound relief. Then he watched as James was carried gently away, accompanied by the doctor. The guards brought Lavinia and the driver forward, and Lord Liverpool stood before them.

"You've committed a serious act of treason here, Lady Winchell," Liverpool announced loudly. "Attempting to assassinate the Prime Minister of England will get you hung very high indeed."

Clutching her broken arm, Lavinia whined, "But I wasn't aiming for you at all, my lord. I meant only to shoot James Cunnington. I am merely a scorned woman determined to punish her lover! I have witnesses who will attest to our relationship. You have no proof otherwise."

"But I do." Agatha stepped forward. Her voice cut clearly through the other woman's protestations.

"You!" Lavinia's face tightened. "Don't listen to that little liar, my lord! She is my rival for Cunnington's affections. She'd say anything to get me out of the way."

Simon watched proudly as Agatha raised her chin to face

Lavinia. "Don't be more foolish than you must, Lavinia. James is not my lover, he is my brother."

She turned to Lord Liverpool. "Lavinia kidnapped me yesterday from in front of the hospital. In the hope, I believe, of distracting my—"

Simon could see her look worriedly around her, searching for him, but he could not step forward now.

Agatha continued, "—my brother from stopping this attempt."

"You and your brother are to be commended, my dear," said Lord Liverpool. "It is not every day that *common citizens* of England take action to defend the government."

Liverpool was obviously trying to tell Agatha not to reveal the Liars' role in the exposure of the plot, and Simon saw her tiny nod of agreement before she went on.

"Lady Winchell revealed her plan to me then, for she assumed I would be long dead by the time she attempted it." Agatha tilted her head and pondered Lavinia. "Rather careless of her, really."

Lavinia snarled. "She may not be James Cunnington's lover, I give you that. But this unmarried woman has been carrying on with a man in her house just the same. Would you believe the word of a whore over that of a lady?"

Liverpool frowned. "What are you saying, woman?"

"I'm saying that she's been lying about being married. She's been living with a hired man dressed up to play her husband. Why wouldn't she lie about me as well?"

There was a murmur of disapproval from the primarily male audience. Dalton Montmorency stepped forward. "I doubt we need take the word of a traitor for any value."

"Fine," Lavinia said with a snarl. "Ask for her wedding license. What clergyman married her?"

Agatha didn't respond, and Simon could see several frowns on the faces in the crowd. The very influential crowd.

Lavinia laughed, an ugly, vindictive sound. "No, there was no marriage. Was there, Agatha? See what a liar she is? But the worst of it is, the lover is nothing but a filthy chimney-sweep!"

Dalton made to speak again, but Liverpool spoke up. "Is this true, Miss—?"

Simon held his breath. *Lie, damsel. Lie!*

Agatha felt ill at the way everyone was looking at her. What had she done that was so wrong? She'd fallen in love, that was all. As she gazed out over the people surrounding her, she saw him.

Simon stood far from her and made no move to come closer. She'd made herself into a public scandal now. And Simon, secret, invisible Simon, could never get close to her again.

She could see the anguish on his face as he met her gaze, and her heart ached for him. She'd never meant to tear at him this way. It would be best to end it now, before she hurt him any further.

Besides, she couldn't lie anymore, and she could never bear to lie about her love. She raised her voice and said the one thing that would separate them forever. The truth.

"I am indeed in love with a chimneysweep." The crowd around her made a mingled noise of shock and titillation. She heard laughter and the beginnings of some very ungentlemanly jests. Agatha ignored them and raised her voice still more. *"And Lady Winchell is indeed a murderous traitor!"*

Even Simon was unprepared for the outcry that followed. Foul names were flung at Lavinia, and the crowd tightened around both women until Agatha was blocked from his view.

Mobs could turn ugly at moments like these. Worried, Simon pushed forward through the crowd. He could only see Dalton towering over the rest, obviously trying to get Agatha to safety.

Someone grabbed Simon's arm. He shook them off and continued on to Agatha. Then Liverpool pulled him roughly to a stop. "Simon, stop this immediately!"

"She'll be hurt!"

"Etheridge has her. See, they've made it into the building. Now remove yourself!"

Simon turned on his superior, a snarl on his lips. "You

simply stood there! You stood there and let her be laid bare to ridicule."

"Not at all," declared Liverpool calmly. "I made sure it happened."

Rage boiled through Simon, and he itched to take Liverpool to pieces with his bare hands. "You made her a laughingstock on purpose? Why?"

"It was necessary. You've become too attached. You can't afford such a point of weakness in your position and you know it." Liverpool smiled then, a chill reptilian smile, and Simon understood the depths of the man's inflexibility.

Liverpool would spare nothing and no one in his defense of England. He had precisely the ruthlessness that Simon had always cultivated within himself.

Until Agatha had come along.

"It was she who saved your life. I won't let her be your sacrificial lamb."

"You must. You belong to England, Simon, not to her. You are irreplaceable. She is not."

Liverpool delivered a flinty stare, then turned away and was lost in the crowd.

Agatha closed the door to James's room and ventured back downstairs, her weariness like a leaden cloak about her shoulders. Despite her joy that James would be all right, she could scarcely feel anything at all.

It was full night now, the end of perhaps the longest day of her life. She had not slept more than a few hours in the past three days, and she wasn't sure how much longer she could force herself to function.

She had yet to pay the physician, who disapproved of her so mightily that he refused to bill her later. She'd not even have been able to force him to come to her house had it not been for Dalton.

It had been Dalton who had stepped in to save her from the crowd and who had arranged for Jamie to be brought home. If it had not been for Dalton's strength, she didn't know how she would have managed.

She needed to rest before she became seriously unhinged.

When she reached the parlor, however, she found that the doctor had gone. Dalton awaited her alone.

When she entered the room, he turned from his contemplation of the fire. She was struck yet again by his picture-book perfection. He was indeed a grand fellow and was proving himself a good friend as well.

"I took care of the doctor for you, Miss Cunnington."

"Thank you."

He stepped forward to take her hands. "Please, you must sit. You appear ready to drop."

"Oh, no. I dropped hours ago. I'm sleeping now, and you are only a dream."

He smiled at that.

"You don't smile often, do you? Neither does Simon." She smiled wistfully. "I always feel as though I've won a prize when I can make him smile."

Dalton led her to the sofa and took the chair alongside. His expression was thoughtful. "What are you going to do now?"

"I suspect I'll stay in for a while. James needs me to care for him, and I'm not feeling very sociable." She tried to make light of her predicament, but in truth she was fast realizing precisely what she had done.

Not that she regretted releasing Simon. It was what he needed, to be free of her. But when she considered her future and the future of the child she might even now be carrying, she felt deep dismay. It was one thing to bear an illegitimate child in sheltering isolation, but now . . .

She herself would likely be well enough at Appleby and in the village where she was known and loved, although if they decided to pity her it might be worse. But her child would always be ostracized by everyone who knew. And now everyone knew.

Bastards were only acceptable if they were from royalty. A chimneysweep's child would have no easy road. And she had purposely done this to her innocent babe. Her selfishness truly knew no bounds.

"What about when James has healed?"

"Home to Lancashire, I suppose. Life in London has lost some of its appeal, I fear."

She decided a change of subject was in order. She attempted a bright smile. "Did you know that James is to be decorated as soon as he can appear before the Prince?"

"Yes, I did know. He is to be congratulated. I believe his act of heroism will go a long way to disproving any hint of his collaboration with the French."

She blinked at him. "You know about his involvement in intelligence?"

His smile was only slight. "Yes. I am rather involved as well."

It was too much. Agatha began to laugh, soft, helpless laughter with a tinge of bitterness. "Of course you are. I declare, if I should pick an attractive man out of a crowd, he'll prove himself to be a spy."

Dalton looked surprised. "You find me attractive?"

Agatha snorted. "Utterly. You are an absolute god. Therefore, you are guaranteed to be wholly committed to something else. It is a basic mathematical formula, proven time and again. I think I'll name it Agatha's Theorem."

Dalton's reflective gaze became sympathetic. "You've really had a time of it, haven't you?"

"Don't pity me," Agatha retorted sharply. "Not unless you wish me to collapse in a puddle at your feet."

He held up both hands. "God forbid. Very well, I shall offer you no pity. I shall, however, offer you an option, as Collis puts it." He took her hand gently in his. Without a speck of passion in his voice he said, "Marry me. Immediately."

She could only stare at him for a long moment. "You are sincere, aren't you?"

"Entirely. I think we'd suit. I need a wife to add stability to my reputation, and you need a powerful husband to salvage yours."

"I hardly think I'll add anything to your reputation except scandal."

He dismissed the notion. "Gossip. It will die away once you've wed me."

The thought snaked through her foggy mind that if she could wed him immediately, and manage to bed him—for he wasn't entirely unappealing—then her possible child would be completely acceptable to the world. As Dalton's coloring was close enough to Simon's, she need never let on otherwise, even to him.

Another lie. She could not do it.

"Dalton, I will answer your question after you answer mine."

"Yes?"

"Would you be able to raise another man's child as your own?"

That threw him, she could see it in his eyes.

"You're increasing?"

"It is a possibility."

"But I thought—Simon didn't seem the sort—"

Agatha smiled wearily. "I was quite determined. Simon didn't stand a chance. Please don't hold it against him."

He shook his head slowly. "I won't. But that does change things."

She couldn't help a pang of disappointment. A quick marriage to a man she respected would have been a bearable solution to her problem. "I rather thought it might."

His eyes narrowed. "But not the way you think. I'd no idea the involvement was so deep. The best arrangement would be for you to work this out with Simon."

She shook her head, a quick, painful denial. "That is not possible."

"Perhaps," he said with a nod. "But first, I must make certain."

Her eyes were threatening to close with exhaustion. Agatha stood abruptly. "Fine. If you decide that your answer is yes, then mine will be yes as well."

She turned blindly to the hall and the stairs that would carry her off to bed. "I must sleep—please excuse me—good night."

The stairs were a mountain and the hall an endless path, but at last Agatha closed herself into her own room. There was a fire in the hearth, but no candles were lit. Nellie must have gone on to bed.

Agatha reached behind her neck to remove the gown she had donned immediately upon reaching the house in Carriage Square. But Nellie had helped her into it, and now Agatha found that her wrenched shoulder would not allow her to undo it.

Almost weeping with frustration, Agatha tried again. She was only able to fumble a few buttons free. Then warm fingers covered hers, moving her hands gently aside.

"Let me."

"S-Simon?" She tried to turn, but he prevented her.

Tenderly he shushed her. "I came to ease my mind about you. Let me help you, damsel."

She stood still in the near darkness while he undressed her and laid her things neatly on a chair. Finally, he led her, clad only in her chemise, to the bed, then made her sit while his fingers worked to free the pins in her hair.

"I'd like to help you wash the Thames from your hair, but I think you need sleep more."

Agatha only whimpered as his warm hands began to knead her shoulders. Then he lifted the covers and helped her slip between them.

"Lie down, sweeting. Go to sleep."

She fumbled for his hand. "Stay."

He smoothed her hair back and dropped a gentle kiss on her forehead, then one on her bruised lips. "I wouldn't dream of leaving."

She couldn't keep her eyes open to watch him in the dimness, but she was aware of the sound of him undressing. Then his large warm body joined hers beneath the counterpane, and she melted wearily into him.

He enclosed her in his arms, tucking her into the curve of his body until he surrounded every bit of her.

Only then, finally, was she able to leave the world behind and sleep.

Chapter Thirty

Simon hadn't meant to sleep. He'd intended only to watch over Agatha for the night. But his own exhaustion had caught up with him as he lay wrapped protectively about her.

When he awoke a few hours later, it took him a moment to recall where he was and why. The only immediate awareness was of warm, sweet woman cradled against him. His body reacted even before his mind truly put a name to the sensation.

Then he remembered the river and the foiled assassination attempt. And, painfully, Agatha's very public downfall at his hands.

The entire city would have the story by morning, he'd no doubt. She'd been ruined beyond the limits of public forgiveness, and would forever be known as "the Chimneysweep's Whore" or some other foul name.

"Let me send you away from England," he whispered against her neck.

"No," she whispered back.

He hadn't known she was awake, but now he was glad she had heard him. "Why not? You could go to the West Indies. It is the perfect solution. No one will know you. You may start over."

She rolled to face him, although he could scarcely see her

in the dim final glow of the coals. He could feel her hand as she raised it to caress his face.

"I'll not run, Simon. I ran from Reggie, and look what happened. This would only follow me, as Reggie did. If I have learned anything, it is that challenging the past is the only way to conquer it."

"You may never truly be part of your world again. I know. I have spent my life on the outside. It is not a good place to be."

She didn't respond for a moment. Then he felt her move, and felt her lips gently on the corner of his mouth. "I shall make my own world," she whispered. "And you will always be part of it, though I never see you again."

He dropped his face into her neck. It was over, almost as soon as it had begun. Yet in their few short weeks together, he had fallen so deeply he thought he might never recover.

Her fingers entwined gently in his hair, and she softly ground her body against his. "We have this night," she murmured.

"Yes," he answered, and took her mouth with his. They had only hours left, and suddenly every moment counted. Every second, every sigh, every muffled cry mattered.

He had so much to prove to her, so much to reveal to her about her own soul and spirit. Assurances that he should have had a lifetime to convince her of.

"You are strong," he whispered as he held her above him and let her ride him at her own speed, confirming her power over his heart.

"You are splendid," he murmured into her as he took her to the peak of pleasure again and again with his mouth, teaching her the limitless pleasures of her own body.

"You are brave," he told her as he stroked deeply into her from behind as she knelt before him, artlessly gasping her orgasm into the pillow.

"You are beautiful," he cried into her mouth as he released into her for the last time and fell gasping to the bed beside her in the first glow of dawn.

Then she kissed him softly and replied to each and every lesson with three simple words.

"I love you," she said. But he could not bear to answer.

. . .

Agatha woke alone, to late-morning sunlight streaming into her room. Her body ached, especially her wrists and shoulder. She was terribly weak and thirsty as well. But most of all, she felt overwhelmed with sadness.

Her eyes burned with ready tears and there was an invisible manacle of anguish about her chest. Blurrily she tried to think. Why should she wake with her heart aching so?

Then she remembered. Her loss exploded within her, and she could only curl into a defensive ball as grief tore through her in expanding waves.

She wanted to howl, to strike out, to throw everything breakable in the world against the stone wall of her pain, yet it was only possible to lie silent as hot tears ran freely onto her pillow.

There was no tantrum powerful enough to alleviate this pain. No fit of spoiled anger would begin to tap into her loss. Without anger to strengthen her, only the soul-killing sadness remained.

No one came to her all morning, and she did not ring for them. There was no room for anyone else, for her pain filled every corner.

Finally she rose to use her chamber pot, and the next blow fell. Her courses had begun.

There would be no child, and the loss of that beautiful possibility was enough to knock her to her knees.

Agatha knelt there with her arms wrapped tightly about her stomach, around what never was, until the blackness passed from before her eyes. She was weak from hunger, she realized. Not a bite had passed her lips since just before Reggie had come.

Two days? Indeed she must eat, although the thought did not appeal. She stumbled to the bell-pull to call for Nellie, then made her way back to the bed.

She was still standing with one hand wrapped about the bedpost, staring at her great empty bed, when Nellie popped into the room seconds later. The little maid must have restrained herself with difficulty all morning, for Agatha could practically see the sympathetic curiosity bubbling inside her.

"I've brought you some tea, miss." Nellie set the tray upon Agatha's small table and arranged the chair for her. Then she saw that Agatha still stood by the bed.

"Would you like your tea in bed, miss?"

The bed seemed to call to Agatha. *Climb in and stay forever. Curl up and forget everything but the last night you spent with him here. You can live a lifetime in this bed, a lifetime in your memories.*

Agatha shuddered. "Now that is quite simply pathetic," she muttered. She cast a challenging glance at Nellie. "Do I strike you as pathetic?"

"No, miss?" The girl gazed at her warily, as if not sure that was the correct response.

"Precisely." Agatha turned away from the bed and moved shakily to the table. "I'll need a bath after breakfast, Nellie, if you please. And I'll wear the yellow gown. The black is rather pointless, now."

"Yes, miss."

"Ask Cook to send up something plain, will you please? I'm not feeling quite myself today."

"Nor should you, miss," ventured Nellie. "You nearly died!"

"Well, I'm not dead yet," resolved Agatha, and set about proving it to herself.

When she was fed, bathed, and dressed, her outlook was somewhat improved. She still felt as though her chest were full of shattered glass, and her eyes had a tendency to leak tears, but her strength and will were returning.

After checking on a sleeping James, who was pale, but not terribly feverish, Agatha restlessly made her way downstairs. There was nothing to do down there, either, but at least she would not feel so very much as though she were hiding out.

The table in the entry that had once overflowed with invitations held nothing but an empty salver and a vase of dimming flowers from the garden. Agatha was unsurprised.

She was a true pariah now. After all her experiences this

week, she found little reason to care about the silly opinions of useless people. The only one with whom she might have enjoyed a closer acquaintance, Clara Simpson, gave her a small pang when she thought of what the young widow must think of her now. But it was only a pang.

She almost entered the parlor but decided not to subject herself to a room in which she and Simon had spent so much time together. The breakfast room was off-limits for the same reason. Finally, she ended up at the kitchen table, sharing a comfortable cup with Sarah Cook.

"I know it all seems dark now, madam, but you're young yet. Men will come and go in a woman's life. Fathers, brothers, husbands, even lovers."

Agatha couldn't help her piqued curiosity. "Did you have lovers, Sarah?"

"Did I have lovers? What a question. I wasn't always just known for my pastries, was I?" The stout woman fluttered her lashes seductively.

Agatha managed a small smile. "But was there ever one man who was . . ."

"The one man?"

Nodding, Agatha ran a fingertip around the rim of her tea-cup. "I simply can't imagine ever not loving him."

"Who said you would ever not love him? The first man you love, well . . . you never really get over him, no matter how it ended."

"Oh, dear. That doesn't sound very promising."

"But that's not to say you couldn't love someone else. Maybe not that easy-hearted way, or so much, but mark my words, you'll love someone else . . . someday."

Agatha pressed her fingertips to her aching eyes. "But not today. And not tomorrow."

"No, can't say that you will."

"Today and tomorrow will be the most difficult, I believe. Then of course, there is the day after that."

The two women sat in silence for a moment, contemplating their tea and their memories. Then Pearson appeared in the doorway, with the attitude that he had been looking for Agatha for some time. She decided not to check his eyebrow gauge.

"Madam, an invitation has come for Mr. Cunnington."

Agatha blinked. "Well, it seems James will still be welcome in some houses."

"Indeed, madam. It is a Royal Invitation."

Agatha smiled, her joy in James's public redemption undiluted by her own reverse situation. "He is to be decorated, I was told. No one deserves it more."

"Yes, madam. The Invitation came by Royal Messenger. He awaits a reply."

"Of course." Agatha held out her hand for It. "How do you manage to capitalize spoken words that way, Pearson?"

"Years of practice, Madam."

"Well, you're very good at it."

Pearson bowed. "Thank you, Madam."

The Invitation came in the form of a rolled scroll of vellum, wrapped in silk ribbon and marked with an ornate seal. Agatha carefully detached the seal to save it for Jamie. One didn't get one of these every day, after all.

The Invitation was for James to attend the Morning Audience at the Palace in order for the Prince Regent to show his official appreciation for an Act of Valor.

In four days.

"Four days? His Royal Highness cannot be serious!"

Even Pearson seemed concerned. "Master James will not be much recovered in four days."

"I shall have to refuse for him, then."

Pearson cleared his throat. "I would not advise it, madam. The audiences are sometimes scheduled months in advance. Someone powerful may have been bumped aside for Master James. It would not do to put His Royal Highness out."

Agatha chewed her lip. "Would it be permissible to have someone accept it in his place?"

"Perhaps. If he were dead."

"Ah. Well, then. I suppose I must reply with a respectful acceptance."

Pearson cleared his throat again. Agatha looked up. "An obsequious acceptance?"

"It may be advisable."

Agatha thought about her own filth-beneath-their-feet position in Society and decided that she would hurt James's chances for recognition as little as possible.

"Thank you, Pearson. Will you be so kind as to bring me my writing case? And come back here. I've a feeling I'll need your expertise to word this properly. I might make a muck of it, myself."

"Most assuredly, madam." Then he was gone before she could figure out precisely which part of her request Pearson was agreeing with.

Simon nodded in response to something Stubbs had said, but he wasn't listening. Instead, his gaze kept returning to the fire in the hearth of Jackham's office. The flames reminded him of the golden lights on Agatha's skin as she reached for him before the fire that first fateful night.

"So d'you think the Griffin will be back to his post soon, sir?"

Simon drew his attention back with a jolt. "What? Oh, perhaps. But he has a bit of healing to do, first."

"True enough. I was thinkin' maybe he might be wanting to take me on as an apprentice-like, while he's laid up."

Stubbs gazed at Simon hopefully.

"Why, Stubbs, I'd no idea your ambitions lay in that direction."

"Oh, yessir. 'Specially after that lovely bit he pulled on Winchell's privy. I 'eard the muck flew near 'alf a mile. Wish't I seen it."

Simon forced his mind to consider the plan. Training an apprentice took time, which was why he never seemed to have enough skilled men. No one really wanted to stay out of the field long enough to do the job, so new men were only trained while injuries healed or when attrition made it a necessity.

"It's a good idea. I know you have the mechanical ability for the job. I'll speak to him, Stubbs."

"Yessir. Thank you, sir! Well, I'd best get back to the door, then." Bobbing awkwardly, Stubbs backed out of the room.

Simon closed his eyes and scrubbed his face with both hands. He was finding it very difficult to care today. Would he never regain his lost enthusiasm?

He heard someone clear their throat. "Stubbs, I said I would speak to him." Simon looked up. "I can't promise—"

It wasn't the delirious Stubbs. Before him stood Dalton Montmorency, who did not look happy at all. He loomed over Simon's desk like a well-dressed angel of Death. It was incredibly irritating. Simon had a serious dislike of being loomed over.

He gave a sour smile. "Well, don't you look every inch the Lord Etheridge this fine morning."

"I want to marry her."

Simon looked away with a spasmodic jerk of his head. "Thanks for the warning," he said tightly.

Dalton shrugged. "But I can't. Not until you tell me face-to-face why you won't."

Simon leaned back in his chair, a bitter bark of laughter escaping him. "My leash has been pulled."

Dalton nodded. "Liverpool."

"Yes. Apparently she is now completely off-limits, even should I overcome my own reservations, for she has become a public oddity. The focus of far too many eyes. He does not want me or the Liar's Club exposed to such scrutiny."

Simon wished fervently for a brandy, though the sun was not yet low in the sky. "Furthermore, should I fail to respect those limitations, he will withdraw all support for the reinstatement of James Cunnington."

Swearing, Dalton sat on the sofa opposite Simon's desk. "The calculating bastard. He's always wanted more of a hold over you."

"He has one now. Agatha would never risk her brother's career."

"And you would never ask her to."

"No."

Dalton leaned forward, elbows on knees, hands steepled before him. "Then this bit of news may interest you. After the attack, I immediately sent word of Cunnington's heroism to the Prince Regent."

Simon raised a brow. "Against Liverpool's wishes, I assume?"

Dalton lifted one corner of his mouth in a cynical smile. "Let's just say I was not officially aware of any objection when I sent the message."

"Quick thinking."

"More like desperation. Since Liverpool's appointment, he has tightened his grip on all the operations overseen by the Royal Four."

"I thought your loyalty to him was boundless."

Dalton steepled his fingers. "My loyalty to England is boundless. My loyalty to Liverpool extends only until it contradicts that."

"I'd say that is a wise stance. Obsession has ruined many great men. Liverpool may yet cross the line."

"True. But more to the point, the Prince Regent has invited James to a Royal Audience. He intends to publicly decorate him for saving Liverpool."

Simon sat up, a swift dart of hope giving strength to his spine. "What?"

Dalton nodded. "Of course, he'll be far too well remembered for covert work for a while, but sabotage doesn't necessarily call for that."

Simon was thinking quickly. "But that will negate any moves that Liverpool makes to remove James from his post! He'll never be able to make good on that threat."

Dalton grinned. "I know."

Plans spun in Simon's head. Marriage. A home. A lifetime of Agatha in the morning—

But there still remained the one insurmountable obstacle. Her life would never be out of danger. Not unless he walked away from the business forever.

You are irreplaceable.

But was he truly? The job required a certain kind of man. A man with no lust for wealth or power. Someone with vision and brilliance, without worries of status or class distinction. Someone with an abiding love of England that would make it worthwhile to give up all else.

A man like the one before him.

It all came down to one question. Should he keep the Liar's Club and let Dalton have Agatha? Or should he hand the job over to Dalton and be an unemployed dependent for the rest of his days? One who went to sleep in Agatha's arms every night?

Simon had always liked the easy ones.

He leaned back in his chair once more and regarded Dalton with a nonchalant smile. Time to do a little Covent Garden–style haggling. "So you miss the fieldwork, eh?"

Chapter Thirty-one

"You'll not miss this. I won't allow it." James pinned Agatha with a vehement glance. The intimidating effect was somewhat ruined by his pallor and the fact that his chin was pointed ceilingward while Button tied his full jabot.

Agatha smiled proudly. "You do look fine in your court costume. I shall have to keep reminding myself about those baggy winter drawers of yours to keep from being overly impressed."

James grimaced at the ceiling. "Hoyden."

"Bookworm," Agatha retorted in an age-old exchange.

All teasing aside, James did look magnificent. His pale blue satin frock coat was heavily trimmed with gold embroidery, and his waistcoat and formal knee breeches were done up in a complementary cream satin. A cream satin sling was draped over Button's shoulder, waiting to support James's injured arm.

She shook her head with wonder. "Button, I believe I shall give you another raise in pay. I cannot believe you were able to locate this and fit it in less than four days."

"Aggie, enough about my clothes. I insist that you come." Freed from his temporary immobility, James gingerly adjusted his lace cuffs with his good hand and turned to her.

Agatha was silent for a moment, her mood gone somber. Then she said, "I don't want to shame you."

His eyes flashing with anger, James crossed the room to her. "I'm hurt that you think you could!"

"But this should be your moment," she protested. "You've earned it. If I appear, all anyone will talk of is the 'Chimneysweep's Doxy.' "

"Where did you hear that?" James was furious. "You shouldn't have to hear that!"

"I asked the servants to find out what they were calling me. I knew it would be something, and I thought it best if I were prepared. So I don't think I should go. I wouldn't want to offend the Prince Regent."

James snorted. "He's not easily shocked. If he hasn't done it, he has paid to watch it done."

Button tittered at that. "He's entirely correct, Miss Agatha. Why, the stories I've heard—"

James held up a hand. "Perhaps not suitable to a lady's ears, Button?"

Button nodded affably. "No, sir. Quite true, sir." Then he turned to Agatha and mouthed, *I shall tell you later.*

James continued. "But more important, the Prince Regent knows Simon well, and likes him very much. I doubt he would hold your 'chimneysweep' much against you."

"Oh." Agatha blinked in surprise. "Simon is a friend of His Royal Highness?" Her heart swelled with pride. "How lovely for him."

"So you must go. I order you to do so."

Agatha propped her fists on her hips. "Order?"

"Insist."

"Oh, really?"

James grinned. "Plead abjectly?"

"Much better. Very well, then. I shall go, but I'll not look nearly as nice as you, for I've nothing suitable to wear."

Button piped up. "Oh, yes, you do, Miss Agatha!"

He reached into James's wardrobe and pulled out an exquisite blue satin gown just shades darker than James's frock coat. It was absolutely laden with gold embroidery.

Enjoying her shock immensely, James grinned at her. "Really, Aggie, do get dressed. Why do women take forever to get ready?"

Her breath finally returned in a delighted shriek. Seizing the magnificent gown, Agatha ran for her room, yelling for Nellie all the way.

The Royal Audience Chamber deserved capital letters. Agatha had never seen such immense artistry and beauteous wealth in all her life. She and James were directed down a long velvet runner to stand near the front of the crowd that had already assembled for the audience.

There was indeed a rush of whispers at her presence, but Agatha kept her head high. Perhaps it was the fine gown or perhaps it was the quick warm clasp of James's fingers as she walked down the carpet at his side, but she felt nothing but pride. In him, in herself—for after all, she'd been part of Lord Liverpool's rescue as well—and in her beloved country's finest hall.

If Agatha did not want to meet the eyes of any courtiers or other attendees—and she didn't—she could easily spend the next week examining the lovely room in which she stood.

The ceiling alone was noteworthy for its astonishing amount of gilt detail. And the colossal chandeliers that hung from it were marvels of shimmering gold and crystal.

A stirring in the crowd forced Agatha's gaze down to the raised and richly draped dais at the end of the long room. The Prince Regent was ascending his throne. Excitement rose within her. She'd been so looking forward to seeing him in person—

Well . . . hmm. Agatha was a bit disappointed. He wasn't precisely impressive at first look, unless one was impressed by girth. He was a very wide sort of fellow. Or perhaps a better word would be *round*.

He was richly dressed, of course. His gold-bedecked waistcoat alone likely cost a year's income from Appleby. Then the Prince Regent turned to settle his generous rear on his throne, and Agatha saw him clearly for the first time. Though his face was round and pale with overindulgence, his intelligent eyes were attentive to all about him.

Agatha liked him immediately.

"Whyever did Lavinia call him brainless?" she whispered to James.

"I've no idea," he whispered back. "He's actually quite brilliant, for all his decadent ways."

Agatha continued to watch the Prince Regent through the next hour or so, as he fulfilled his audience's various petitions and rewards. Sometimes bored and rude, sometimes lively and interested, often scathingly amusing—George IV seemed a fascinating fellow.

She could see him enjoying a man like Simon. And she could see why Simon would in turn enjoy the Prince Regent.

Then James's name was called by an outrageously dressed man—perhaps a herald?—and James slowly made his way to the front of the chamber to stand before the Prince Regent.

Agatha cried proud tears as her monarch spoke over her brother's bowed head, then draped a beribboned medal about James's neck. When it was done, she remembered not a word, but she would never forget the fierce gladness on James's face when he turned to face the audience and bowed to tumultuous applause.

She was happily sniffling still when James made his way back to where she stood.

"Did you hear what he said to me?" he asked her.

Shaking her head, Agatha laughed. "Not a bit of it. I was too occupied with crying."

James ran a wondering hand over the medal on his chest. "He said that he was demanding my continued service. For life! I'm to be reinstated to my post!"

Agatha bit back her instant worry for his safety and smiled joyously at him. "Of course you are. What would they do without you?"

Then Agatha's heart leaped as the herald stepped forward and called out, "His Royal Highness will now hear the petition of Simon Rain!"

• • •

Simon walked the long path up the velvet carpet to stand before his sovereign. He bowed deeply as he was presented and remained low until the Prince Regent called his name.

Then he stepped close to the dais when a lazy wave of the royal hand indicated he should.

George IV regarded him coolly for a moment. Then he smiled. "What's afoot, Simon?" he asked, in a natural tone that did not reach the first row of the audience.

Relief filled Simon that the capricious Prince Regent seemed inclined to remember their past friendship. "Your Majesty, I am here to petition my release from your service."

The Prince Regent's eyes narrowed. "Really? Why?"

"I wish to marry, Your Majesty."

There was no answer for a long moment, then the Prince barked, "Who?"

"Miss Agatha Cunnington."

"Cunnington. He was just up here. The sister?"

"Yes, Your Majesty."

The Prince's eyebrows rose, and he chortled with delight. "*You* are the infamous chimneysweep?"

"I am."

Simon was forced to wait while the Prince took several long moments for hilarity. Finally, the Prince wiped his eyes, still chuckling weakly. "Oh, that's rich. I needed a good joke. I may grant your petition simply in thanks for that." Then the sharp-eyed ruler was back. "Bring this woman to me."

Before Simon could protest, the herald stepped forward. "His Royal Highness calls Miss Agatha Cunnington."

Astonished whispers swept the assembled crowd. Simon heard "Chimneysweep's Doxy" more than once. The name enraged him further every time he heard it, and it seemed he could go nowhere without hearing it.

Yet Agatha seemed entirely unaffected by the clearly audible mockery. She walked gracefully through it to stand beside Simon, then curtsied flawlessly to her sovereign.

The herald formally presented her. The Prince recognized her, and she stood to face him serenely.

"Your Majesty," she said.

The Prince regarded her closely for a moment, and Simon could see that he liked what he saw. For a moment, Simon regretted bringing her to the attention of the Royal Rake.

Then the Prince returned his attention to Simon. "I smell a story here. Tell me."

So Simon told him, sparing himself nothing in the telling. From the first clue in the active bank account to the moment outside Parliament when he was forced to walk away, Simon laid out the facts for the Prince. He wanted the Prince to know precisely what Agatha had sacrificed for her country. Perhaps royal favor might protect her even should his petition be rejected.

The Prince listened attentively, apparently fascinated. Agatha listened as well, never losing her serene expression, although Simon did hear one tiny peep of protest when he claimed the blame for seducing her. He ignored it, for the last thing he wanted the lascivious Prince to learn of was Agatha's natural . . . ah, talents.

When Simon finished, all three were silent for a long moment. Then the Prince turned to Agatha.

"Well? Speak up, woman! You are a lady, born to marry a gentleman and have a life of ease. Will you give it all up for a bastard chimneysweep?"

"I'd prefer a life of adventure, Your Majesty."

"You're willing to marry this man?"

Agatha dimpled and tilted her head. "Yes, Your Majesty. Should I ever be asked."

The Prince turned to Simon. "You haven't asked the woman?" he inquired in surprise. "Have you no romance in your soul, man?"

"I didn't think it wise to marry in my position. Rather dangerous for her."

"Hmm. I know whereof you speak." He turned back to Agatha, clearly fascinated. "So this man, this lowborn chimneysweep without a single romantic bone in his body, this is the man you want?"

"I fear so, Your Majesty. I have never been known for my taste."

"You could do better."

Agatha smiled and batted her long lashes. "Yes, I know. However, inasmuch as Your Majesty is already romantically occupied, I'm afraid I must satisfy myself with second-best."

He liked that, Simon could see. The Prince flicked his gaze to Simon without moving his head. "She's a bit saucy. Are you sure you're man enough?"

"I ask myself that all the time."

The Prince sat back with a chuckle. "It's too amusing. The lady and the chimneysweep. I cannot resist. You're released, Simon Rain, on the condition that you marry this enchantress before she takes on my court."

He turned to his chamberlain with a gesture and nod. The man's eyes widened, but he handed his master a bejeweled sword that had lain alongside the throne.

"As entertaining as it might be to let the two of you tame London on your own terms, I should hate to see the offspring of such a loyal union feel shame in the face of any man. Therefore"—he gestured for Simon to come closer—"kneel, man! Now is not the time to become dense."

Agatha's heart nearly stopped with pride as Simon knelt before the Prince Regent.

"With the powers vested in me as Prince Regent of the British Empire, so on and so forth, I dub thee Sir Rain."

Simon tipped his head up. The Prince scarcely missed lopping off Simon's ear as he jerked the blade up just in time.

"I beg your pardon, Your Majesty, but my true name is Simon Montague Raines."

The Prince blinked. "You're French?"

"My mother was."

"Fine, fine, let's get on with it." He cleared his throat and intoned, "I dub thee Sir Simon Montague Raines."

Agatha had no idea that tears were streaming down her face until they dripped on her hands clasped before her.

"Now get thee to a bishop and marry the little madwoman before she gets herself into any more trouble." The Prince gave them a cynical smirk. "I don't think you'll find too many doors in Society closed to the two of you now. These silly fribbles do so love a romantic tale."

Agatha curtsied blindly to the Prince and took Simon's arm. She'd no memory of leaving the audience chamber at all but found herself in the outer hall with Simon and James.

"Oh, Simon!" She threw her arms about him, then kissed him deeply, surrounding guards be damned. Then she hit him in the shoulder with her fist. "I cannot believe you never told me your real name!"

He smiled gently at her and took both her hands in his. "It's not much of a name, but I shall share it with you if you like."

"Hmm. Lady Raines. Has a lovely lilt to it, don't you think? I accept."

"I should bloody well hope so!"

She rolled her eyes. "Unromantic to the end."

Slowly he drew both her gloves free of her hands. From his pocket he pulled a golden ring adorned with sapphires. Agatha held her breath as he slipped it onto her betrothal finger, then lifted her hands to his lips and kissed each knuckle, gazing deeply into her eyes all the while.

"Marry me, for I love you with everything that I am," he murmured huskily, "and I shall continue to love you until the end of time."

She froze for a moment, her heart expanding until it threatened to spring her ribs. Then she drew a fractured breath. "I take it back. You are romantic."

He grinned swiftly. She raised her fingers to trace the outline of his lips. "Someday, Sir Simon Montague Raines, I vow I will make that smile stay."

He quirked an eyebrow at her. "What do you mean?"

"Oh, nothing. Nothing at all." She turned to her brother. "Jamie, I am getting married. Will you do me the honor of giving me away?"

James was grinning, unabashedly watching their intimate exchange. "I'd be delighted, Aggie."

Simon protested. "Wait a moment. I need James to be my best man."

Agatha tilted her head and pursed her lips. "Hmm. This is a pickle. What do you say we draw for him?"

Simon tucked her arm into his and walked her past the bemused guards, James following along. "Very well. But we'll use *my* cards and *I'll* deal."

She smiled sweetly up at her beloved chimneysweep-thief-spy-knight.

"Of course."

Chapter Thirty-two

The wedding was small but lovely.

The stone chapel was very old, with a simple grace that can only be granted by the centuries. The double doors were left open during the ceremony and the perfume of ripening apples swept down from the orchards, causing all within to reflect upon the harvest, both from the laden trees and from the devotion of two people in love.

The sniffling servants of Carriage Square and Appleby stood to one side for the bride, and on the groom's side there ranged an outrageous mix of openly weeping thieves and assassins.

The groom was accompanied by his good friend, a handsome gentleman who shared the bonds of his work.

And the bride was given away by her brother.

Of course.

Epilogue

Sir Simon Raines sat by the fire in his newly redecorated house reading the day's news over an after-dinner brandy. The fire was delightful against the autumn chill, the news was good, and the brandy was sublime. Simon was extremely comfortable.

He was also extremely bored.

Oh, marriage suited him well, delightfully so. His life with Agatha was so happy that he waited constantly to wake up from his blissful dream. His beloved wife could never be the cause of his current state.

Simon's problem was that he had nothing to *do*. Never in his life had he not worked. From his first memories of pawing through refuse for cloth to sell to the ragman, Simon had earned his keep. Now he was the one being kept.

True, he stuck a hand in with the Liars now and then. But he dared not do too much, for he wanted Dalton to earn the same undying loyalty from the men that he himself had enjoyed. So he kept his presence to a minimum, only offering advice when asked.

Currently the men were fighting over who would foster the little orphaned chimneysweep. Robbie had been absorbed into the Liar's Club without a ripple from the outside world and by all accounts was enjoying the battle in full. Simon's money was on Kurt, with James a close second.

Simon stretched in his luxurious chair, took a sip of magnificent brandy, and contemplated his predicament.

"Hello, darling man." Agatha burst into the room, trailed by her maid, who was trying to gather up her mistress's bonnet and cloak. The fresh air of autumn tinged with coal smoke came with her. Suddenly Simon was no longer bored.

"Shopping again, damsel?"

"Heavens, no. I've just been to the hospital for a meeting." She shuddered theatrically. "After refurbishing every inch of this monastery of yours, I hope I shall never have to shop again."

"Good. I was afraid you were going to try to replace my carpet." Simon gestured in the general direction of their scandalously shared bedchamber, whereupon resided the jewel-toned rug from the house on Carriage Square. It most decidedly did not match the new decor. Simon didn't care one whit.

Agatha sniffed. "That's odd. I thought it was my carpet. I won it from you fair and square."

"You did not. You cheated."

Agatha handed the last of her outerwear to her maid. "Thank you, Nellie. Would you please ask Pearson for a pot of tea? It's gone very brisk out there. And I'm a bit hungry. Would you ask Sarah Cook to send in something light?"

Nellie bobbed cheerfully and left. Agatha turned back to Simon and fisted her hands on her hips.

"I did not cheat. It isn't my fault that you played badly."

"I played badly because you were naked."

"It is still your loss," she teased. She came closer to warm her hands at the fire. Simon made a long arm and swept her into his lap instead.

"I'll warm you."

She snuggled close. "Better already. Now, I want you to listen carefully, for I have something I'd like you to consider."

"I won't do it." He nuzzled her neck instead.

"Simon, please. I need your undivided attention."

"Then get naked."

"Simon, I've rushed home to tell you something splendid. I have an idea what we can do with your skills and my money."

Defeated by her tightly attached collar, Simon leaned back with a sigh and a silent vow to toss her lace betsy into the fire later. "I hope this is better than your plan for the beaver-breeding farm."

"I still believe that would have raked in the pounds, what with beaver hats coming back into fashion."

"Nonetheless, I do not believe beaver enjoy being bred."

"Never mind that. I have decided that we should open a school!"

"Of fish?"

"No, and do stop teasing. I'm quite serious. We shall open the Lillian Raines School for the Less Fortunate."

"Hmm. I appreciate the tribute to my mother, damsel, but the rest of the title sounds a bit . . . well . . . unappealing. I hardly think the parents of London will be lining up to register their little pets with us."

She hopped off his lap to face him, by her expression very pleased with herself. "Precisely! It's perfect."

"Sorry, my love. You've lost me again."

"We won't be teaching little pets. We'll be teaching those who want to improve their speech and their table manners. We'll teach dancing and etiquette—"

"You are a wonderful teacher, Agatha, but—"

"—and pocket-picking, safe-breaking, and map-making—"

Simon's chair squeaked as he abruptly sat up off the base of his spine. "And sabotage!"

"Yes! A training program for the Liar's Club! Do you like it?"

With a laugh, Simon jumped up to gather Agatha into his arms and swung her around in a joyous spin. "It's perfect. And we may actively recruit. The Liars will never be short-handed again! All the men will have the necessary skills."

"And the women."

That halted him for a moment. He gave her a wary look. "That's been your goal all along, hasn't it?"

"Well, you could use a few likely girls. Women are so overlooked, maids and governesses and so forth, that people say all sorts of things in front of them."

He flashed her a grin. "Angling for a bit of work yourself, are you?"

"No," she said smugly.

"No? I'm surprised. I thought you'd want to be right in the thick of the action."

"Oh, no. I shall be far too busy teaching. Furthermore, the thick of the action is no place for a woman when she's increasing."

His mouth dropped open and threatened to stay that way. She tipped it shut with one finger. "A child, my love. Your child. Small. Occasionally loud. Usually wet."

A child. Simon's heart began to beat with a new resonance. His child.

A family of his own.

A slow smile began then, a smile that crossed his face and remained there for a very long time.

TURN THE PAGE FOR AN EXCERPT FROM

The Impostor
(Book Two in the Liar's Club)

by
Celeste Bradley

COMING FROM ST. MARTIN'S PAPERBACKS
OCTOBER 2003

With one hand, Clara dragged Beatrice into the ladies' retiring room.

Bea put a hand to her hair to protect her array of ostrich plumes as she ducked through the doorway. "What are you on about, Clara?"

Clara didn't bother to correct her sister-in-law's use of the hated nickname. Instead she towed Bea through the crowded room to a free corner.

"I need to look different," she whispered urgently to Bea. "I need to look like them." She gestured toward the other ladies. "Only better.".

A smug gleam lit Beatrice's eyes. "I knew it. I knew you'd regret not coming out of mourning sooner. It's that Thorogood fellow, isn't it? He's a handsome one, I'll grant you that."

Clara shook off the question. "Help me, Bea."

Bea looked her up and down. "Well, we can visit Madame Fontaine tomorrow morning and order some things, though I'm sure it will take weeks at this time of year—"

"No, Bea. *Now*."

Beatrice blinked. "Now? You want to impress a man in that gown, with that hair, and your face unpowdered—"

It was time to bring out the big cannon. Clara half-turned

away, letting her shoulders sag. "If you don't think you can, I suppose I could ask Cora Teagarden—"

"That goose? Are you mad? She doesn't have the fashion sense of a flea! You'd look a sight worse—" Sputtering in indignation, Beatrice grabbed Clara's arm and dragged her to a mirror.

"The gown's well enough, if we abandon the collar—heavens, girl, why bother with a corset if you're not gong to lace it nice and tight?—pull the shoulders down—no, lower. Hmm . . ."

She turned to gesture at a waiting chambermaid, assigned to help ladies who wished to unlace or freshen up a bit. "You there! Fetch some rice powder and kohl. And some pins!" she called after the retreating maid.

Turning back to Clara, Beatrice smiled with fierce glee. "I've been dying to get my hands on you for years."

Clara swallowed. Oh, dear holy *drat*. What had she gotten herself into now?

Dalton's feet hurt and his cheeks ached, but he smiled insincerely at yet another fawning female. "I'm entirely shocked, my lady. How could one so lovely as yourself ever have had any doubt . . ." Blah, blah, blah. He could hardly keep track of all the ninny-ish things he'd said this evening.

Time to leave this party and move on to another, anyway. He was determined to smear Sir Thorogood into the faces of everyone in London who moved among the elite, for surely the daring cartoonist was one of them. No one on the outside could ever know so much about the scandals and goings-on among the members of the *ton*.

Enough. He made a pretty excuse to the lady currently monopolizing his attention and turned away before she could capture it once again.

Only to nearly trip on another. Catching himself quickly from trodding upon the gown of yet one more overdressed female, he made an apologetic bow. "Please pardon my clumsiness, dear creature. Might I beg an introduction?"

"On your knees, for a start."

Dalton looked up quickly. He couldn't have heard those crisp acid words in truth, could he?

But the lady before him was as overdone and silly as any in the room. Sillier, in fact, for her hair was piled high upon her head in a tumbled style and sported three ostrich plumes that topped even his own height.

She was probably attractive enough, if one could forget the face paint and rouge long enough to see it. But her gown, dear heavens! The silly things ladies got up to!

She'd pulled the small cap sleeves down to her elbows, and her breasts were thrust up nearly beneath her chin, likely by a corset too tight to allow breathing.

She stood with her head tilted, batting her overly kohled eyes at him slowly. No, not a sharp tack, this one. More like a dull pin.

"I am Mrs. Bentley Simpson, sir. I don't think we really need an introduction, do you? After all, you're the famous Sir Thorogood, so there, you see?"

He didn't see at all, but rallying to his cause, he bent deeply over the silly twit's hand. "It is my pleasure, Mrs. Simpson. Might I add that Mr. Simpson is undoubtedly the luckiest man in this room tonight?"

He was answered by a decidedly unladylike snort. Was that sarcasm? Once more, he looked up in doubt, only to see the brainless creature tilting her head so far to the right to meet his eyes that she appeared about to fall right over.

Dalton straightened quickly, and Mrs. Simpson bobbed right up with him. One of her plumes had come unfixed, and now bent gracefully forward to dangle before his nose.

Backing away while retaining his smile, Dalton gave the thing a surreptitious bat. The lady only smiled and stepped closer, bringing the damned feather to tickle his cheek and ear.

"I know how you can make it up to me," Mrs. Simpson said with a gleeful little clapping of hands. "You can draw me a picture!"

Good lord, was she twelve? Glancing down at those admittedly mature breasts again, Dalton had to say no to that. But her girlish squeal had brought the attention of several other ladies nearby, and soon he was once again surrounded by trilling ninnies galore.

All clamoring for him to demonstrate a talent which he did not possess.

And at the center of it all, eyes alight, stood the ninniest female of them all, Mrs. Bentley Simpson.

Oh, he was a smooth one. Even as Clara urged the other ladies to plead for drawings, she had to admit that the impostor was a very good liar.

With charming smiles and pretty words, he begged off from displaying his talents here at the musicale, when they had all come to hear the players and singers. Not for him was it to steal their applause, he said.

That was rich. Clara almost kicked him in the shin on the spot. Stealing applause was precisely what he was up to, that or worse.

For the first time, she was forced to admit to herself that she had enjoyed the public's response to her work. Although her original purpose had truly been to stop injustice, over the last months she had begun to cherish Sir Thorogood's popularity like a secret jewel.

She didn't like knowing that she was less than entirely altruistic in her purpose. She didn't like it one little bit. One more reason to hate the outrageous poseur. Scarcely able to hide her sneer, Clara stood amongst the teeming ladies and added her pleas to the clamor.

She'd force him to expose himself. One drawing was all it would take, she was sure. Her talent might not be much more than a parlor trick, but it was a parlor trick that she was very good at.

And it was something that not everyone could do. Caricature was not a straightforward representation of a person. It was an exaggeration of a few key features, and a minimization of all others. To know *what* to draw was the difficult skill.

The press of ladies behind her thrust Clara even closer to the fiend in question, and a whiff of his scent came to her. She wanted to hate it, to claim to herself that he smelled of pungent cologne and lies, but he smelled rather nicely of sandalwood soap and clean, healthy male.

Was there no end to his perfidy? Even his scent was a lie!

Look at him. Tall and handsome, and by his wardrobe—outrageous as it might be—more than comfortably wealthy. Why did he have to come to steal the one thing that she had ever been able to call her very own?

Her anger seemed almost to be choking her. Clara tried to shake off a sudden spell of dizziness, but it only worsened. Or was it her corset that wasn't allowing her to breathe?

Bea had pulled the dratted laces much too tight. Clara tried to take deep even breaths to stem the dizziness, and it seemed to help for a moment. She turned her attention back to the crowd around the impostor.

Over the shoulders of the ladies, Dalton saw a man enter the ballroom. He was a lean, older fellow, not very tall, but the guests seem to part before him like a well-trained sea.

Lord Liverpool.

Dalton knew his godfather rarely made appearances at anything but royal events. Apparently, he was about to find himself in some trouble.

Sure enough, after greeting a few of the more important men in the room, the Prime Minister of England raised his gaze directly to Dalton's.

Oh, yes, trouble indeed. When Lord Liverpool's gaze flicked to a nearby set of balcony doors and back, Dalton gave a tiny nod.

With sugary platitudes he excused himself from the company of his fawning admirers. He'd thought the clinging Mrs. Simpson would put up more of a struggle, but she seemed a bit distracted and pale.

Dalton made his escape and strolled leisurely to the balcony doors.

As this was a town house, the scale of the balconies was small. Each had its own entry into the ballroom, and a set of stone stairs leading to the gardens below.

Dalton found Lord Liverpool leaning against the balustrade, gazing down to where a box-hedge maze cleverly gave the small area of gardens more scale for the wandering admirer.

Dalton hadn't made a noise but Liverpool began speaking immediately, though he remained turned away.

"What in the seven reaches of hell do you think you're doing?"

If Liverpool was resorting to bad language, Dalton was in even more trouble than he'd thought. "I'm investigating the latest case given to the Liar's Club," he replied stiffly.

Liverpool snorted. "*Personally*. You left out 'personally.' Which you are not supposed to be doing. Have you given any thought to the repercussions if your true identity is revealed? You've lived quietly these last few years, but not that quietly!"

"It isn't likely that anyone will associate the somber, reclusive Lord Etheridge with the flamboyant Sir Thorogood. In the event that they do, I shall admit my identity, claim Thorogood was merely my nom-de-plume, and laugh it all off as a very good joke."

"Laugh it off? Laugh off the humiliation and degradation of more than a dozen peers of the realm at the hands of that reformist agitator? Laugh off the connection that will inevitably be made to *me*?" Liverpool turned swiftly, his black eyes glittering in the half-light. "It is no secret among those that matter that I raised you when your father died!"

Dalton looked down at his godfather. "Raised" was perhaps too strong a word for the man's participation in Dalton's childhood. *Supervised*, perhaps. *Conducted*, even.

Liverpool had personally selected a highly distinguished school, and every six months had made an appearance there to check on the young Lord Etheridge's progress. Dalton knew this because the faculty had never failed to inform him of his esteemed guardian's visits.

He himself had never had much conversation with the man until he'd finally left Oxford to take his place in the House of Lords.

Once there, he'd been expected to back Liverpool at every turn, to vote with his godfather's vote, and generally add to the power and influence that the man had already accumulated.

Liverpool would have had his support anyway. The man was the glue holding the government together, what with a mad king and a profligate prince who was more interested in art and women than in government.

But he was not Dalton's intimidating guardian anymore.

"I fail to see how any of this could come to reflect on you, my lord. My true identity will not be revealed. I had the best of costumers, and honestly, would anyone dream that the sober Lord Etheridge would use a quizzing glass?"

The attempt at levity fell flat in the silence. Though the gathering was plainly audible in the background, the balcony seemed very much like a chill mountaintop at that moment.

"Watch yourself, boy. Just watch yourself."

Before Dalton could protest that he was no longer a boy and had not been for fifteen years, Liverpool had slipped back through the doors, leaving him in the darkness.

"Well, that went quite well, I'd say," Dalton murmured to the night as he pulled a cheroot from his pocket. "Much better than I expected."

Clara was finding it more and more difficult to take a breath. The ballroom seemed to waver about her, and the oppressive air seemed to have been entirely used up by the people swirling about her. It gave her lungs no nourishment.

And she'd lost the dratted impostor, to boot.

She would find him later. Now she needed her sister-in-law. As she cast her gaze desperately around for Beatrice, she saw a wiry older gentleman entering the ballroom through a set of doors. The cool night beckoned her for a moment before he closed them behind him.

Clear night air.

Air.

Clara stumbled the short distance to the balcony exit. Leaning against the gilded doors, she dimly tried to manage the latch. After fumbling for a moment, the door fell open before her. She staggered through to the balcony, trying to pull deep dragging breaths into her lungs.

It wasn't working. The corset was too tight. Tiny particles of gray began to come between her and her view of the evening gardens. Blindly, she reached for the stone balustrade, only dimly aware that she was in danger of falling to the ground far below.

Dalton couldn't believe it. This was no dainty feminine show. The silly twit was *fainting* her way off the balcony! Tossing his cheroot to one side, he made a grab for her.

His right hand caught only a wisp of silk, but his left managed to wrap itself around one pale arm. With a yank, he pulled her away from danger, back against his own body. She sagged, forcing him to shift his grip hurriedly.

Unfortunately, that left him with one arm wrapped around her ribs and a handful of soft breast.

"Damn." All he could think of was facing her likely equally brainless—though undoubtedly well-armed—husband at dawn. Quickly, he spun her and tossed her over one shoulder.

Back into the house? The draped doorway led directly to the ballroom, her husband . . . and Liverpool. Not an excellent option.

Instead, Dalton headed for the stone stairs at the end of the balcony that led to the gardens below.

Bloody ladies and their bloody fashion. Whatever possessed them to sacrifice sensible comfort for some illogical physical ideal? Then he winced as he nearly turned his ankle when his high-heeled shoes failed to take purchase on the graveled pathway.

Of course, *he'd* never be dressed so by choice.

The white gravel path shone in the lamplight coming from the windows of the house, making it fairly easy to see. The brightness also made it easy to be seen.

Damn. What the hell was he to do with the woman?

She stirred on his shoulder. Having her head down was apparently bringing her back to life. Dalton ducked down a darkened path, hauling his irritating burden away from the betraying light.

The maze of hedges led him to a turn, then opened to display a gazebo of some sort ahead, barely outlined in the dimness.

Perfect. He'd dump the woman, fix her bloody corset prison for her, then slip away before she came to. She hadn't seen him, so she'd likely think she'd wandered off in her daze. If she bothered to think at all, which he doubted.

Stepping up onto the marble floor of the garden structure, Dalton heaved Mrs. Simpson off his shoulder to half-sit her on a crescent-shaped bench.

He supported her upper body with one arm wrapped beneath her breasts, this time avoiding taking a handful of soft flesh into his hands. She lay limp against him, her breath shallow on his neck.

She smelled good at least. Stupid she may be, slovenly she was not. Dalton had never understood the habit of some people layering costly clothing over unwashed bodies. Mrs. Simpson smelled sweetly clean. Even her hair smelled pleasant as it tickled his ear.

Oh, that was those damn plumes. With a growl, Dalton pulled them from her hair and tossed them to the ground. Then he turned his free hand to unfastening the tiny buttons that ran the length of her back.

With skillful fingers he soon had them free, even in the dark. Then he tugged at the knot in her corset strings to no avail. Some idiot maid had tied them into a great snarl that he had no hope of undoing without plenty of light and time.

He could leave her here and let someone know . . .

With the shrug of one shoulder, he flipped her head from

its roost and changed the angle of her body to look into her face. It was too dark to see well, but he was very much afraid that she was paler than ever, right down to the color of her lips. There was no time.

Cursing the stupidity of slaves to fashion, Dalton held her tightly with one arm while he tore the corset strings with one mighty yank. With a series of pops, the garment gave way.

Even unconscious, her body sensed its freedom and drew in a giant breath. When he was sure she was breathing normally, Dalton lay her flat on the bench.

Standing, he arranged her as comfortably as possible, aware that she was likely to awaken at any moment and take umbrage at his liberties.

She was somewhat pretty in the faint starlight, he had to admit. Without the overuse of cosmetics—not to mention the fervent glint in her eye and that annoying titter—she might even be attractive.

Then again, almost any woman would look good lying sprawled wantonly on a bench with her bodice gaping, nearly revealing a pair of small but intriguing—

Her head rolled to one side, then back, and her eyelids quivered.

Time to go. Dalton stepped back into the shadow of the hedge, then quickly made his way back around the turn, walking close to the maze wall to avoid the crunch of gravel under his feet. Then he paused, unwilling to leave her untended until she was fully conscious.

Clara drew one breath after another of cool blessed air deeply into her lungs. At first content only to breathe with ease, it was a moment before she realized that the only sound was her own breathing against a backdrop of rustling greenery and chirping of crickets.

She was outside? She opened her eyes, looking about her in bewilderment. The gardens? She'd come so far in her search for air?

Sitting up swiftly, she felt the bodice of her gown slide away and the cool air of night caress her breasts. Swiftly, she grabbed it back and covered herself. Her face was hot against the cool breeze as she realized that she may not have come to the gardens on her own.

Fumbling behind her with one hand, she discovered the snarl of corset strings and the torn lacing holes. Had she been attacked? Deep inside her, something cried out with age-old feminine fear.

Yet she was unhurt, and her gown had been carefully unbuttoned, not a single tiny pearl gone astray.

The back of her neck tingled. She looked about frantically, but there was no sign of anyone. Only her crumpled plumes, trod negligently onto the inlaid marble floor of the gazebo. The sight almost reminded her of something, or someone . . .

Well, whoever had brought her here had disappeared for the moment. She'd best do likewise in case they decided to come back. With quick movements she retied the corset loosely halfway down, then did up her buttons as well as she could.

She looked a scandal, she was sure. She'd go round the house and wait in the carriage, she decided, unwilling to search for Beatrice in the crowd. Picking up her skirts, she ran from the gazebo, back down the path toward the noise and light of the assembly, that same prickle down her neck speeding her on her way.